VAGRANT QUEEN. VOLUME ONE. SECOND PRINT. APRIL 2019.
Copyright © 2019 MAGDALENE VISAGGIO & JASON SMITH.
Originally published in single magazine form. VAGRANT
QUEEN, #1-6. All rights reserved. "VAGRANT QUEEN", the VA-
GRANT QUEEN logo, and the likenesses of all characters
herein are trademarks of MAGDALENE VISAGGIO & JASON
SMITH, unless otherwise noted. "VAULT" and the VAULT
logo are trademarks of CREATIVE MIND ENERGY, LLC., No
part of this work may be reproduced, transmitted, stored
or used in any form or by any means graphic, electronic,
or mechanical, including but not limited to photocopying,
recording, scanning, digitizing, taping, Web distribution,
information networks, or information storage and re-
trieval systems, except as permitted under Section 107 or
108 of the 1976 United States Copyright Act, without the
prior written permission of the publisher.

VAULT

VAULTCOMICS.COM

DAMIAN A. WASSEL
PUBLISHER

ADRIAN F. WASSEL
EDITOR-IN-CHIEF

NATHAN C. GOODEN
ART DIRECTOR

TIM DANIEL
VP BRANDING/DESIGN

KIM McLEAN
DIRECTOR OF MARKETING

DAMIAN A. WASSEL, SR.
PRINCIPAL

All names, characters, events, and locales in this publica-
tion are entirely fictional. Any resemblance to actual per-
sons (living or dead, or exiled Queens), events, institu-
tions, or places, without satiric intent, is coincidental.
Printed in the USA. For information about foreign or multi-
media rights, contact: rights@vaultcomics.com

WRITTEN BY
MAGDALENE VISAGGIO

ILLUSTRATED BY
JASON SMITH

COLORED BY
HARRY SAXON

LETTERED BY
ZAKK SAAM

VAULT COMICS
PRESENTS

VAGRANT QUEEN

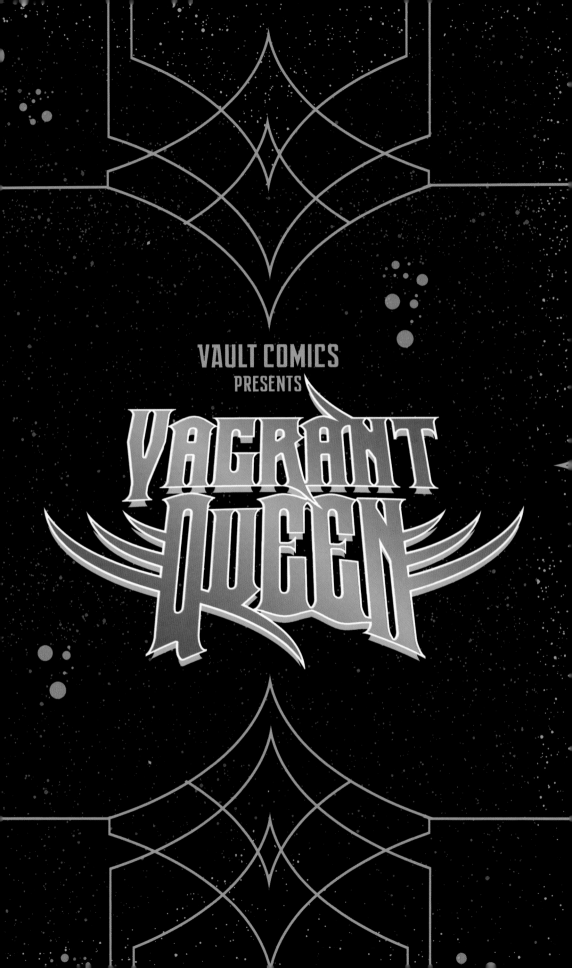

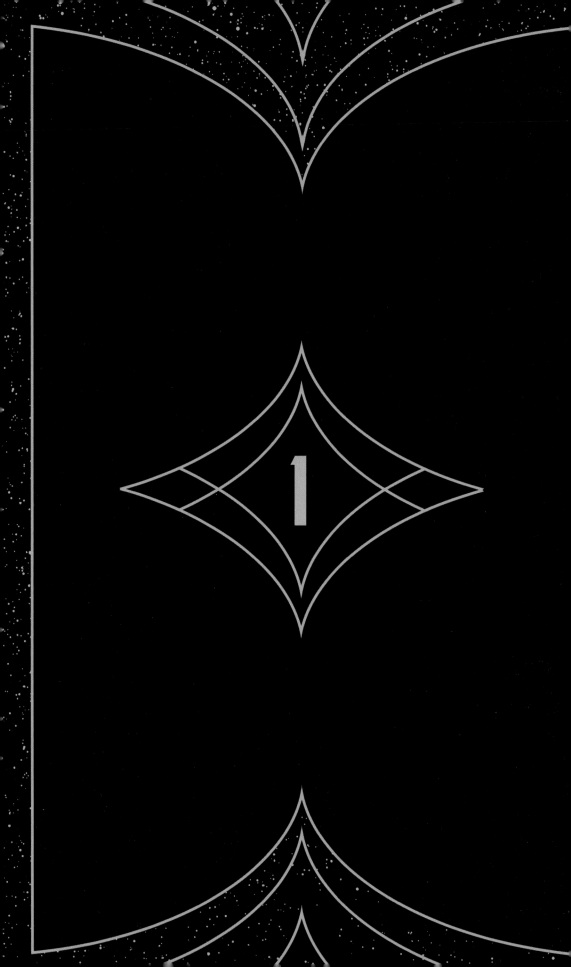

1

THE OTHER SIDE OF THE GALAXY. WEEKS AGO.

TURN!

DAMN YOUR BLOOD! **TURN!**

WONKWONKWONKWONKWONKWONKWONK

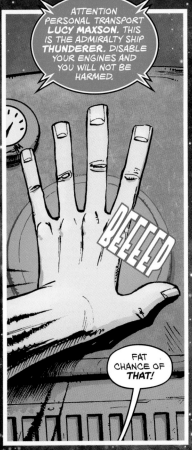

ATTENTION PERSONAL TRANSPORT *LUCY MAXSON.* THIS IS THE ADMIRALTY SHIP *THUNDERER.* DISABLE YOUR ENGINES AND YOU WILL NOT BE HARMED.

BEEEP

FAT CHANCE OF *THAT!*

BSSSHOOOO

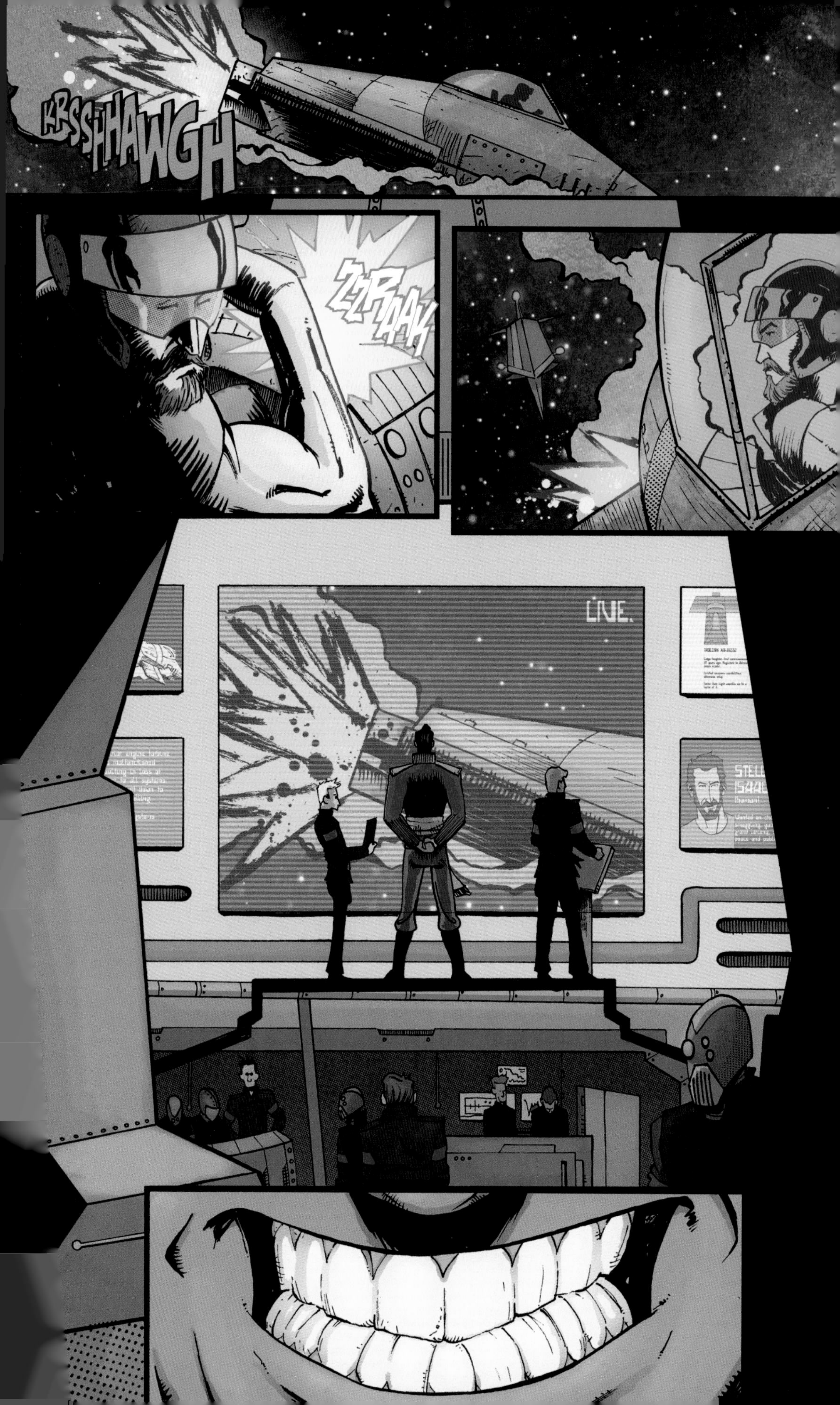
KRSSHHAWGH
ZZRAAK
LIVE.

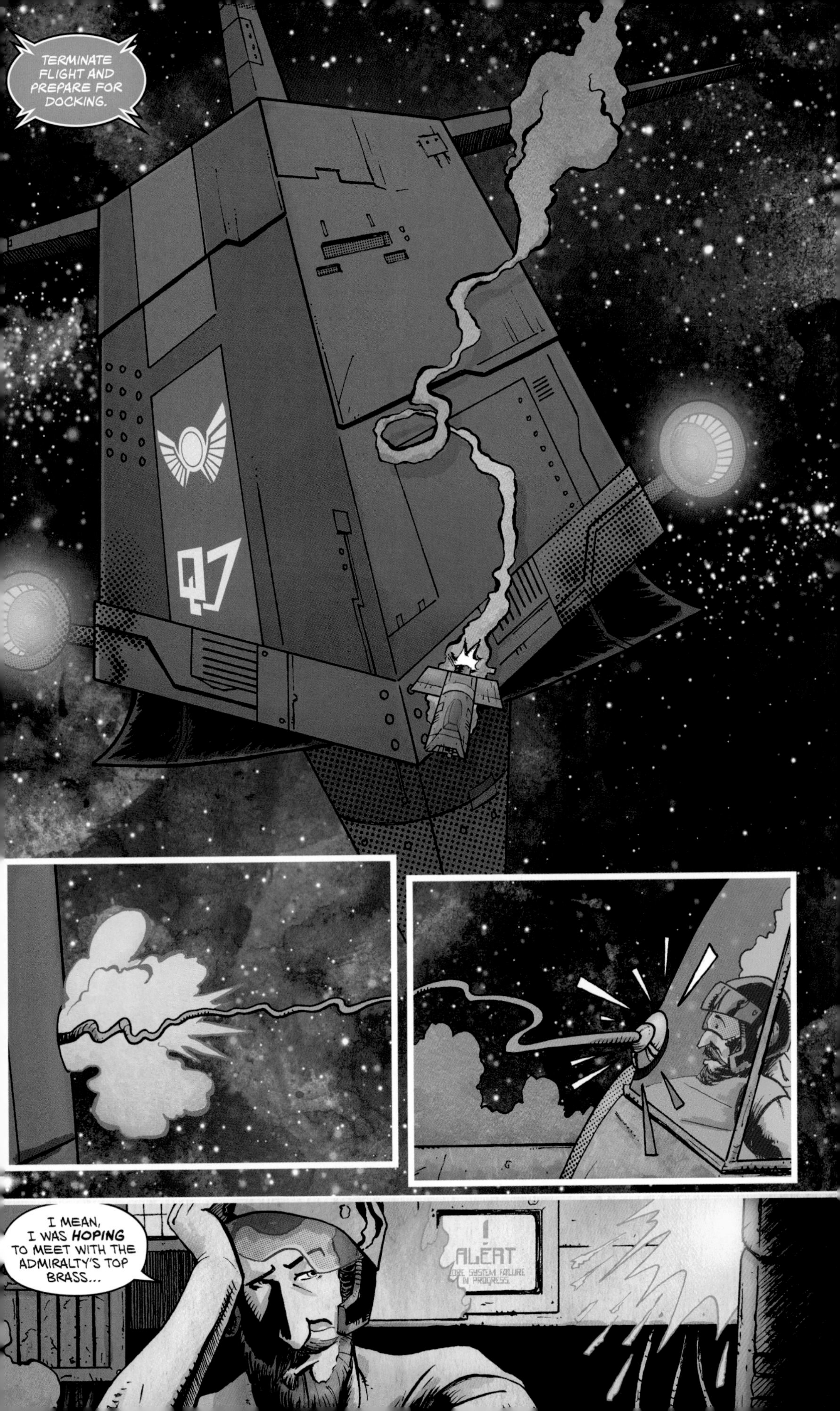

TERMINATE FLIGHT AND PREPARE FOR DOCKING.
Q7
I MEAN, I WAS **HOPING** TO MEET WITH THE ADMIRALTY'S TOP BRASS...
!
ALERT
ORE SYSTEM FAILURE
IN PROGRESS.

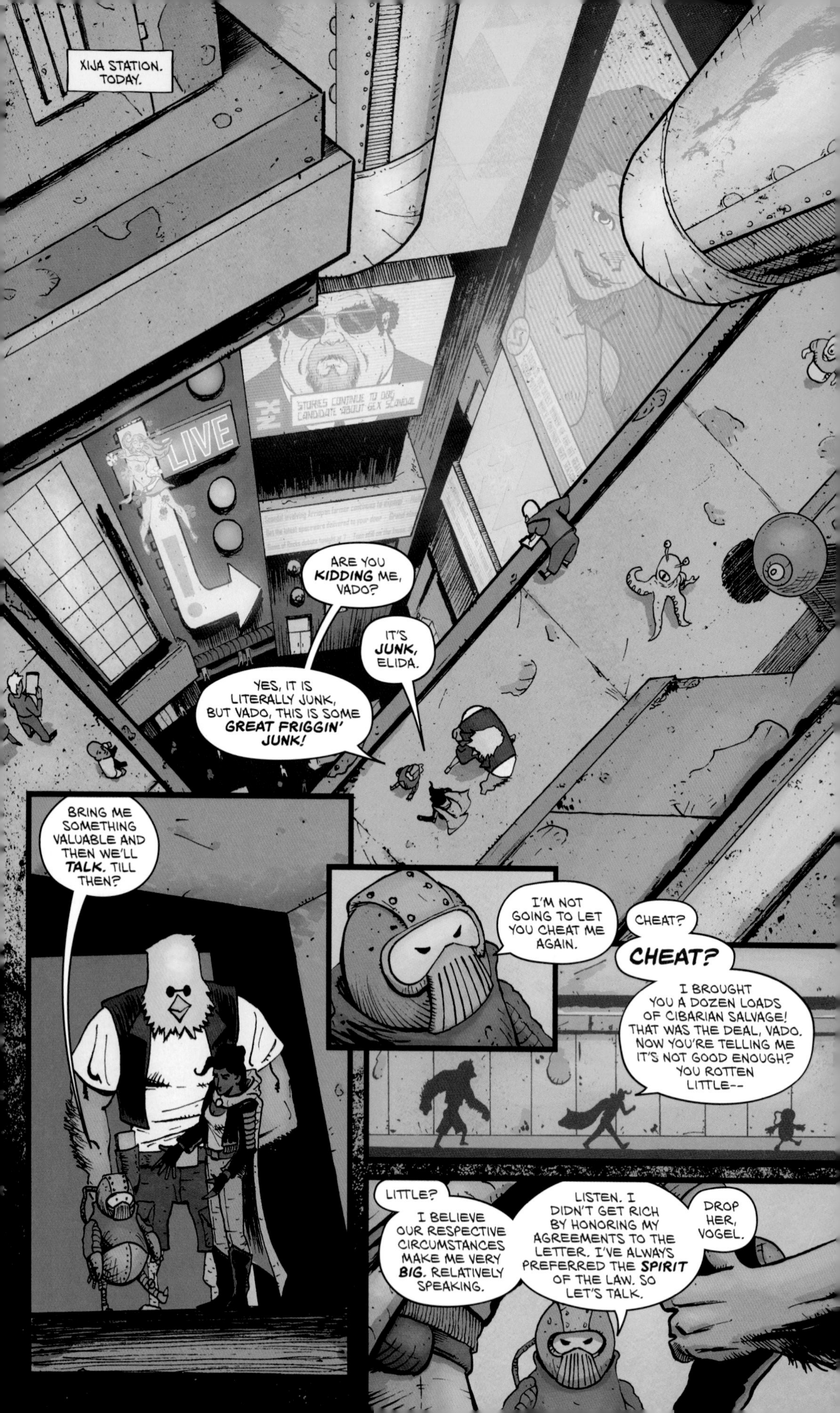

XIJA STATION. TODAY.
LIVE
STORIES CONTINUE TO DOG CANDIDATE ABOUT SEX SCANDAL
ARE YOU KIDDING ME, VADO?
IT'S JUNK, ELIDA.
YES, IT IS LITERALLY JUNK, BUT VADO, THIS IS SOME GREAT FRIGGIN' JUNK!
BRING ME SOMETHING VALUABLE AND THEN WE'LL TALK. TILL THEN?
I'M NOT GOING TO LET YOU CHEAT ME AGAIN.
CHEAT?
CHEAT?
I BROUGHT YOU A DOZEN LOADS OF CIBARIAN SALVAGE! THAT WAS THE DEAL, VADO. NOW YOU'RE TELLING ME IT'S NOT GOOD ENOUGH? YOU ROTTEN LITTLE--
LITTLE?
I BELIEVE OUR RESPECTIVE CIRCUMSTANCES MAKE ME VERY BIG. RELATIVELY SPEAKING.
LISTEN. I DIDN'T GET RICH BY HONORING MY AGREEMENTS TO THE LETTER. I'VE ALWAYS PREFERRED THE SPIRIT OF THE LAW. SO LET'S TALK.
DROP HER, VOGEL.

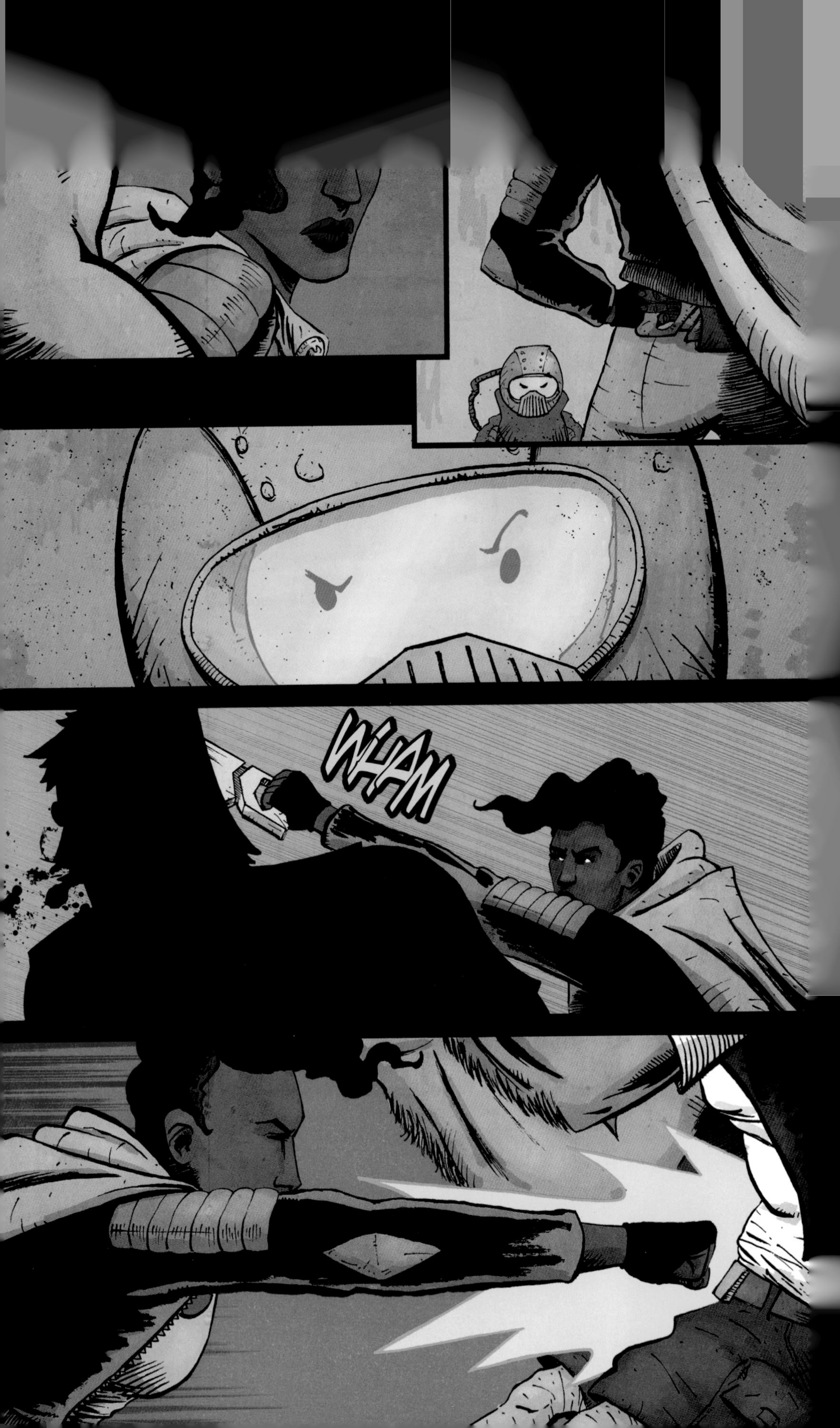
WHAM

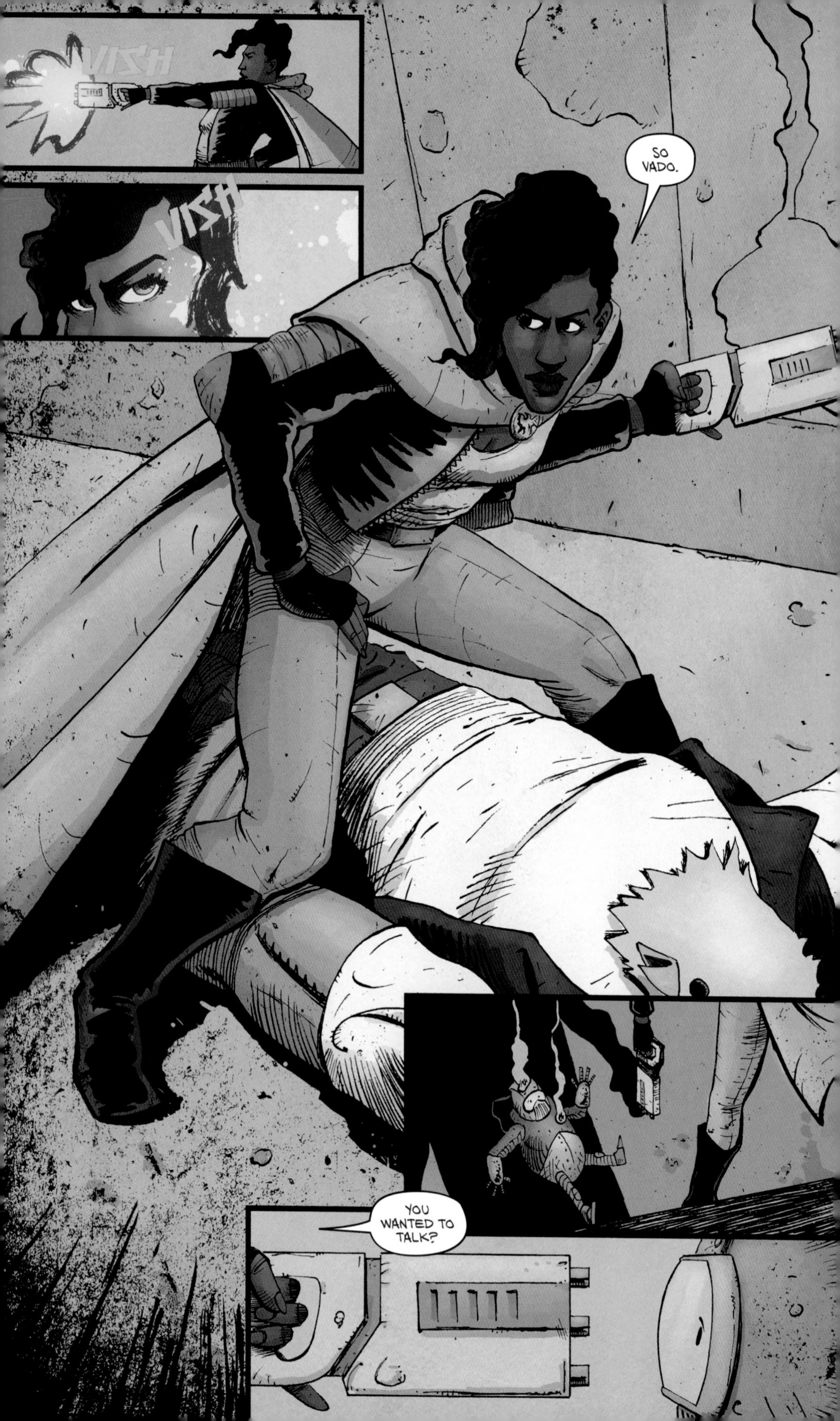
VISH
VISH
SO VADO.
YOU WANTED TO TALK?

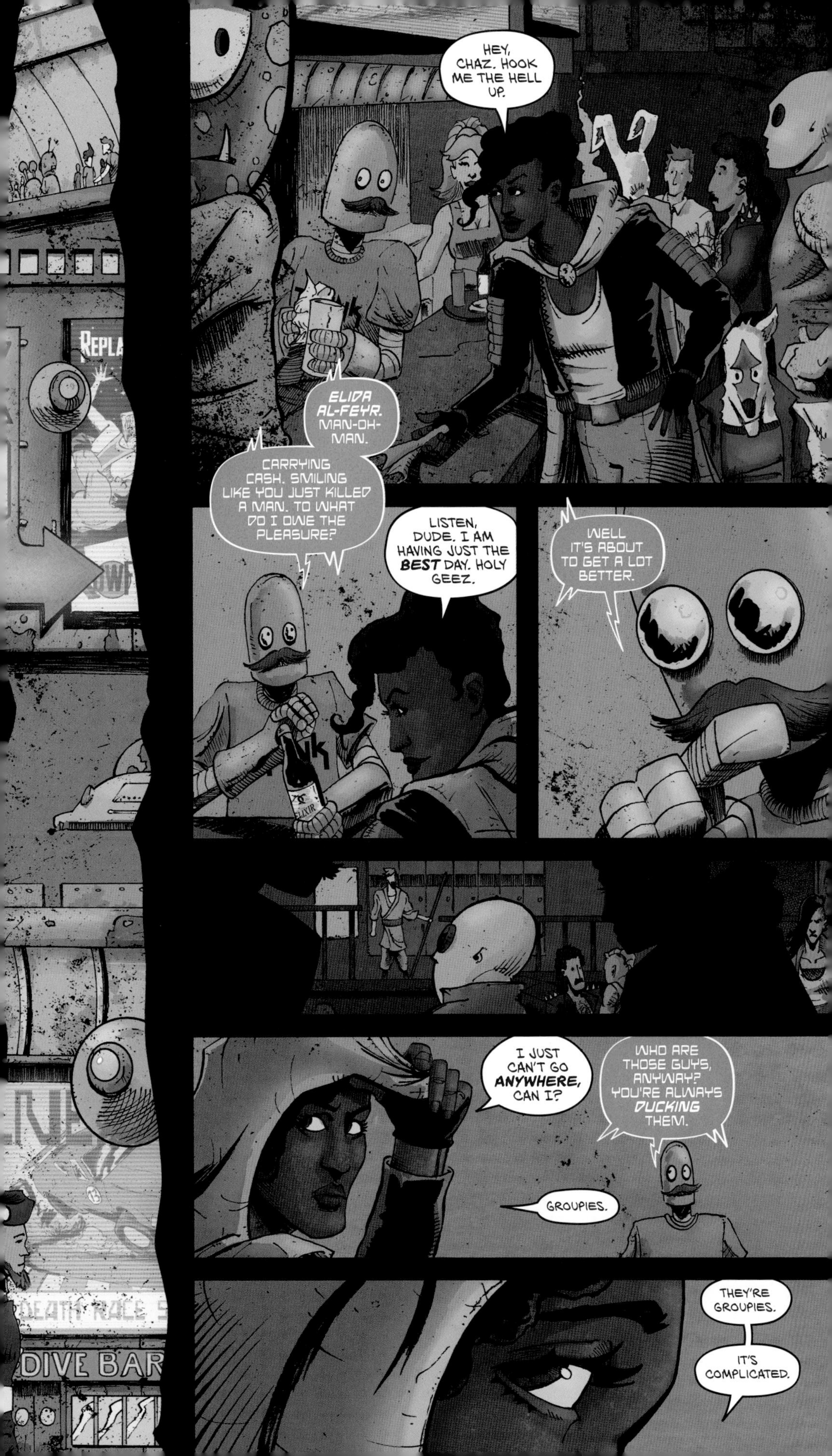

REPLA
HEY, CHAZ. HOOK ME THE HELL UP.
ELIDA AL-FEYR. MAN-OH-MAN.
CARRYING CASH. SMILING LIKE YOU JUST KILLED A MAN. TO WHAT DO I OWE THE PLEASURE?
LISTEN, DUDE. I AM HAVING JUST THE BEST DAY. HOLY GEEZ.
ELIXIR
WELL IT'S ABOUT TO GET A LOT BETTER.
I JUST CAN'T GO ANYWHERE, CAN I?
WHO ARE THOSE GUYS, ANYWAY? YOU'RE ALWAYS DUCKING THEM.
GROUPIES.
THEY'RE GROUPIES.
IT'S COMPLICATED.
DIVE BAR

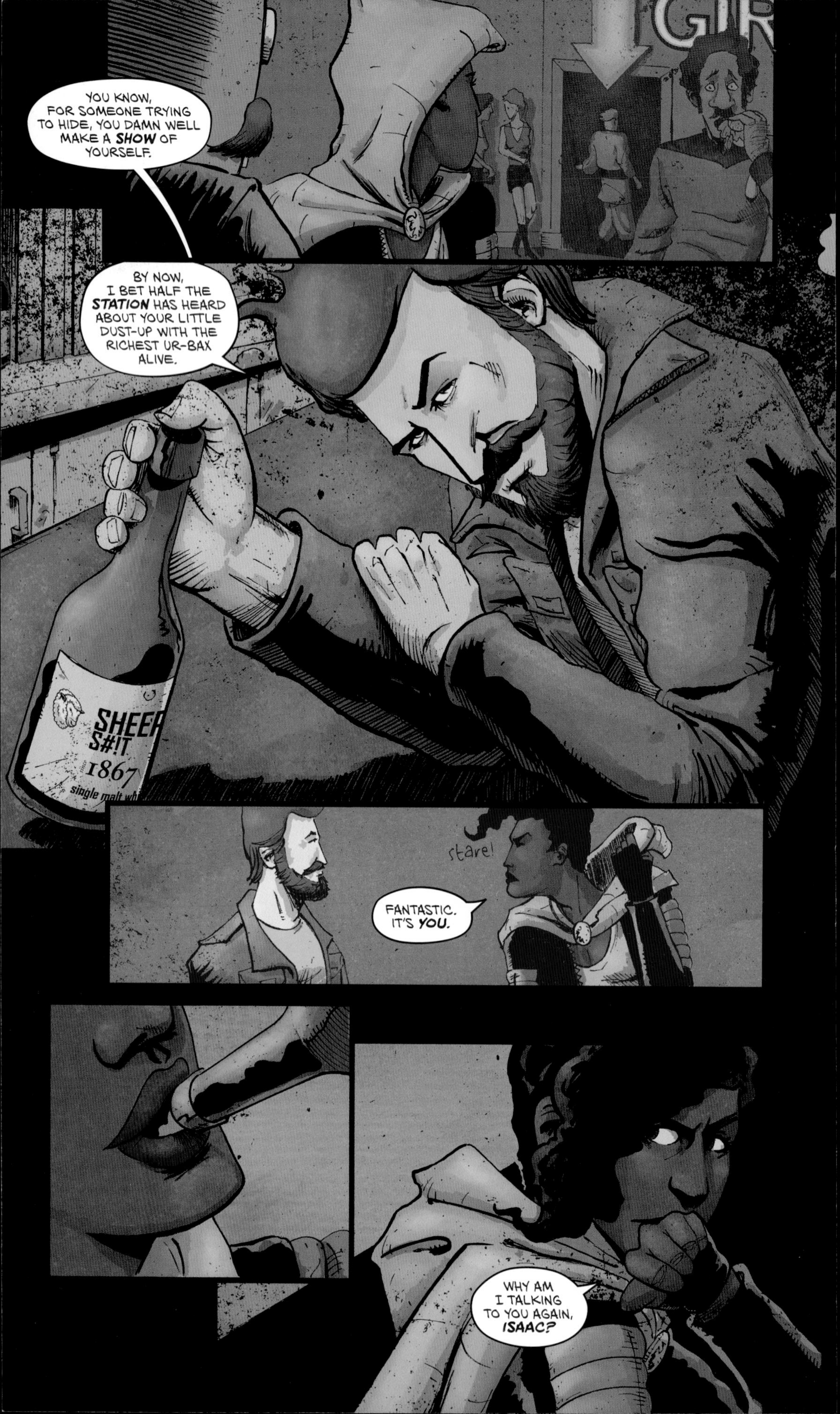
GIR
YOU KNOW, FOR SOMEONE TRYING TO HIDE, YOU DAMN WELL MAKE A **SHOW** OF YOURSELF.
BY NOW, I BET HALF THE **STATION** HAS HEARD ABOUT YOUR LITTLE DUST-UP WITH THE RICHEST UR-BAX ALIVE.
SHEEP S#!T 1867 single malt wh
stare!
FANTASTIC. IT'S **YOU.**
WHY AM I TALKING TO YOU AGAIN, **ISAAC?**

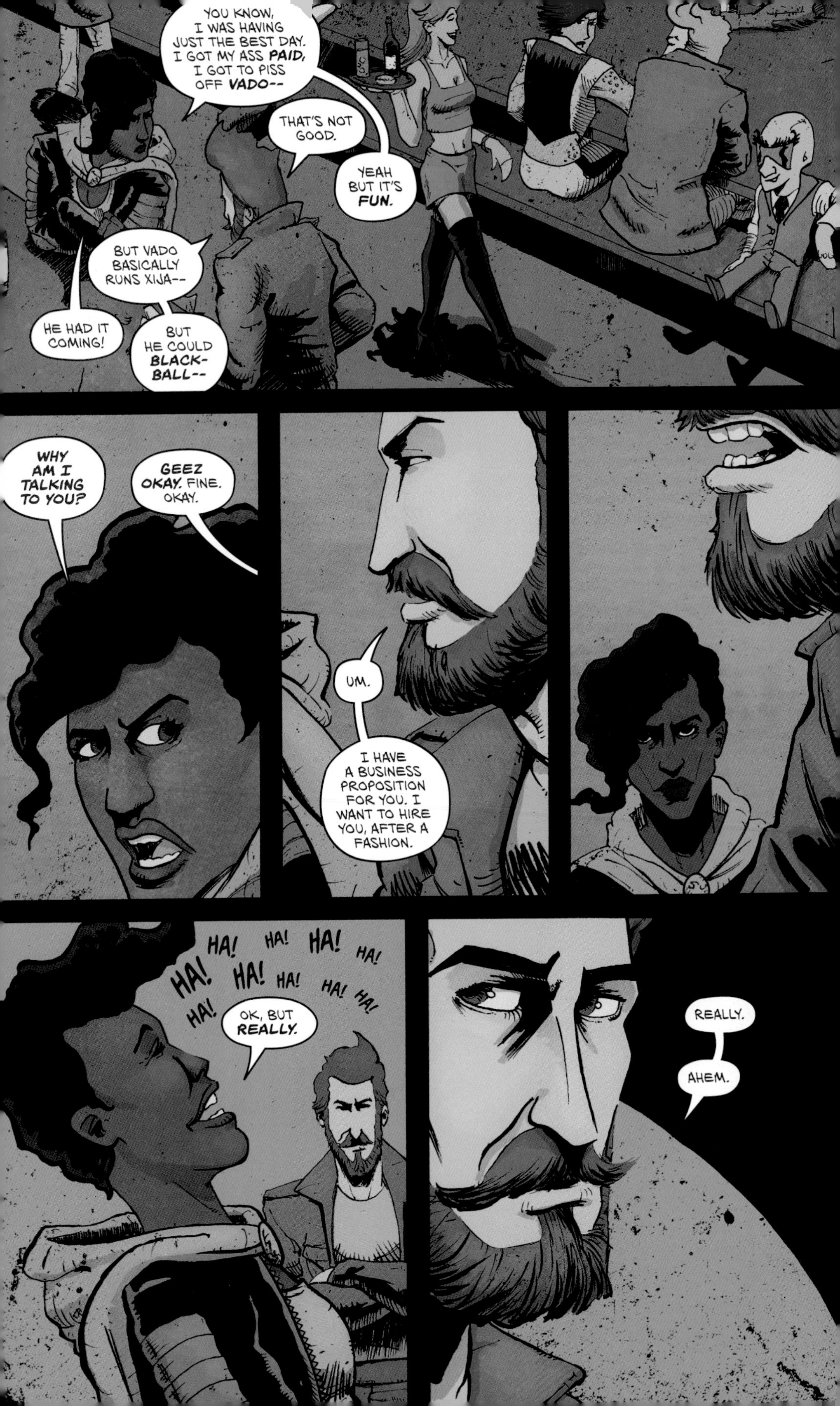

YOU KNOW, I WAS HAVING JUST THE BEST DAY. I GOT MY ASS PAID, I GOT TO PISS OFF VADO--
THAT'S NOT GOOD.
YEAH BUT IT'S FUN.
BUT VADO BASICALLY RUNS XIJA--
HE HAD IT COMING!
BUT HE COULD BLACK-BALL--
WHY AM I TALKING TO YOU?
GEEZ OKAY. FINE. OKAY.
UM.
I HAVE A BUSINESS PROPOSITION FOR YOU. I WANT TO HIRE YOU, AFTER A FASHION.
HA! HA! HA! HA! HA! HA! HA! HA! HA! HA!
OK, BUT REALLY.
REALLY.
AHEM.

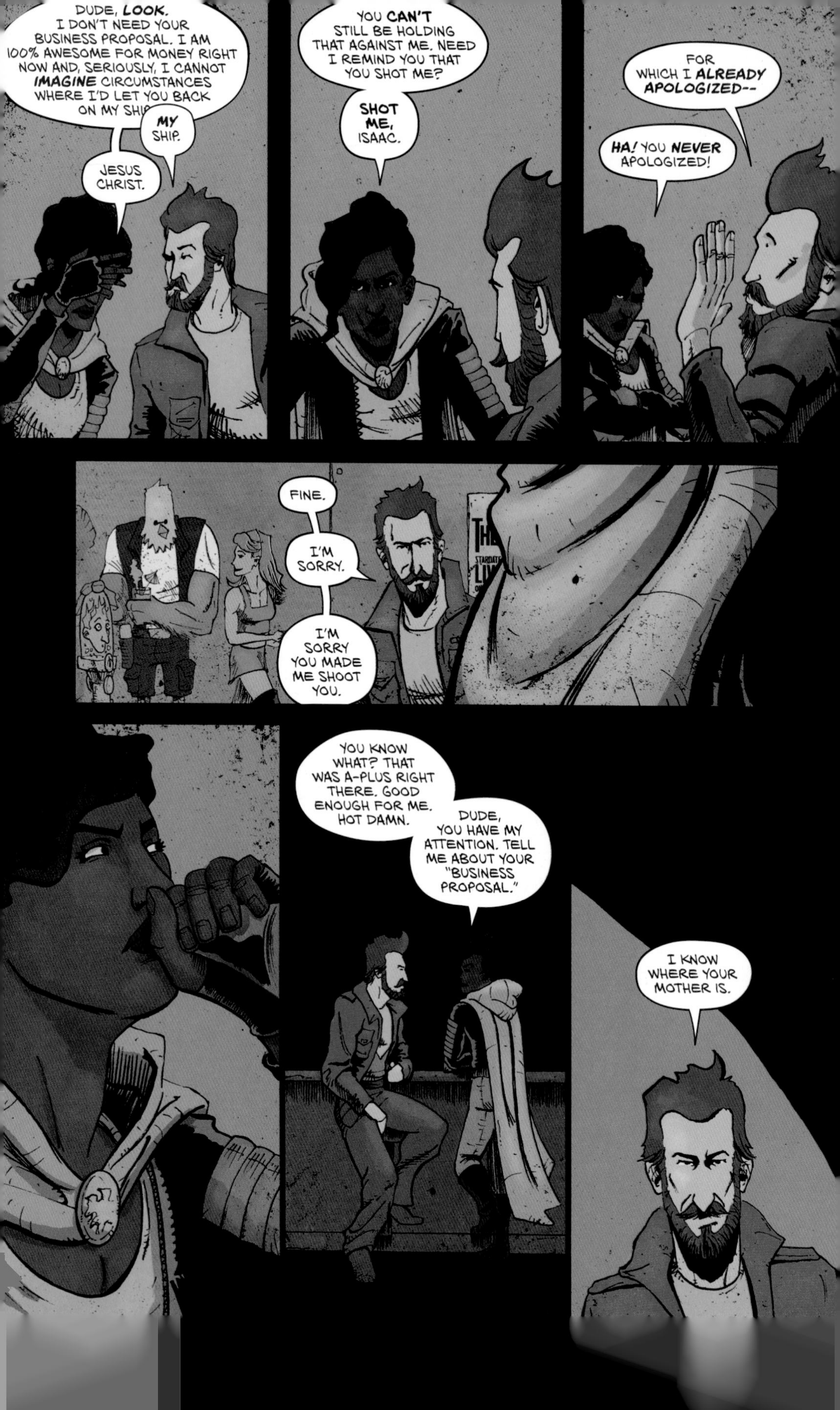
DUDE, **LOOK.** I DON'T NEED YOUR BUSINESS PROPOSAL. I AM 100% AWESOME FOR MONEY RIGHT NOW AND, SERIOUSLY, I CANNOT **IMAGINE** CIRCUMSTANCES WHERE I'D LET YOU BACK ON MY SHI--
MY SHIP.
JESUS CHRIST.
YOU **CAN'T** STILL BE HOLDING THAT AGAINST ME. NEED I REMIND YOU THAT YOU SHOT ME?
SHOT ME, ISAAC.
FOR WHICH I **ALREADY APOLOGIZED--**
HA! YOU **NEVER** APOLOGIZED!
FINE.
I'M SORRY.
I'M SORRY YOU MADE ME SHOOT YOU.
YOU KNOW WHAT? THAT WAS A-PLUS RIGHT THERE. GOOD ENOUGH FOR ME. HOT DAMN.
DUDE, YOU HAVE MY ATTENTION. TELL ME ABOUT YOUR "BUSINESS PROPOSAL."
I KNOW WHERE YOUR MOTHER IS.

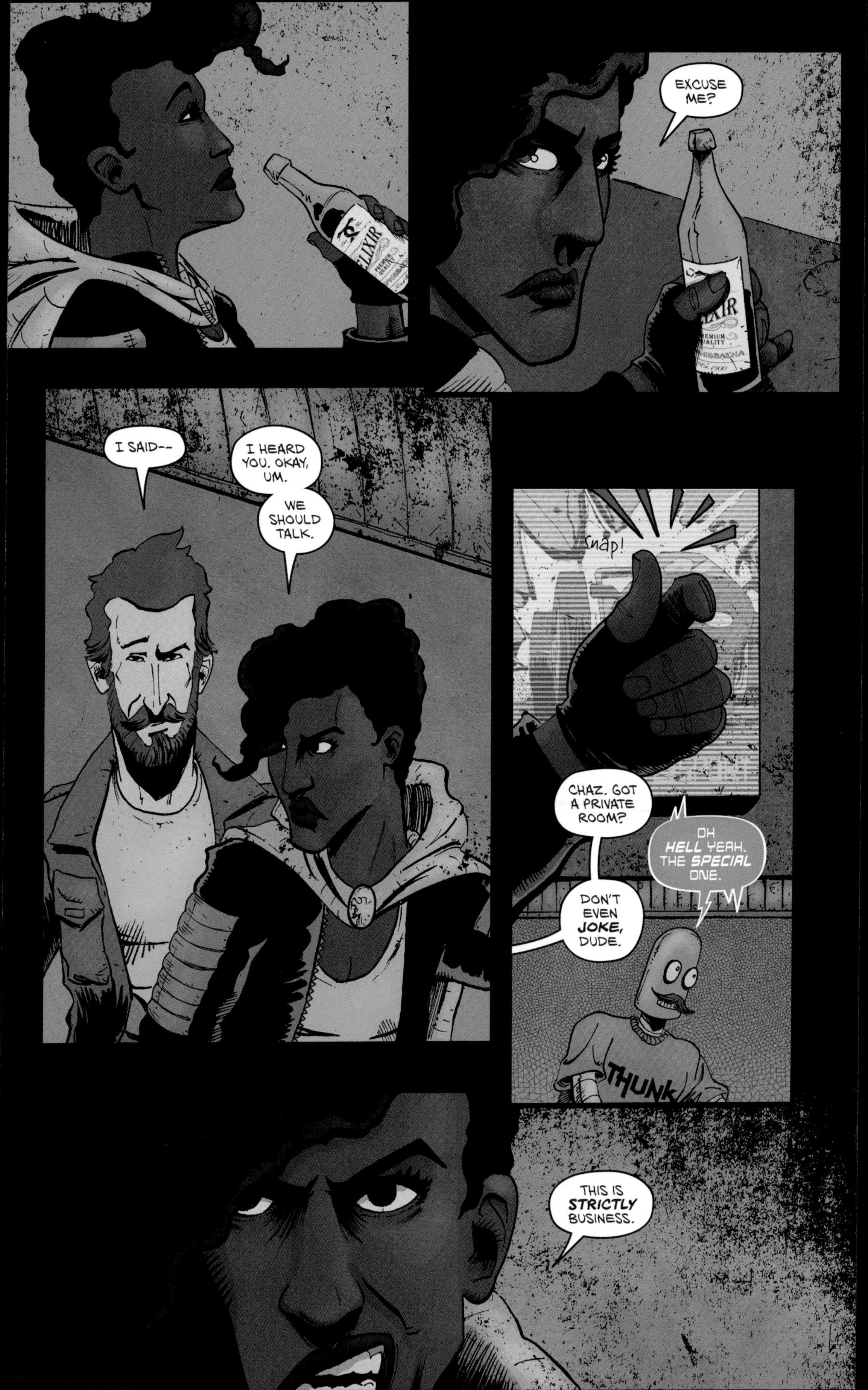
ELIXIR
PREMIUM QUALITY
EXCUSE ME?
I SAID--
I HEARD YOU. OKAY, UM.
WE SHOULD TALK.
Snap!
CHAZ. GOT A PRIVATE ROOM?
OH HELL YEAH. THE SPECIAL ONE.
DON'T EVEN JOKE, DUDE.
THUNK
THIS IS STRICTLY BUSINESS.

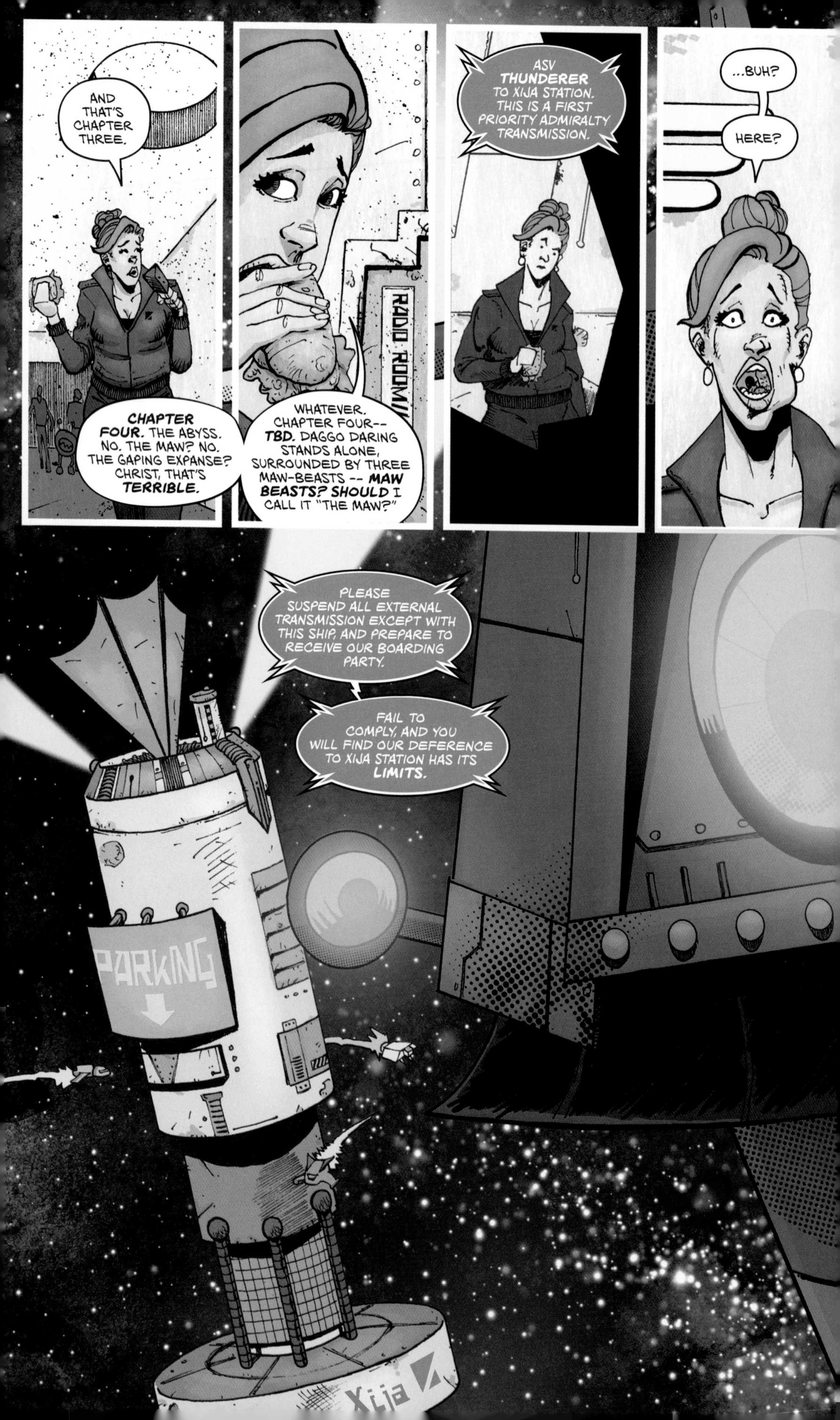
AND THAT'S CHAPTER THREE.
CHAPTER FOUR. THE ABYSS. NO. THE MAW? NO. THE GAPING EXPANSE? CHRIST, THAT'S TERRIBLE.
RADIO ROOM
WHATEVER. CHAPTER FOUR-- TBD. DAGGO DARING STANDS ALONE, SURROUNDED BY THREE MAW-BEASTS -- MAW BEASTS? SHOULD I CALL IT "THE MAW?"
ASV THUNDERER TO XIJA STATION. THIS IS A FIRST PRIORITY ADMIRALTY TRANSMISSION.
...BUH?
HERE?
PLEASE SUSPEND ALL EXTERNAL TRANSMISSION EXCEPT WITH THIS SHIP, AND PREPARE TO RECEIVE OUR BOARDING PARTY.
FAIL TO COMPLY, AND YOU WILL FIND OUR DEFERENCE TO XIJA STATION HAS ITS LIMITS.
PARKING
Xija

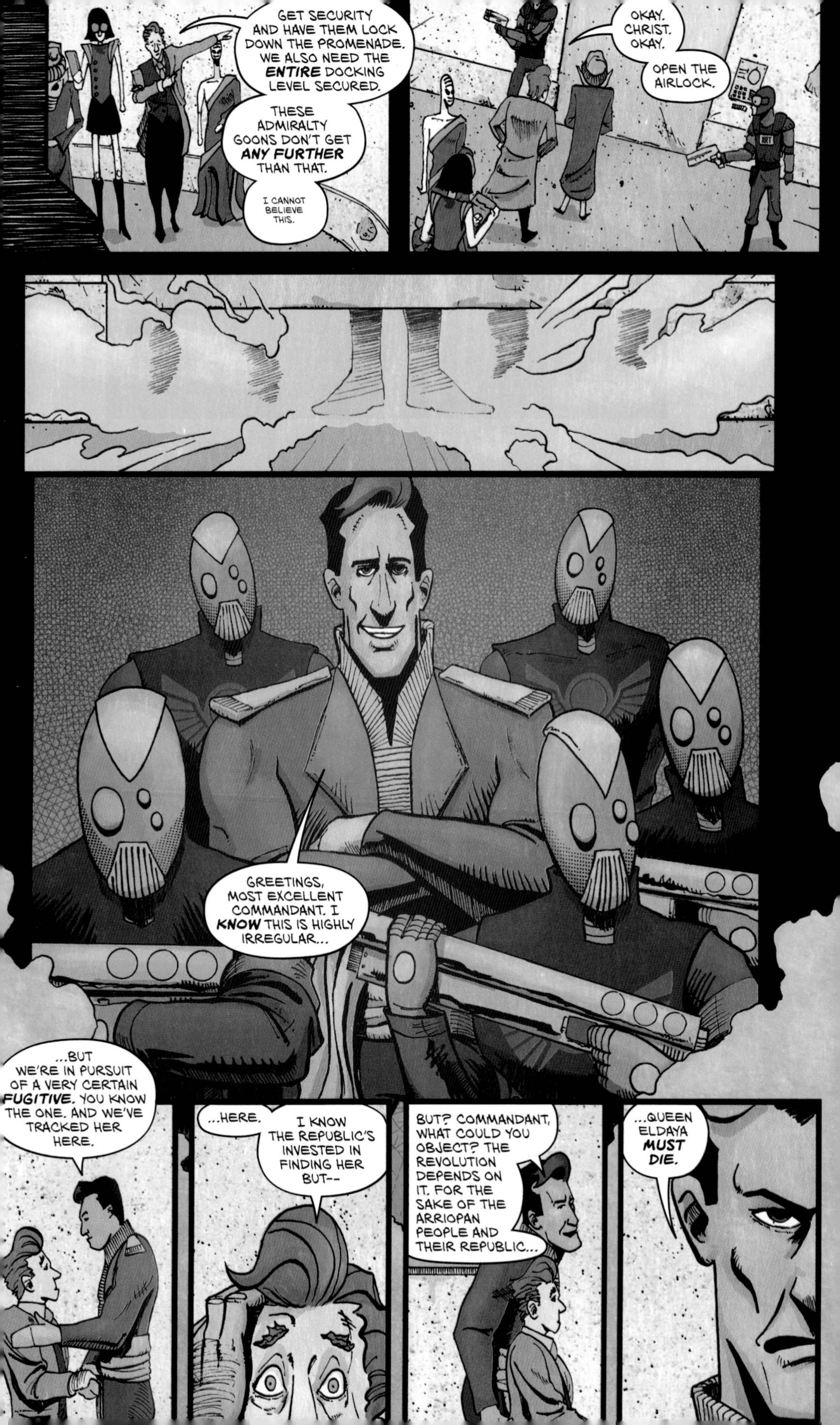
GET SECURITY AND HAVE THEM LOCK DOWN THE PROMENADE. WE ALSO NEED THE **ENTIRE** DOCKING LEVEL SECURED.
THESE ADMIRALTY GOONS DON'T GET **ANY FURTHER** THAN THAT.
I CANNOT BELIEVE THIS.
OKAY. CHRIST. OKAY.
OPEN THE AIRLOCK.
GREETINGS, MOST EXCELLENT COMMANDANT. I **KNOW** THIS IS HIGHLY IRREGULAR...
...BUT WE'RE IN PURSUIT OF A VERY CERTAIN **FUGITIVE.** YOU KNOW THE ONE. AND WE'VE TRACKED HER HERE.
...HERE.
I KNOW THE REPUBLIC'S INVESTED IN FINDING HER BUT--
BUT? COMMANDANT, WHAT COULD YOU OBJECT? THE REVOLUTION DEPENDS ON IT. FOR THE SAKE OF THE ARRIOPAN PEOPLE AND THEIR REPUBLIC...
...QUEEN ELDAYA **MUST DIE.**

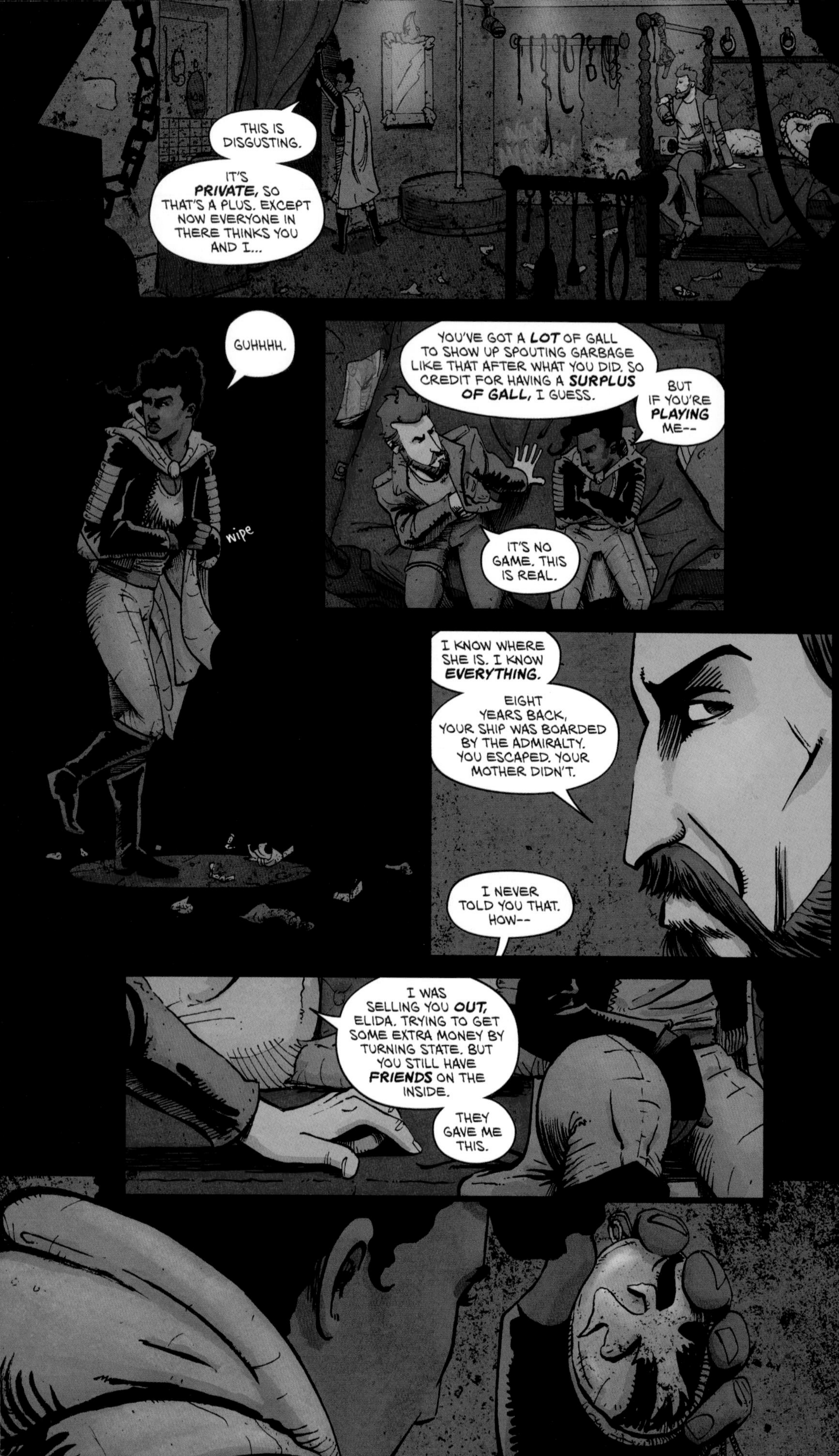

THIS IS DISGUSTING.
IT'S PRIVATE, SO THAT'S A PLUS. EXCEPT NOW EVERYONE IN THERE THINKS YOU AND I...
GUHHHH.
wipe
YOU'VE GOT A LOT OF GALL TO SHOW UP SPOUTING GARBAGE LIKE THAT AFTER WHAT YOU DID. SO CREDIT FOR HAVING A SURPLUS OF GALL, I GUESS.
BUT IF YOU'RE PLAYING ME--
IT'S NO GAME. THIS IS REAL.
I KNOW WHERE SHE IS. I KNOW EVERYTHING.
EIGHT YEARS BACK, YOUR SHIP WAS BOARDED BY THE ADMIRALTY. YOU ESCAPED. YOUR MOTHER DIDN'T.
I NEVER TOLD YOU THAT. HOW--
I WAS SELLING YOU OUT, ELIDA. TRYING TO GET SOME EXTRA MONEY BY TURNING STATE. BUT YOU STILL HAVE FRIENDS ON THE INSIDE.
THEY GAVE ME THIS.

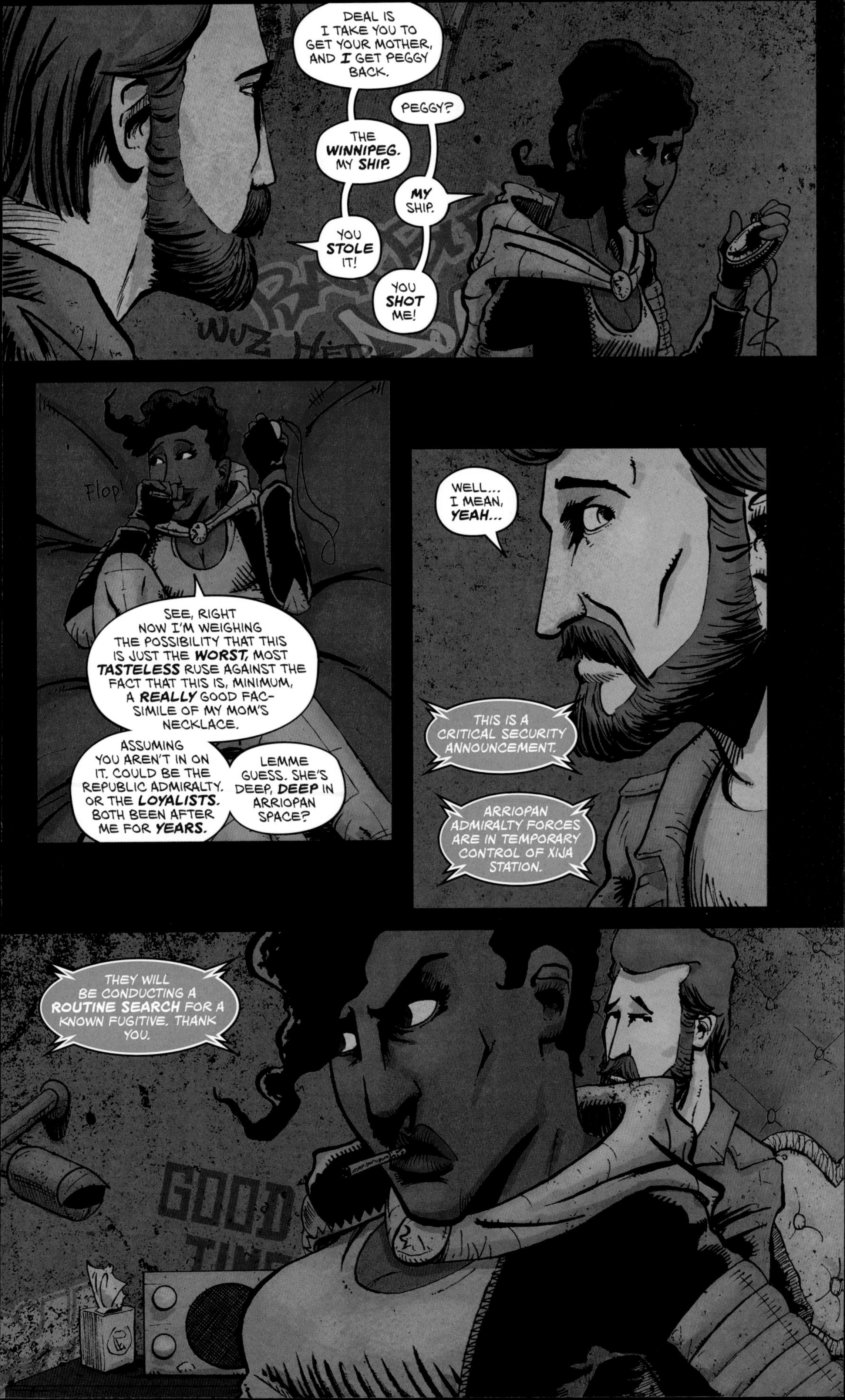
DEAL IS I TAKE YOU TO GET YOUR MOTHER, AND I GET PEGGY BACK.
PEGGY?
THE WINNIPEG. MY SHIP.
MY SHIP.
YOU STOLE IT!
YOU SHOT ME!
WUZ HER
Flop!
SEE, RIGHT NOW I'M WEIGHING THE POSSIBILITY THAT THIS IS JUST THE WORST, MOST TASTELESS RUSE AGAINST THE FACT THAT THIS IS, MINIMUM, A REALLY GOOD FAC-SIMILE OF MY MOM'S NECKLACE.
ASSUMING YOU AREN'T IN ON IT. COULD BE THE REPUBLIC ADMIRALTY. OR THE LOYALISTS. BOTH BEEN AFTER ME FOR YEARS.
LEMME GUESS. SHE'S DEEP, DEEP IN ARRIOPAN SPACE?
WELL... I MEAN, YEAH...
THIS IS A CRITICAL SECURITY ANNOUNCEMENT.
ARRIOPAN ADMIRALTY FORCES ARE IN TEMPORARY CONTROL OF XIJA STATION.
THEY WILL BE CONDUCTING A ROUTINE SEARCH FOR A KNOWN FUGITIVE. THANK YOU.
GOOD

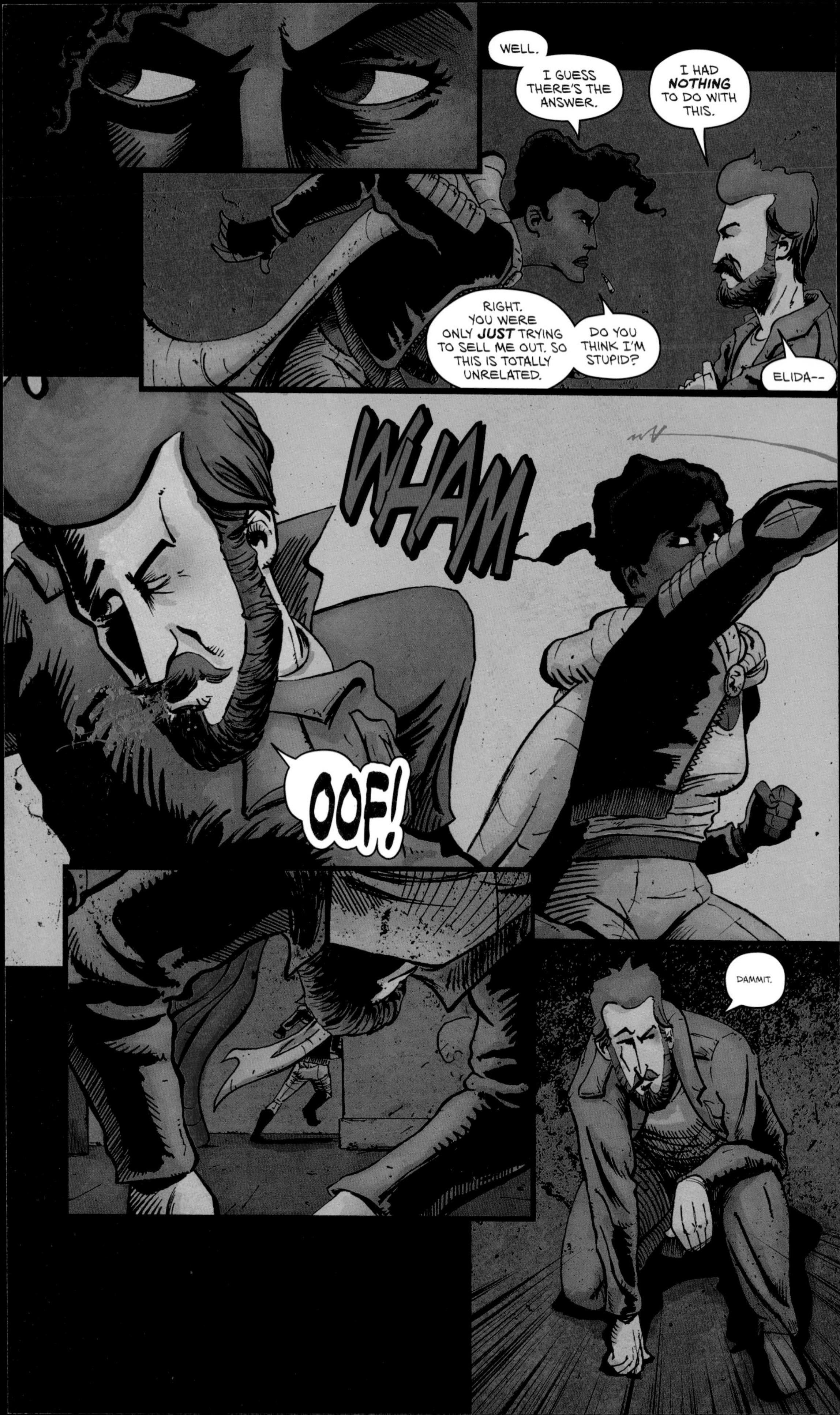
WELL.
I GUESS THERE'S THE ANSWER.
I HAD NOTHING TO DO WITH THIS.
RIGHT. YOU WERE ONLY JUST TRYING TO SELL ME OUT. SO THIS IS TOTALLY UNRELATED.
DO YOU THINK I'M STUPID?
ELIDA--
WHAM
OOF!
DAMMIT.

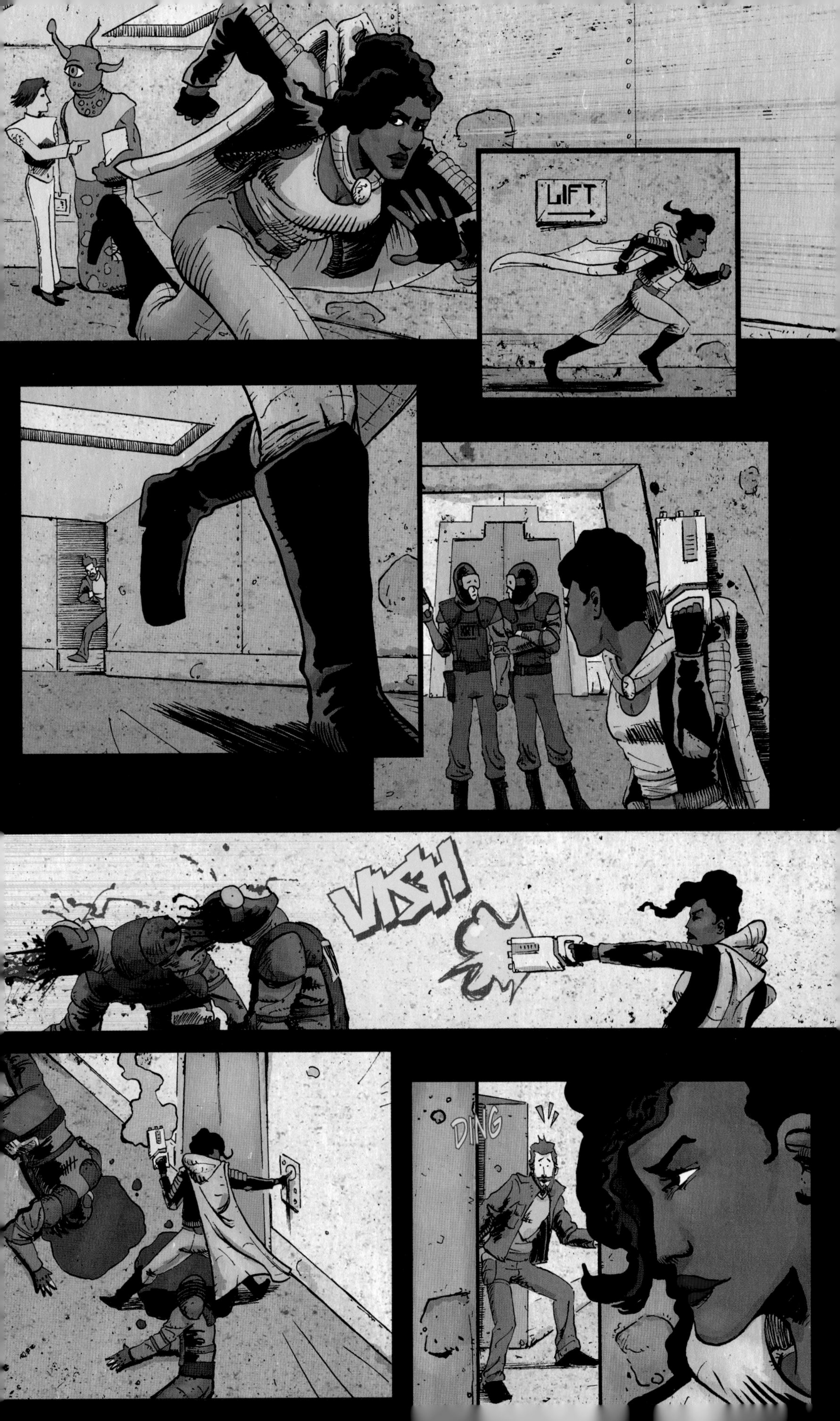

LIFT
VISH
DING

GOOD DAY, MADAME.

IT WAS.

I TAKE IT YOU ARE *ELIDA AL-FEYR?* WE'VE BEEN TRACKING THIS SHIP FOR SOME TIME. NOT ONE THAT'S HARD TO MISS, EITHER.

IT'S A BIT OF A *CLASSIC*, THE TROEZAN S900. SIXTY YEARS OLD, DISTINCTIVE SHAPE, SIGNATURE RESONANCE FREQUENCY.

DISCONTINUED SOME YEARS BACK BECAUSE THE *ENGINE* HAS A THETA RAY *LEAKAGE PROBLEM*. IN CERTAIN CIRCUMSTANCES... *KABOOM.*

STILL DETECTABLE FRO[M] SOME DISTANCE EVE[N] AFTER IT'S BEEN FIX[ED,] ESPECIALLY IF YOU['RE] KNOW WHAT YOU'RE LOOKING FOR.

I WOULDN'T.

VISH VISH VISH VISH

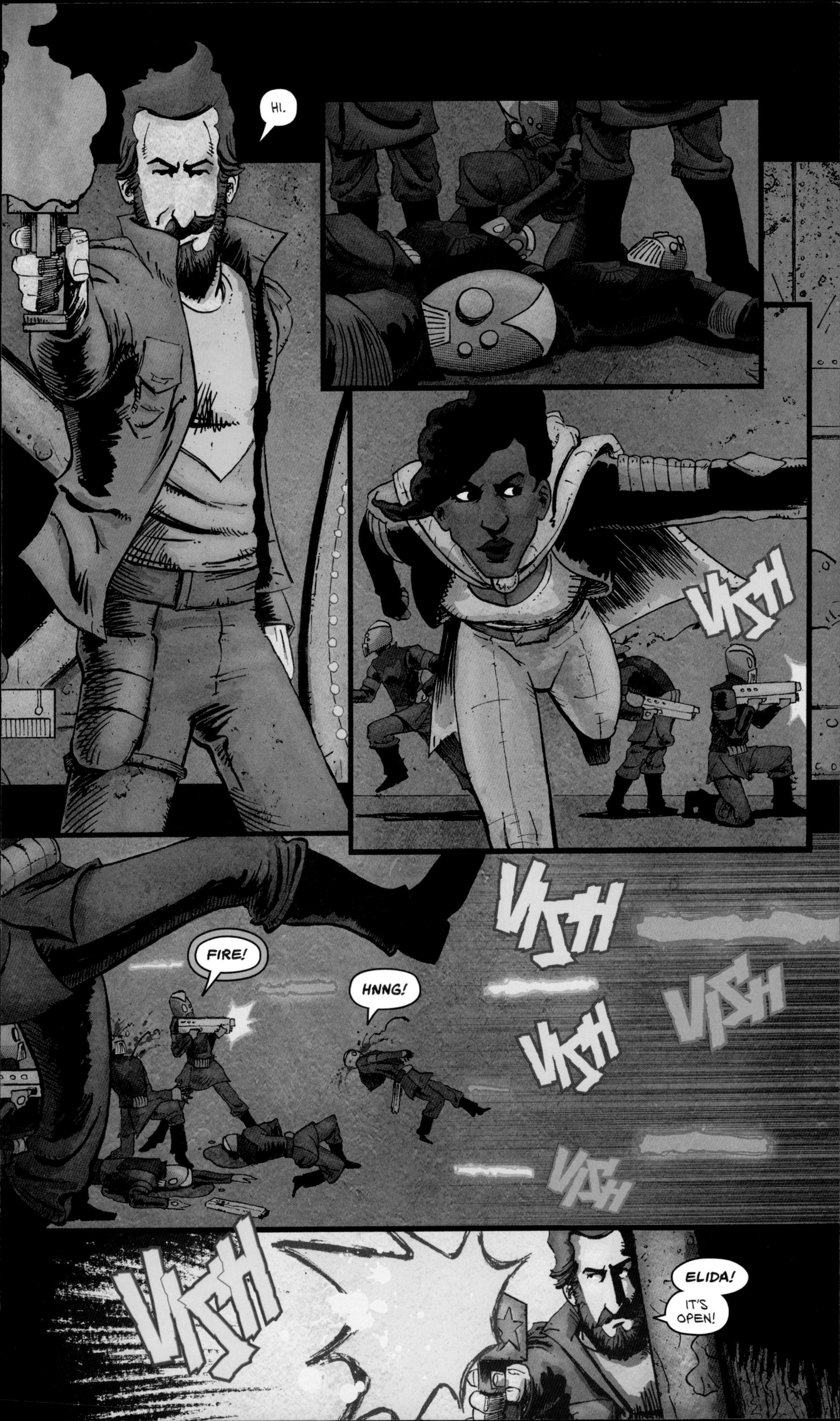
HI.
VISH
VISH
FIRE!
HNNG!
VISH
VISH
VISH
VISH
ELIDA!
IT'S OPEN!

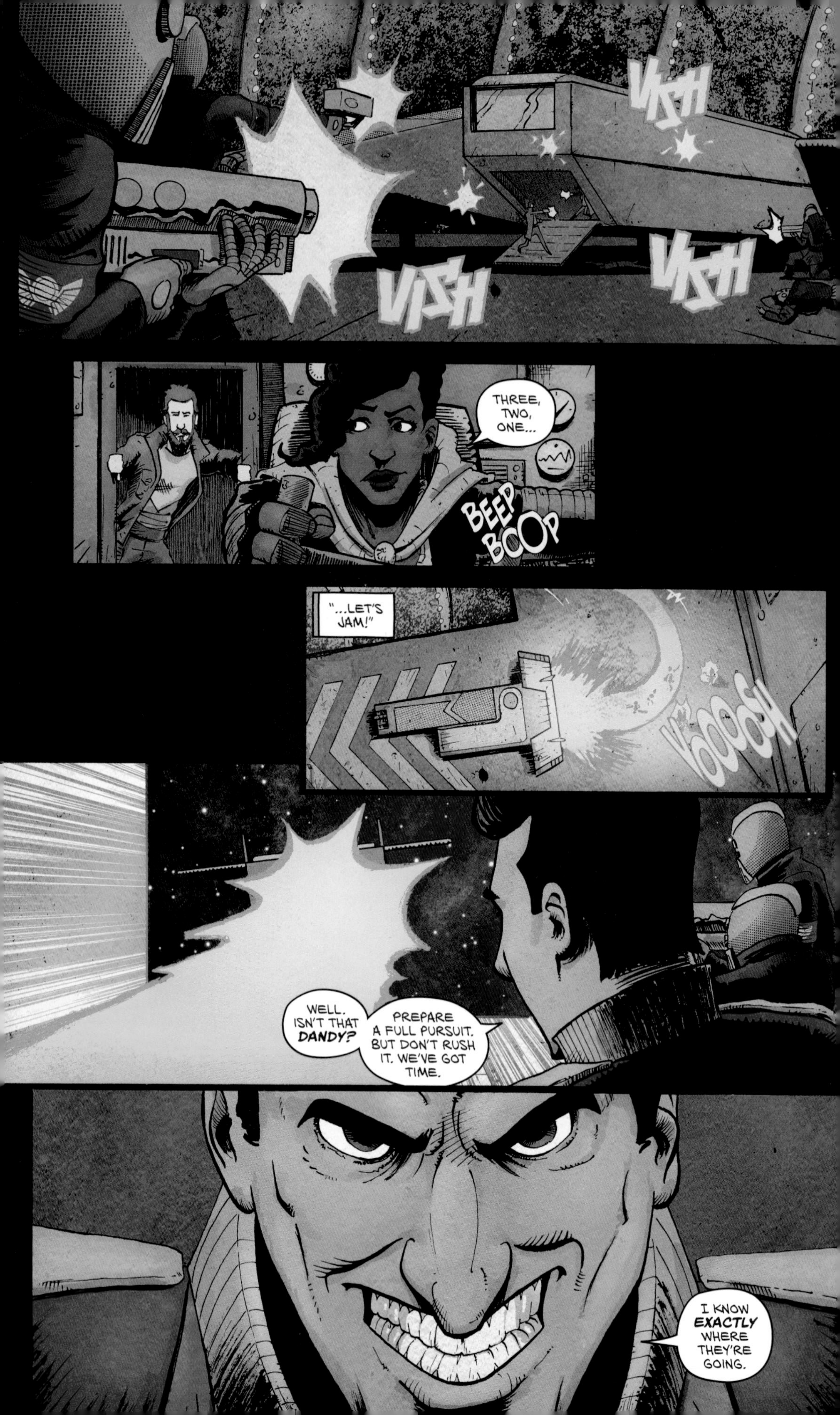

VISH
VISH
VISH
THREE, TWO, ONE...
BEEP BOOP
"...LET'S JAM!"
VOOOSH
WELL. ISN'T THAT DANDY?
PREPARE A FULL PURSUIT. BUT DON'T RUSH IT. WE'VE GOT TIME.
I KNOW EXACTLY WHERE THEY'RE GOING.

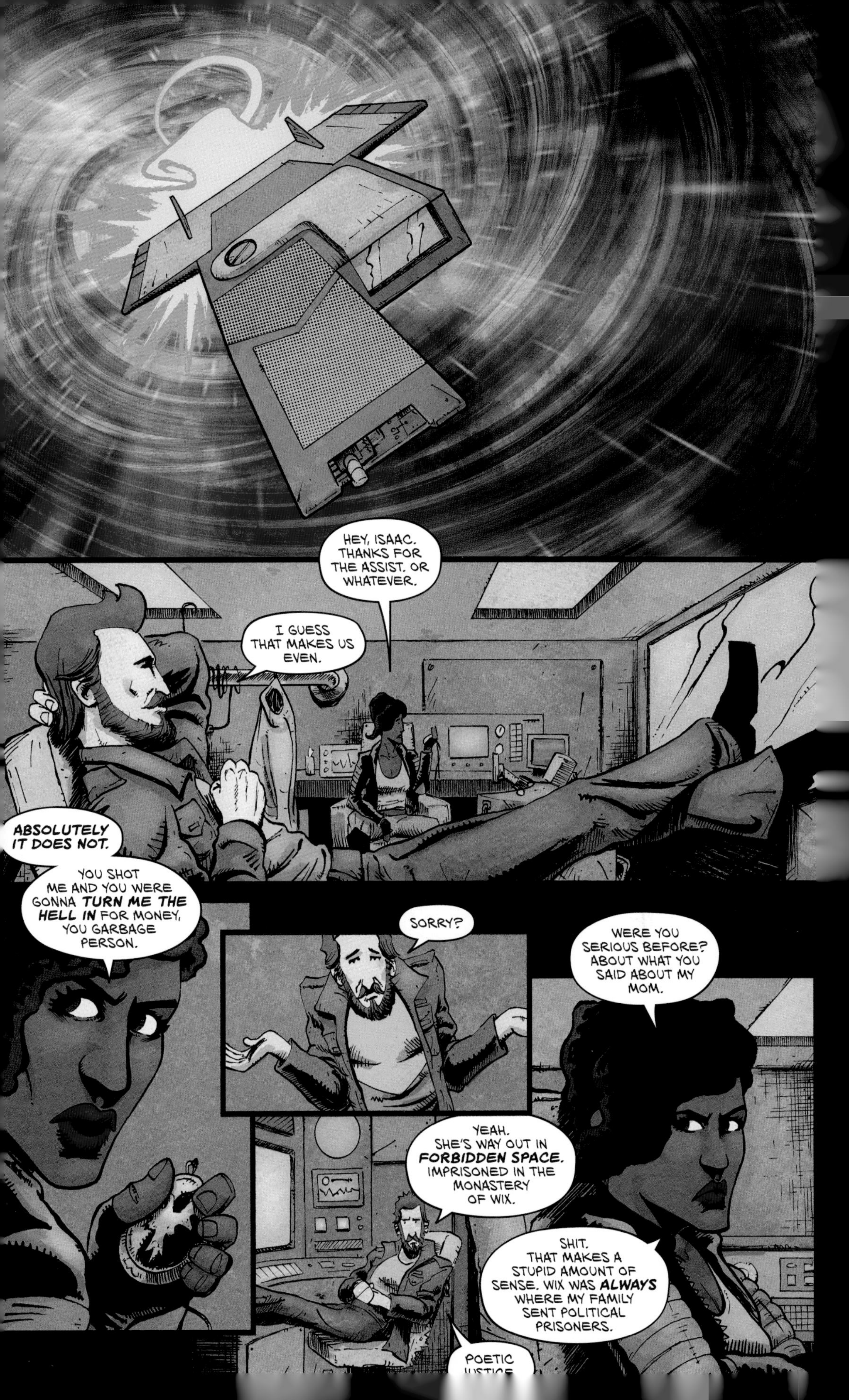

HEY, ISAAC. THANKS FOR THE ASSIST. OR WHATEVER.
I GUESS THAT MAKES US EVEN.
ABSOLUTELY IT DOES NOT.
YOU SHOT ME AND YOU WERE GONNA TURN ME THE HELL IN FOR MONEY, YOU GARBAGE PERSON.
SORRY?
WERE YOU SERIOUS BEFORE? ABOUT WHAT YOU SAID ABOUT MY MOM.
YEAH. SHE'S WAY OUT IN FORBIDDEN SPACE. IMPRISONED IN THE MONASTERY OF WIX.
SHIT. THAT MAKES A STUPID AMOUNT OF SENSE. WIX WAS ALWAYS WHERE MY FAMILY SENT POLITICAL PRISONERS.
POETIC

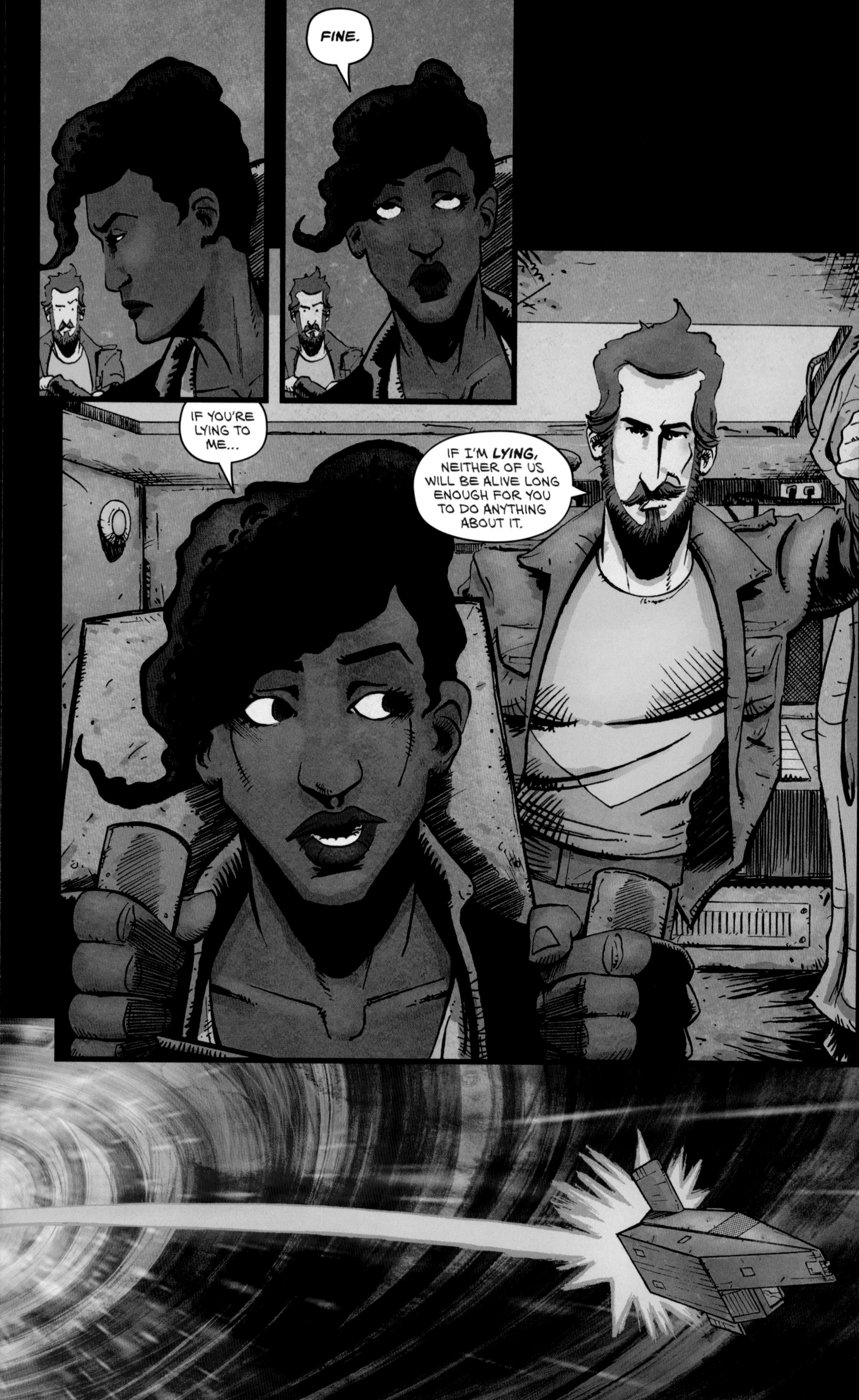
FINE.
IF YOU'RE LYING TO ME...
IF I'M LYING, NEITHER OF US WILL BE ALIVE LONG ENOUGH FOR YOU TO DO ANYTHING ABOUT IT.

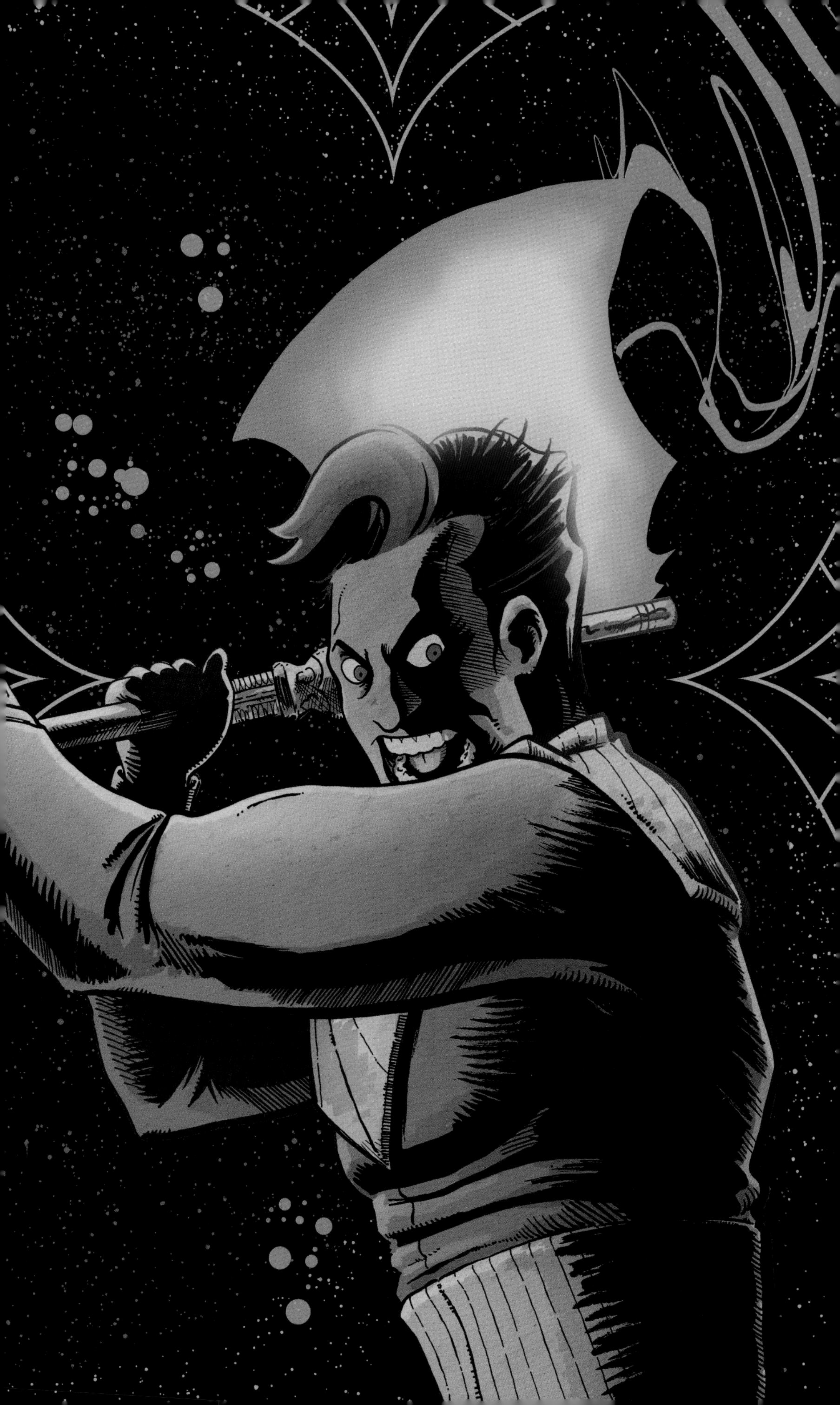

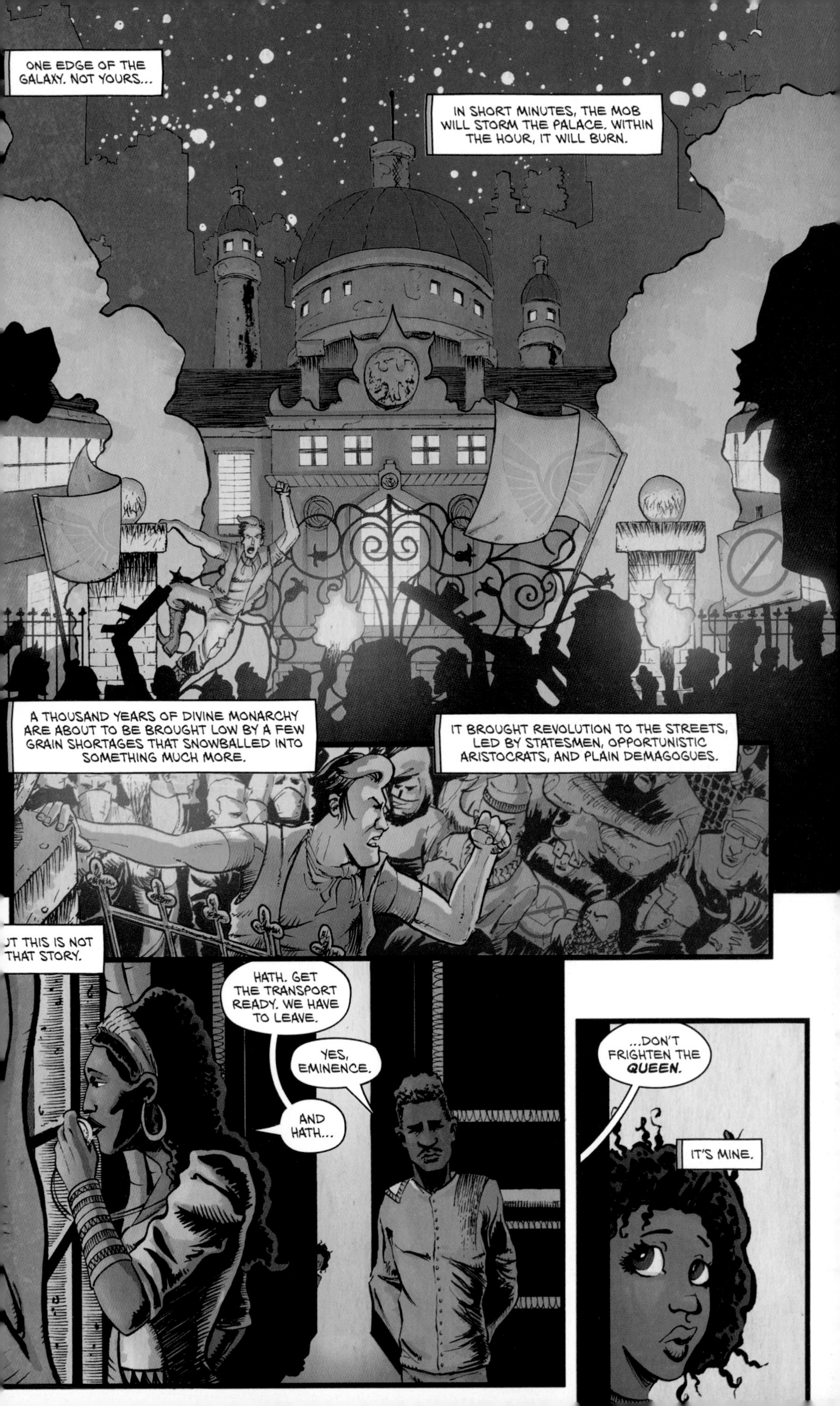
ONE EDGE OF THE GALAXY. NOT YOURS...
IN SHORT MINUTES, THE MOB WILL STORM THE PALACE. WITHIN THE HOUR, IT WILL BURN.
A THOUSAND YEARS OF DIVINE MONARCHY ARE ABOUT TO BE BROUGHT LOW BY A FEW GRAIN SHORTAGES THAT SNOWBALLED INTO SOMETHING MUCH MORE.
IT BROUGHT REVOLUTION TO THE STREETS, LED BY STATESMEN, OPPORTUNISTIC ARISTOCRATS, AND PLAIN DEMAGOGUES.
UT THIS IS NOT THAT STORY.
HATH. GET THE TRANSPORT READY. WE HAVE TO LEAVE.
YES, EMINENCE.
AND HATH...
...DON'T FRIGHTEN THE **QUEEN**.
IT'S MINE.

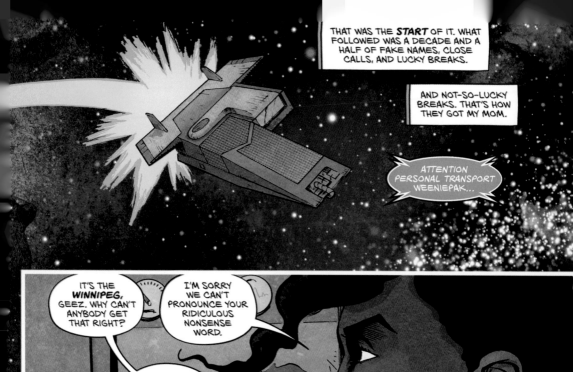

THAT WAS THE **START** OF IT. WHAT FOLLOWED WAS A DECADE AND A HALF OF FAKE NAMES, CLOSE CALLS, AND LUCKY BREAKS.

AND NOT-SO-LUCKY BREAKS. THAT'S HOW THEY GOT MY MOM.

ATTENTION PERSONAL TRANSPORT WEENIEPAK...

IT'S THE **WINNIPEG**, GEEZ. WHY CAN'T ANYBODY GET THAT RIGHT?

I'M SORRY WE CAN'T PRONOUNCE YOUR RIDICULOUS NONSENSE WORD.

THAT'S MY HOMETOWN, YOU INCONSIDERATE **ASS**.

REPEAT, ATTENTION. YOU HAVE ENTERED A NO-FLY ZONE.

YOU **KNOW** THEY'RE GONNA TOW US IN, RIGHT?

DON'T WORRY. I HAVE A PLAN.

DO YOU?

shrug!

MOSTLY.

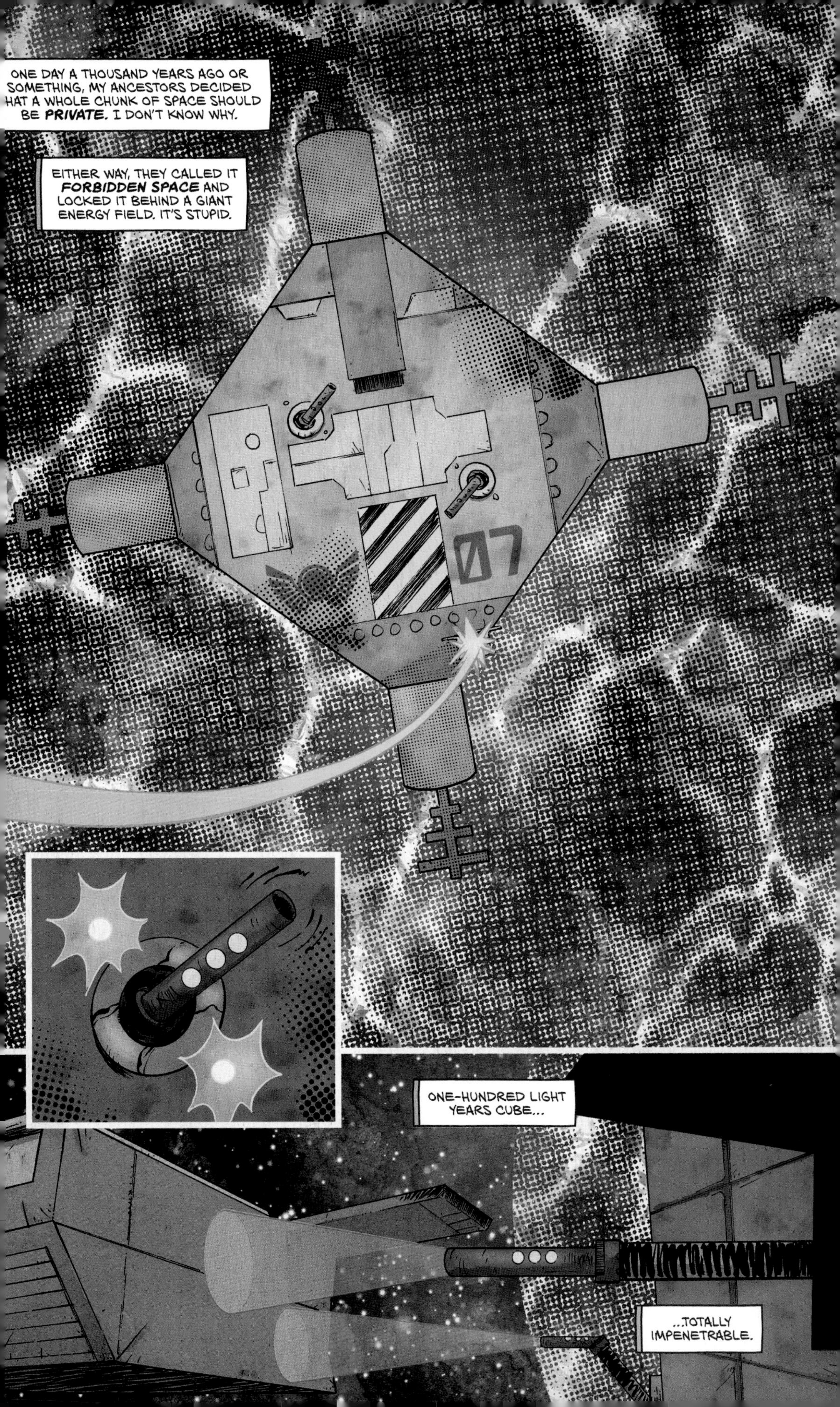

ONE DAY A THOUSAND YEARS AGO OR SOMETHING, MY ANCESTORS DECIDED HAT A WHOLE CHUNK OF SPACE SHOULD BE **PRIVATE.** I DON'T KNOW WHY.
EITHER WAY, THEY CALLED IT **FORBIDDEN SPACE** AND LOCKED IT BEHIND A GIANT ENERGY FIELD. IT'S STUPID.
07
ONE-HUNDRED LIGHT YEARS CUBE...
...TOTALLY IMPENETRABLE.

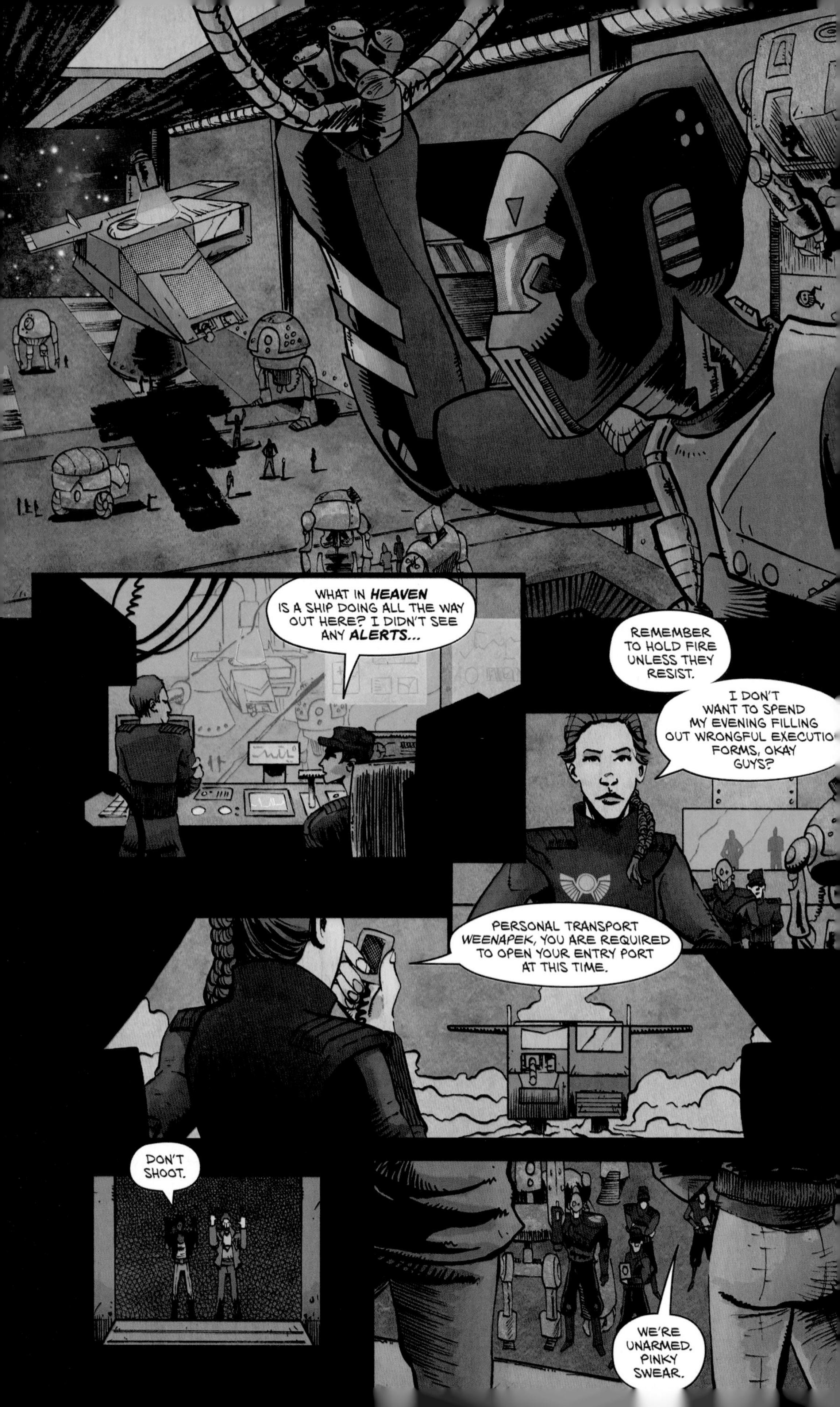
WHAT IN **HEAVEN** IS A SHIP DOING ALL THE WAY OUT HERE? I DIDN'T SEE ANY **ALERTS...**
REMEMBER TO HOLD FIRE UNLESS THEY RESIST.
I DON'T WANT TO SPEND MY EVENING FILLING OUT WRONGFUL EXECUTIO FORMS, OKAY GUYS?
PERSONAL TRANSPORT *WEENAPEK*, YOU ARE REQUIRED TO OPEN YOUR ENTRY PORT AT THIS TIME.
DON'T SHOOT.
WE'RE UNARMED. PINKY SWEAR.

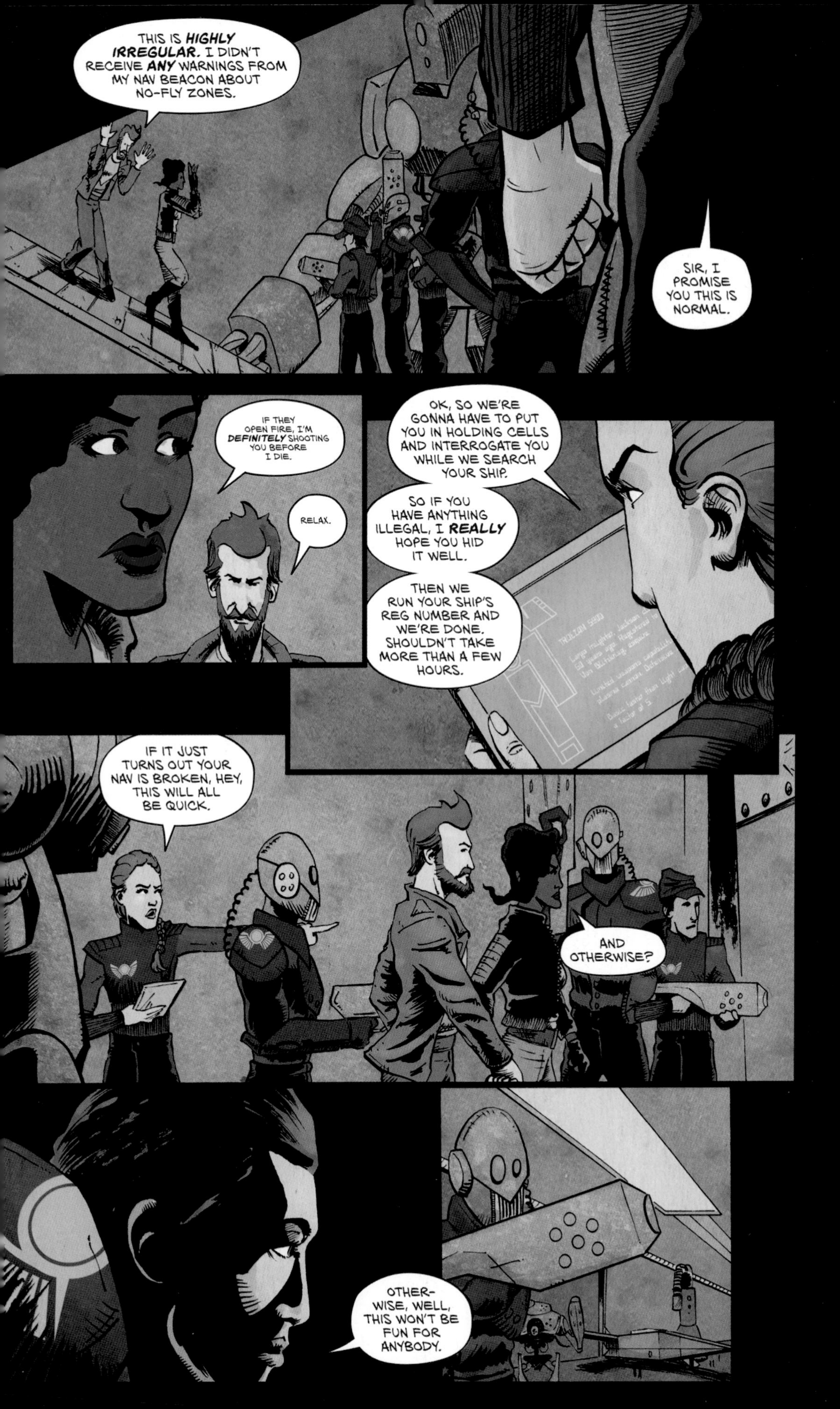
THIS IS HIGHLY IRREGULAR. I DIDN'T RECEIVE ANY WARNINGS FROM MY NAV BEACON ABOUT NO-FLY ZONES.
SIR, I PROMISE YOU THIS IS NORMAL.
IF THEY OPEN FIRE, I'M DEFINITELY SHOOTING YOU BEFORE I DIE.
RELAX.
OK, SO WE'RE GONNA HAVE TO PUT YOU IN HOLDING CELLS AND INTERROGATE YOU WHILE WE SEARCH YOUR SHIP.
SO IF YOU HAVE ANYTHING ILLEGAL, I REALLY HOPE YOU HID IT WELL.
THEN WE RUN YOUR SHIP'S REG NUMBER AND WE'RE DONE. SHOULDN'T TAKE MORE THAN A FEW HOURS.
IF IT JUST TURNS OUT YOUR NAV IS BROKEN, HEY, THIS WILL ALL BE QUICK.
AND OTHERWISE?
OTHER-WISE, WELL, THIS WON'T BE FUN FOR ANYBODY.

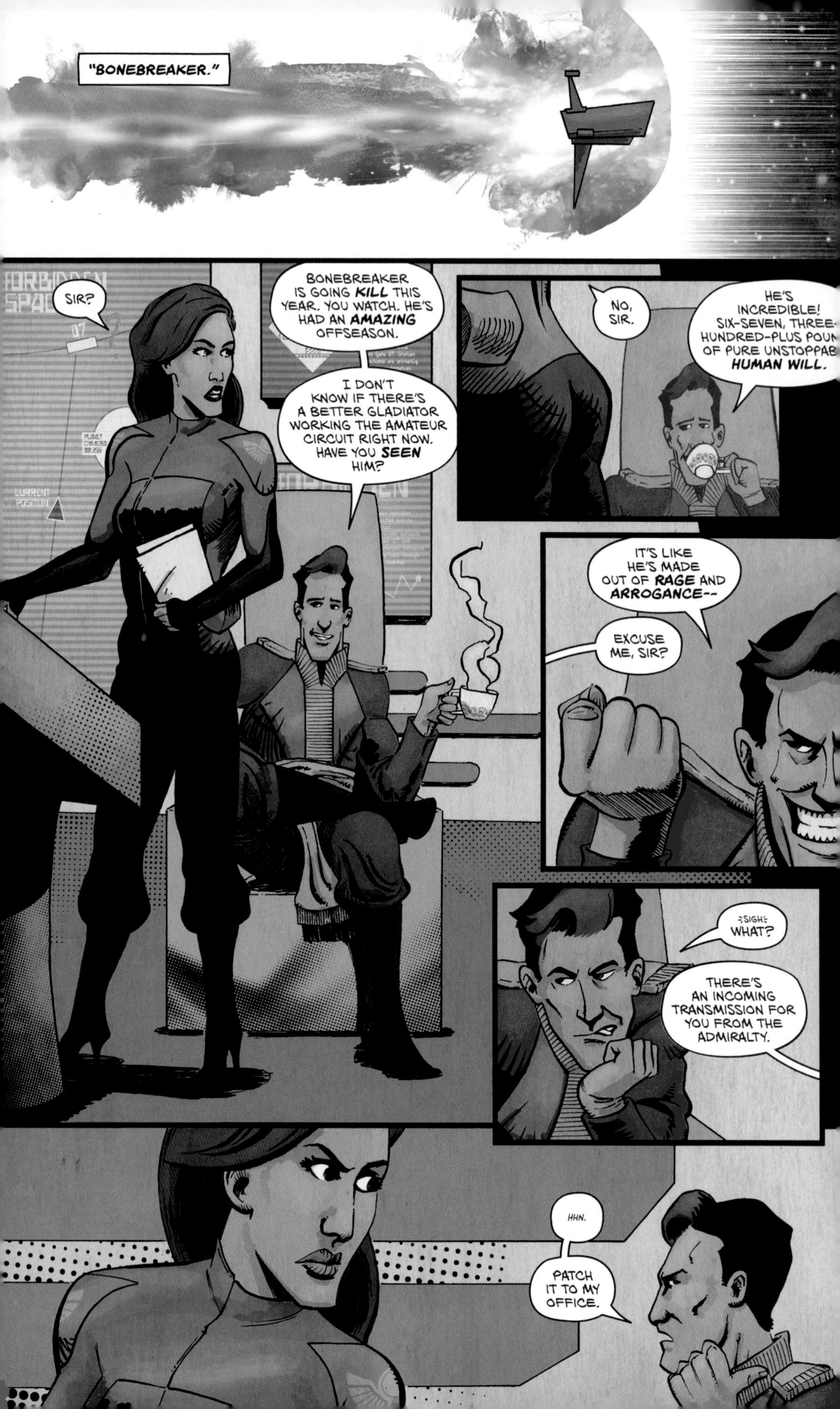

"BONEBREAKER."
FORBIDDEN SPACE
PLANET CHIMERA
CURRENT POSITION
SIR?
BONEBREAKER IS GOING KILL THIS YEAR. YOU WATCH. HE'S HAD AN AMAZING OFFSEASON.
I DON'T KNOW IF THERE'S A BETTER GLADIATOR WORKING THE AMATEUR CIRCUIT RIGHT NOW. HAVE YOU SEEN HIM?
NO, SIR.
HE'S INCREDIBLE! SIX-SEVEN, THREE-HUNDRED-PLUS POUN OF PURE UNSTOPPAB HUMAN WILL.
IT'S LIKE HE'S MADE OUT OF RAGE AND ARROGANCE--
EXCUSE ME, SIR?
SIGH WHAT?
THERE'S AN INCOMING TRANSMISSION FOR YOU FROM THE ADMIRALTY.
HHN.
PATCH IT TO MY OFFICE.

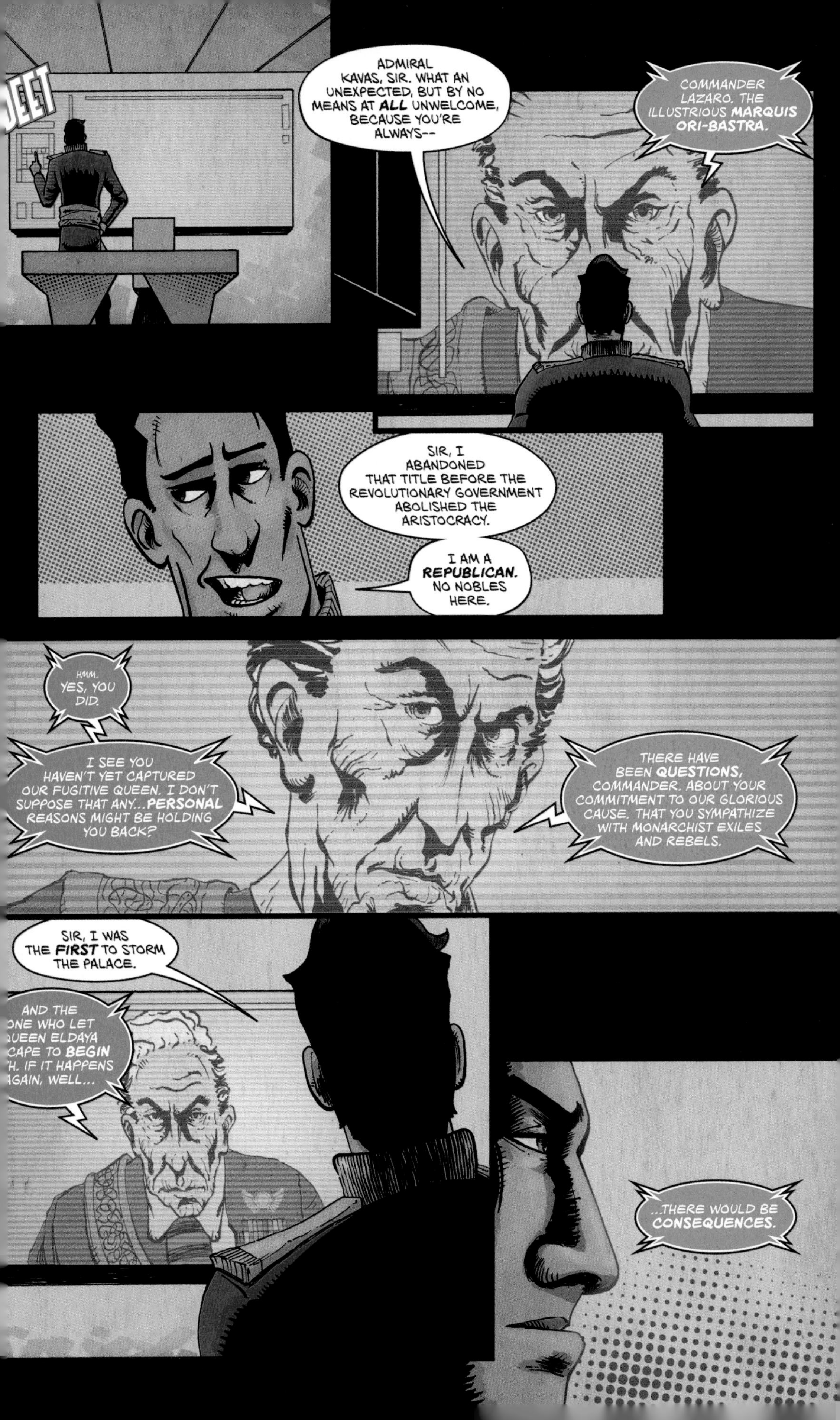
JEET
ADMIRAL KAVAS, SIR. WHAT AN UNEXPECTED, BUT BY NO MEANS AT **ALL** UNWELCOME, BECAUSE YOU'RE ALWAYS--
COMMANDER LAZARO. THE ILLUSTRIOUS **MARQUIS ORI-BASTRA.**
SIR, I ABANDONED THAT TITLE BEFORE THE REVOLUTIONARY GOVERNMENT ABOLISHED THE ARISTOCRACY.
I AM A **REPUBLICAN.** NO NOBLES HERE.
HMM. YES, YOU DID.
I SEE YOU HAVEN'T YET CAPTURED OUR FUGITIVE QUEEN. I DON'T SUPPOSE THAT ANY... **PERSONAL** REASONS MIGHT BE HOLDING YOU BACK?
THERE HAVE BEEN **QUESTIONS,** COMMANDER. ABOUT YOUR COMMITMENT TO OUR GLORIOUS CAUSE. THAT YOU SYMPATHIZE WITH MONARCHIST EXILES AND REBELS.
SIR, I WAS THE **FIRST** TO STORM THE PALACE.
AND THE ONE WHO LET QUEEN ELDAYA CAPE TO **BEGIN** H. IF IT HAPPENS AGAIN, WELL...
...THERE WOULD BE **CONSEQUENCES.**

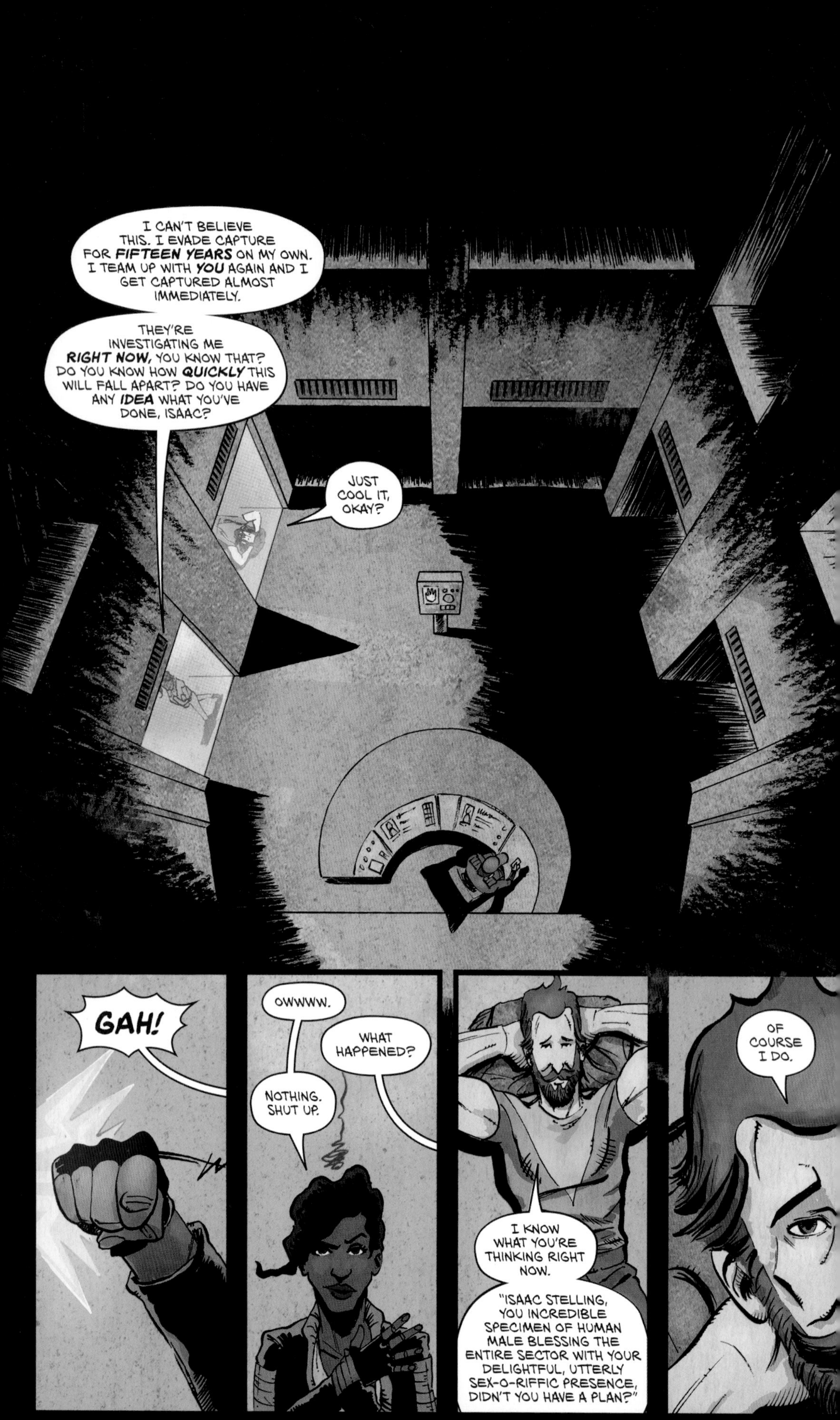
I CAN'T BELIEVE THIS. I EVADE CAPTURE FOR FIFTEEN YEARS ON MY OWN. I TEAM UP WITH YOU AGAIN AND I GET CAPTURED ALMOST IMMEDIATELY.
THEY'RE INVESTIGATING ME RIGHT NOW, YOU KNOW THAT? DO YOU KNOW HOW QUICKLY THIS WILL FALL APART? DO YOU HAVE ANY IDEA WHAT YOU'VE DONE, ISAAC?
JUST COOL IT, OKAY?
GAH!
OWWWW.
WHAT HAPPENED?
NOTHING. SHUT UP.
I KNOW WHAT YOU'RE THINKING RIGHT NOW.
"ISAAC STELLING, YOU INCREDIBLE SPECIMEN OF HUMAN MALE BLESSING THE ENTIRE SECTOR WITH YOUR DELIGHTFUL, UTTERLY SEX-O-RIFFIC PRESENCE, DIDN'T YOU HAVE A PLAN?"
OF COURSE I DO.

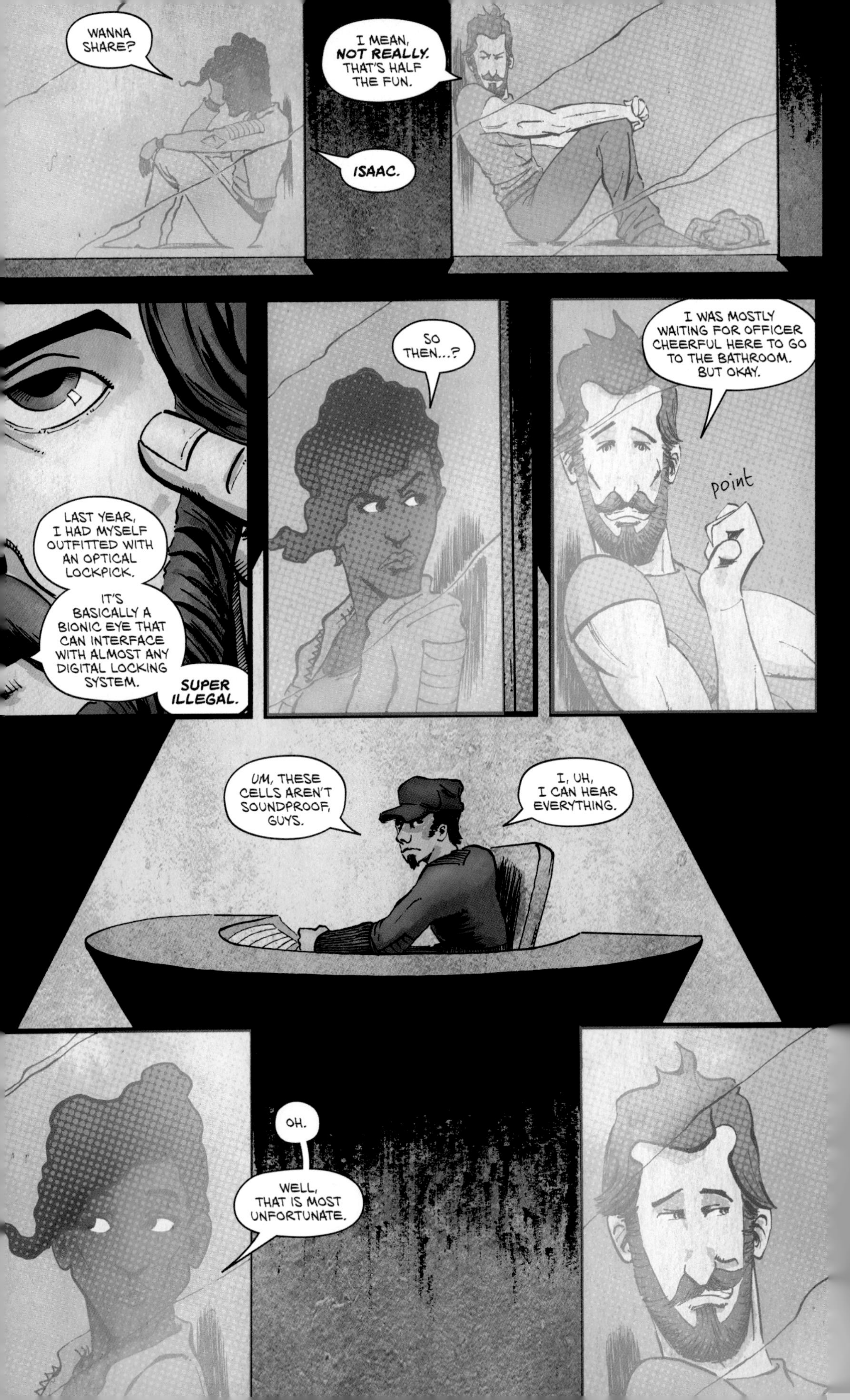
WANNA SHARE?
I MEAN, **NOT REALLY.** THAT'S HALF THE FUN.
ISAAC.
SO THEN...?
I WAS MOSTLY WAITING FOR OFFICER CHEERFUL HERE TO GO TO THE BATHROOM. BUT OKAY.
point
LAST YEAR, I HAD MYSELF OUTFITTED WITH AN OPTICAL LOCKPICK.
IT'S BASICALLY A BIONIC EYE THAT CAN INTERFACE WITH ALMOST ANY DIGITAL LOCKING SYSTEM.
SUPER ILLEGAL.
UM, THESE CELLS AREN'T SOUNDPROOF, GUYS.
I, UH, I CAN HEAR EVERYTHING.
OH.
WELL, THAT IS MOST UNFORTUNATE.

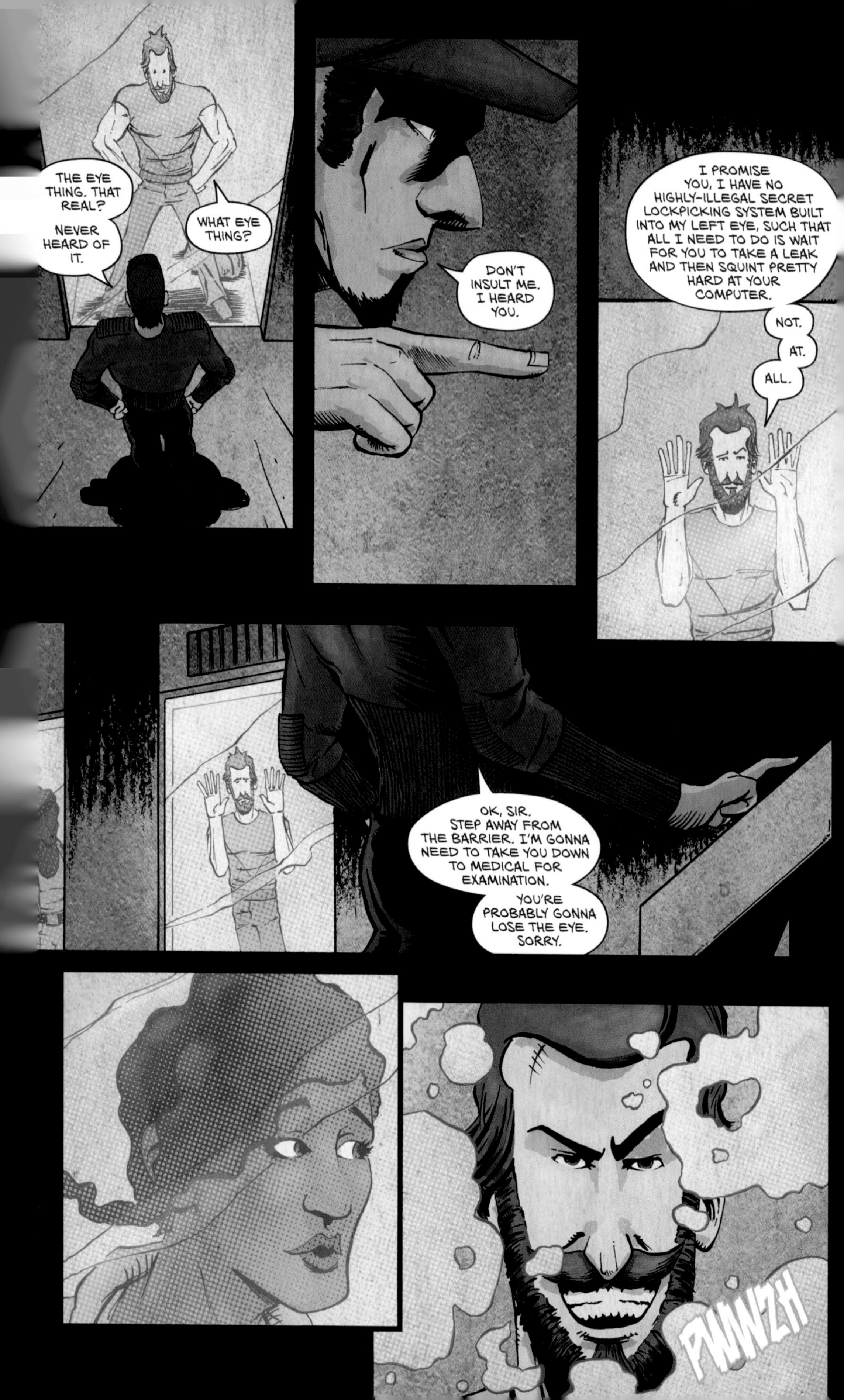
THE EYE THING. THAT REAL?
NEVER HEARD OF IT.
WHAT EYE THING?
DON'T INSULT ME. I HEARD YOU.
I PROMISE YOU, I HAVE NO HIGHLY-ILLEGAL SECRET LOCKPICKING SYSTEM BUILT INTO MY LEFT EYE, SUCH THAT ALL I NEED TO DO IS WAIT FOR YOU TO TAKE A LEAK AND THEN SQUINT PRETTY HARD AT YOUR COMPUTER.
NOT.
AT.
ALL.
OK, SIR. STEP AWAY FROM THE BARRIER. I'M GONNA NEED TO TAKE YOU DOWN TO MEDICAL FOR EXAMINATION.
YOU'RE PROBABLY GONNA LOSE THE EYE. SORRY.
PWWZH

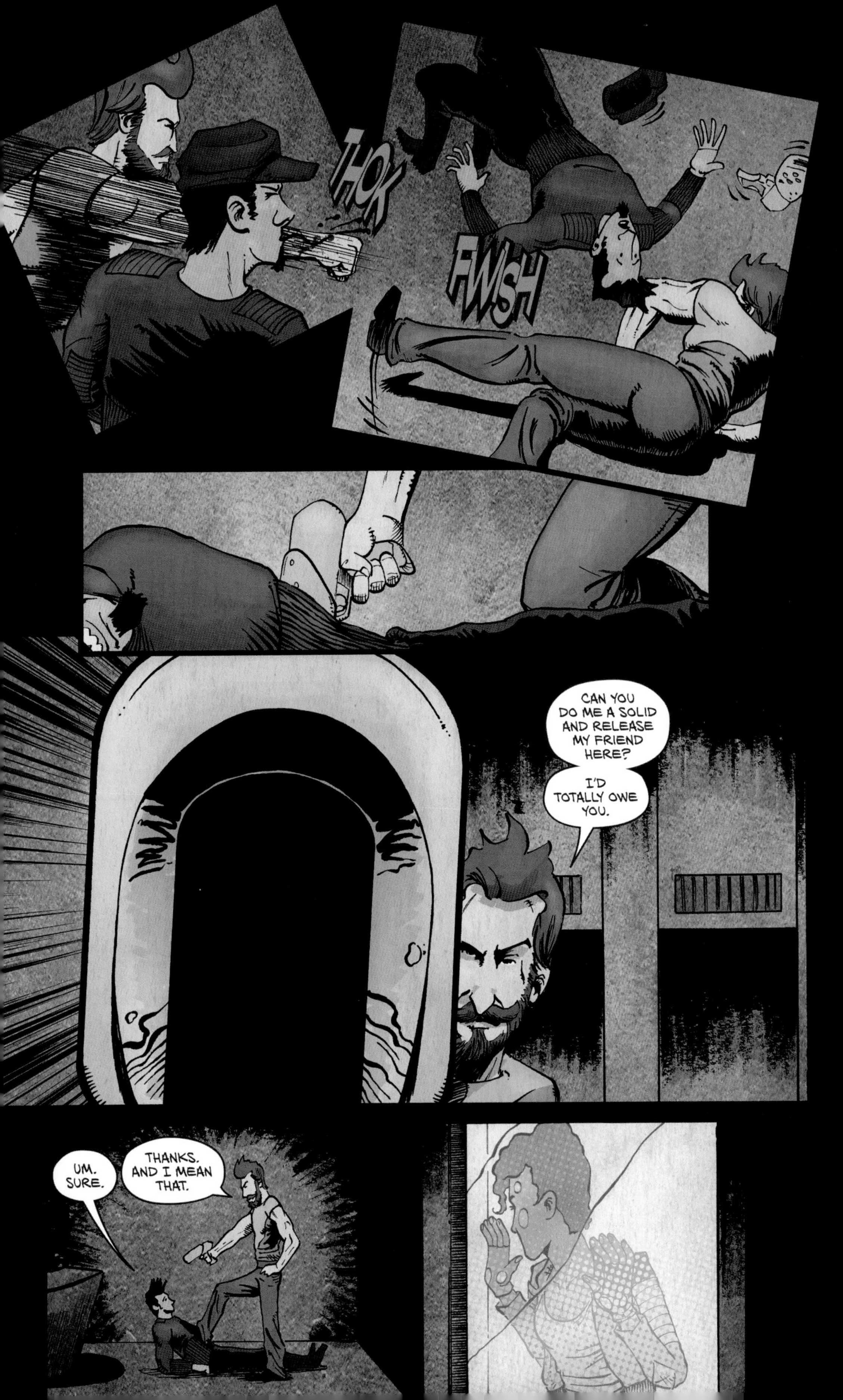
THOK
FWISH
CAN YOU DO ME A SOLID AND RELEASE MY FRIEND HERE?
I'D TOTALLY OWE YOU.
THANKS. AND I MEAN THAT.
UM. SURE.

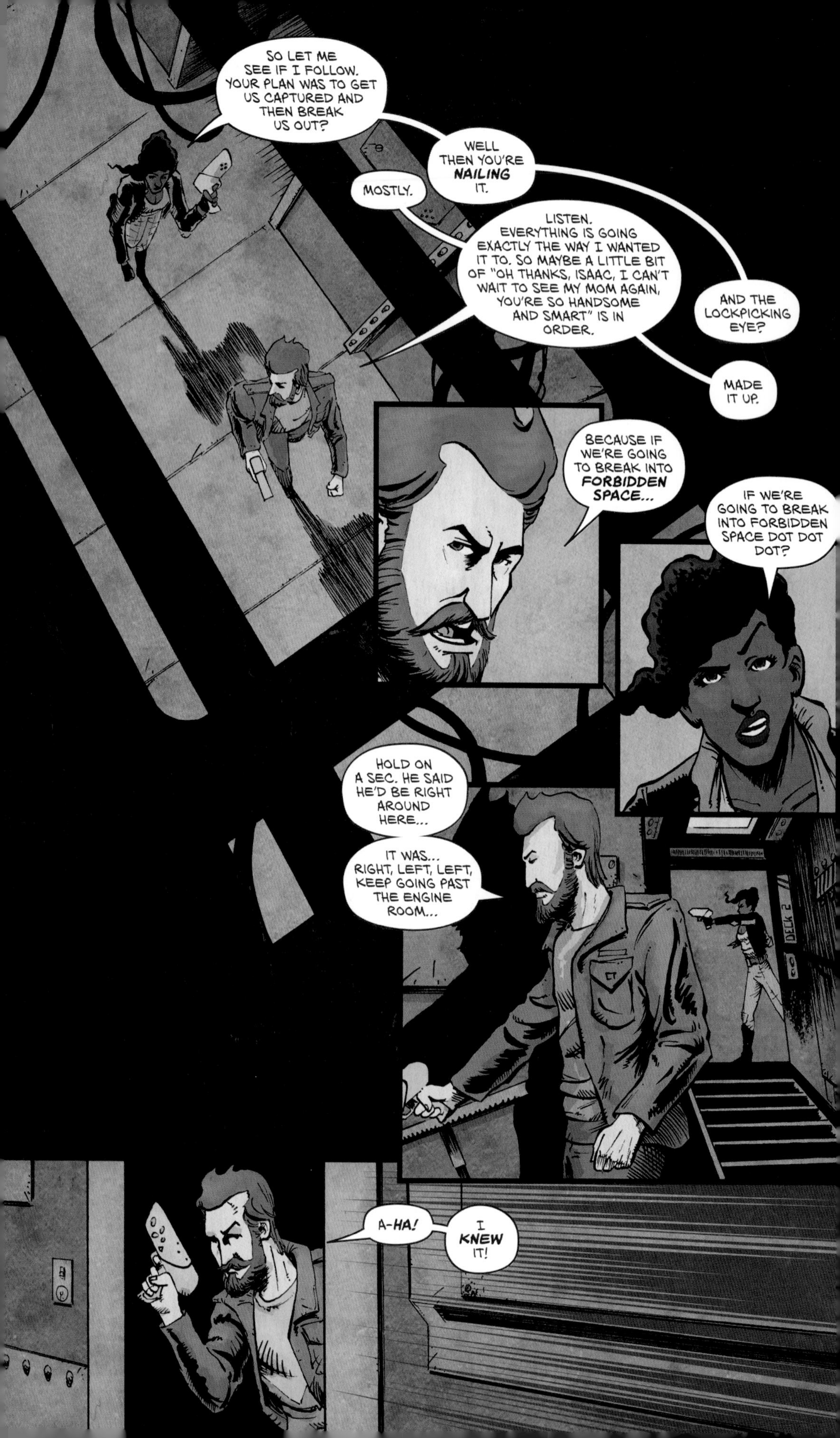
SO LET ME SEE IF I FOLLOW. YOUR PLAN WAS TO GET US CAPTURED AND THEN BREAK US OUT?
WELL THEN YOU'RE NAILING IT.
MOSTLY.
LISTEN. EVERYTHING IS GOING EXACTLY THE WAY I WANTED IT TO. SO MAYBE A LITTLE BIT OF "OH THANKS, ISAAC, I CAN'T WAIT TO SEE MY MOM AGAIN, YOU'RE SO HANDSOME AND SMART" IS IN ORDER.
AND THE LOCKPICKING EYE?
MADE IT UP.
BECAUSE IF WE'RE GOING TO BREAK INTO FORBIDDEN SPACE...
IF WE'RE GOING TO BREAK INTO FORBIDDEN SPACE DOT DOT DOT?
HOLD ON A SEC. HE SAID HE'D BE RIGHT AROUND HERE...
IT WAS... RIGHT, LEFT, LEFT, KEEP GOING PAST THE ENGINE ROOM...
DECK 2
A-HA!
I KNEW IT!

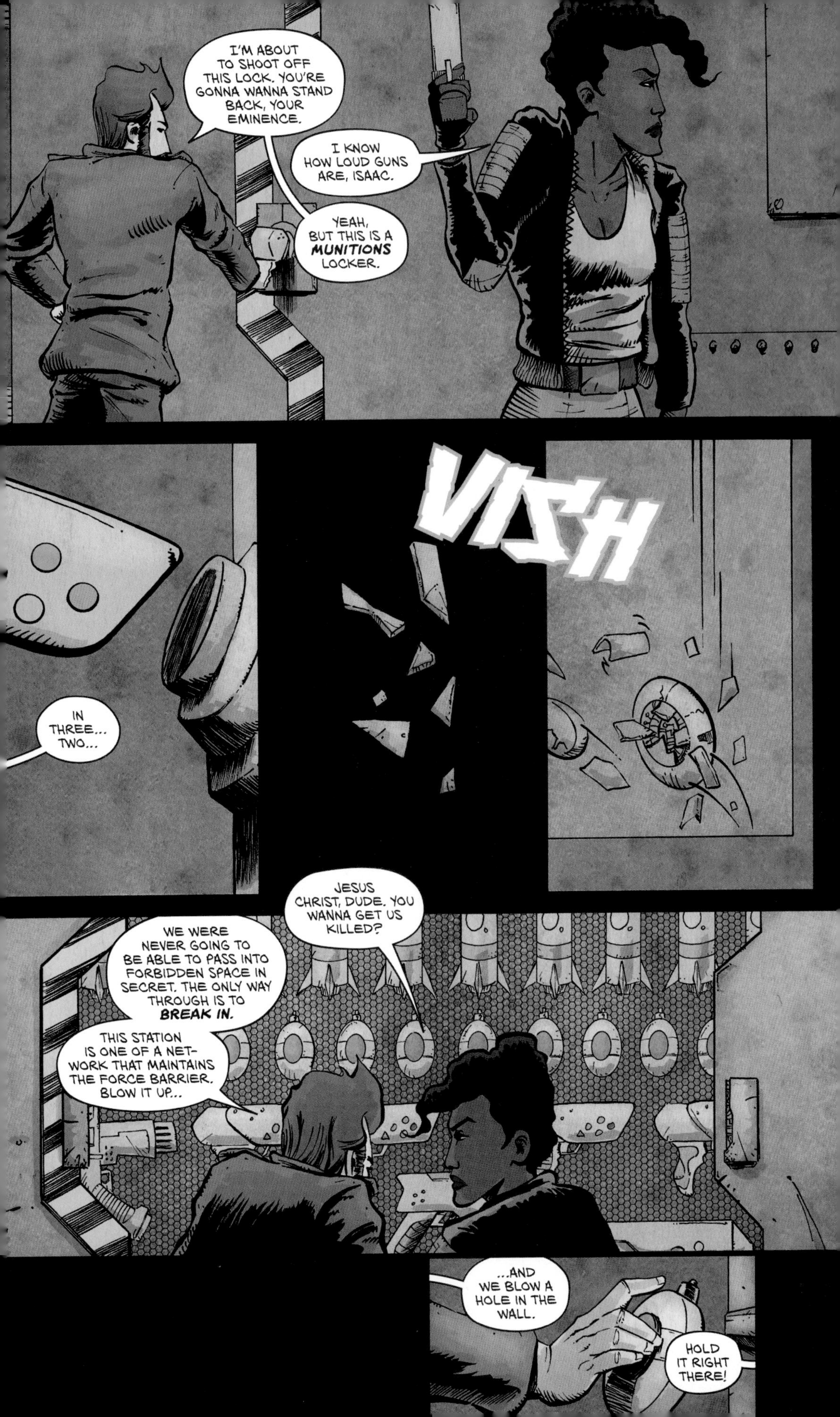
I'M ABOUT TO SHOOT OFF THIS LOCK. YOU'RE GONNA WANNA STAND BACK, YOUR EMINENCE.
I KNOW HOW LOUD GUNS ARE, ISAAC.
YEAH, BUT THIS IS A **MUNITIONS** LOCKER.
IN THREE... TWO...
VISH
JESUS CHRIST, DUDE. YOU WANNA GET US KILLED?
WE WERE NEVER GOING TO BE ABLE TO PASS INTO FORBIDDEN SPACE IN SECRET. THE ONLY WAY THROUGH IS TO **BREAK IN.**
THIS STATION IS ONE OF A NET-WORK THAT MAINTAINS THE FORCE BARRIER. BLOW IT UP...
...AND WE BLOW A HOLE IN THE WALL.
HOLD IT RIGHT THERE!

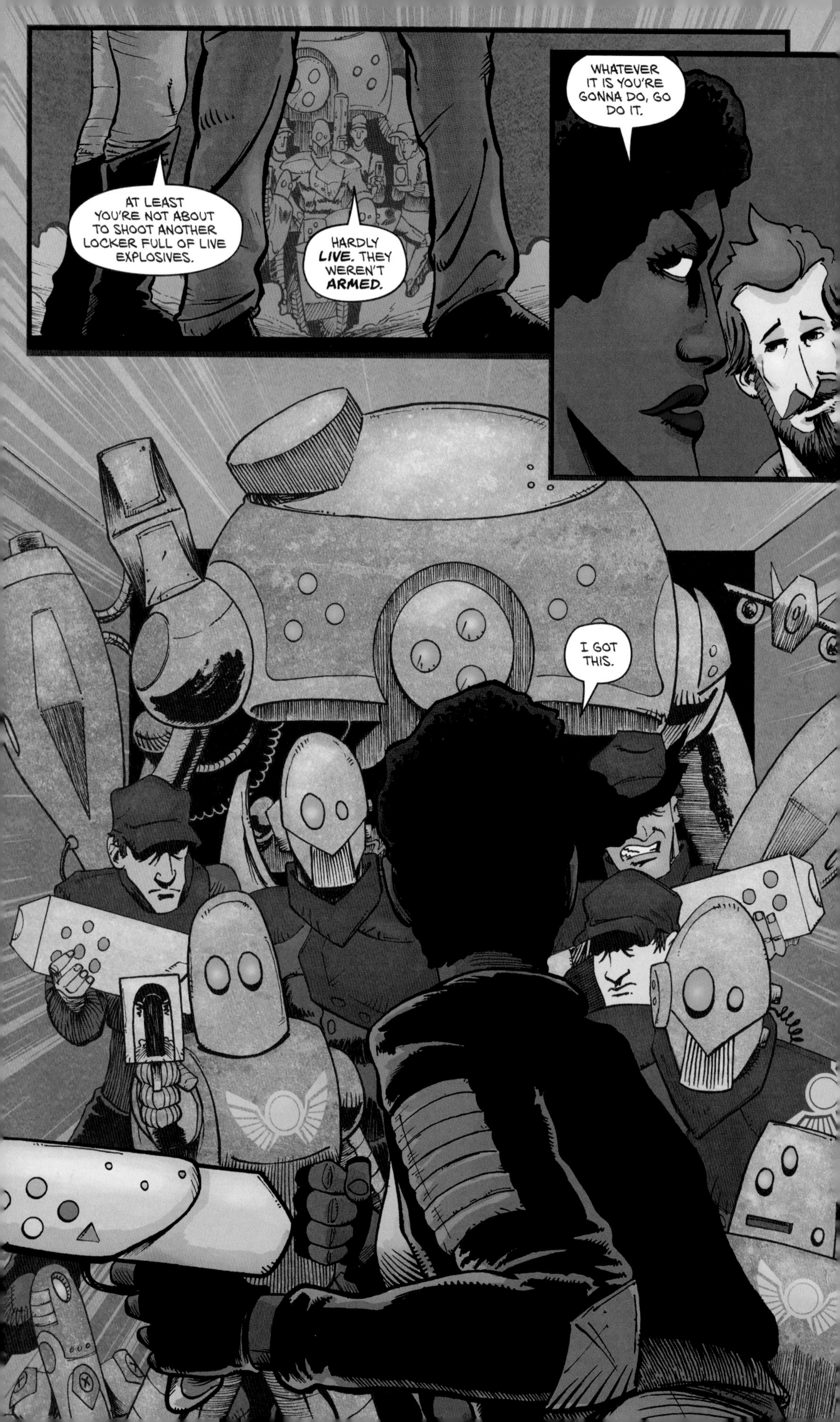
AT LEAST YOU'RE NOT ABOUT TO SHOOT ANOTHER LOCKER FULL OF LIVE EXPLOSIVES.
HARDLY LIVE. THEY WEREN'T ARMED.
WHATEVER IT IS YOU'RE GONNA DO, GO DO IT.
I GOT THIS.

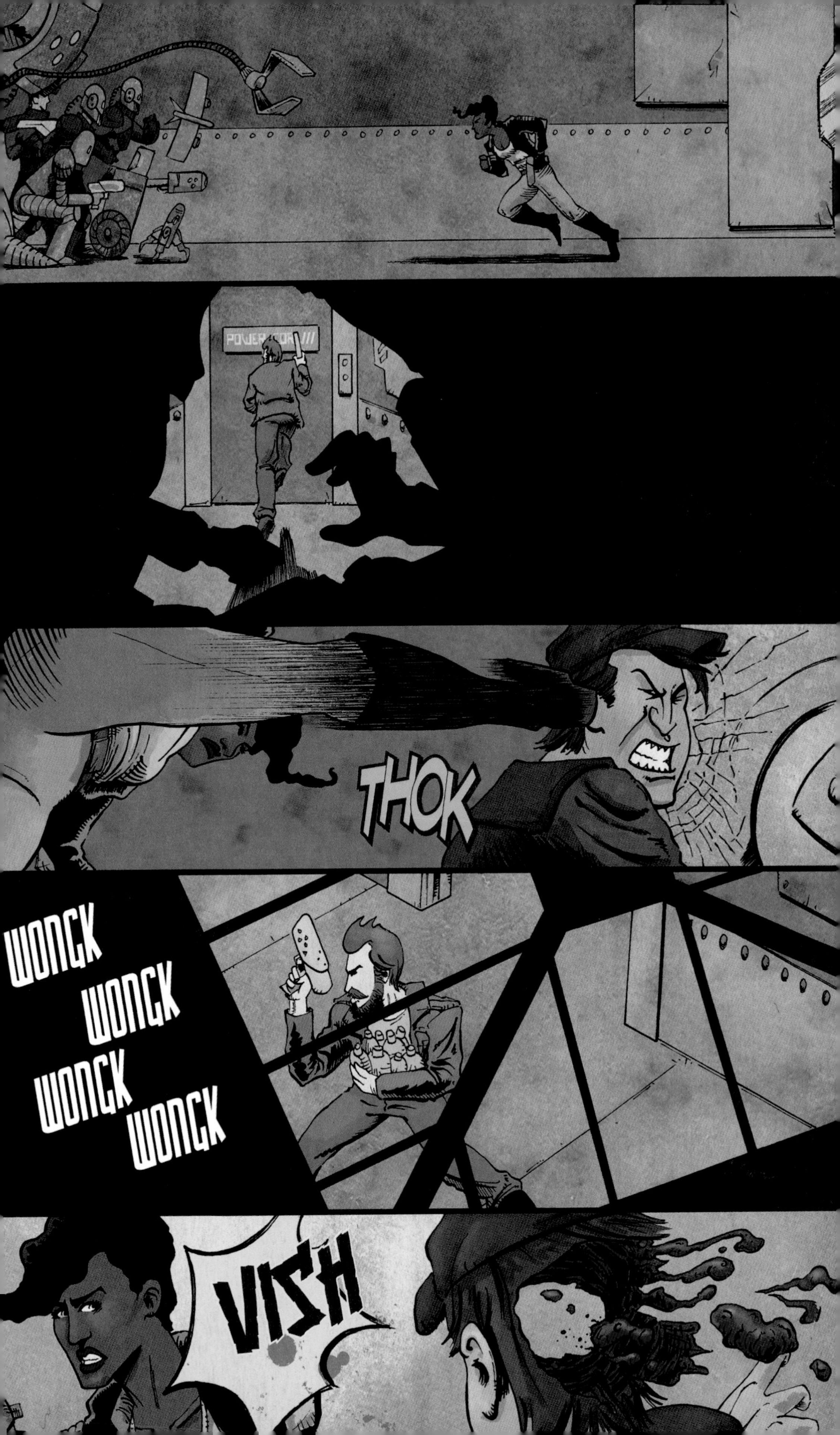
POWER CORE ///
THOK
WONGK
WONGK
WONGK
WONGK
VISH

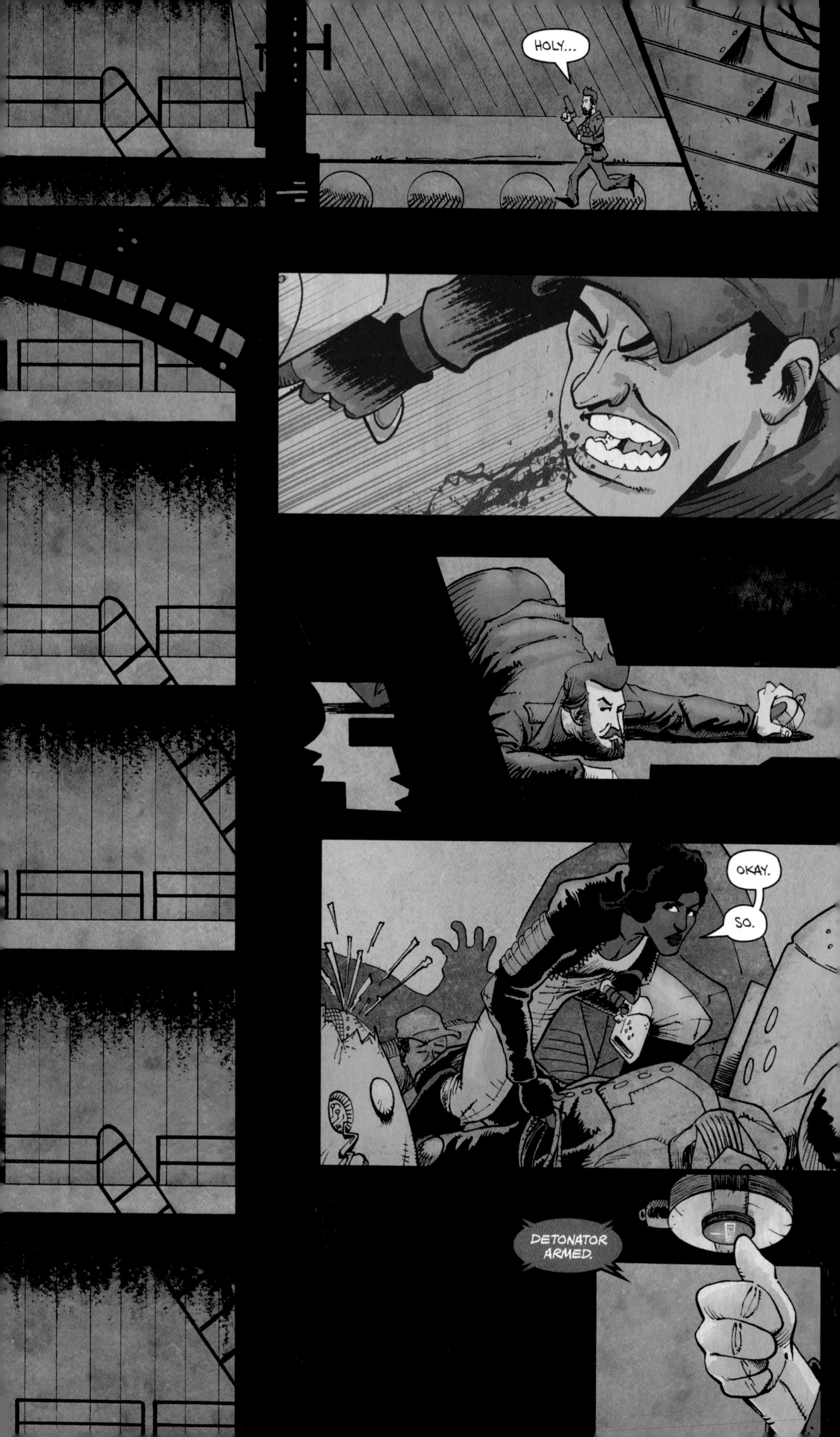
HOLY...
OKAY.
SO.
DETONATOR ARMED.

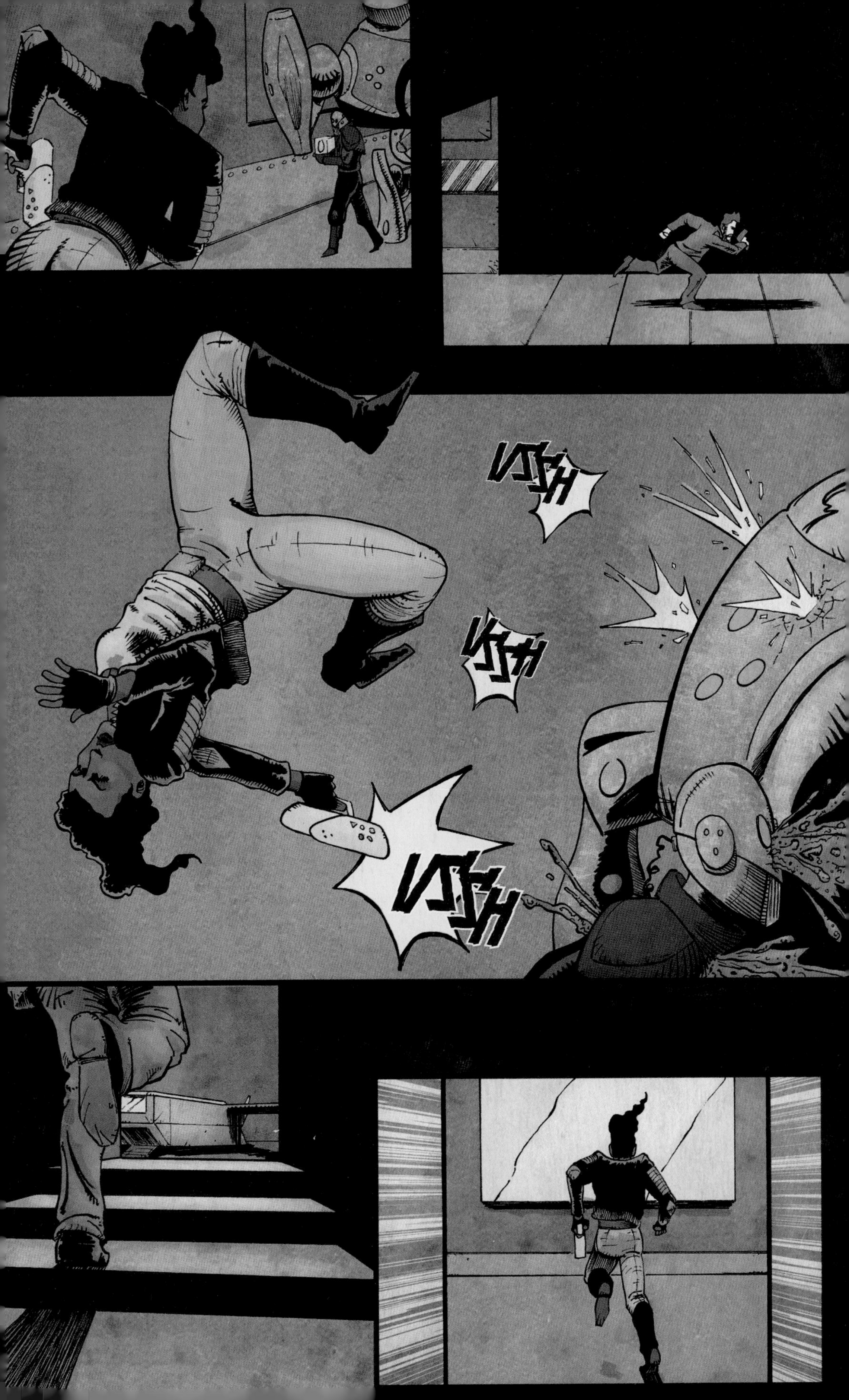
VSSH
VSSH
VSSH

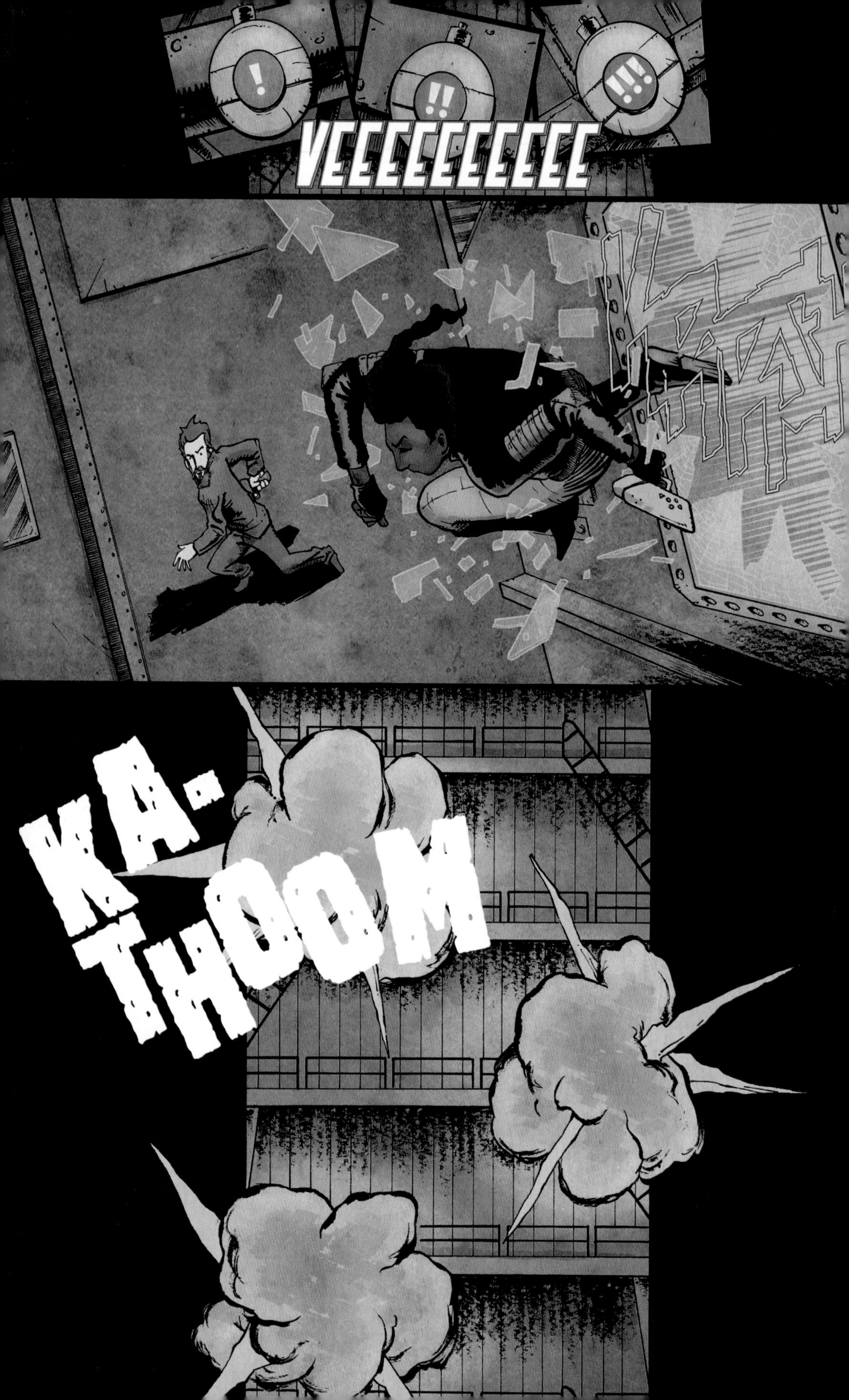
!
!!
!!!
VEEEEEEEEEE
KA-
THOOM

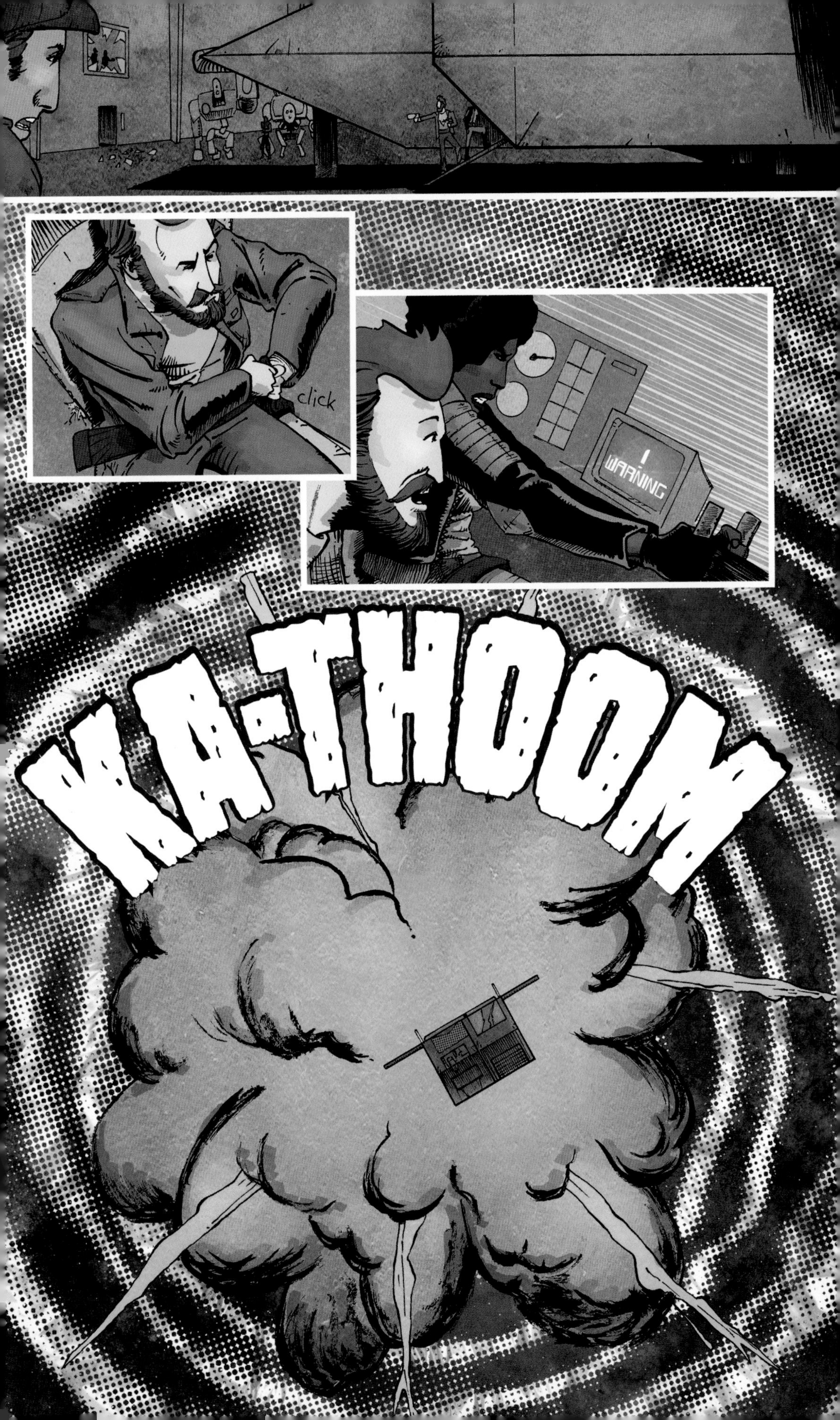

click
!
WARNING
KA-THOOM

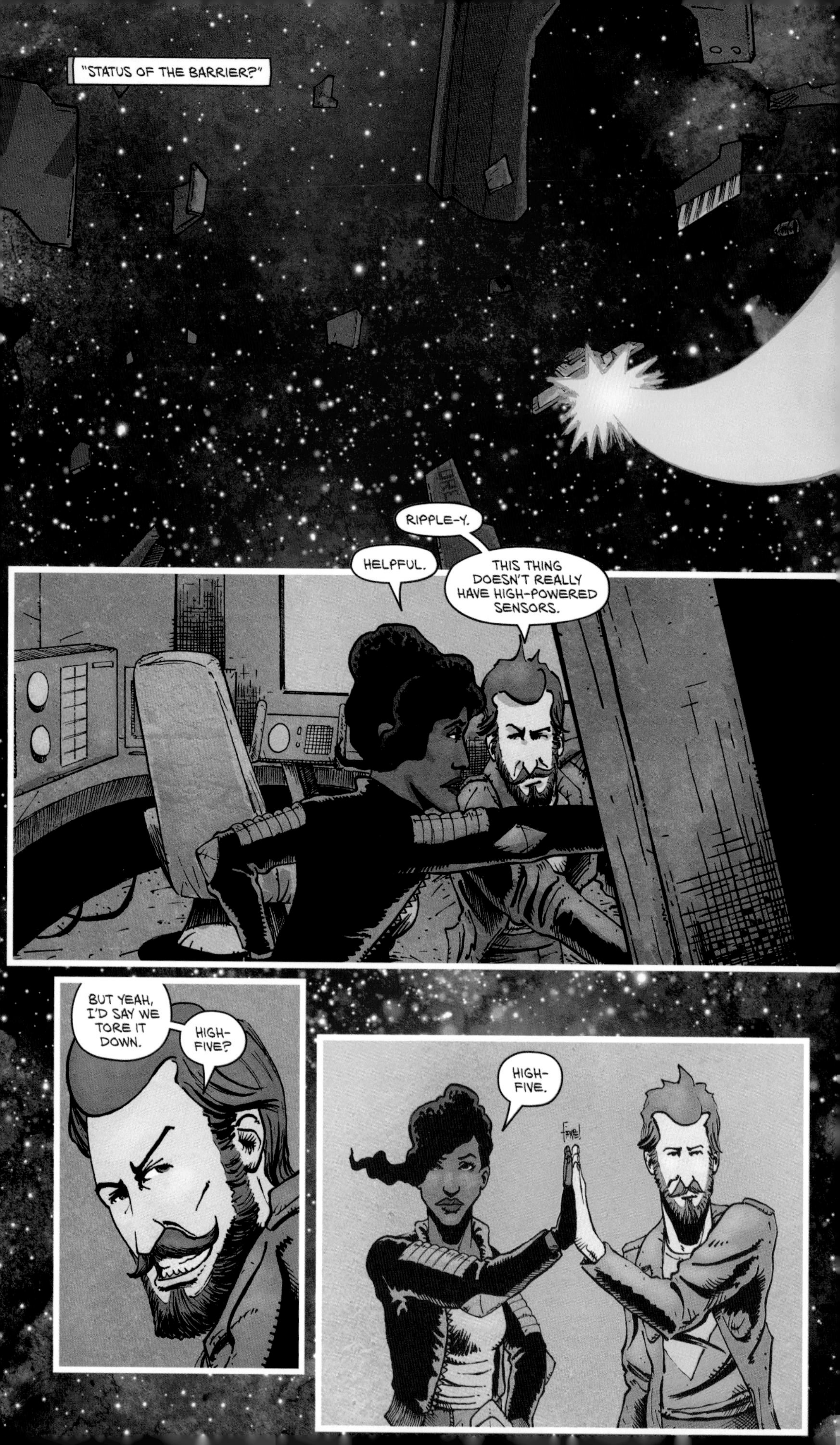
"STATUS OF THE BARRIER?"
HELPFUL.
RIPPLE-Y.
THIS THING DOESN'T REALLY HAVE HIGH-POWERED SENSORS.
BUT YEAH, I'D SAY WE TORE IT DOWN.
HIGH-FIVE?
HIGH-FIVE.

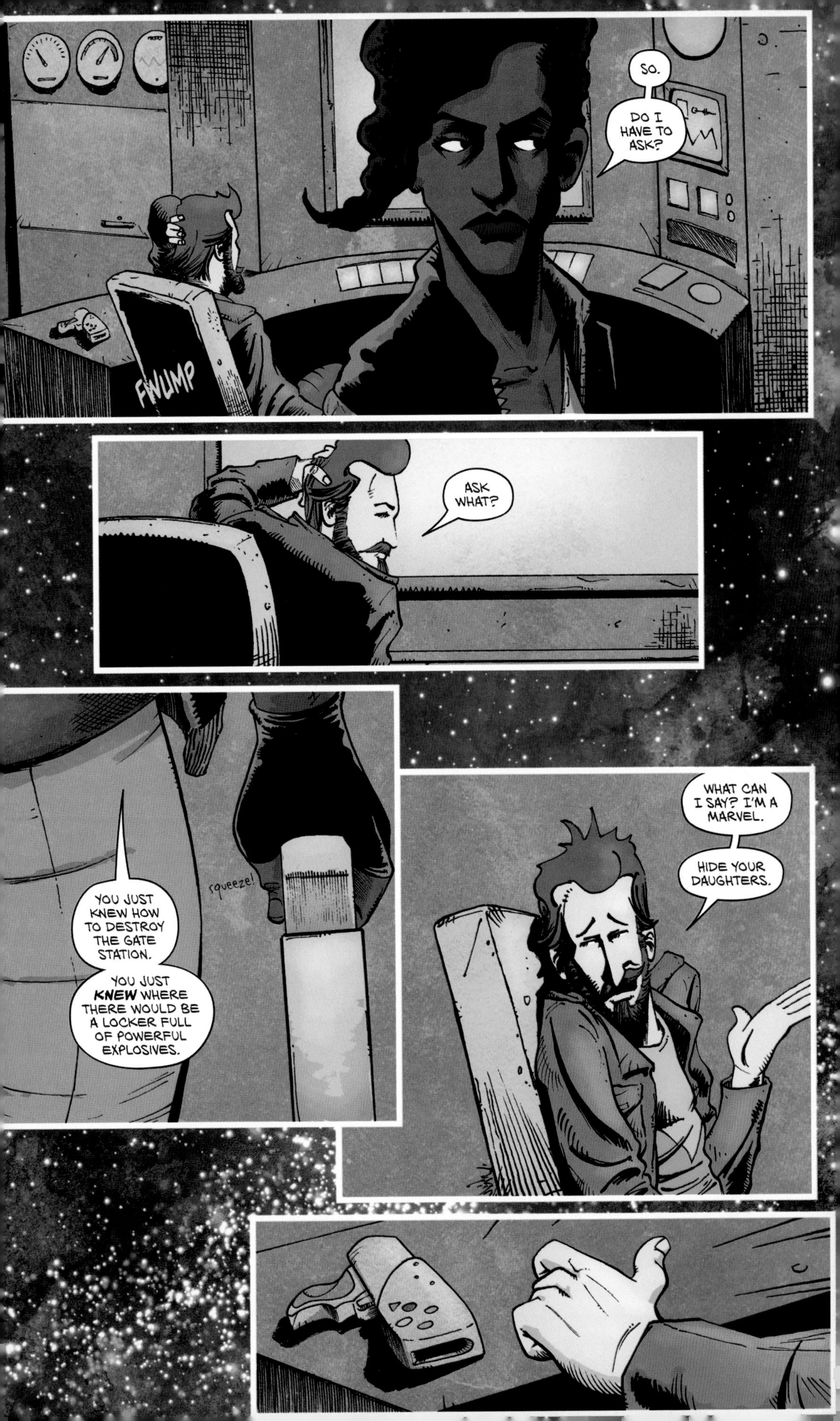

SO.
DO I HAVE TO ASK?
FWUMP
ASK WHAT?
squeeze!
YOU JUST KNEW HOW TO DESTROY THE GATE STATION.
YOU JUST **KNEW** WHERE THERE WOULD BE A LOCKER FULL OF POWERFUL EXPLOSIVES.
WHAT CAN I SAY? I'M A MARVEL.
HIDE YOUR DAUGHTERS.

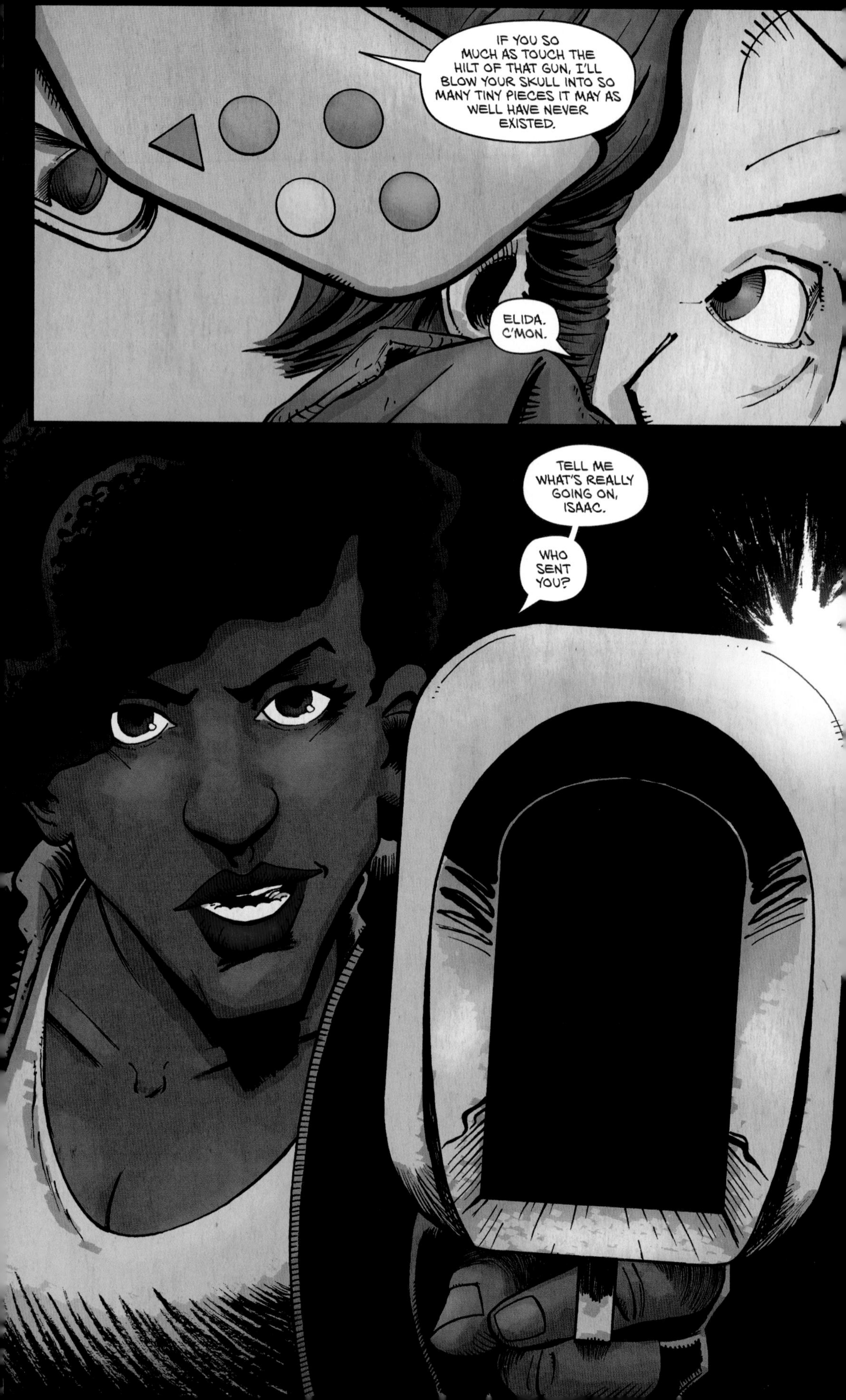
IF YOU SO MUCH AS TOUCH THE HILT OF THAT GUN, I'LL BLOW YOUR SKULL INTO SO MANY TINY PIECES IT MAY AS WELL HAVE NEVER EXISTED.
ELIDA. C'MON.
TELL ME WHAT'S REALLY GOING ON, ISAAC.
WHO SENT YOU?

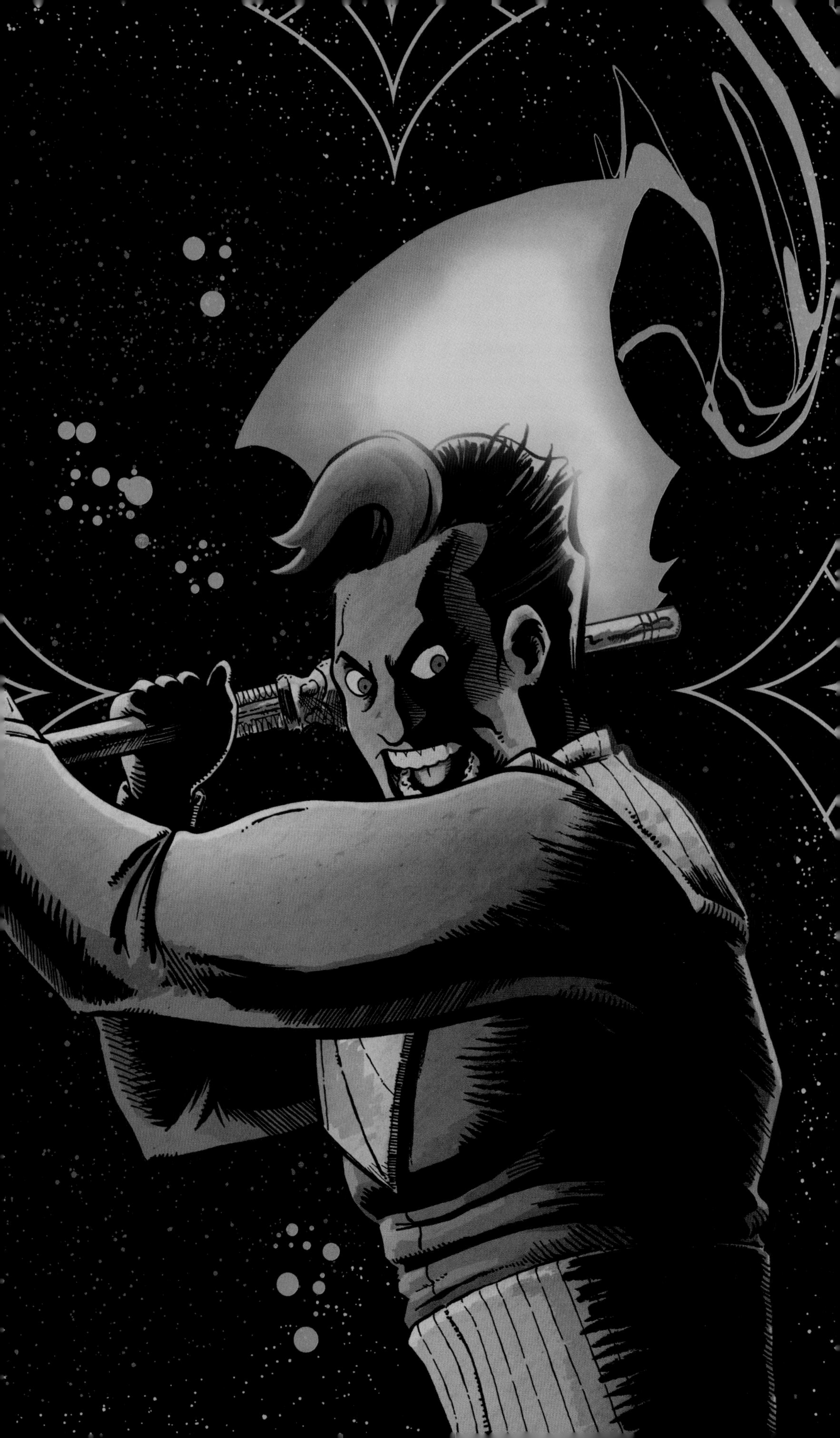

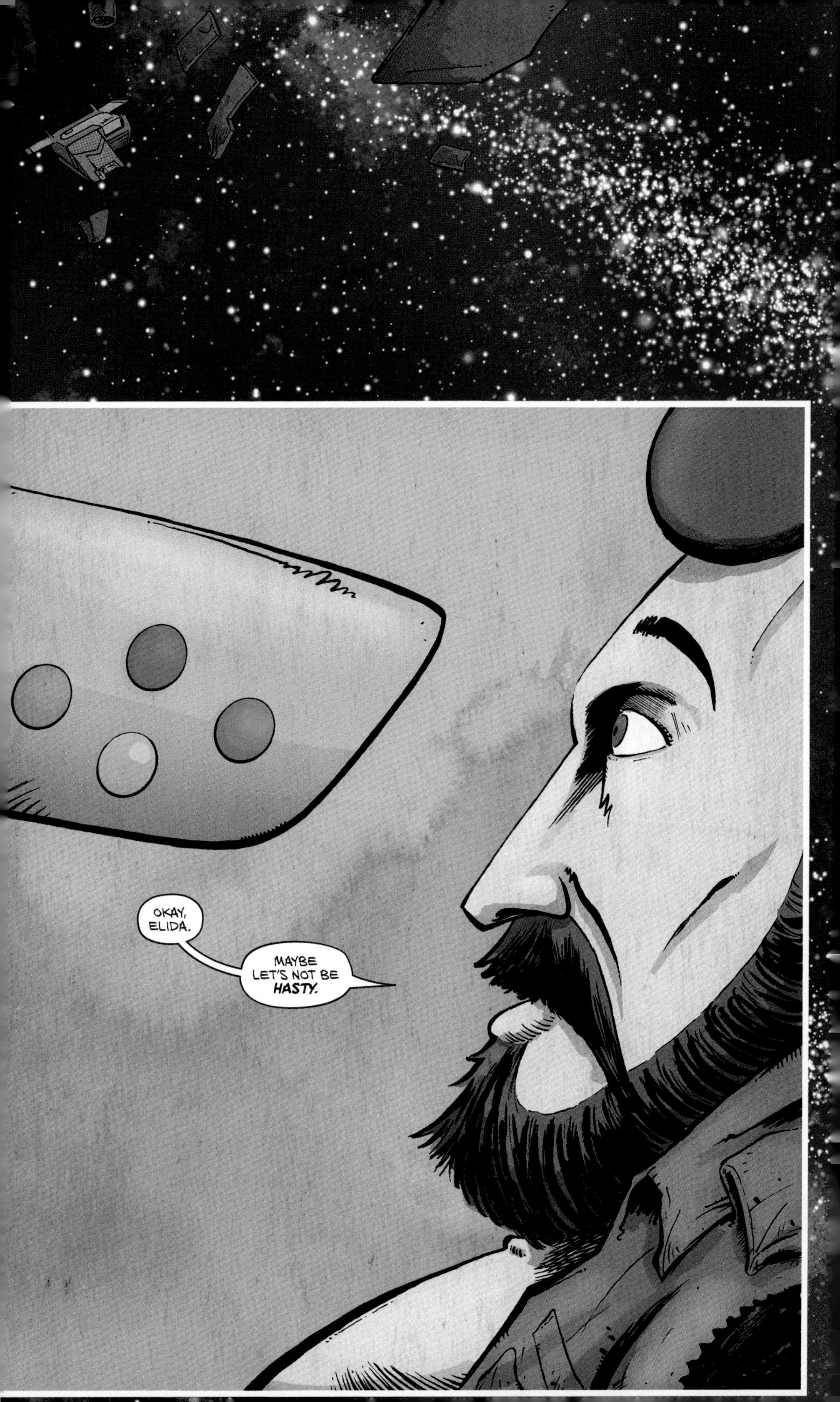
OKAY, ELIDA.
MAYBE LET'S NOT BE HASTY.

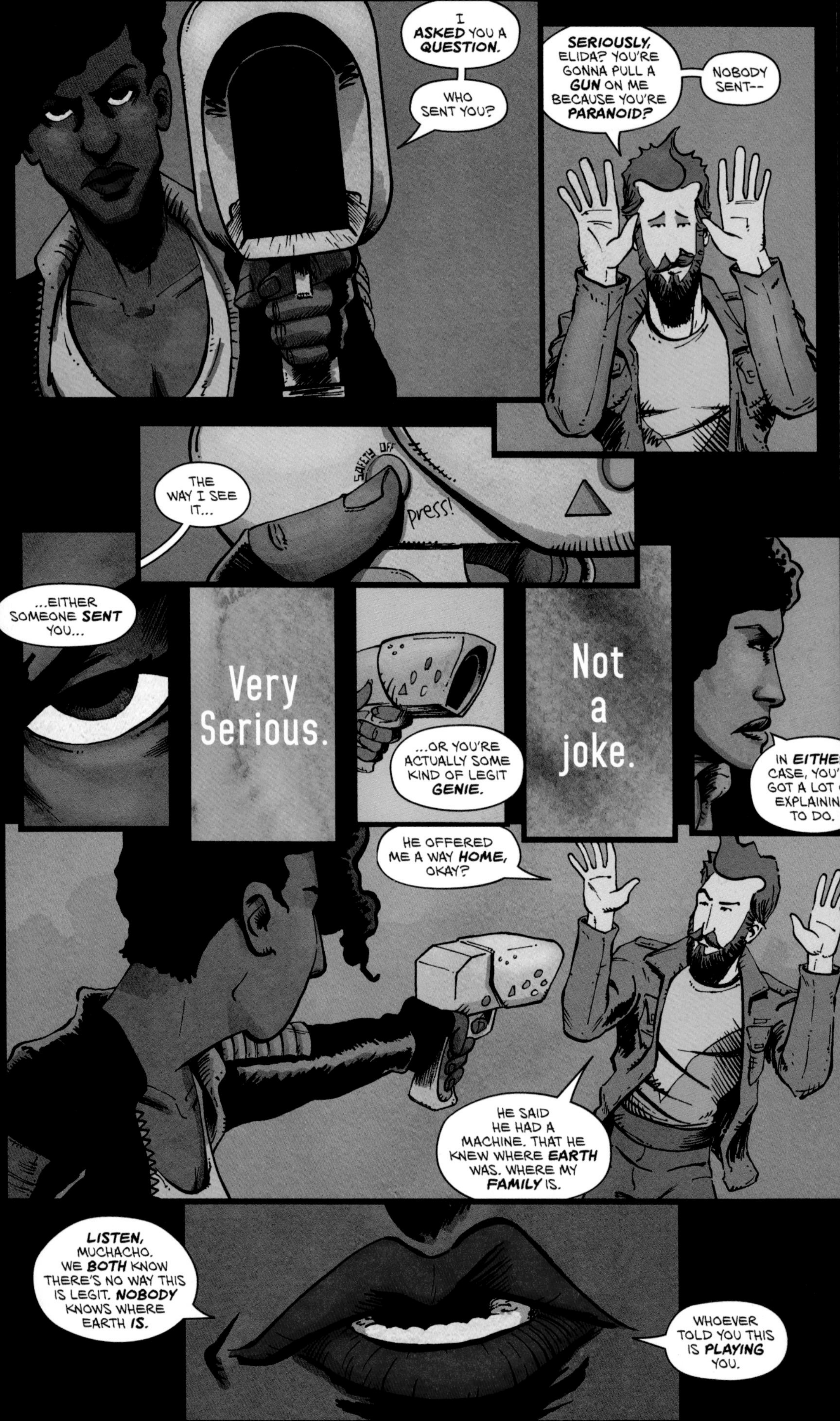
I ASKED YOU A QUESTION.
WHO SENT YOU?
SERIOUSLY, ELIDA? YOU'RE GONNA PULL A GUN ON ME BECAUSE YOU'RE PARANOID?
NOBODY SENT--
SAFETY OFF
THE WAY I SEE IT...
press!
...EITHER SOMEONE SENT YOU...
Very Serious.
...OR YOU'RE ACTUALLY SOME KIND OF LEGIT GENIE.
Not a joke.
IN EITHE CASE, YOU' GOT A LOT EXPLAININ TO DO.
HE OFFERED ME A WAY HOME, OKAY?
HE SAID HE HAD A MACHINE. THAT HE KNEW WHERE EARTH WAS. WHERE MY FAMILY IS.
LISTEN, MUCHACHO. WE BOTH KNOW THERE'S NO WAY THIS IS LEGIT. NOBODY KNOWS WHERE EARTH IS.
WHOEVER TOLD YOU THIS IS PLAYING YOU.

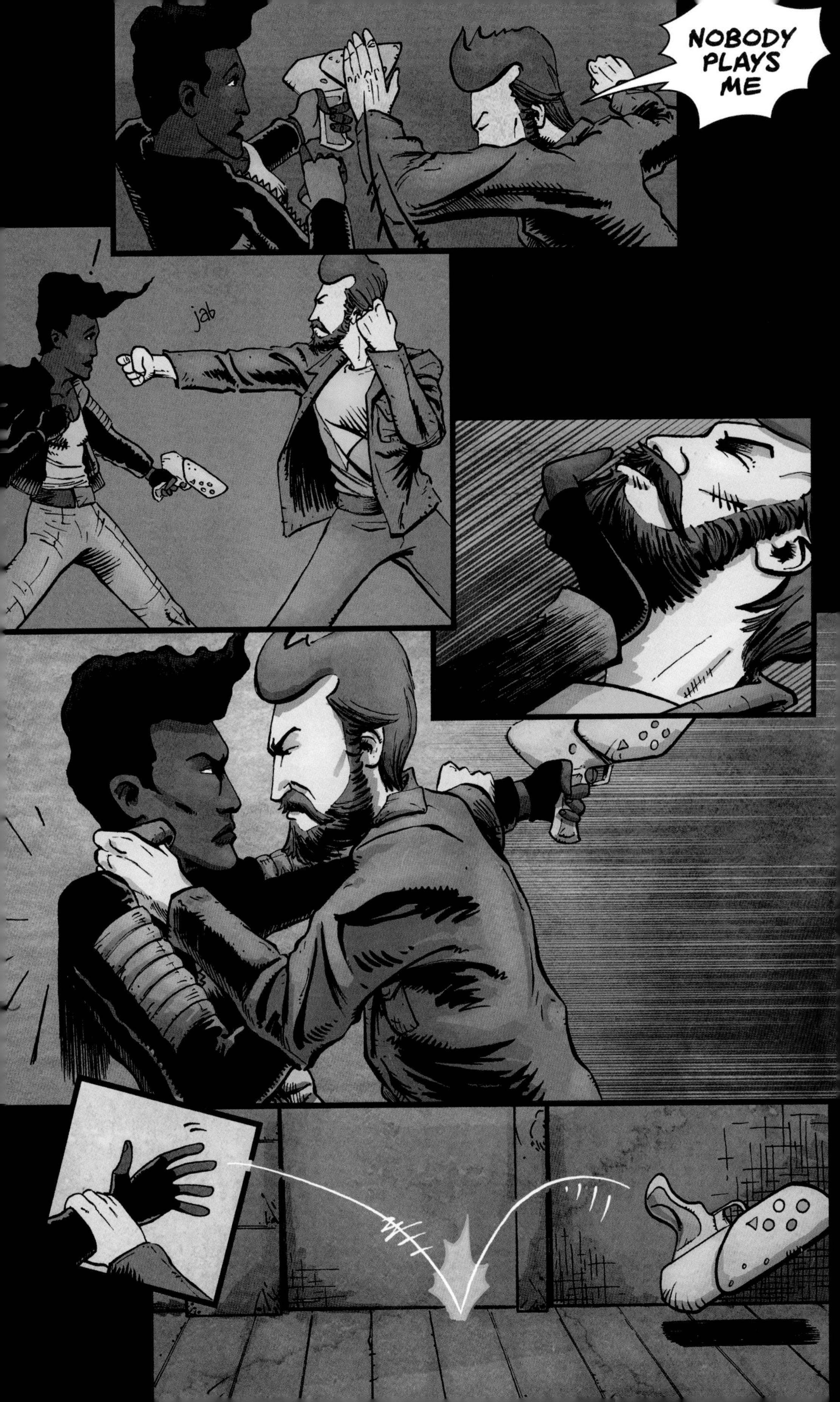
NOBODY PLAYS ME
!
jab

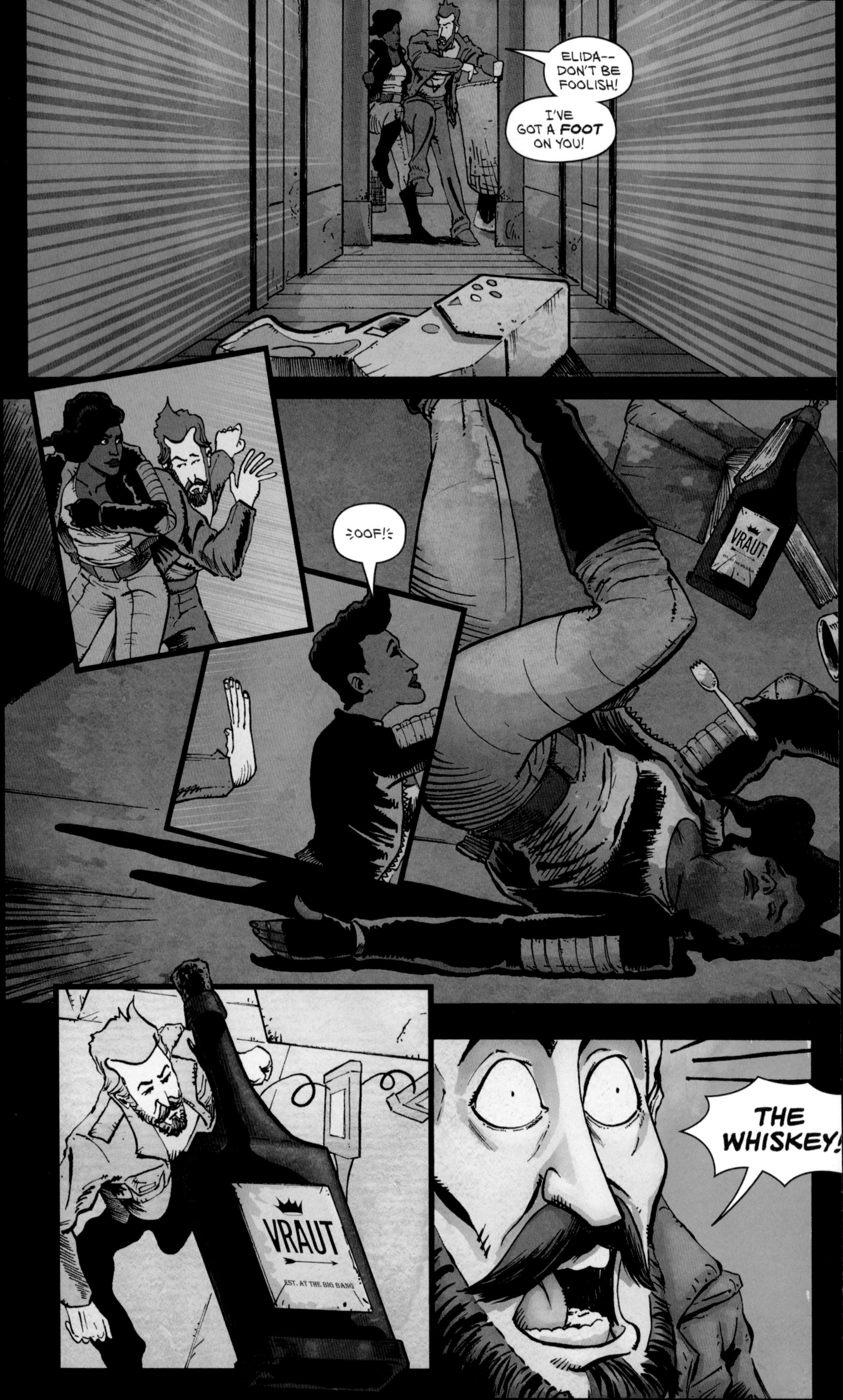
ELIDA-- DON'T BE FOOLISH!
I'VE GOT A FOOT ON YOU!
OOF!
VRAUT
VRAUT
EST. AT THE BIG BANG
THE WHISKEY!

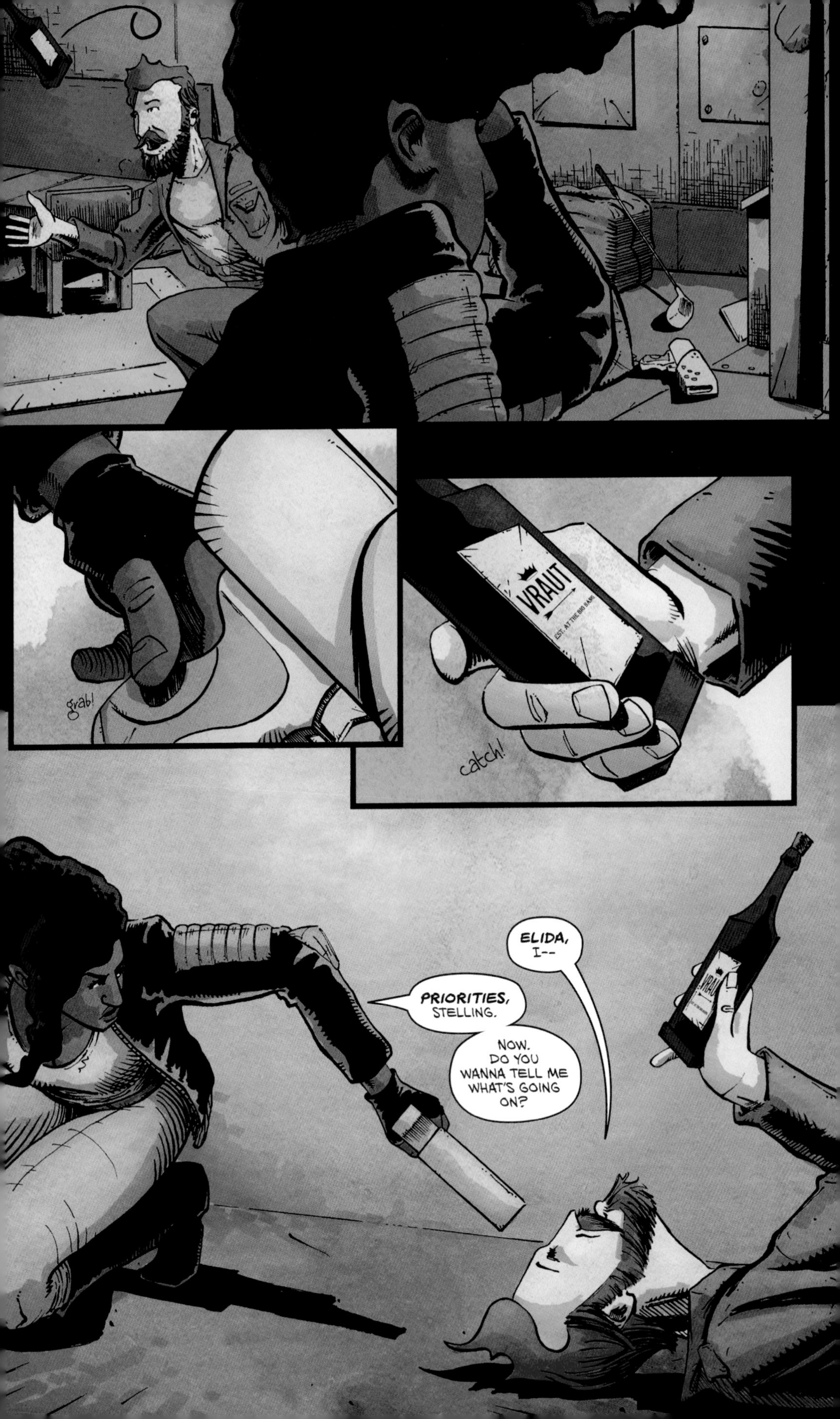
grab!
VRAUT
EST. AT THE BIG BANG
catch!
ELIDA, I--
PRIORITIES, STELLING.
NOW. DO YOU WANNA TELL ME WHAT'S GOING ON?

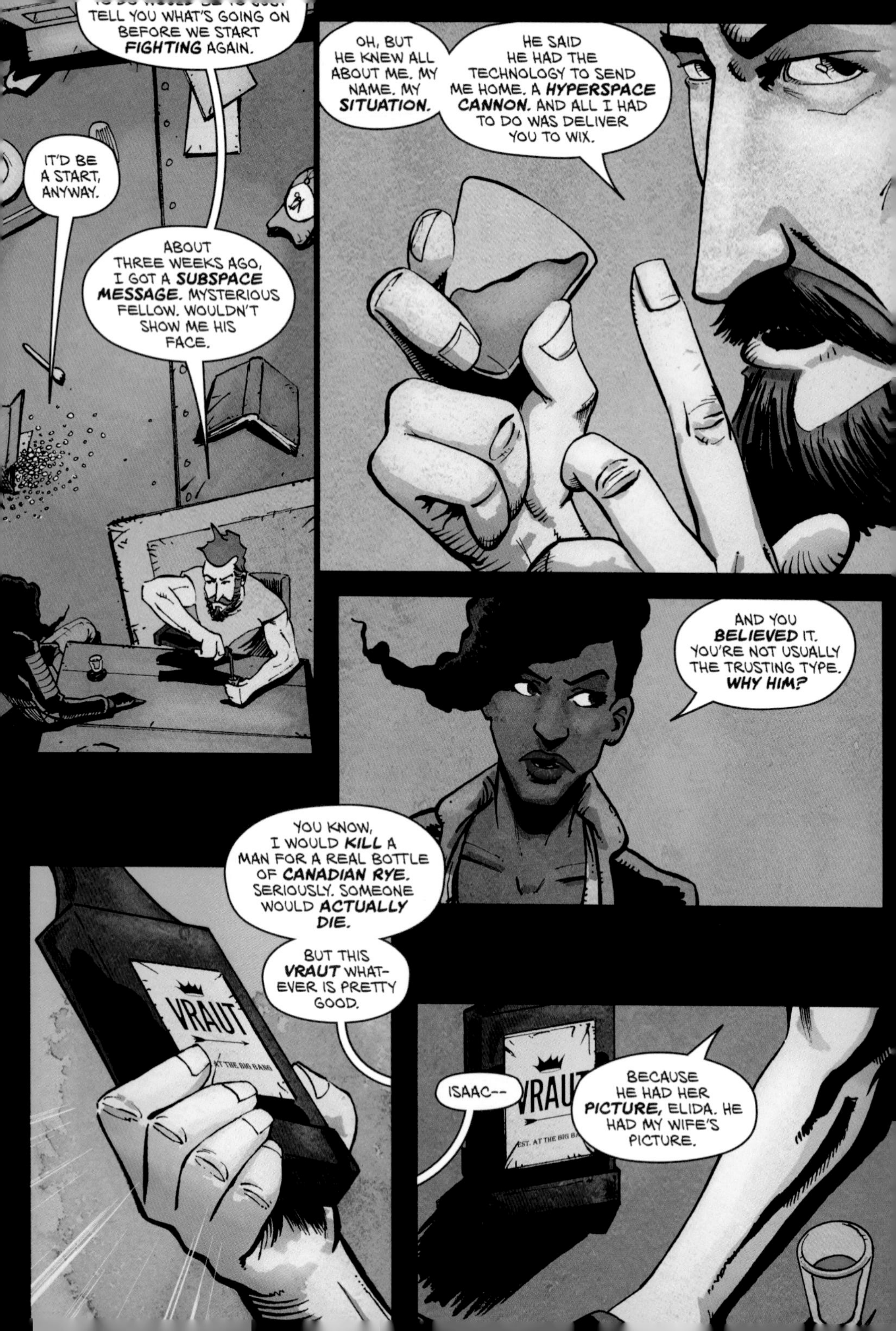
TELL YOU WHAT'S GOING ON BEFORE WE START FIGHTING AGAIN.
IT'D BE A START, ANYWAY.
ABOUT THREE WEEKS AGO, I GOT A SUBSPACE MESSAGE. MYSTERIOUS FELLOW. WOULDN'T SHOW ME HIS FACE.
OH, BUT HE KNEW ALL ABOUT ME. MY NAME. MY SITUATION.
HE SAID HE HAD THE TECHNOLOGY TO SEND ME HOME. A HYPERSPACE CANNON. AND ALL I HAD TO DO WAS DELIVER YOU TO WIX.
AND YOU BELIEVED IT. YOU'RE NOT USUALLY THE TRUSTING TYPE. WHY HIM?
YOU KNOW, I WOULD KILL A MAN FOR A REAL BOTTLE OF CANADIAN RYE. SERIOUSLY. SOMEONE WOULD ACTUALLY DIE.
BUT THIS VRAUT WHAT-EVER IS PRETTY GOOD.
VRAUT
ISAAC--
BECAUSE HE HAD HER PICTURE, ELIDA. HE HAD MY WIFE'S PICTURE.

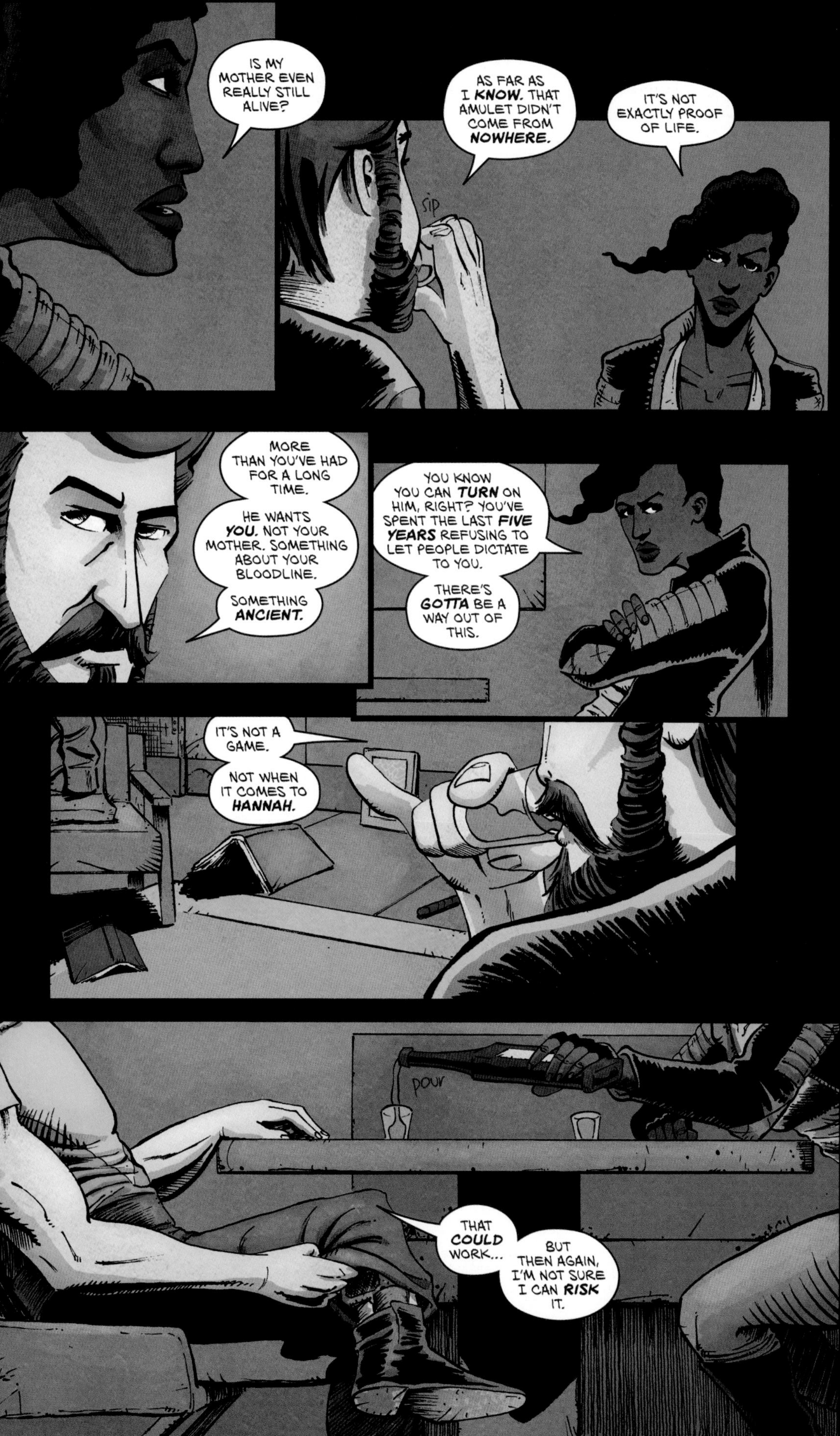
IS MY MOTHER EVEN REALLY STILL ALIVE?
AS FAR AS I **KNOW.** THAT AMULET DIDN'T COME FROM **NOWHERE.**
sip
IT'S NOT EXACTLY PROOF OF LIFE.
MORE THAN YOU'VE HAD FOR A LONG TIME.
HE WANTS **YOU.** NOT YOUR MOTHER. SOMETHING ABOUT YOUR BLOODLINE.
SOMETHING **ANCIENT.**
YOU KNOW YOU CAN **TURN** ON HIM, RIGHT? YOU'VE SPENT THE LAST **FIVE YEARS** REFUSING TO LET PEOPLE DICTATE TO YOU.
THERE'S **GOTTA** BE A WAY OUT OF THIS.
IT'S NOT A GAME.
NOT WHEN IT COMES TO **HANNAH.**
pour
THAT **COULD** WORK...
BUT THEN AGAIN, I'M NOT SURE I CAN **RISK** IT.

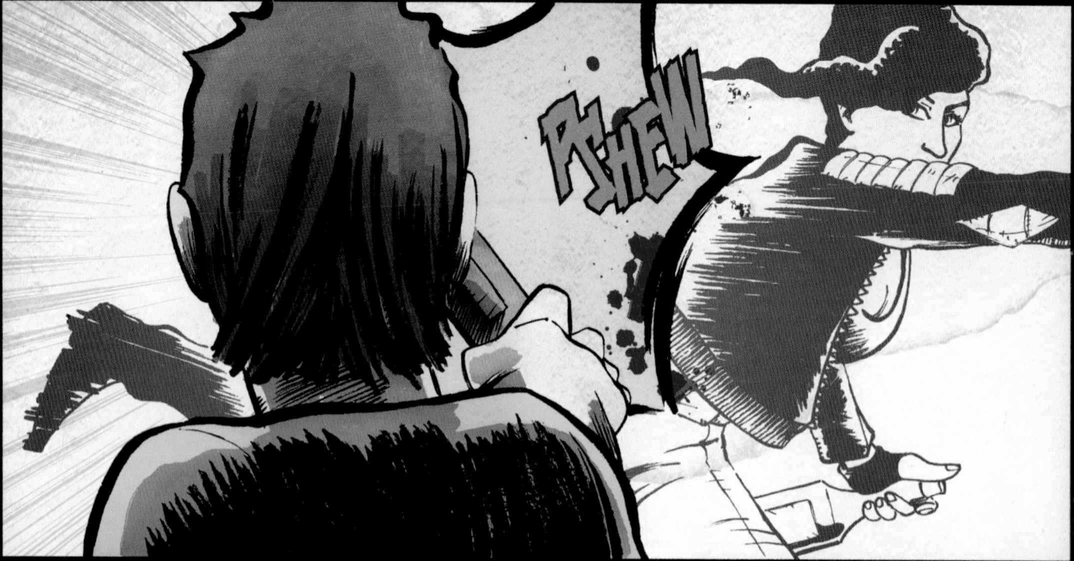
PSHEW

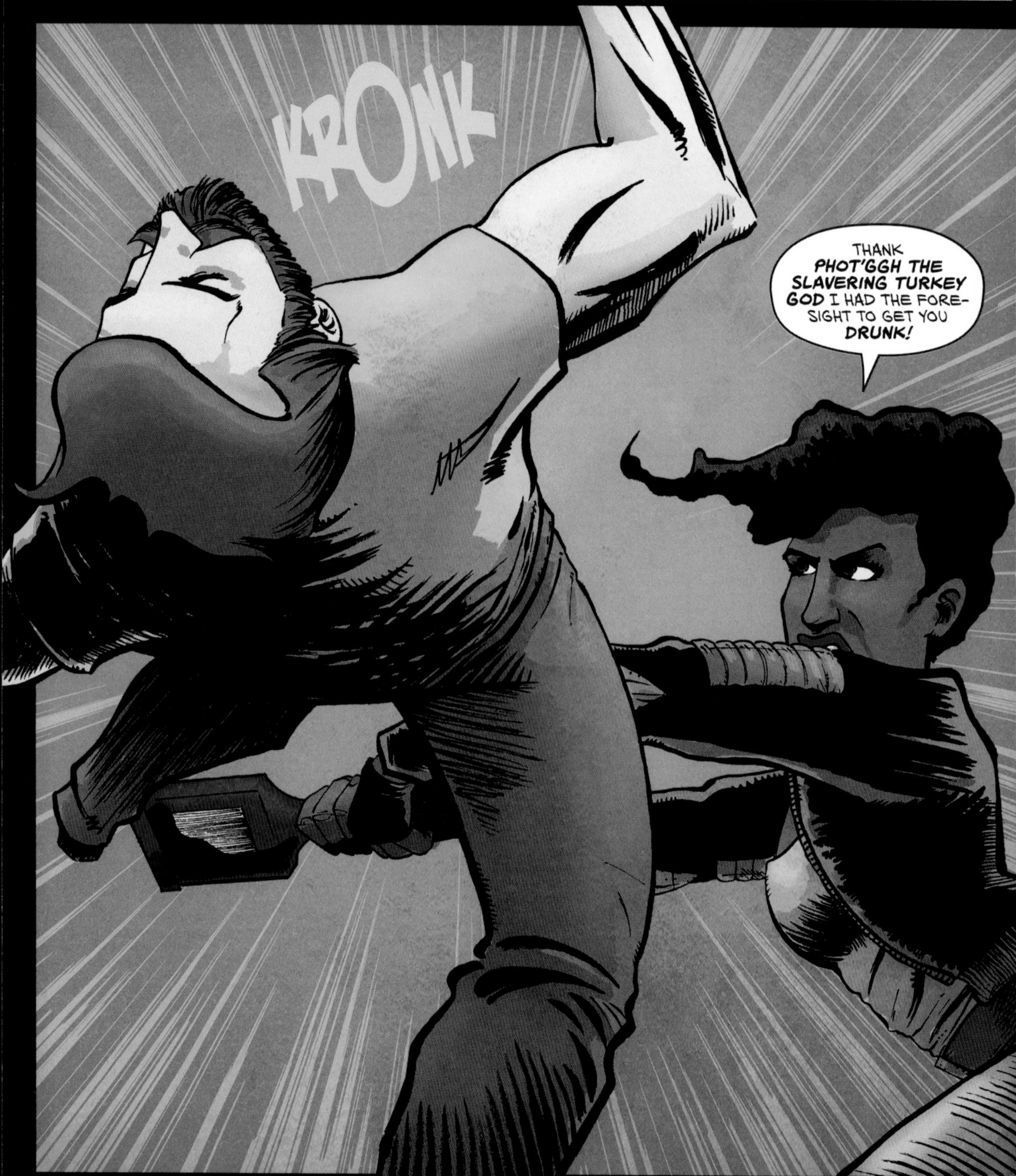
KRONK
THANK PHOT'GGH THE SLAVERING TURKEY GOD I HAD THE FORESIGHT TO GET YOU DRUNK!

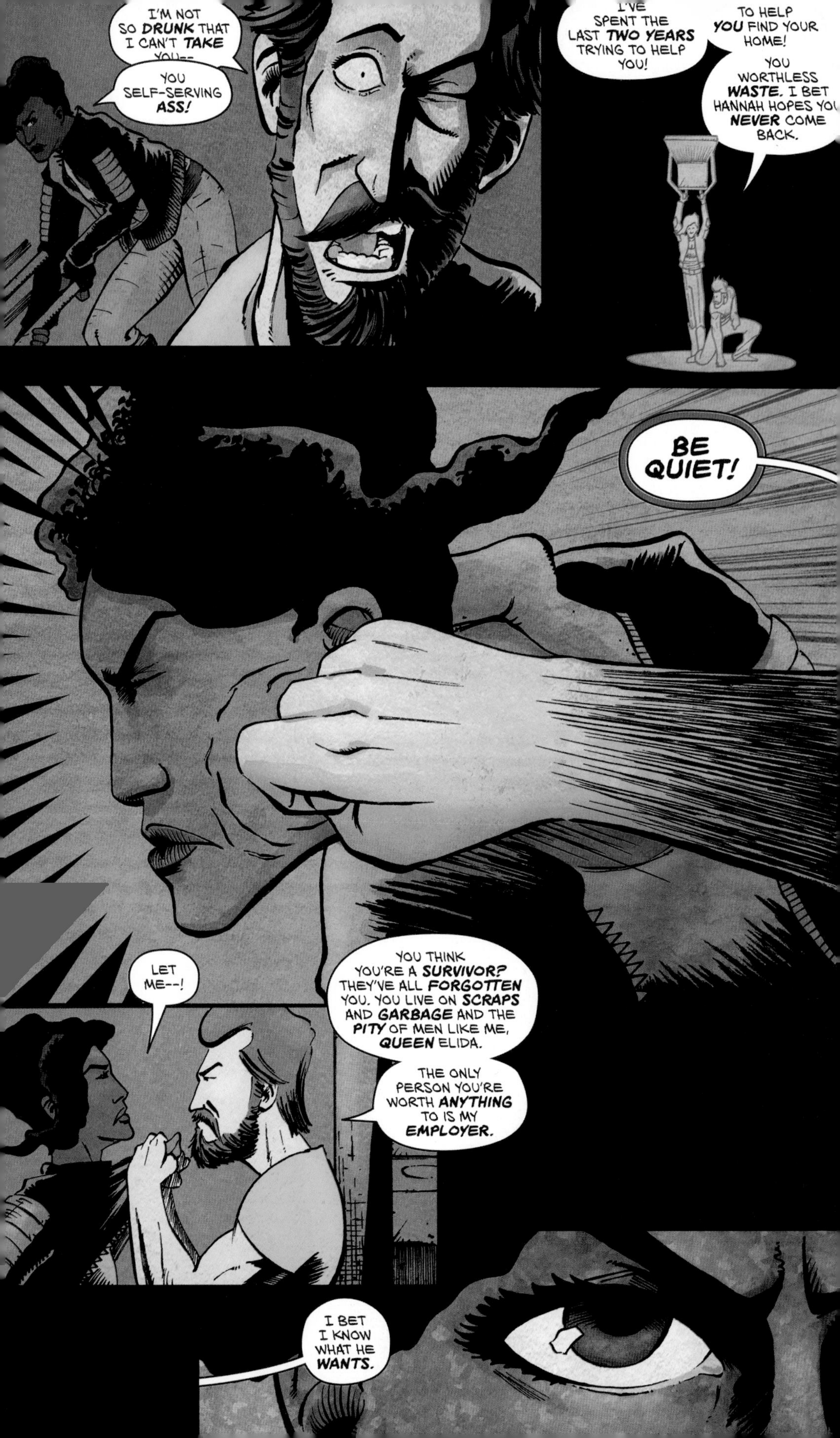

I'M NOT SO **DRUNK** THAT I CAN'T **TAKE** YOU--
YOU SELF-SERVING **ASS!**
I'VE SPENT THE LAST **TWO YEARS** TRYING TO HELP YOU!
TO HELP **YOU** FIND YOUR HOME!
YOU WORTHLESS **WASTE.** I BET HANNAH HOPES YOU **NEVER** COME BACK.
BE QUIET!
LET ME--!
YOU THINK YOU'RE A **SURVIVOR?** THEY'VE ALL **FORGOTTEN** YOU. YOU LIVE ON **SCRAPS** AND **GARBAGE** AND THE **PITY** OF MEN LIKE ME, **QUEEN** ELIDA.
THE ONLY PERSON YOU'RE WORTH **ANYTHING** TO IS MY **EMPLOYER.**
I BET I KNOW WHAT HE **WANTS.**

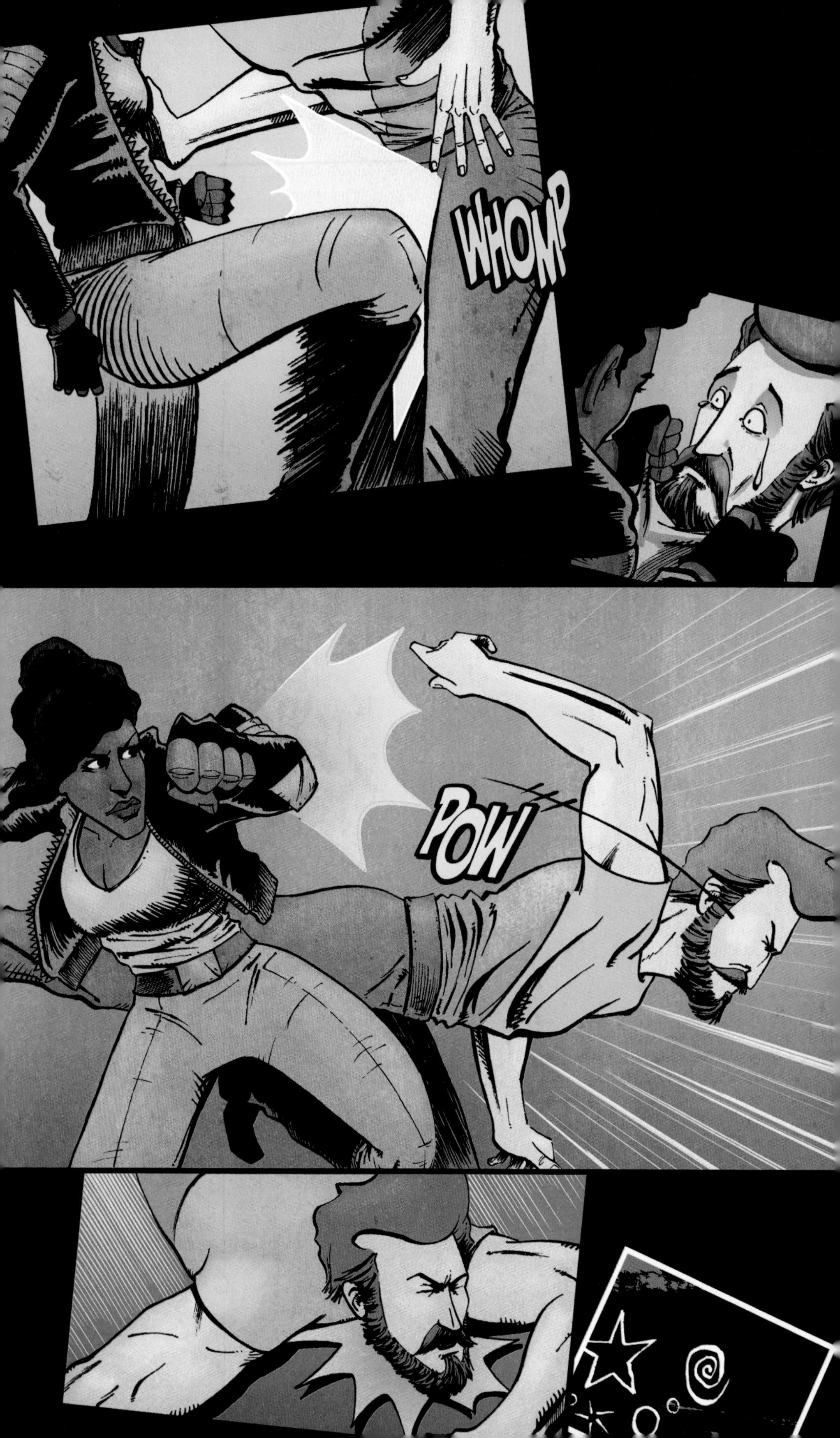
WHOMP
POW

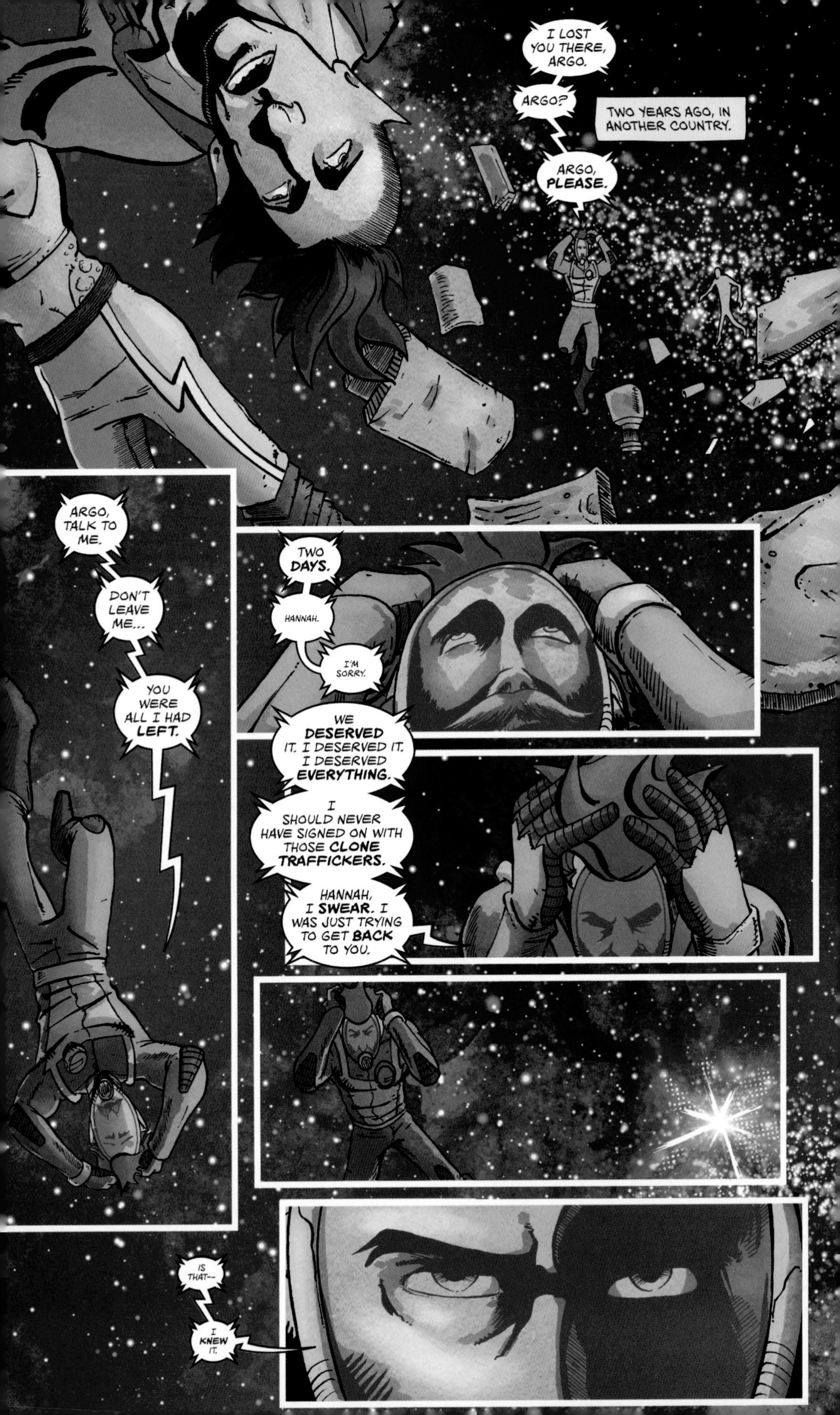

I LOST YOU THERE, ARGO.
ARGO?
TWO YEARS AGO, IN ANOTHER COUNTRY.
ARGO, PLEASE.
ARGO, TALK TO ME.
DON'T LEAVE ME...
YOU WERE ALL I HAD LEFT.
TWO DAYS.
HANNAH.
I'M SORRY.
WE DESERVED IT. I DESERVED IT. I DESERVED EVERYTHING.
I SHOULD NEVER HAVE SIGNED ON WITH THOSE CLONE TRAFFICKERS.
HANNAH, I SWEAR. I WAS JUST TRYING TO GET BACK TO YOU.
IS THAT--
I KNEW IT.

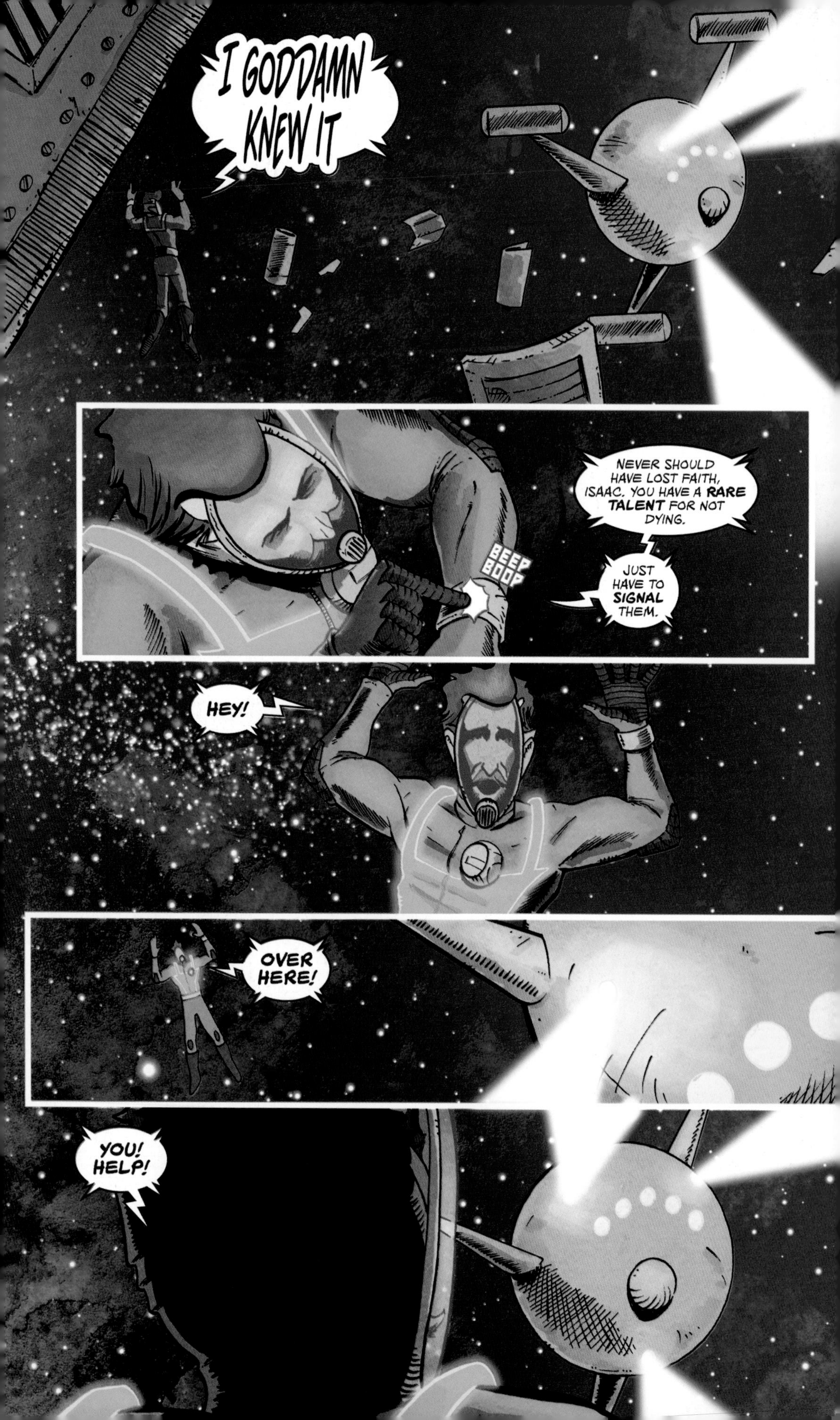
I GODDAMN KNEW IT
NEVER SHOULD HAVE LOST FAITH, ISAAC. YOU HAVE A RARE TALENT FOR NOT DYING.
BEEP BOOP
JUST HAVE TO SIGNAL THEM.
HEY!
OVER HERE!
YOU! HELP!

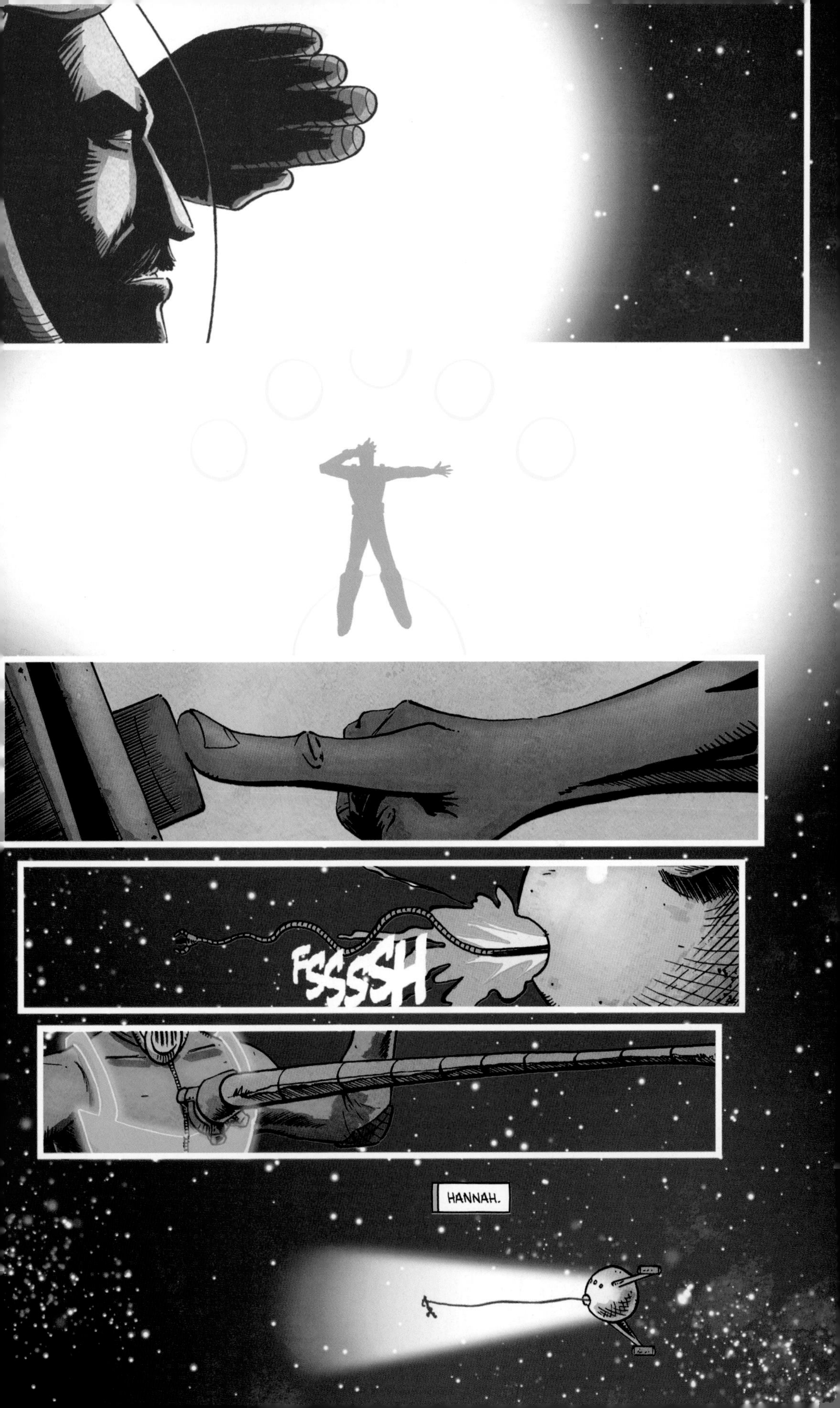
FSSSSH
HANNAH.

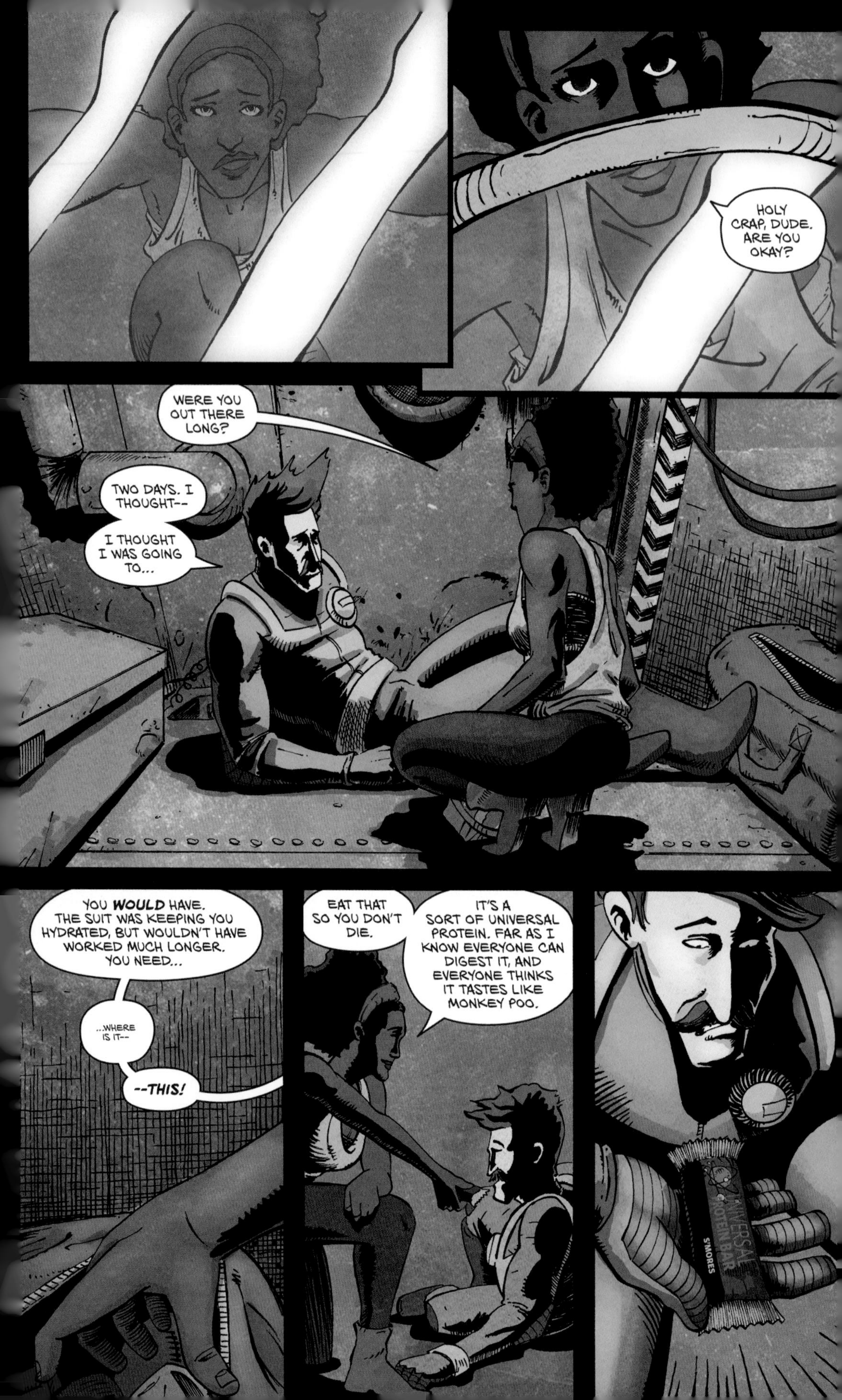
HOLY CRAP, DUDE. ARE YOU OKAY?
WERE YOU OUT THERE LONG?
TWO DAYS. I THOUGHT--
I THOUGHT I WAS GOING TO...
YOU WOULD HAVE. THE SUIT WAS KEEPING YOU HYDRATED, BUT WOULDN'T HAVE WORKED MUCH LONGER. YOU NEED...
...WHERE IS IT--
--THIS!
EAT THAT SO YOU DON'T DIE.
IT'S A SORT OF UNIVERSAL PROTEIN. FAR AS I KNOW EVERYONE CAN DIGEST IT, AND EVERYONE THINKS IT TASTES LIKE MONKEY POO.
UNIVERSAL PROTEIN BAR
S'MORES

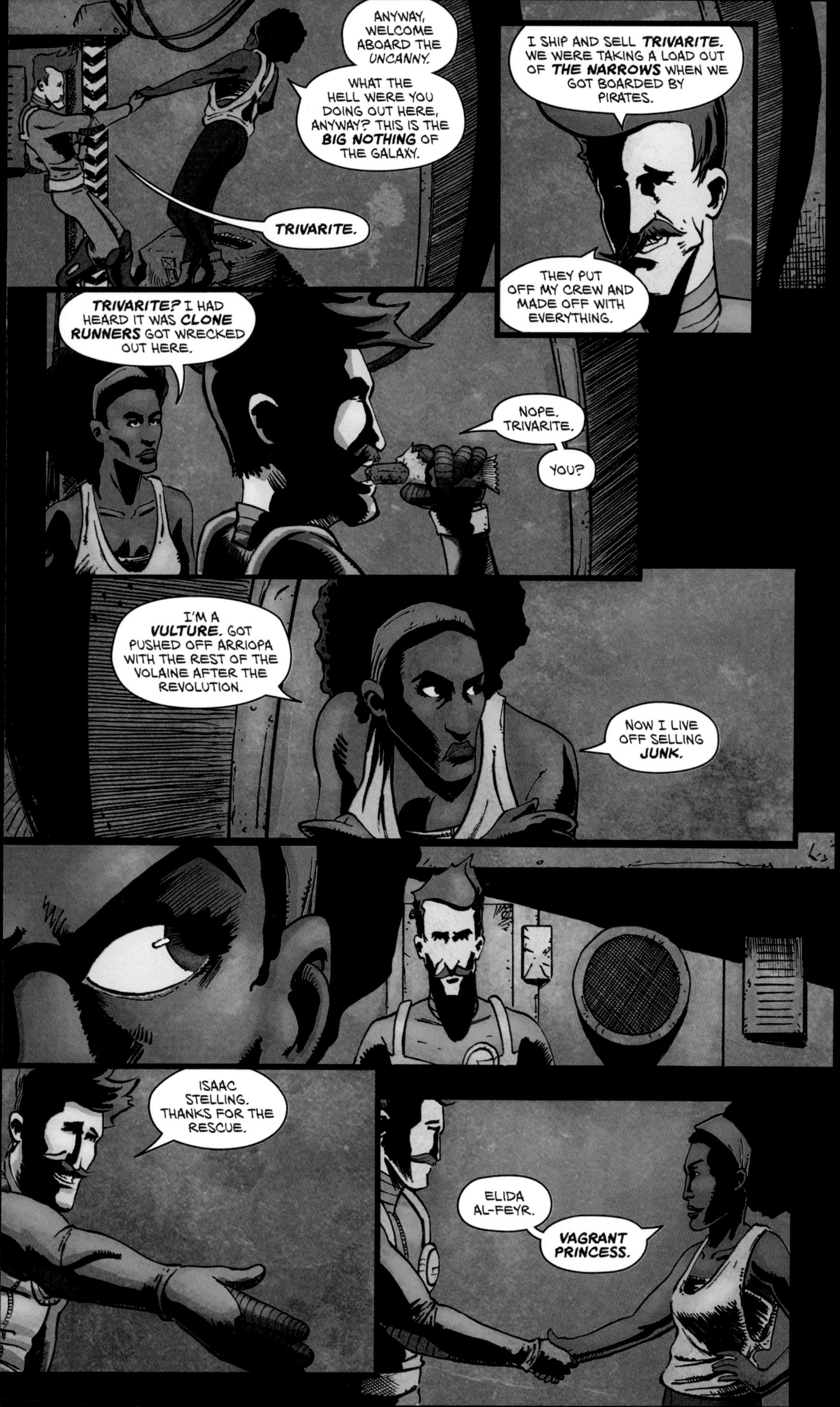

ANYWAY, WELCOME ABOARD THE *UNCANNY.*
WHAT THE HELL WERE YOU DOING OUT HERE, ANYWAY? THIS IS THE **BIG NOTHING** OF THE GALAXY.
TRIVARITE.
I SHIP AND SELL **TRIVARITE.** WE WERE TAKING A LOAD OUT OF **THE NARROWS** WHEN WE GOT BOARDED BY PIRATES.
THEY PUT OFF MY CREW AND MADE OFF WITH EVERYTHING.
TRIVARITE? I HAD HEARD IT WAS **CLONE RUNNERS** GOT WRECKED OUT HERE.
NOPE. TRIVARITE.
YOU?
I'M A **VULTURE.** GOT PUSHED OFF ARRIOPA WITH THE REST OF THE VOLAINE AFTER THE REVOLUTION.
NOW I LIVE OFF SELLING **JUNK.**
ISAAC STELLING. THANKS FOR THE RESCUE.
ELIDA AL-FEYR.
VAGRANT PRINCESS.

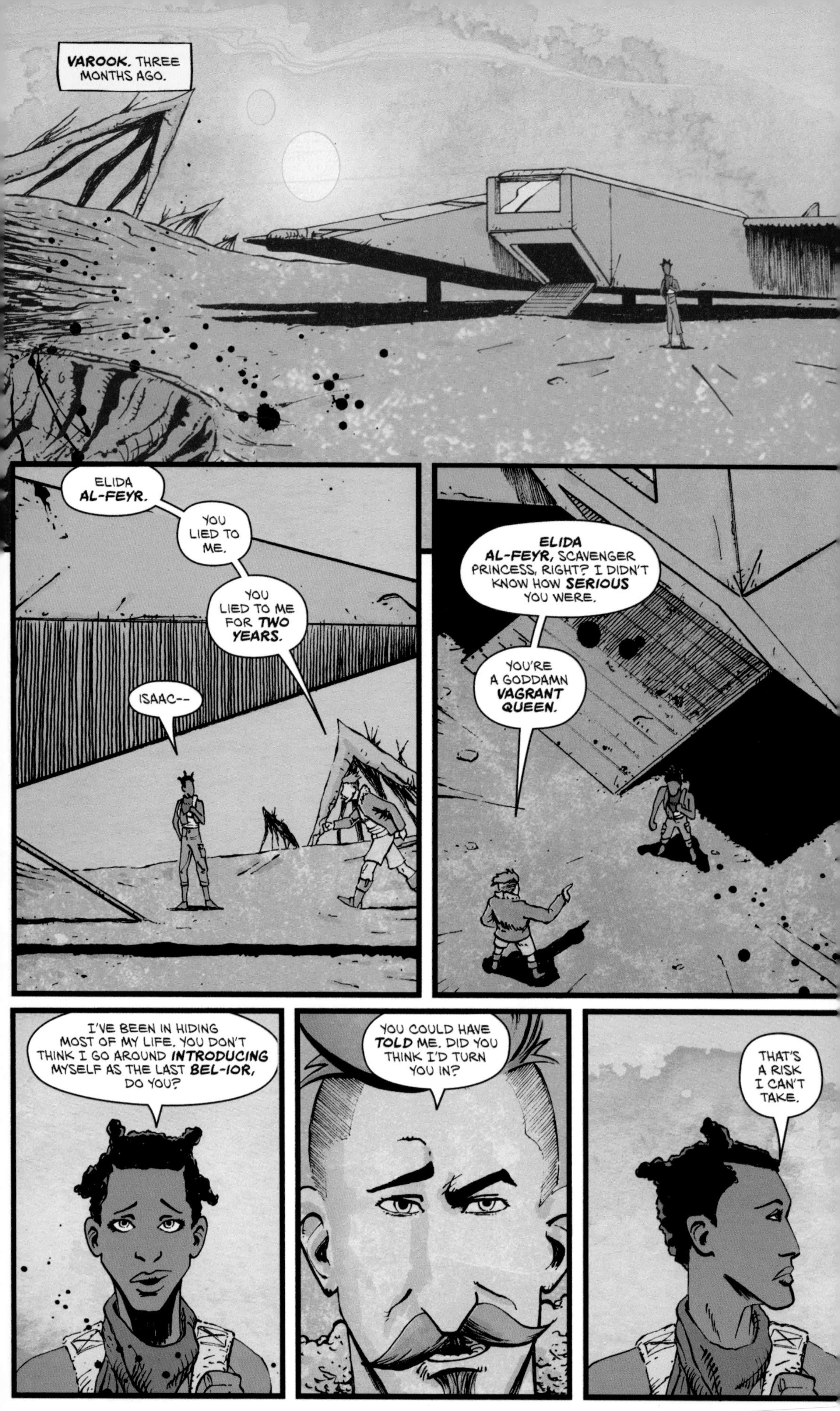
VAROOK. THREE MONTHS AGO.
ELIDA AL-FEYR.
YOU LIED TO ME.
YOU LIED TO ME FOR TWO YEARS.
ISAAC--
ELIDA AL-FEYR, SCAVENGER PRINCESS, RIGHT? I DIDN'T KNOW HOW SERIOUS YOU WERE.
YOU'RE A GODDAMN VAGRANT QUEEN.
I'VE BEEN IN HIDING MOST OF MY LIFE. YOU DON'T THINK I GO AROUND INTRODUCING MYSELF AS THE LAST BEL-IOR, DO YOU?
YOU COULD HAVE TOLD ME. DID YOU THINK I'D TURN YOU IN?
THAT'S A RISK I CAN'T TAKE.

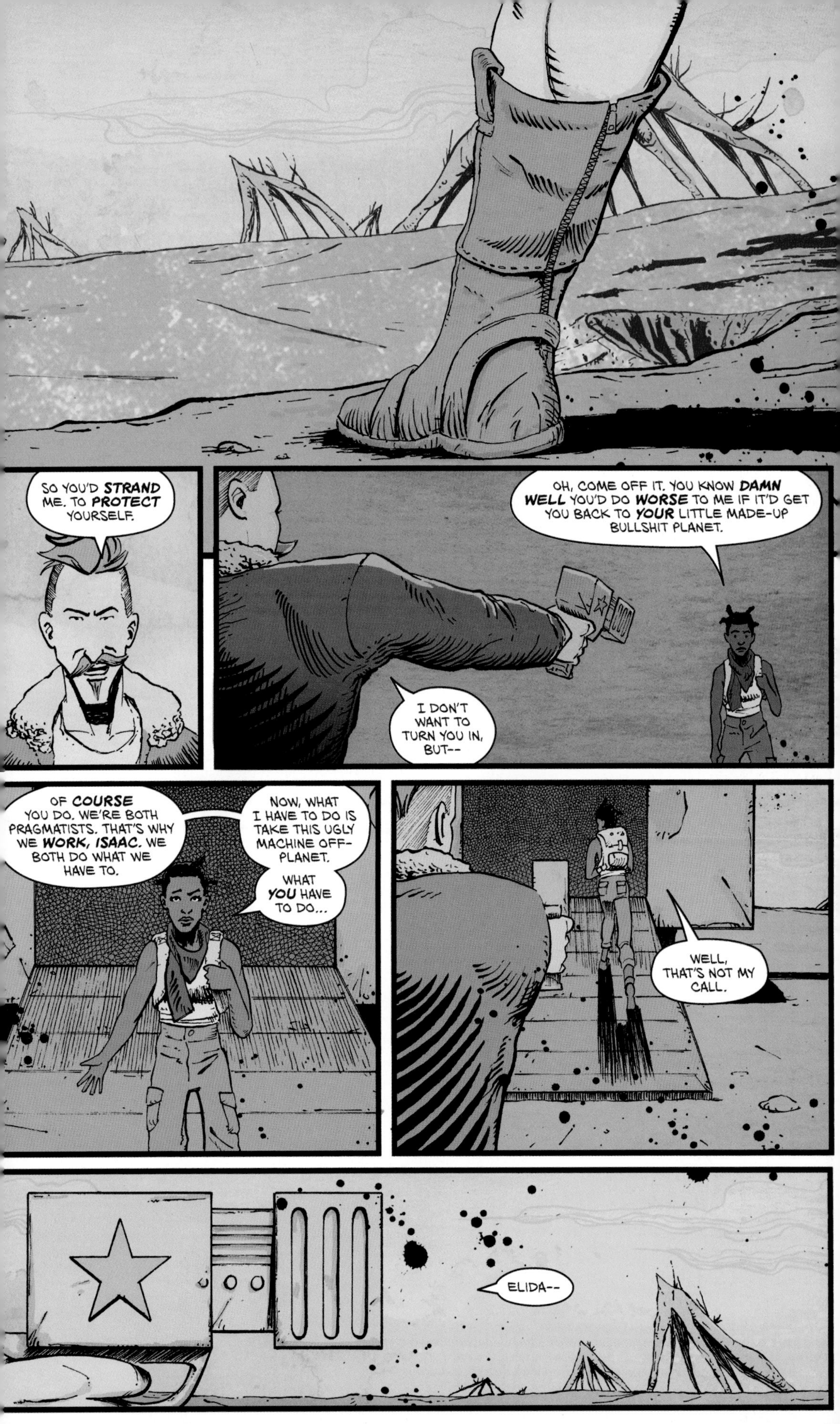
SO YOU'D STRAND ME. TO PROTECT YOURSELF.
OH, COME OFF IT. YOU KNOW DAMN WELL YOU'D DO WORSE TO ME IF IT'D GET YOU BACK TO YOUR LITTLE MADE-UP BULLSHIT PLANET.
I DON'T WANT TO TURN YOU IN, BUT--
OF COURSE YOU DO. WE'RE BOTH PRAGMATISTS. THAT'S WHY WE WORK, ISAAC. WE BOTH DO WHAT WE HAVE TO.
NOW, WHAT I HAVE TO DO IS TAKE THIS UGLY MACHINE OFF-PLANET.
WHAT YOU HAVE TO DO...
WELL, THAT'S NOT MY CALL.
ELIDA--

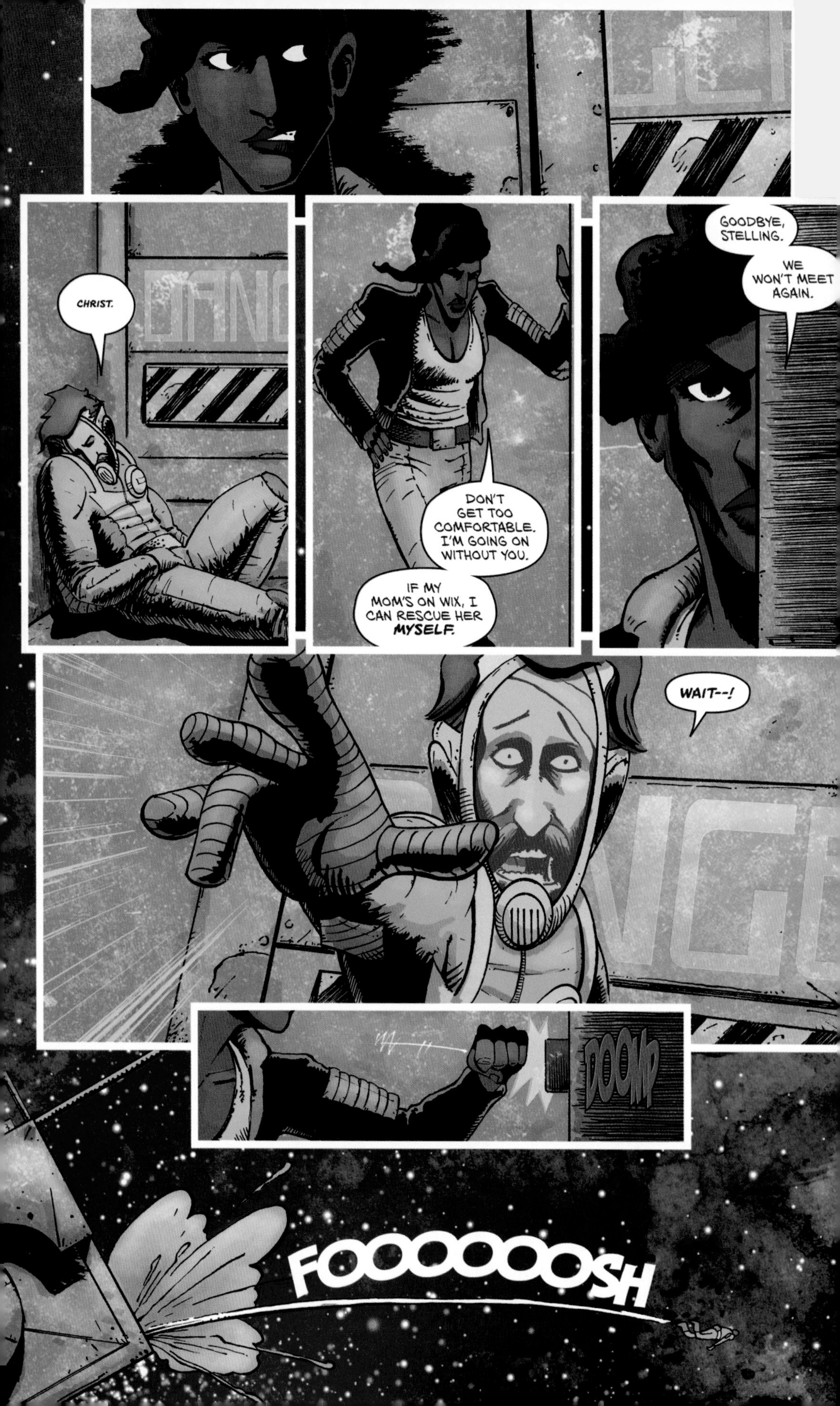
CHRIST.
DON'T GET TOO COMFORTABLE. I'M GOING ON WITHOUT YOU.
IF MY MOM'S ON WIX, I CAN RESCUE HER **MYSELF**.
GOODBYE, STELLING.
WE WON'T MEET AGAIN.
WAIT--!
DOOMP
FOOOOOOSH

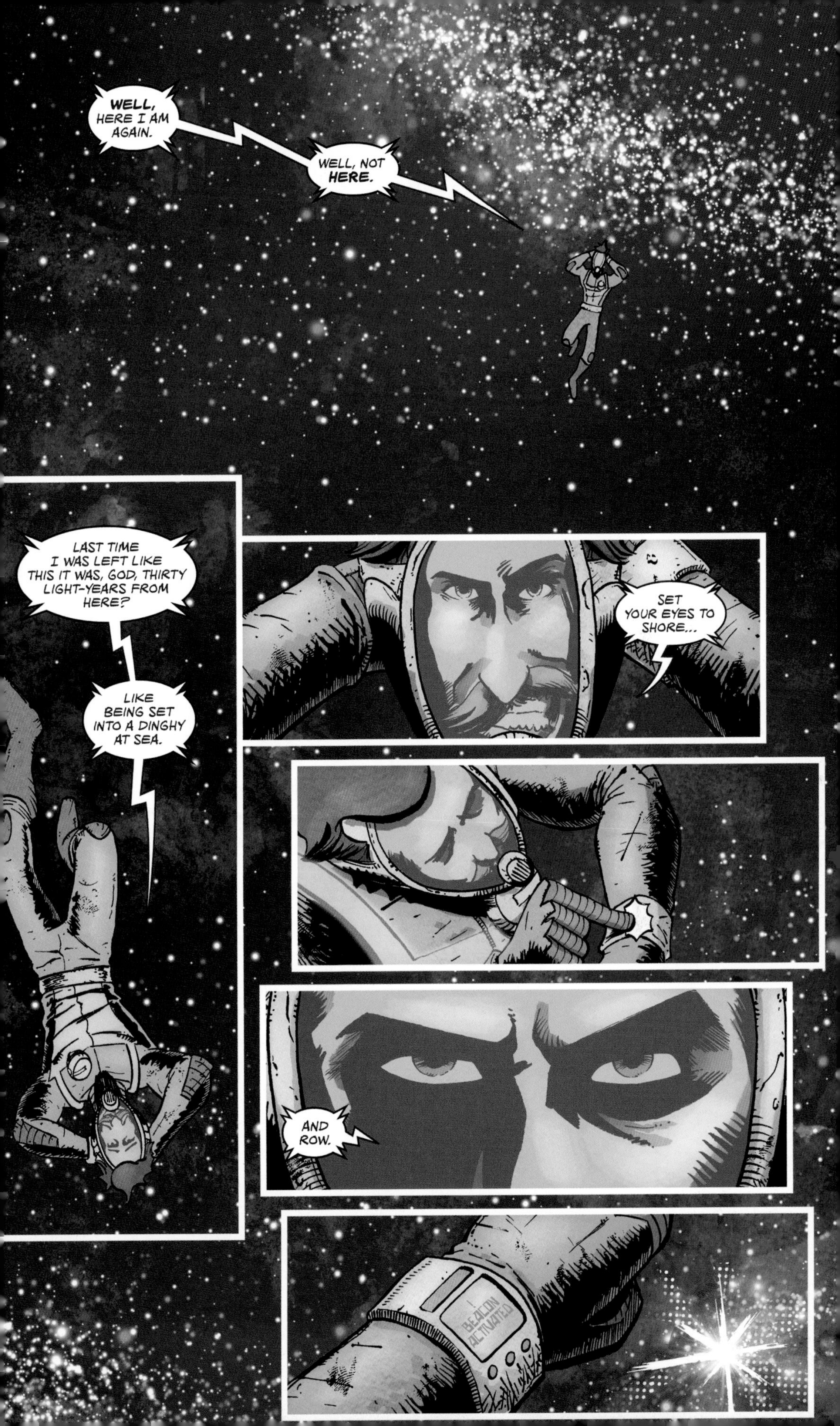
WELL, HERE I AM AGAIN.
WELL, NOT HERE.
LAST TIME I WAS LEFT LIKE THIS IT WAS, GOD, THIRTY LIGHT-YEARS FROM HERE?
LIKE BEING SET INTO A DINGHY AT SEA.
SET YOUR EYES TO SHORE...
AND ROW.
! BEACON ACTIVATED

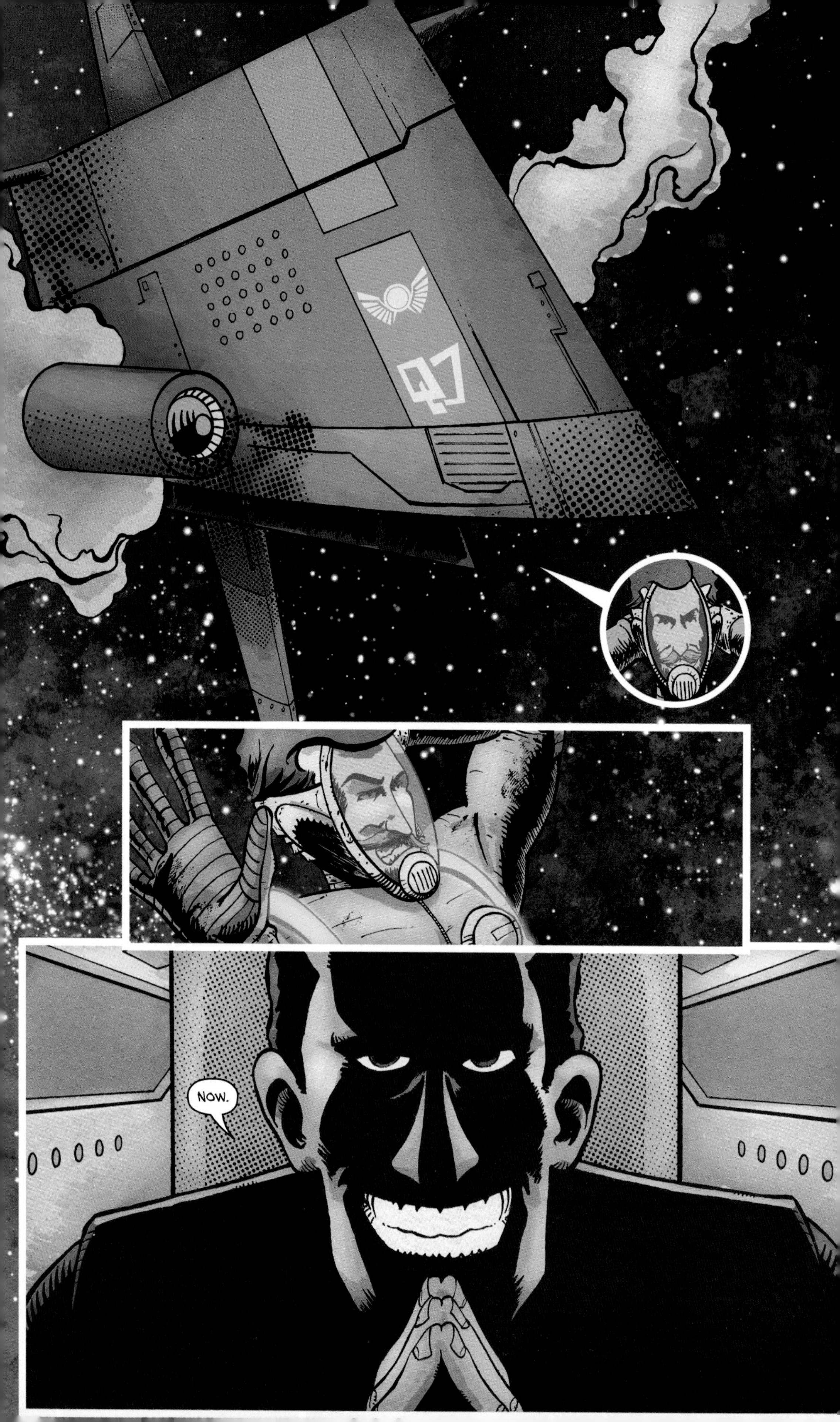
NOW.

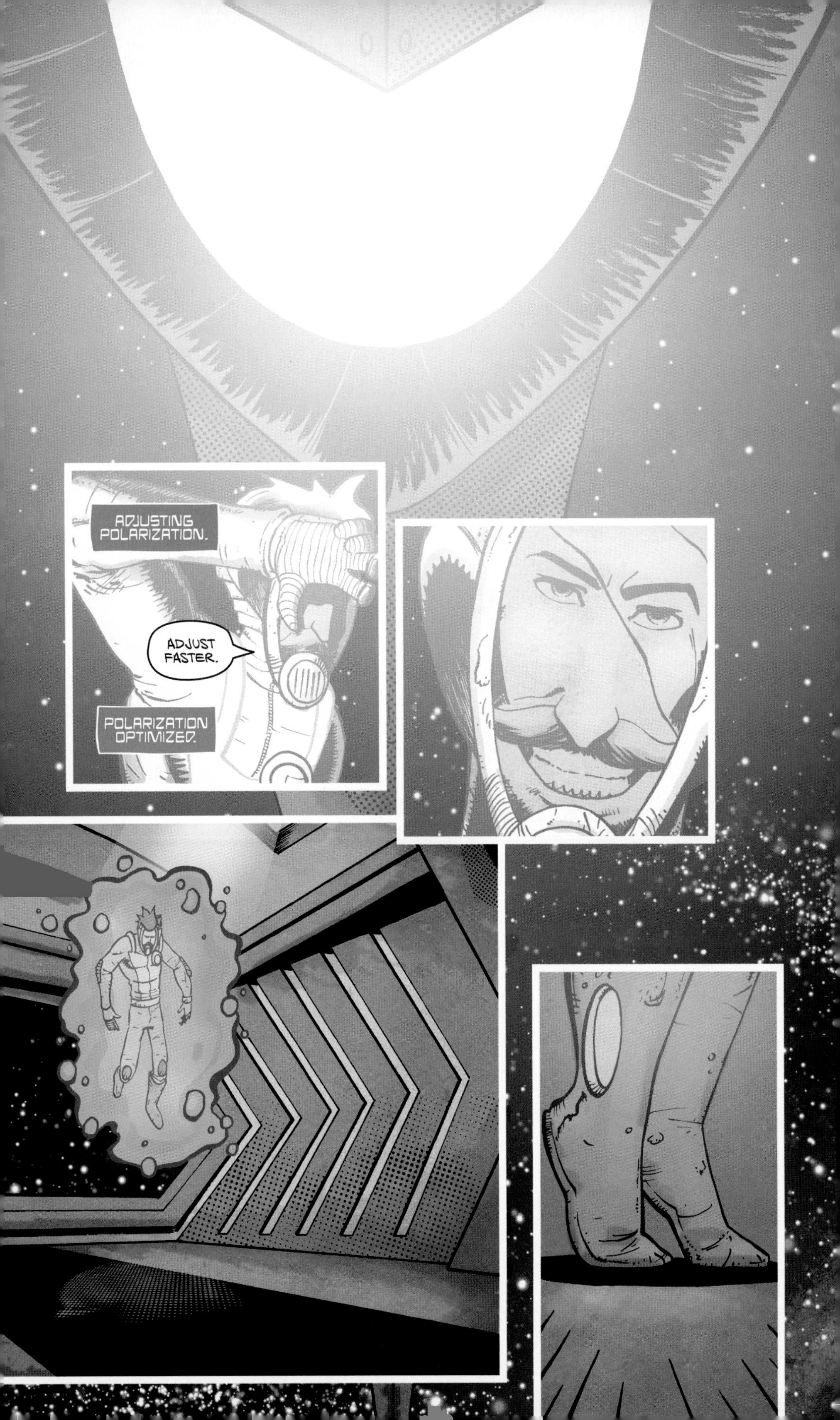
ADJUSTING POLARIZATION.
ADJUST FASTER.
POLARIZATION OPTIMIZED.

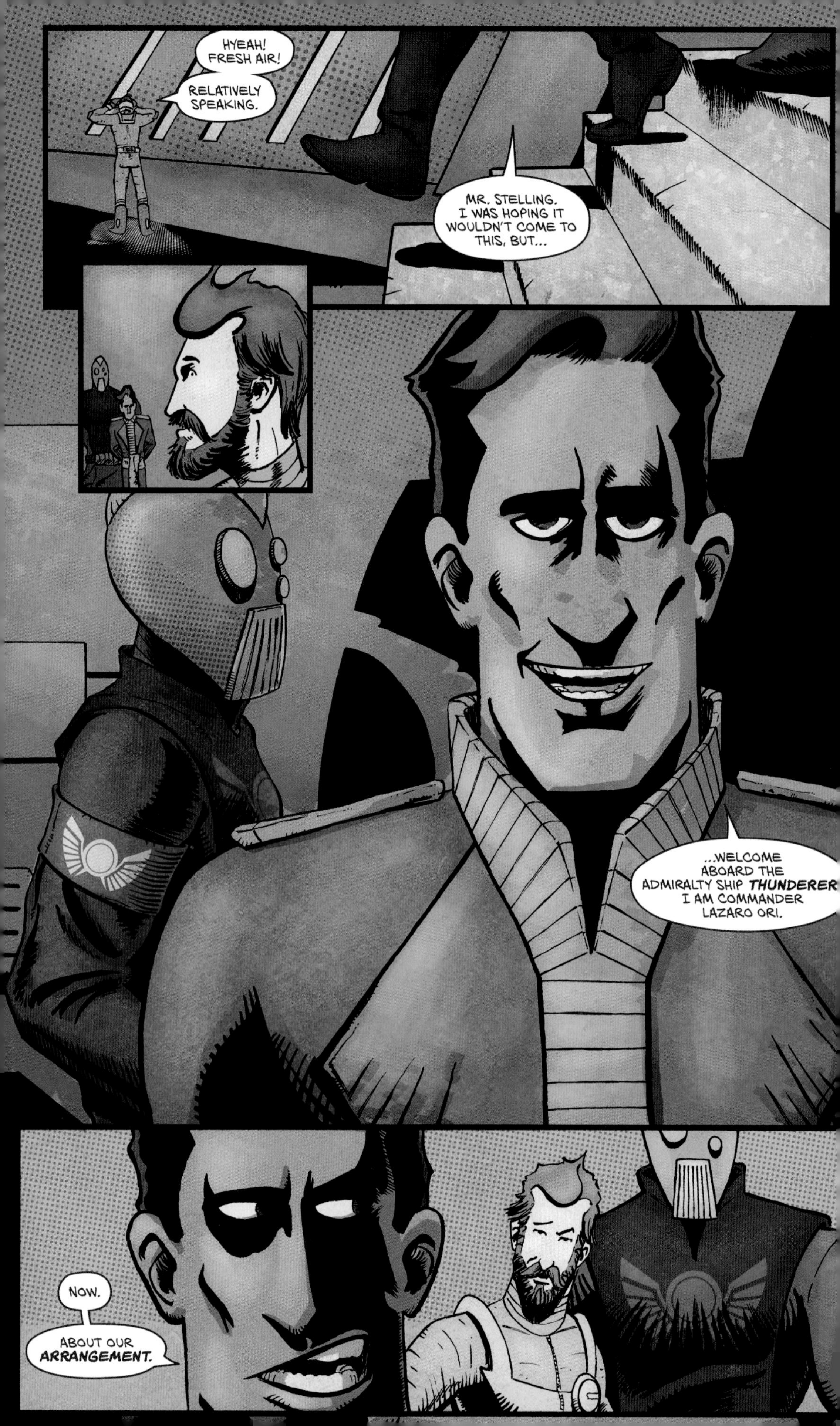
HYEAH! FRESH AIR!
RELATIVELY SPEAKING.
MR. STELLING. I WAS HOPING IT WOULDN'T COME TO THIS, BUT...
...WELCOME ABOARD THE ADMIRALTY SHIP THUNDERER. I AM COMMANDER LAZARO ORI.
NOW.
ABOUT OUR ARRANGEMENT.

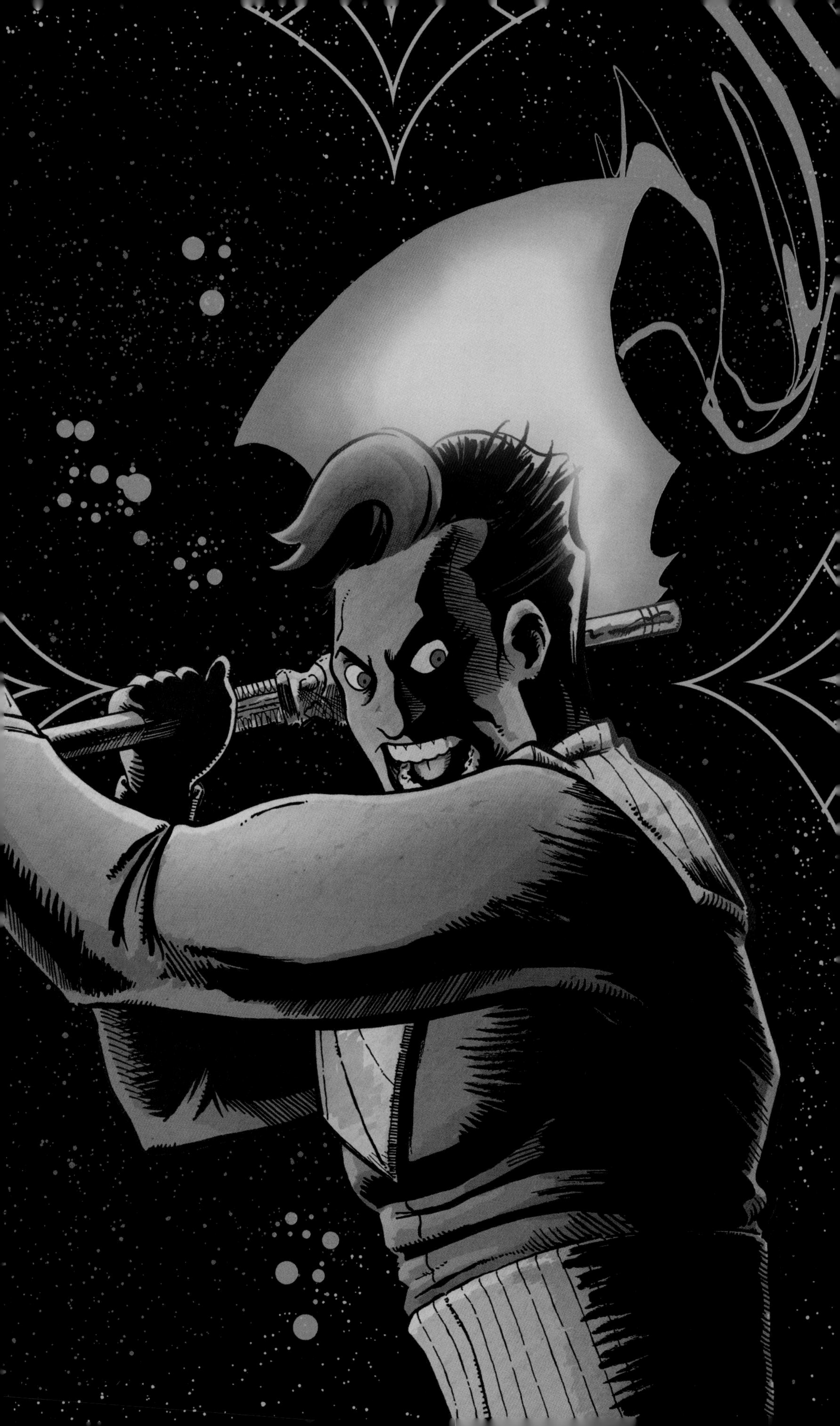

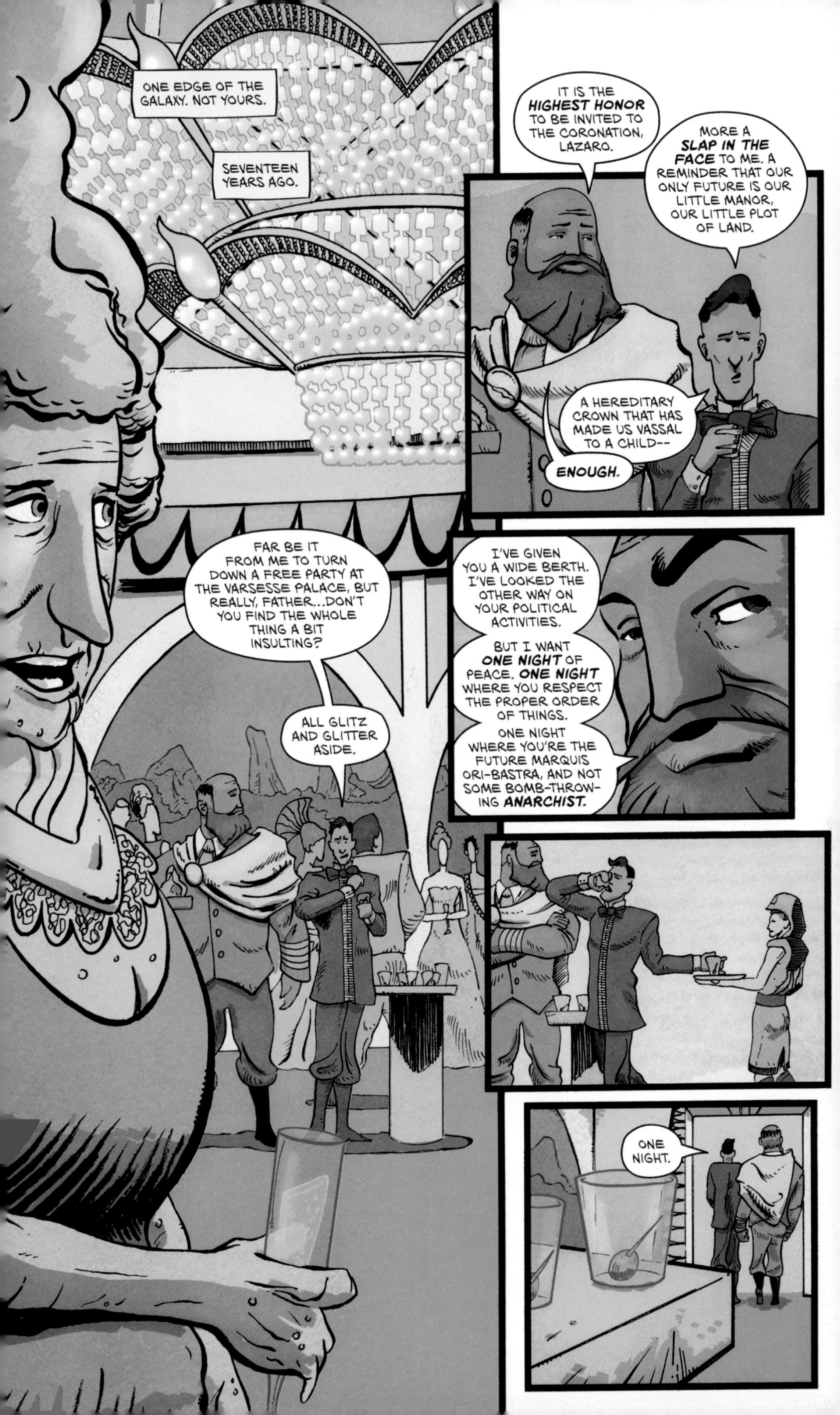
ONE EDGE OF THE GALAXY. NOT YOURS.
SEVENTEEN YEARS AGO.
IT IS THE **HIGHEST HONOR** TO BE INVITED TO THE CORONATION, LAZARO.
MORE A **SLAP IN THE FACE** TO ME. A REMINDER THAT OUR ONLY FUTURE IS OUR LITTLE MANOR, OUR LITTLE PLOT OF LAND.
A HEREDITARY CROWN THAT HAS MADE US VASSAL TO A CHILD--
ENOUGH.
FAR BE IT FROM ME TO TURN DOWN A FREE PARTY AT THE VARSESSE PALACE, BUT REALLY, FATHER...DON'T YOU FIND THE WHOLE THING A BIT INSULTING?
ALL GLITZ AND GLITTER ASIDE.
I'VE GIVEN YOU A WIDE BERTH. I'VE LOOKED THE OTHER WAY ON YOUR POLITICAL ACTIVITIES.
BUT I WANT **ONE NIGHT** OF PEACE. **ONE NIGHT** WHERE YOU RESPECT THE PROPER ORDER OF THINGS.
ONE NIGHT WHERE YOU'RE THE FUTURE MARQUIS ORI-BASTRA, AND NOT SOME BOMB-THROWING **ANARCHIST.**
ONE NIGHT.

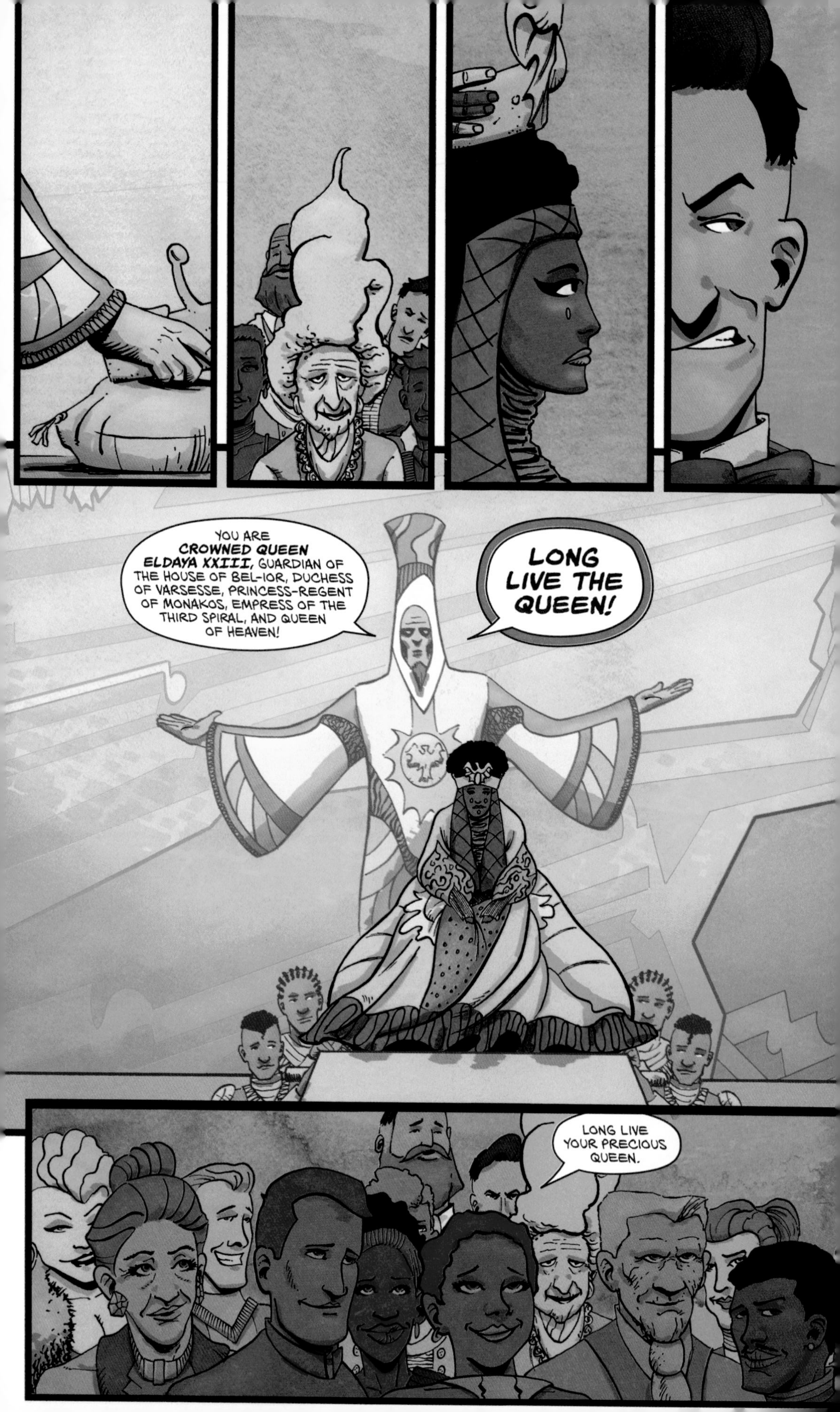
YOU ARE **CROWNED QUEEN ELDAYA XXIII,** GUARDIAN OF THE HOUSE OF BEL-IOR, DUCHESS OF VARSESSE, PRINCESS-REGENT OF MONAKOS, EMPRESS OF THE THIRD SPIRAL, AND QUEEN OF HEAVEN!
LONG LIVE THE QUEEN!
LONG LIVE YOUR PRECIOUS QUEEN.

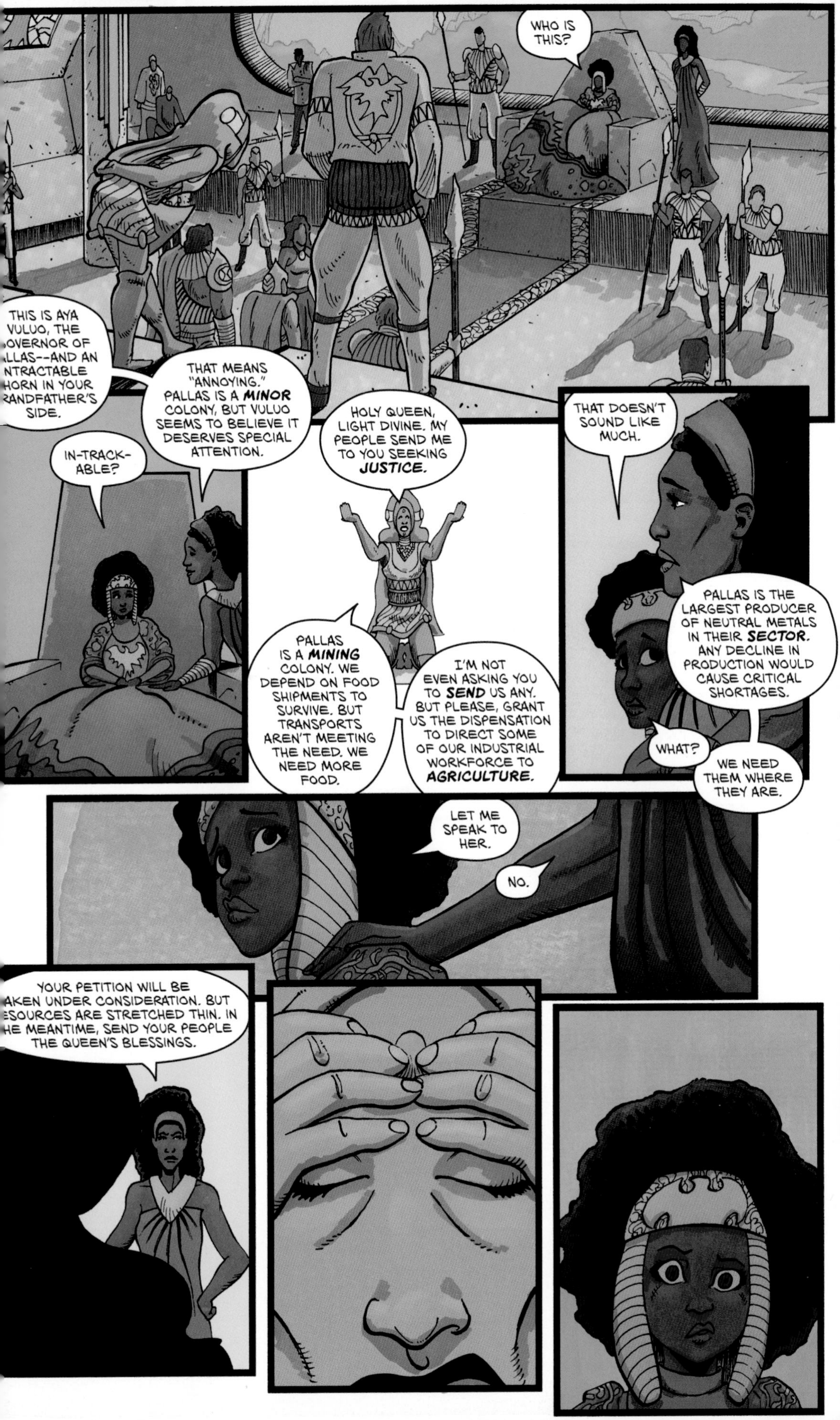
WHO IS THIS?
THIS IS AYA VULUO, THE OVERNOR OF LLAS--AND AN NTRACTABLE HORN IN YOUR RANDFATHER'S SIDE.
THAT MEANS "ANNOYING." PALLAS IS A MINOR COLONY, BUT VULUO SEEMS TO BELIEVE IT DESERVES SPECIAL ATTENTION.
IN-TRACK-ABLE?
HOLY QUEEN, LIGHT DIVINE. MY PEOPLE SEND ME TO YOU SEEKING JUSTICE.
PALLAS IS A MINING COLONY. WE DEPEND ON FOOD SHIPMENTS TO SURVIVE. BUT TRANSPORTS AREN'T MEETING THE NEED. WE NEED MORE FOOD.
I'M NOT EVEN ASKING YOU TO SEND US ANY. BUT PLEASE, GRANT US THE DISPENSATION TO DIRECT SOME OF OUR INDUSTRIAL WORKFORCE TO AGRICULTURE.
THAT DOESN'T SOUND LIKE MUCH.
PALLAS IS THE LARGEST PRODUCER OF NEUTRAL METALS IN THEIR SECTOR. ANY DECLINE IN PRODUCTION WOULD CAUSE CRITICAL SHORTAGES.
WHAT?
WE NEED THEM WHERE THEY ARE.
LET ME SPEAK TO HER.
NO.
YOUR PETITION WILL BE AKEN UNDER CONSIDERATION. BUT ESOURCES ARE STRETCHED THIN. IN HE MEANTIME, SEND YOUR PEOPLE THE QUEEN'S BLESSINGS.

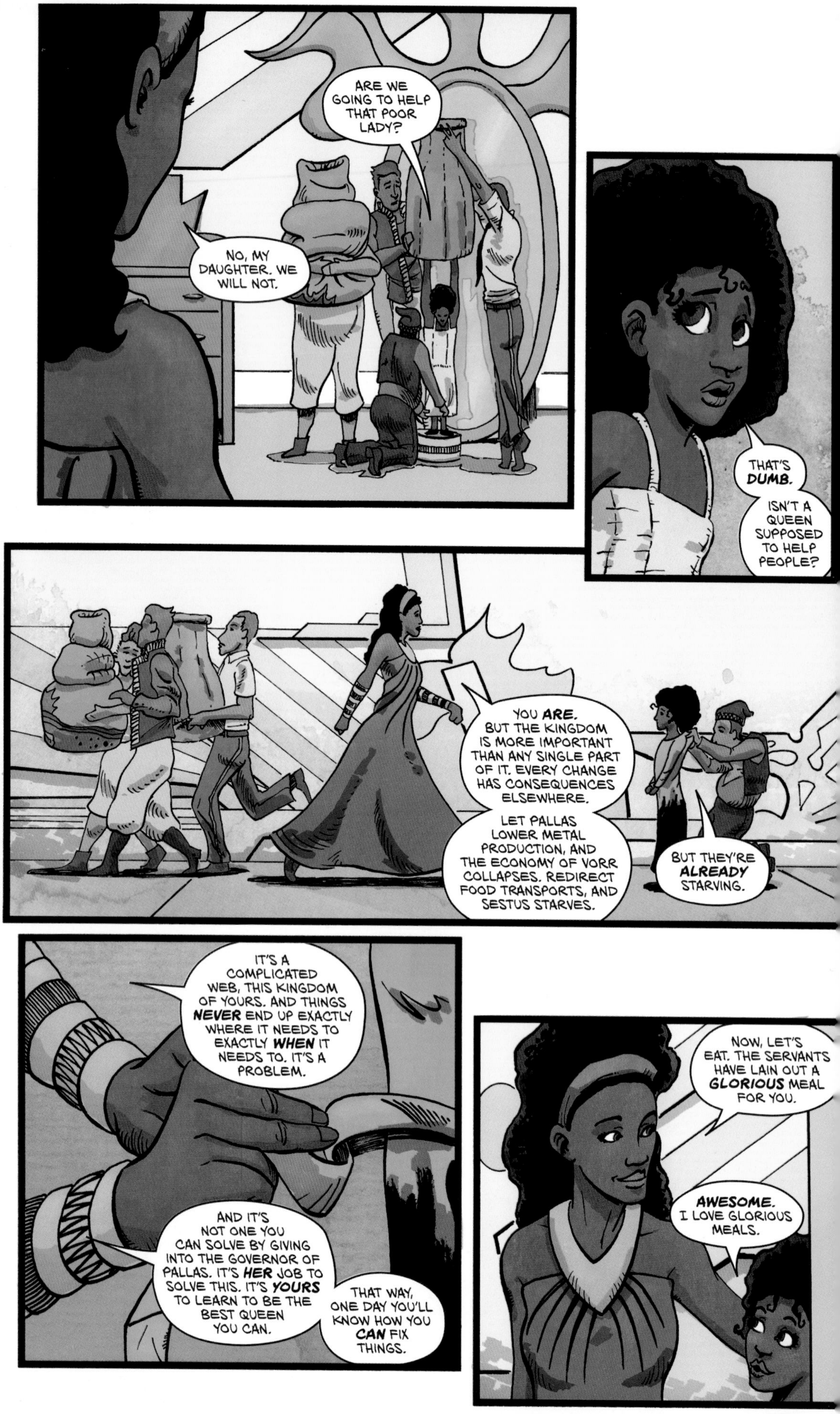
ARE WE GOING TO HELP THAT POOR LADY?
NO, MY DAUGHTER. WE WILL NOT.
THAT'S **DUMB.**
ISN'T A QUEEN SUPPOSED TO HELP PEOPLE?
YOU **ARE.** BUT THE KINGDOM IS MORE IMPORTANT THAN ANY SINGLE PART OF IT. EVERY CHANGE HAS CONSEQUENCES ELSEWHERE.
LET PALLAS LOWER METAL PRODUCTION, AND THE ECONOMY OF VORR COLLAPSES. REDIRECT FOOD TRANSPORTS, AND SESTUS STARVES.
BUT THEY'RE ***ALREADY*** STARVING.
IT'S A COMPLICATED WEB, THIS KINGDOM OF YOURS. AND THINGS ***NEVER*** END UP EXACTLY WHERE IT NEEDS TO EXACTLY ***WHEN*** IT NEEDS TO. IT'S A PROBLEM.
AND IT'S NOT ONE YOU CAN SOLVE BY GIVING INTO THE GOVERNOR OF PALLAS. IT'S ***HER*** JOB TO SOLVE THIS. IT'S ***YOURS*** TO LEARN TO BE THE BEST QUEEN YOU CAN.
THAT WAY, ONE DAY YOU'LL KNOW HOW YOU ***CAN*** FIX THINGS.
NOW, LET'S EAT. THE SERVANTS HAVE LAIN OUT A ***GLORIOUS*** MEAL FOR YOU.
AWESOME. I LOVE GLORIOUS MEALS.

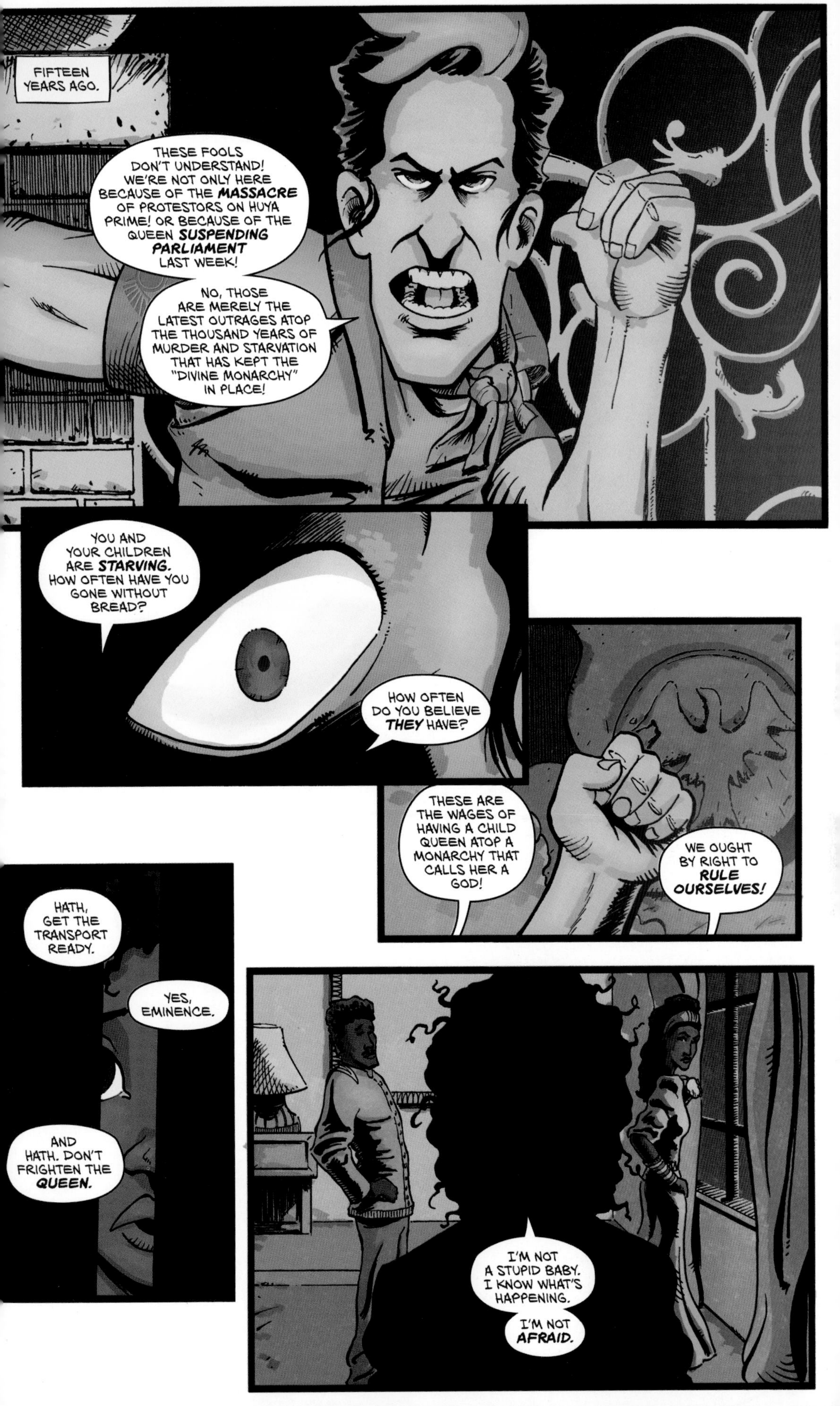
FIFTEEN YEARS AGO.
THESE FOOLS DON'T UNDERSTAND! WE'RE NOT ONLY HERE BECAUSE OF THE MASSACRE OF PROTESTORS ON HUYA PRIME! OR BECAUSE OF THE QUEEN SUSPENDING PARLIAMENT LAST WEEK!
NO, THOSE ARE MERELY THE LATEST OUTRAGES ATOP THE THOUSAND YEARS OF MURDER AND STARVATION THAT HAS KEPT THE "DIVINE MONARCHY" IN PLACE!
YOU AND YOUR CHILDREN ARE STARVING. HOW OFTEN HAVE YOU GONE WITHOUT BREAD?
HOW OFTEN DO YOU BELIEVE THEY HAVE?
THESE ARE THE WAGES OF HAVING A CHILD QUEEN ATOP A MONARCHY THAT CALLS HER A GOD!
WE OUGHT BY RIGHT TO RULE OURSELVES!
HATH, GET THE TRANSPORT READY.
YES, EMINENCE.
AND HATH. DON'T FRIGHTEN THE QUEEN.
I'M NOT A STUPID BABY. I KNOW WHAT'S HAPPENING.
I'M NOT AFRAID.

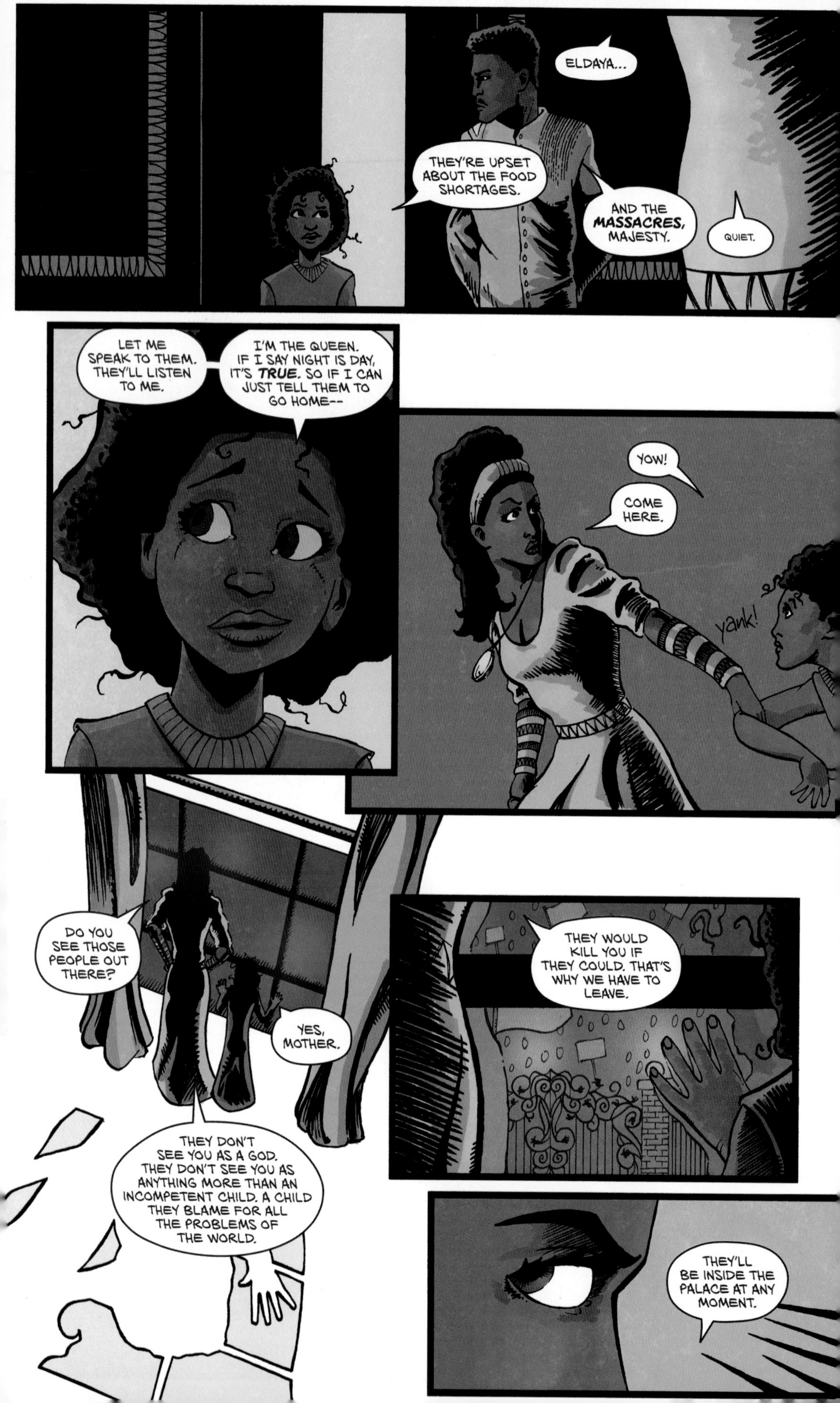
ELDAYA...
THEY'RE UPSET ABOUT THE FOOD SHORTAGES.
AND THE MASSACRES, MAJESTY.
QUIET.
LET ME SPEAK TO THEM. THEY'LL LISTEN TO ME.
I'M THE QUEEN. IF I SAY NIGHT IS DAY, IT'S TRUE. SO IF I CAN JUST TELL THEM TO GO HOME--
YOW!
COME HERE.
yank!
DO YOU SEE THOSE PEOPLE OUT THERE?
YES, MOTHER.
THEY DON'T SEE YOU AS A GOD. THEY DON'T SEE YOU AS ANYTHING MORE THAN AN INCOMPETENT CHILD. A CHILD THEY BLAME FOR ALL THE PROBLEMS OF THE WORLD.
THEY WOULD KILL YOU IF THEY COULD. THAT'S WHY WE HAVE TO LEAVE.
THEY'LL BE INSIDE THE PALACE AT ANY MOMENT.

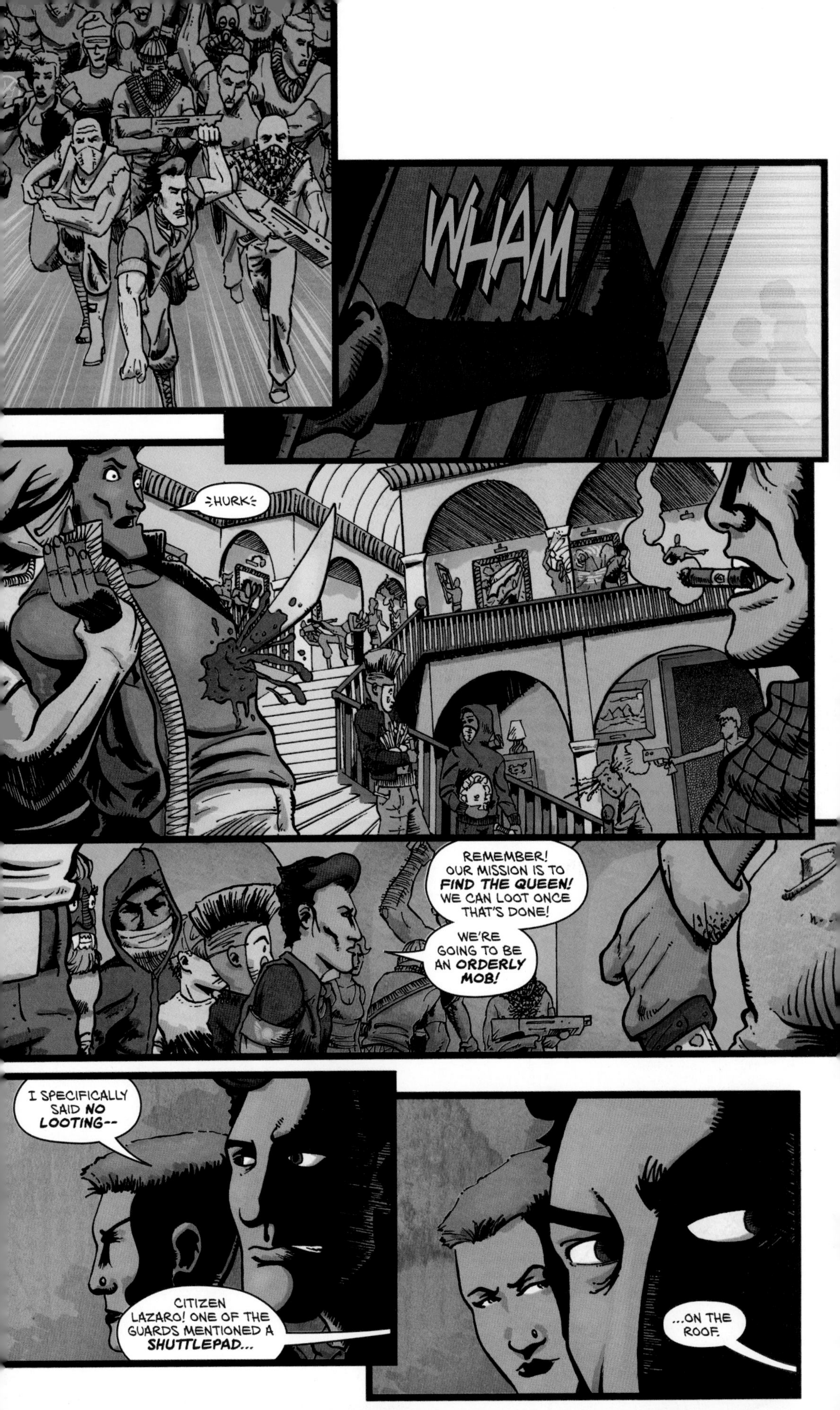
WHAM
HURK
REMEMBER! OUR MISSION IS TO FIND THE QUEEN! WE CAN LOOT ONCE THAT'S DONE!
WE'RE GOING TO BE AN ORDERLY MOB!
I SPECIFICALLY SAID NO LOOTING--
CITIZEN LAZARO! ONE OF THE GUARDS MENTIONED A SHUTTLEPAD...
...ON THE ROOF.

THERE!

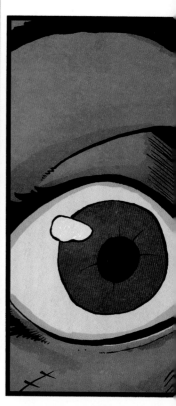

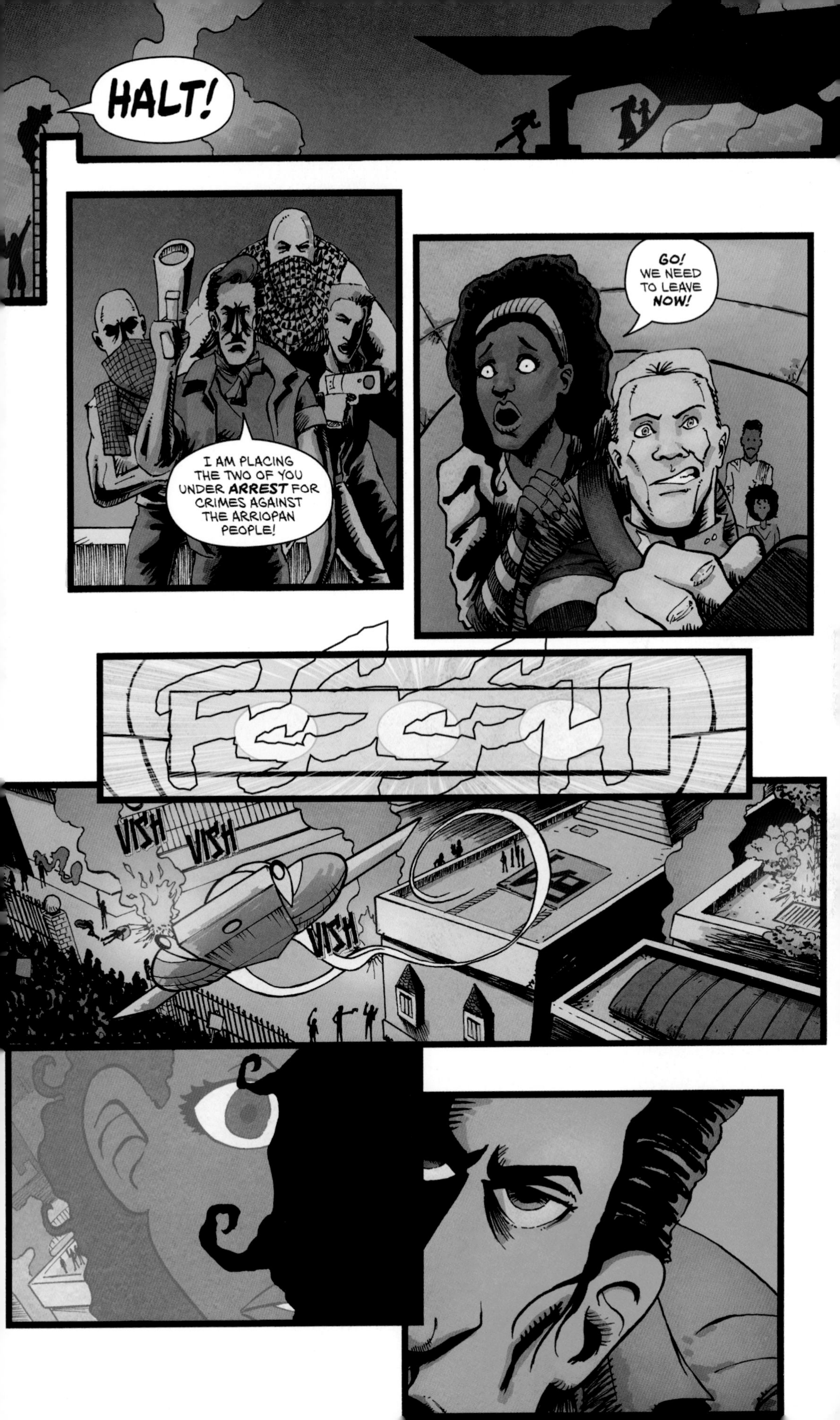
HALT!
I AM PLACING THE TWO OF YOU UNDER ARREST FOR CRIMES AGAINST THE ARRIOPAN PEOPLE!
GO! WE NEED TO LEAVE NOW!
FSSSH
VISH
VISH
VISH

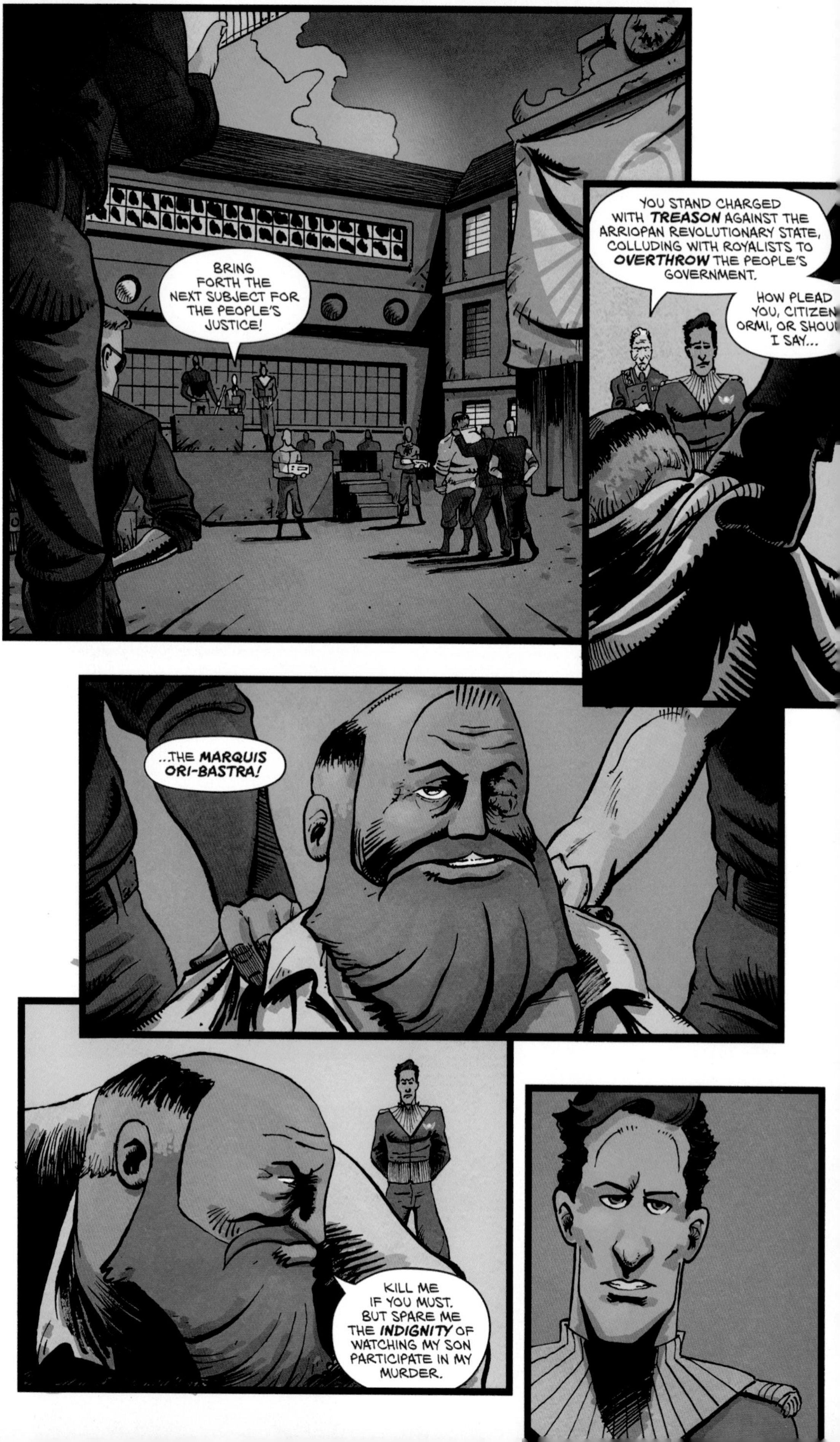
BRING FORTH THE NEXT SUBJECT FOR THE PEOPLE'S JUSTICE!
YOU STAND CHARGED WITH TREASON AGAINST THE ARRIOPAN REVOLUTIONARY STATE, COLLUDING WITH ROYALISTS TO OVERTHROW THE PEOPLE'S GOVERNMENT.
HOW PLEAD YOU, CITIZEN ORMI, OR SHOU I SAY...
...THE MARQUIS ORI-BASTRA!
KILL ME IF YOU MUST. BUT SPARE ME THE INDIGNITY OF WATCHING MY SON PARTICIPATE IN MY MURDER.

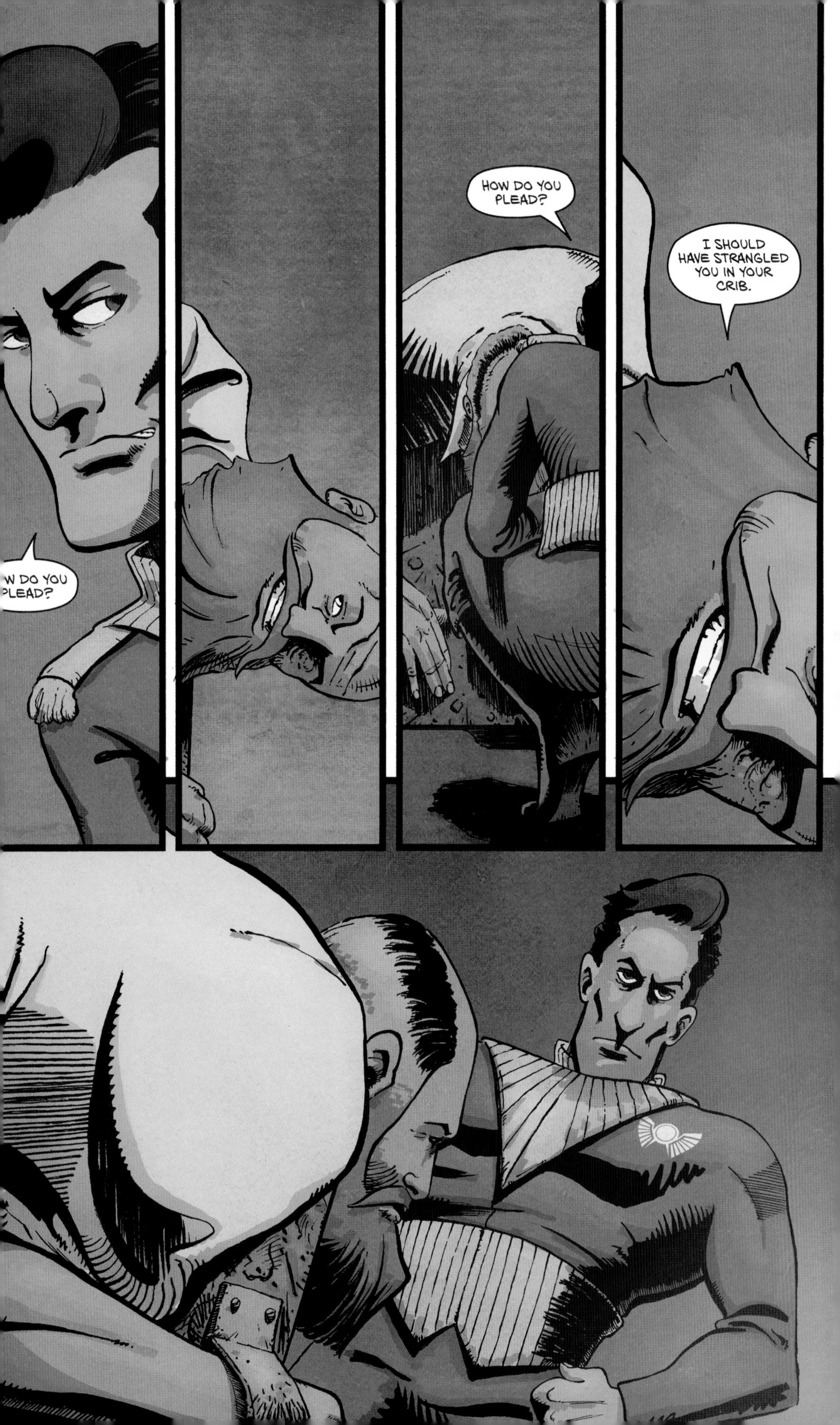
W DO YOU PLEAD?
HOW DO YOU PLEAD?
I SHOULD HAVE STRANGLED YOU IN YOUR CRIB.

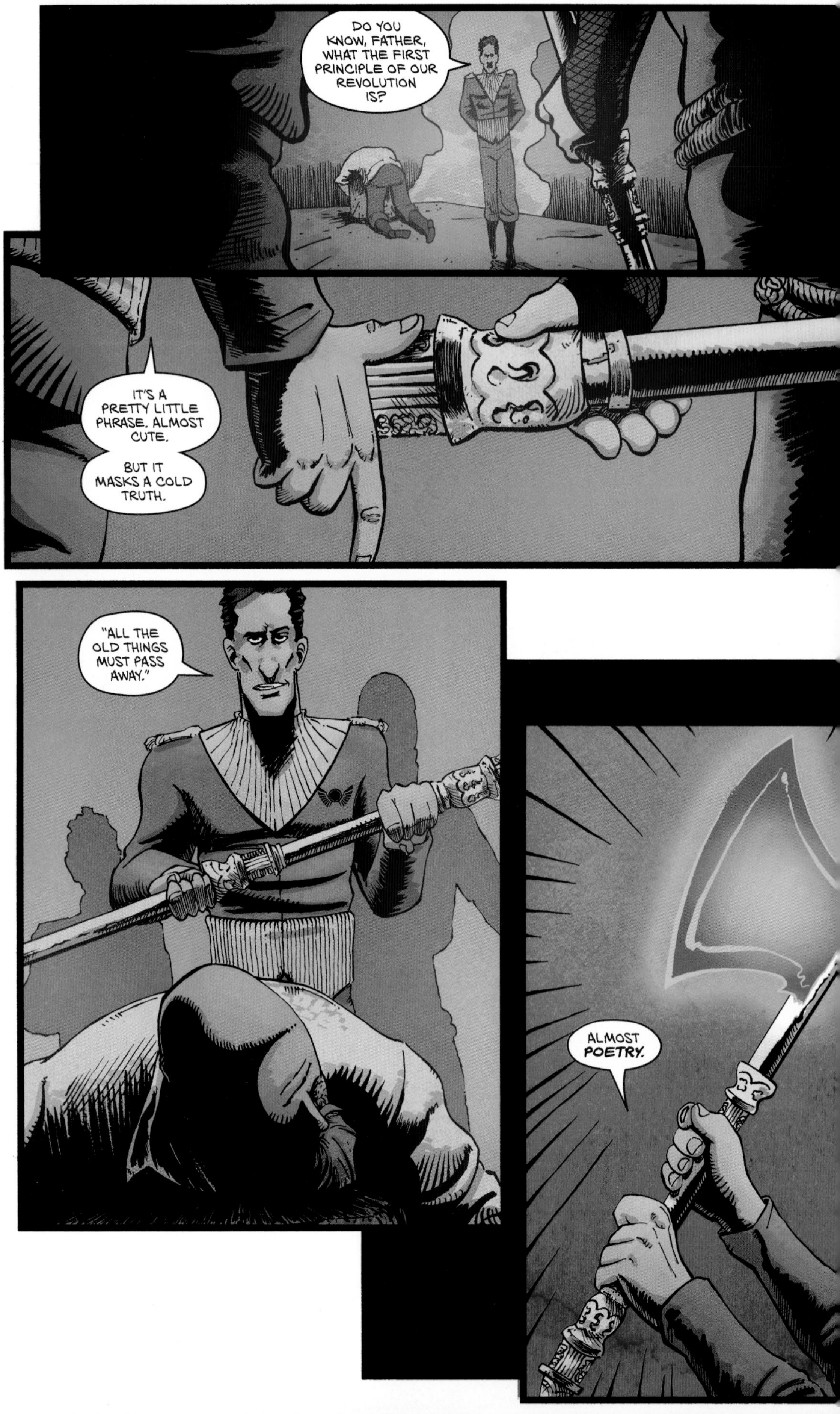
DO YOU KNOW, FATHER, WHAT THE FIRST PRINCIPLE OF OUR REVOLUTION IS?
IT'S A PRETTY LITTLE PHRASE. ALMOST CUTE.
BUT IT MASKS A COLD TRUTH.
"ALL THE OLD THINGS MUST PASS AWAY."
ALMOST **POETRY.**

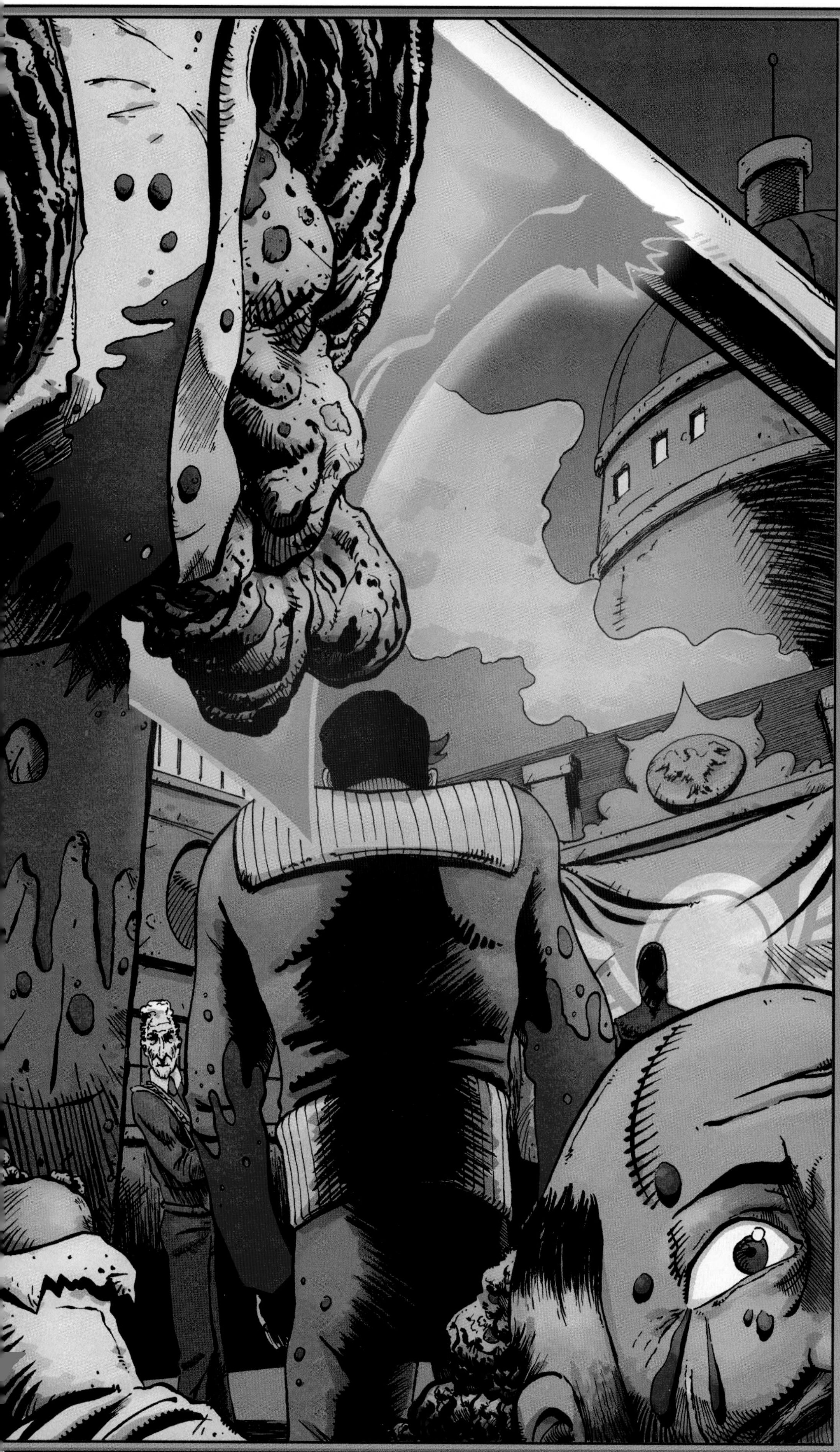

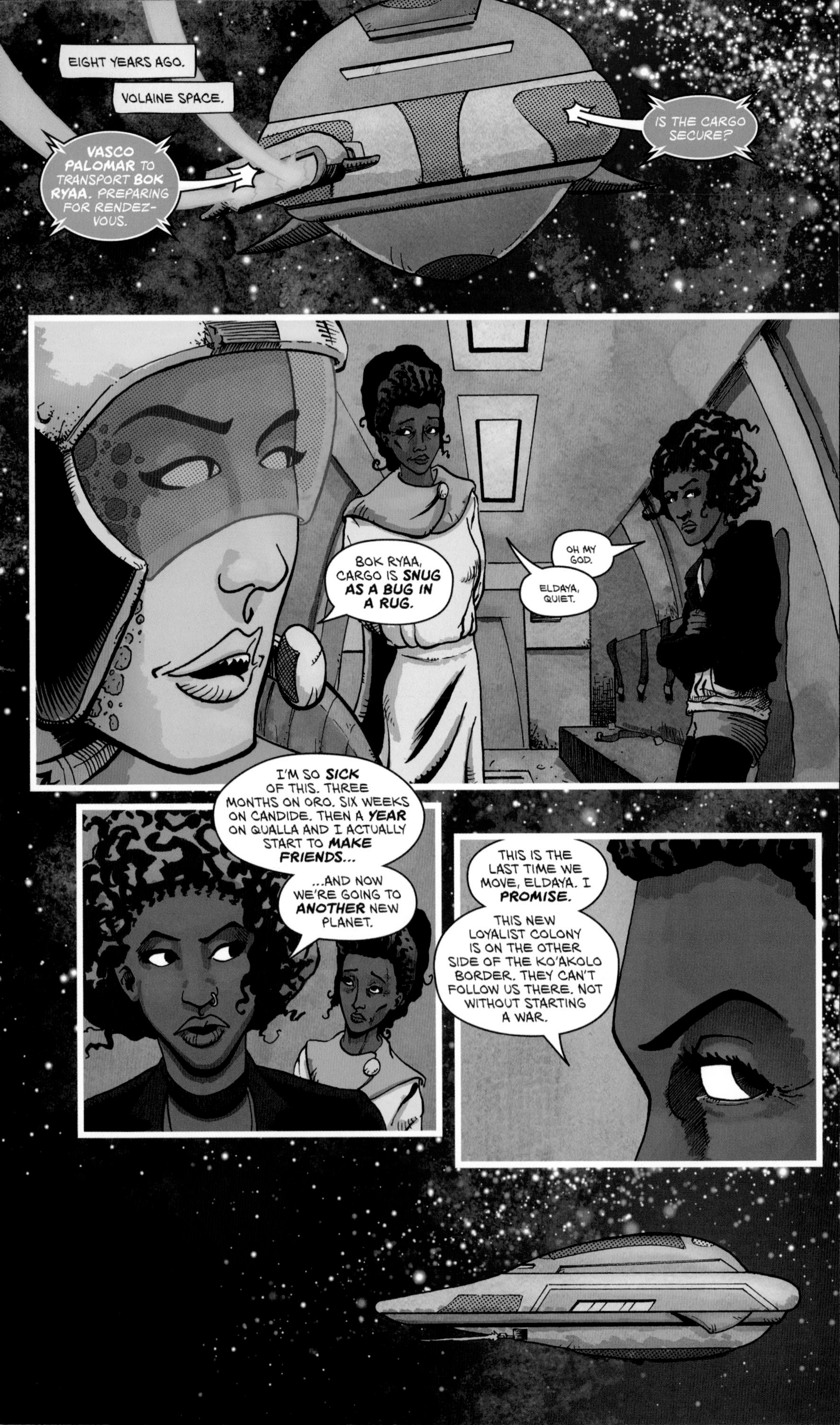
EIGHT YEARS AGO.
VOLAINE SPACE.
VASCO PALOMAR TO TRANSPORT BOK RYAA. PREPARING FOR RENDEZ-VOUS.
IS THE CARGO SECURE?
BOK RYAA, CARGO IS SNUG AS A BUG IN A RUG.
OH MY GOD.
ELDAYA, QUIET.
I'M SO SICK OF THIS. THREE MONTHS ON ORO. SIX WEEKS ON CANDIDE. THEN A YEAR ON QUALLA AND I ACTUALLY START TO MAKE FRIENDS...
...AND NOW WE'RE GOING TO ANOTHER NEW PLANET.
THIS IS THE LAST TIME WE MOVE, ELDAYA. I PROMISE.
THIS NEW LOYALIST COLONY IS ON THE OTHER SIDE OF THE KO'AKOLO BORDER. THEY CAN'T FOLLOW US THERE. NOT WITHOUT STARTING A WAR.

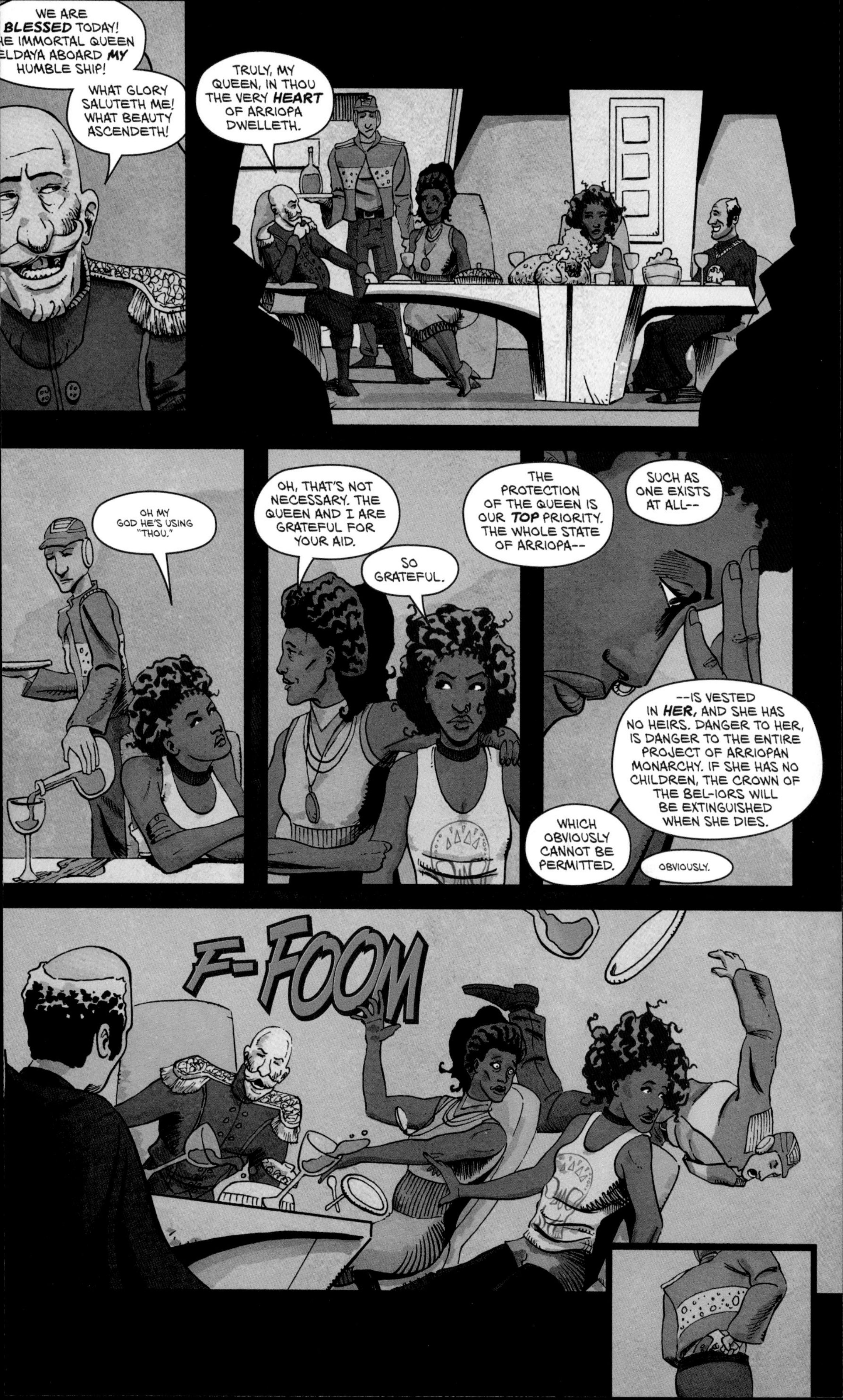

WE ARE **BLESSED** TODAY! HE IMMORTAL QUEEN ELDAYA ABOARD **MY** HUMBLE SHIP!
WHAT GLORY SALUTETH ME! WHAT BEAUTY ASCENDETH!
TRULY, MY QUEEN, IN THOU THE VERY **HEART** OF ARRIOPA DWELLETH.
OH MY GOD HE'S USING "THOU."
OH, THAT'S NOT NECESSARY. THE QUEEN AND I ARE GRATEFUL FOR YOUR AID.
SO GRATEFUL.
THE PROTECTION OF THE QUEEN IS OUR **TOP** PRIORITY. THE WHOLE STATE OF ARRIOPA--
SUCH AS ONE EXISTS AT ALL--
--IS VESTED IN **HER,** AND SHE HAS NO HEIRS. DANGER TO HER, IS DANGER TO THE ENTIRE PROJECT OF ARRIOPAN MONARCHY. IF SHE HAS NO CHILDREN, THE CROWN OF THE BEL-IORS WILL BE EXTINGUISHED WHEN SHE DIES.
WHICH OBVIOUSLY CANNOT BE PERMITTED.
OBVIOUSLY.
F-FOOM

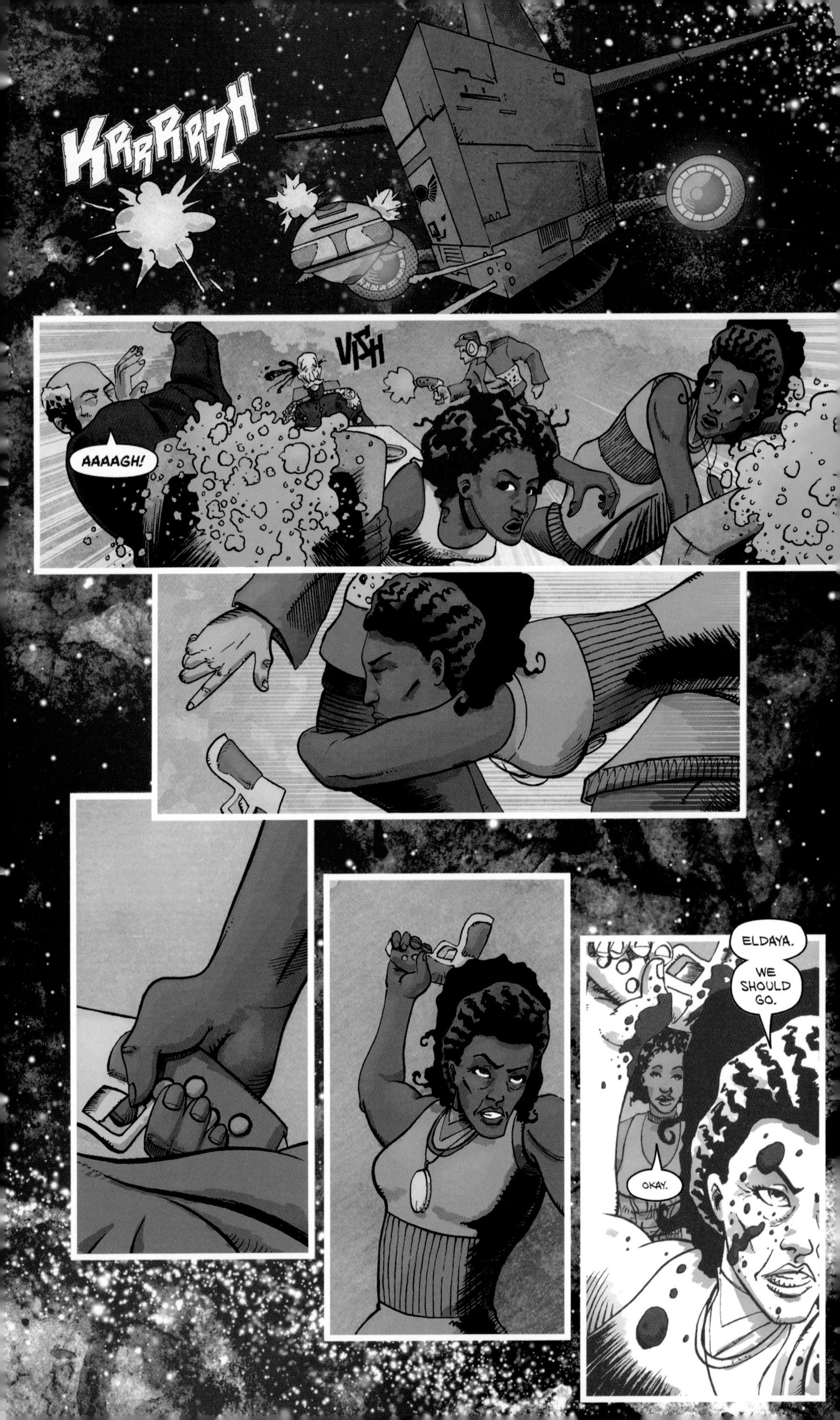
KRRRRZH
VISH
AAAAGH!
ELDAYA.
WE SHOULD GO.
OKAY.

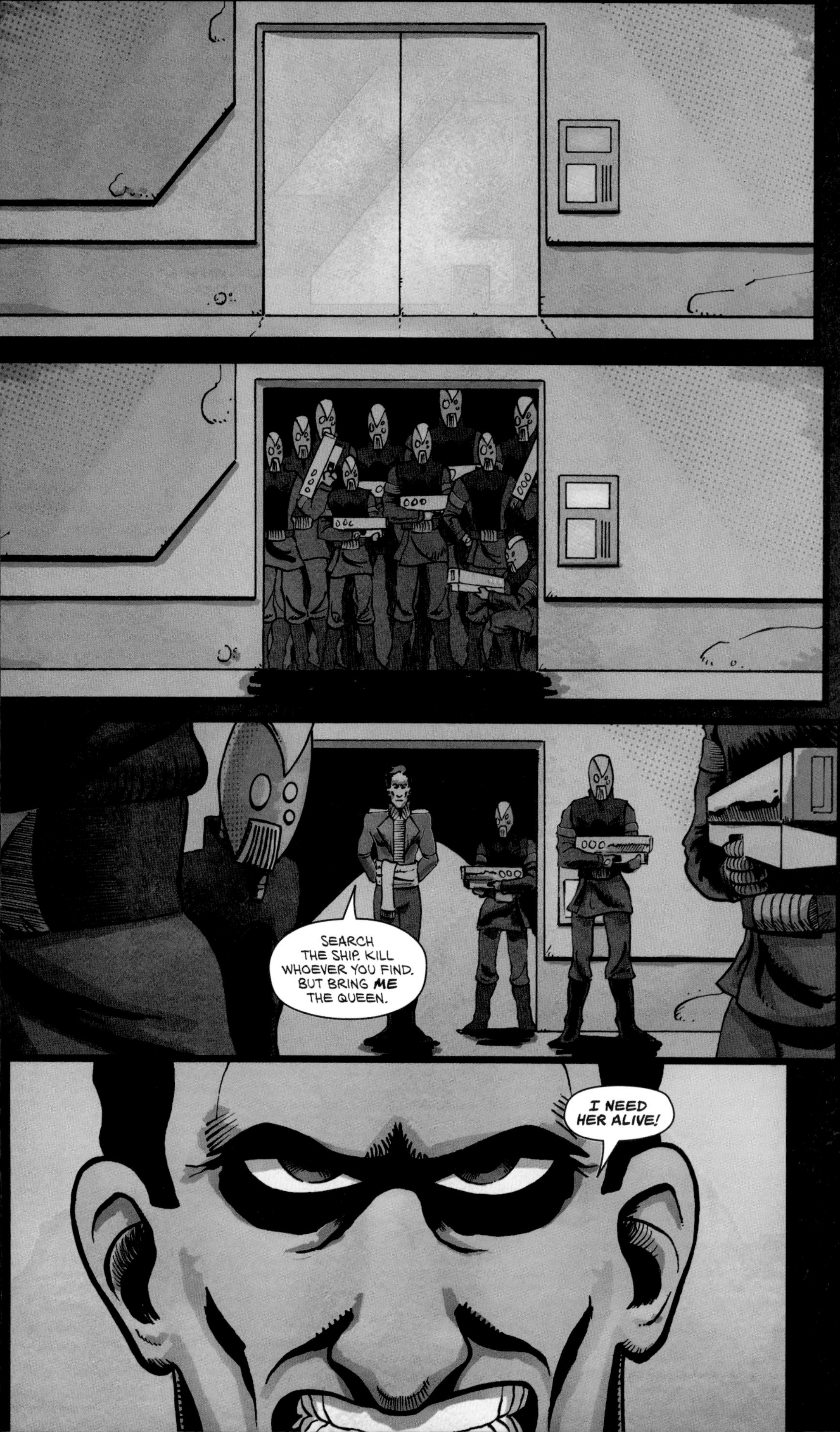
SEARCH THE SHIP. KILL WHOEVER YOU FIND. BUT BRING ME THE QUEEN.
I NEED HER ALIVE!

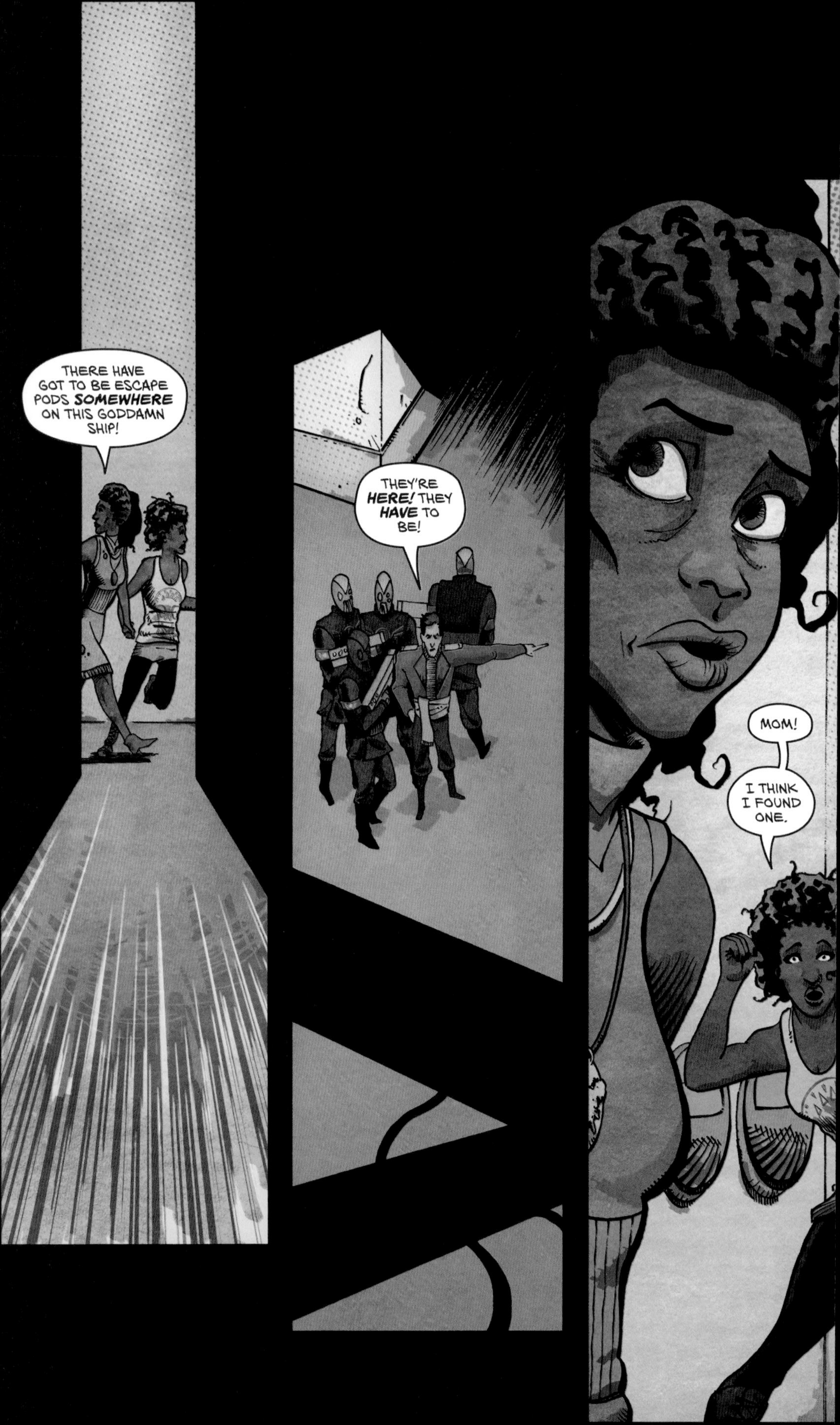
THERE HAVE GOT TO BE ESCAPE PODS **SOMEWHERE** ON THIS GODDAMN SHIP!
THEY'RE **HERE!** THEY **HAVE** TO BE!
MOM!
I THINK I FOUND ONE.

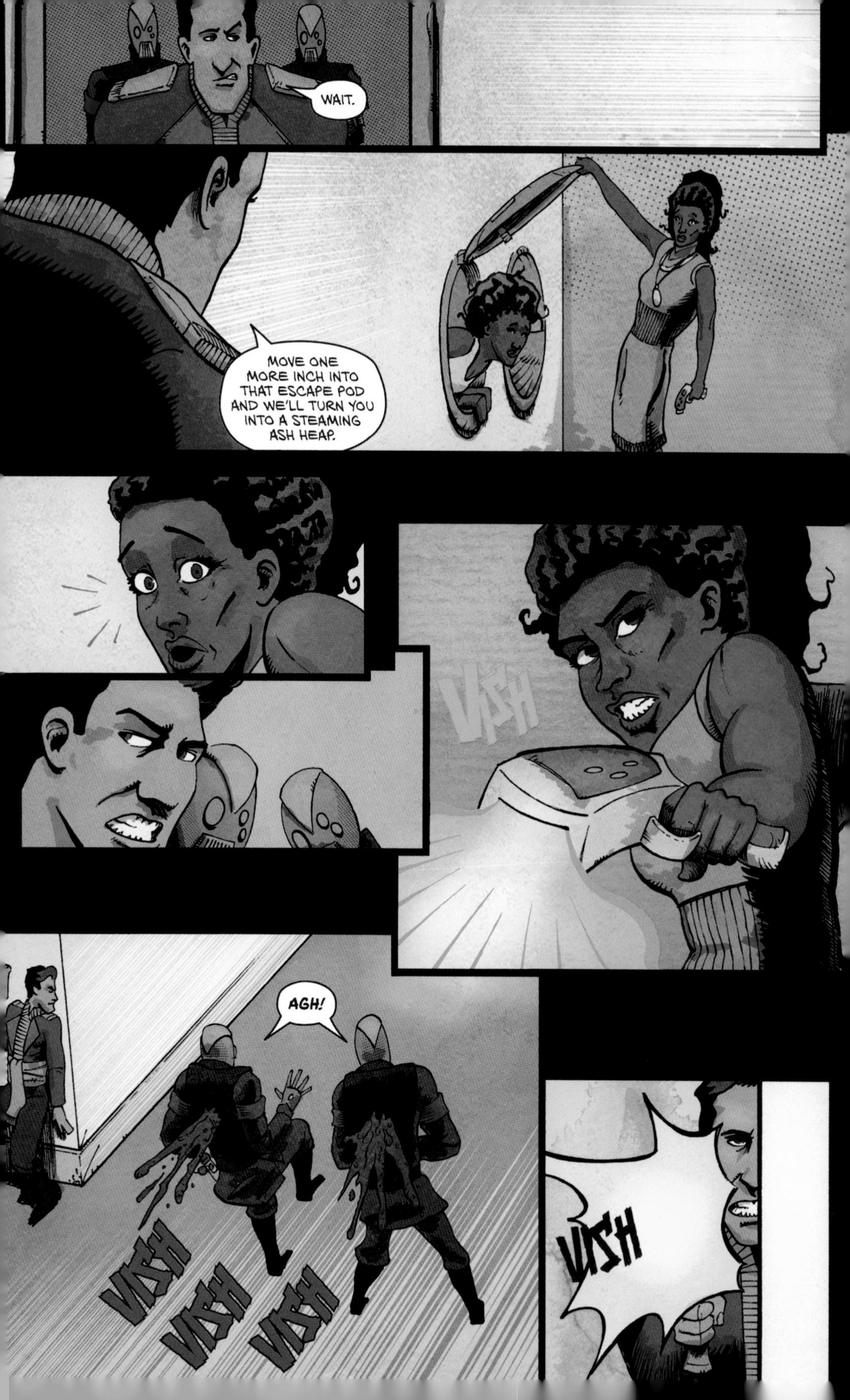
WAIT.
MOVE ONE MORE INCH INTO THAT ESCAPE POD AND WE'LL TURN YOU INTO A STEAMING ASH HEAP.
VISH
AGH!
VISH
VISH
VISH
VISH

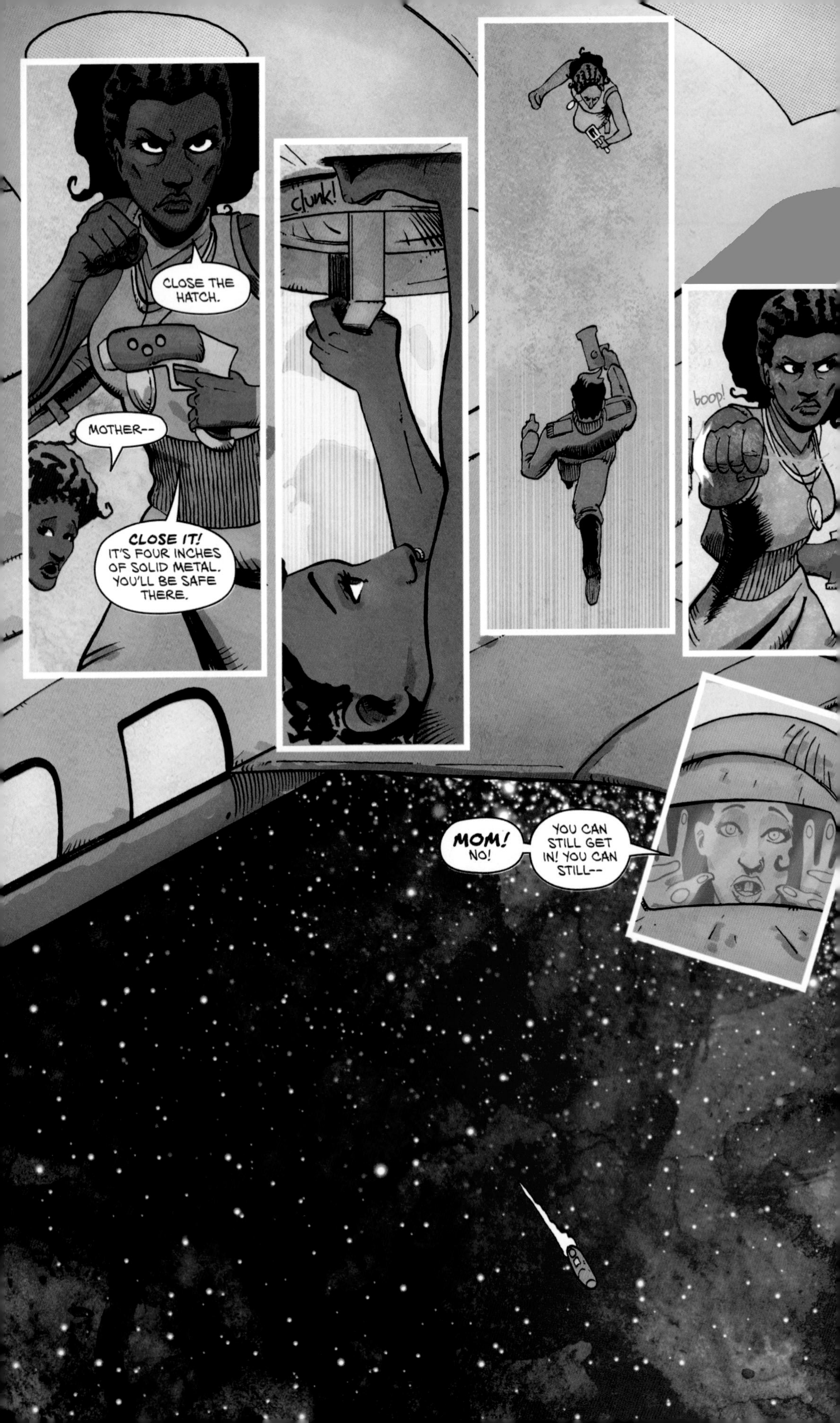
CLOSE THE HATCH.
MOTHER--
CLOSE IT! IT'S FOUR INCHES OF SOLID METAL. YOU'LL BE SAFE THERE.
clunk!
boop!
MOM! NO!
YOU CAN STILL GET IN! YOU CAN STILL--

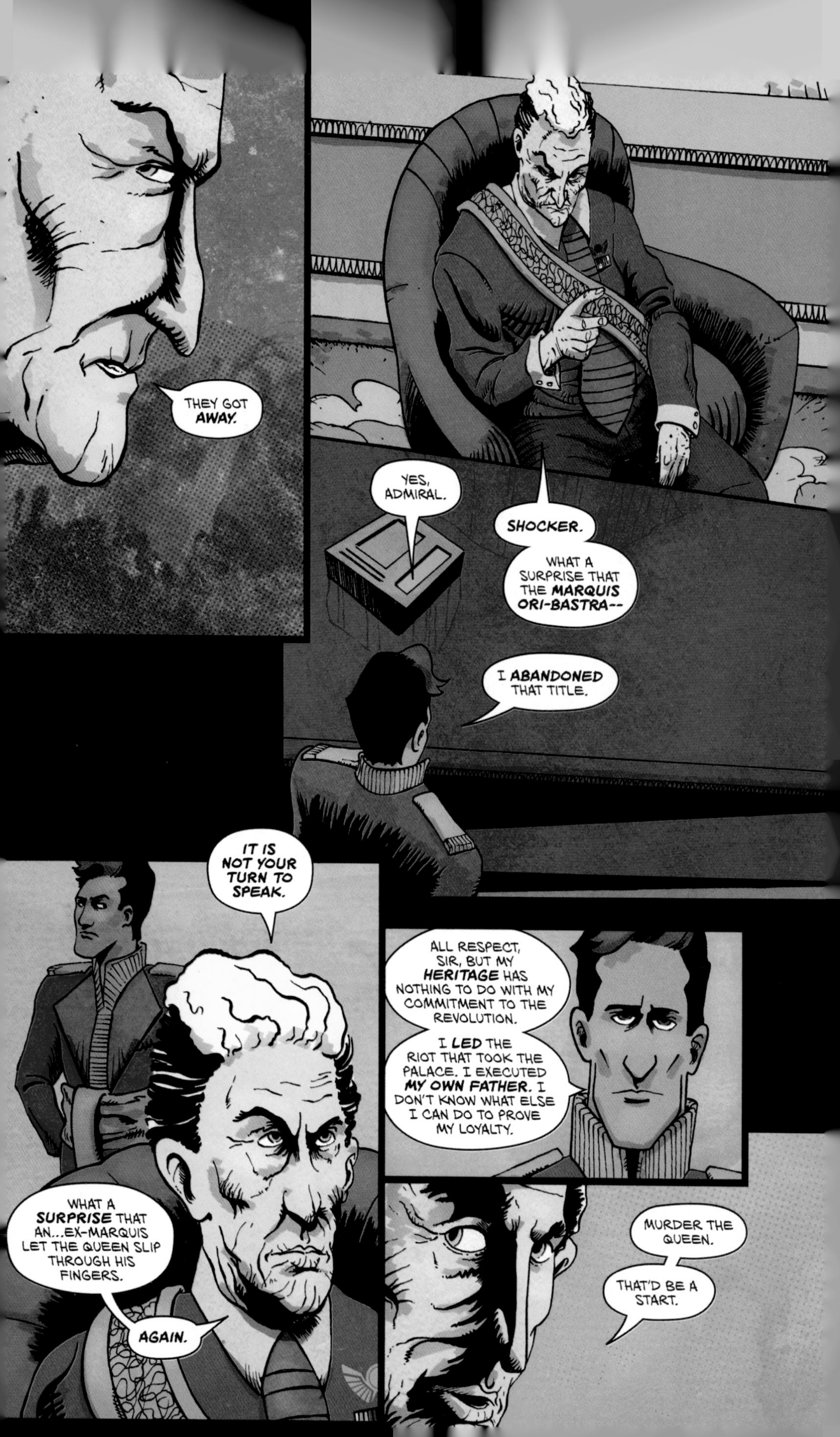
THEY GOT AWAY.
YES, ADMIRAL.
SHOCKER.
WHAT A SURPRISE THAT THE MARQUIS ORI-BASTRA--
I ABANDONED THAT TITLE.
IT IS NOT YOUR TURN TO SPEAK.
WHAT A SURPRISE THAT AN...EX-MARQUIS LET THE QUEEN SLIP THROUGH HIS FINGERS.
AGAIN.
ALL RESPECT, SIR, BUT MY HERITAGE HAS NOTHING TO DO WITH MY COMMITMENT TO THE REVOLUTION.
I LED THE RIOT THAT TOOK THE PALACE. I EXECUTED MY OWN FATHER. I DON'T KNOW WHAT ELSE I CAN DO TO PROVE MY LOYALTY.
MURDER THE QUEEN.
THAT'D BE A START.

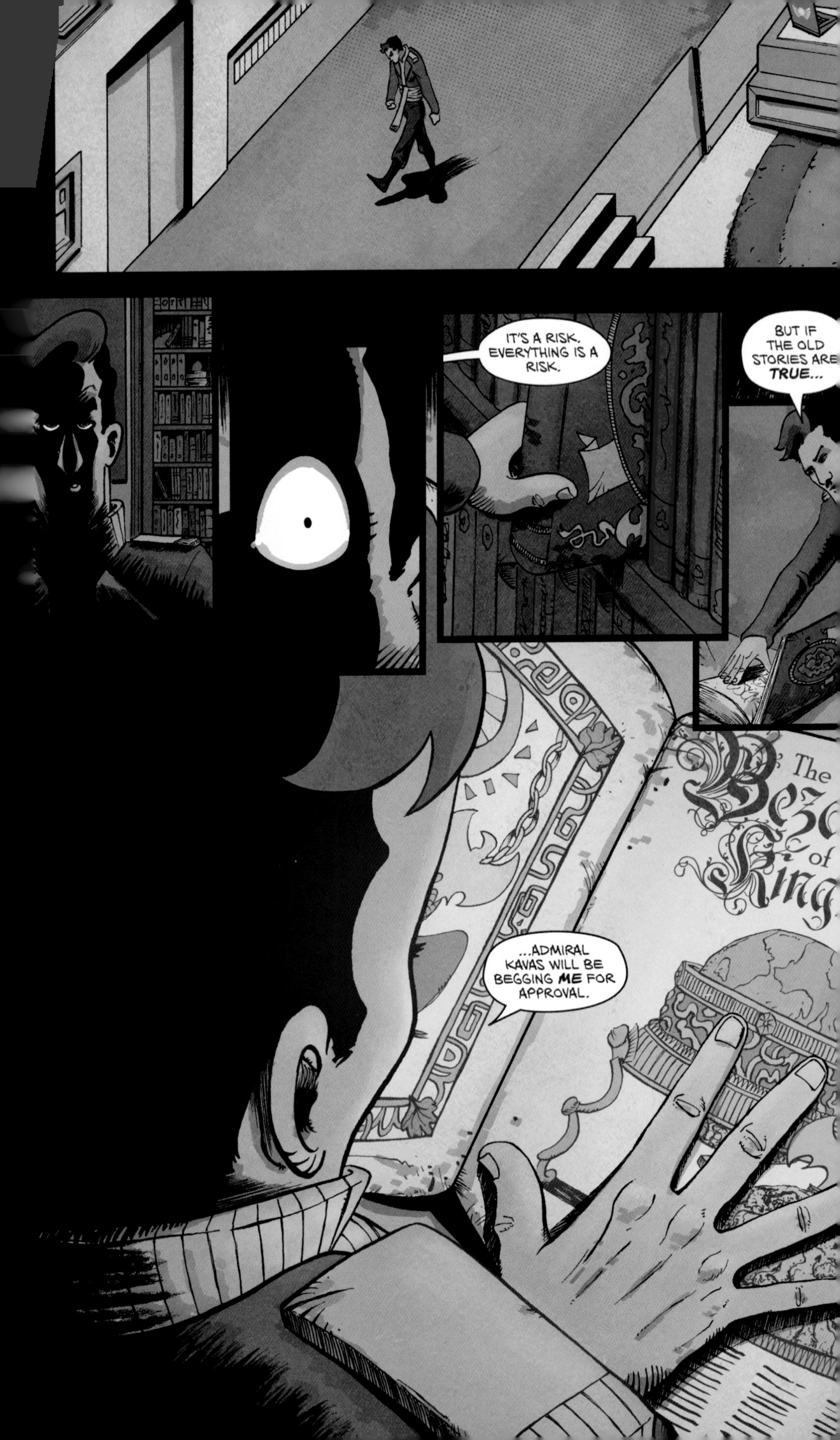
IT'S A RISK. EVERYTHING IS A RISK.
BUT IF THE OLD STORIES ARE TRUE...
...ADMIRAL KAVAS WILL BE BEGGING ME FOR APPROVAL.

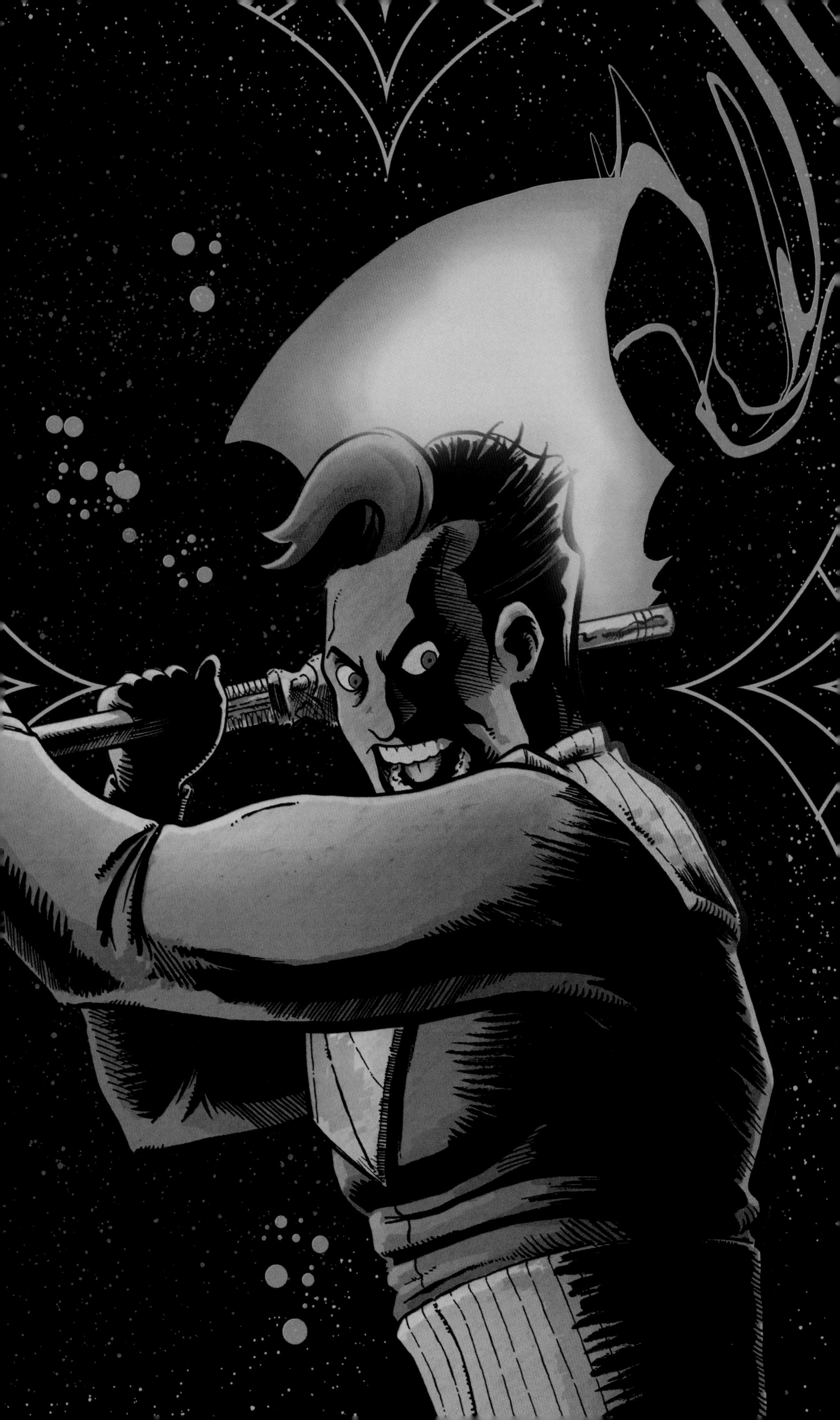

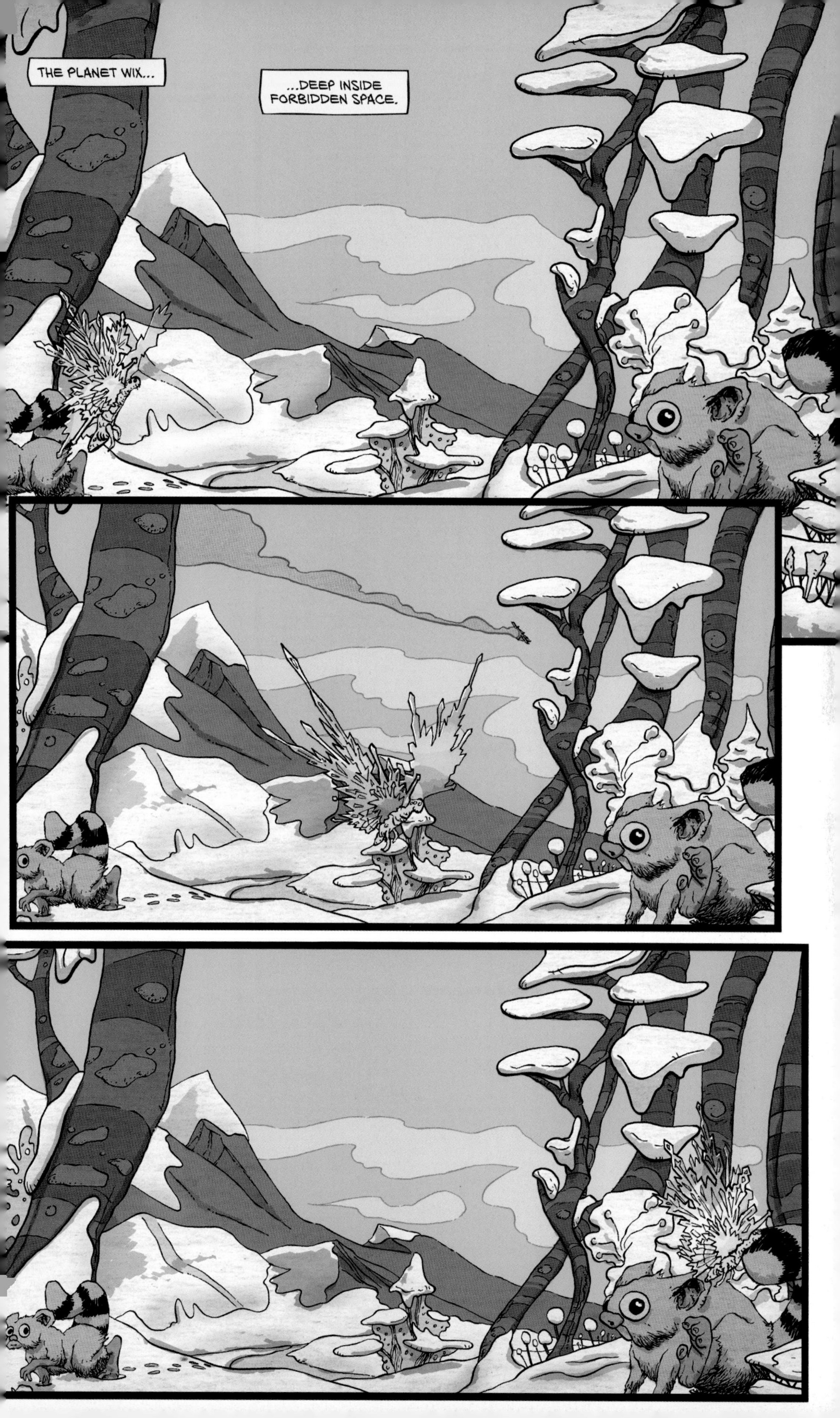
THE PLANET WIX...
...DEEP INSIDE FORBIDDEN SPACE.

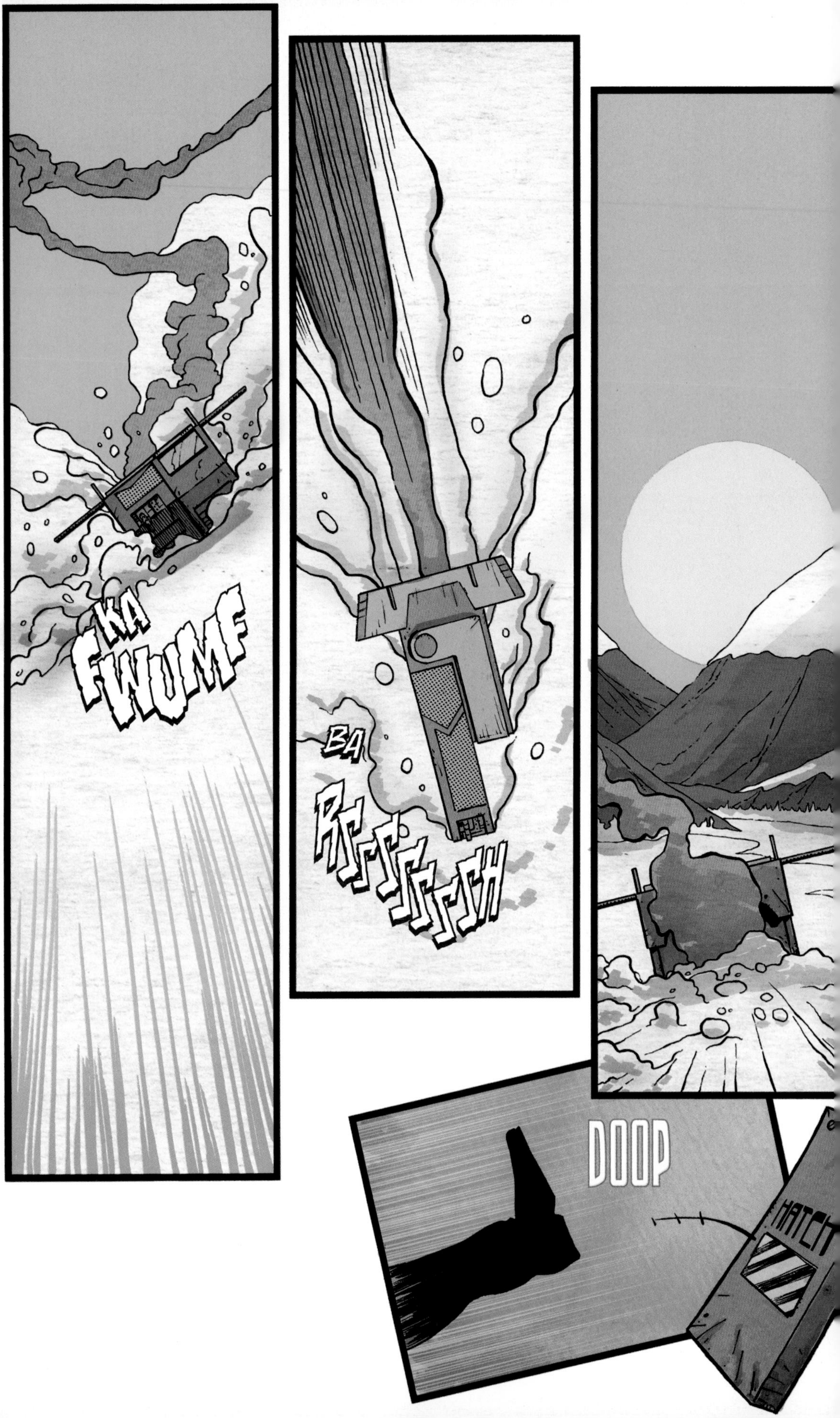
KA
FWUMF
BA
RSSSSSSSH
DOOP
HATCH

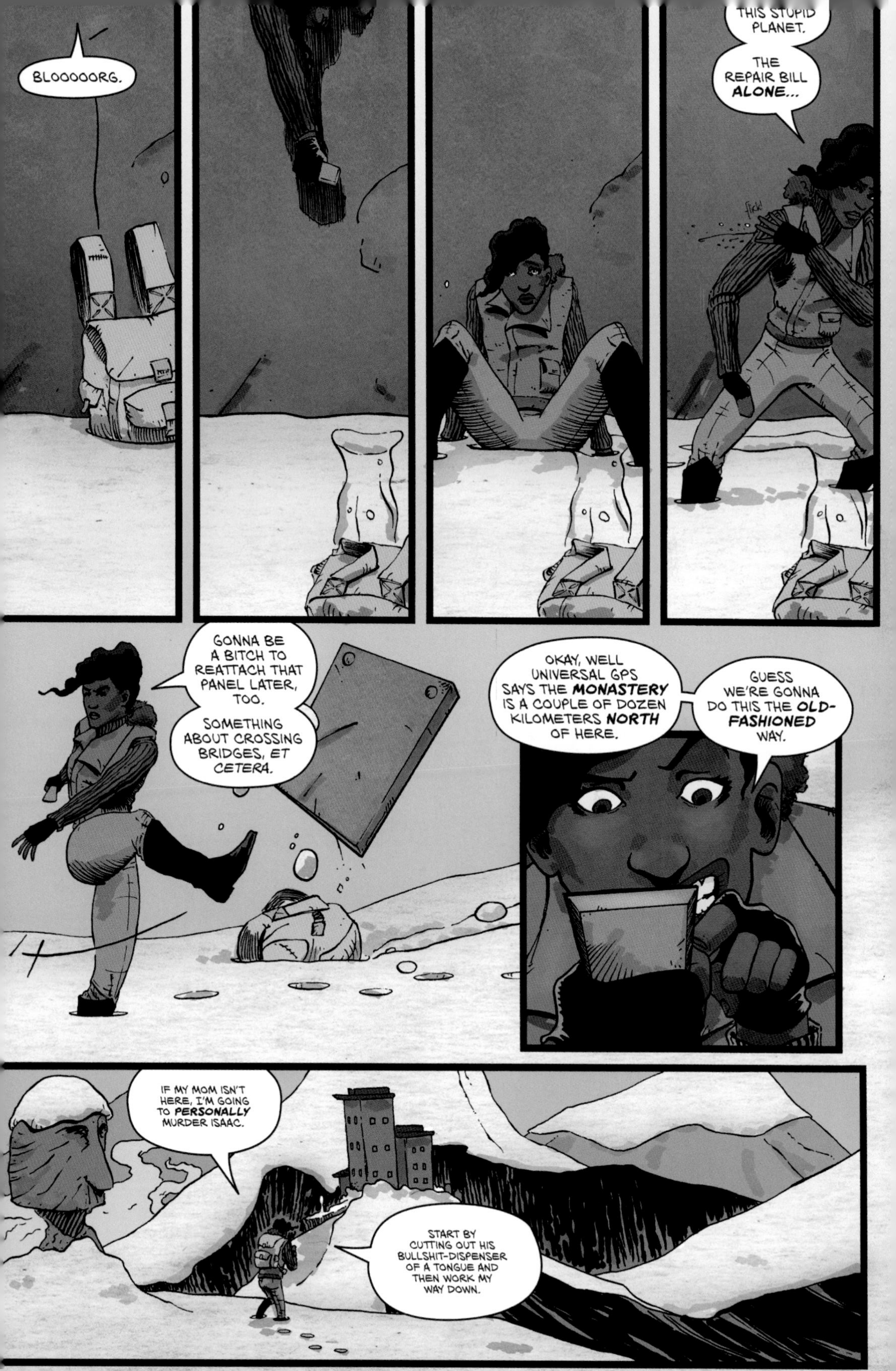
BLOOOOORG.
THIS STUPID PLANET.
THE REPAIR BILL ALONE...
flick!
GONNA BE A BITCH TO REATTACH THAT PANEL LATER, TOO.
SOMETHING ABOUT CROSSING BRIDGES, ET CETERA.
OKAY, WELL UNIVERSAL GPS SAYS THE MONASTERY IS A COUPLE OF DOZEN KILOMETERS NORTH OF HERE.
GUESS WE'RE GONNA DO THIS THE OLD-FASHIONED WAY.
IF MY MOM ISN'T HERE, I'M GOING TO PERSONALLY MURDER ISAAC.
START BY CUTTING OUT HIS BULLSHIT-DISPENSER OF A TONGUE AND THEN WORK MY WAY DOWN.

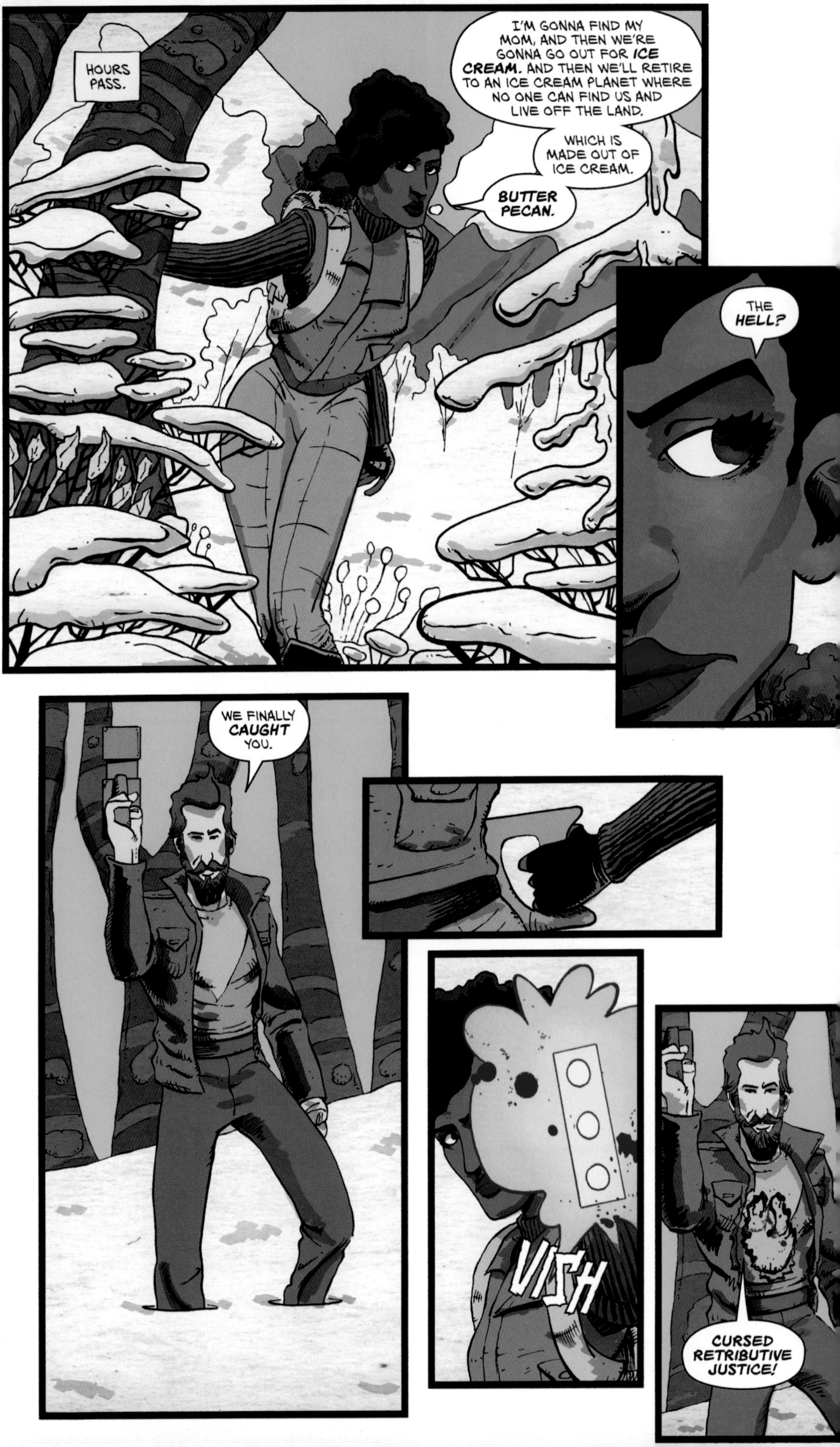
HOURS PASS.
I'M GONNA FIND MY MOM, AND THEN WE'RE GONNA GO OUT FOR ICE CREAM. AND THEN WE'LL RETIRE TO AN ICE CREAM PLANET WHERE NO ONE CAN FIND US AND LIVE OFF THE LAND.
WHICH IS MADE OUT OF ICE CREAM.
BUTTER PECAN.
THE HELL?
WE FINALLY CAUGHT YOU.
VISH
CURSED RETRIBUTIVE JUSTICE!

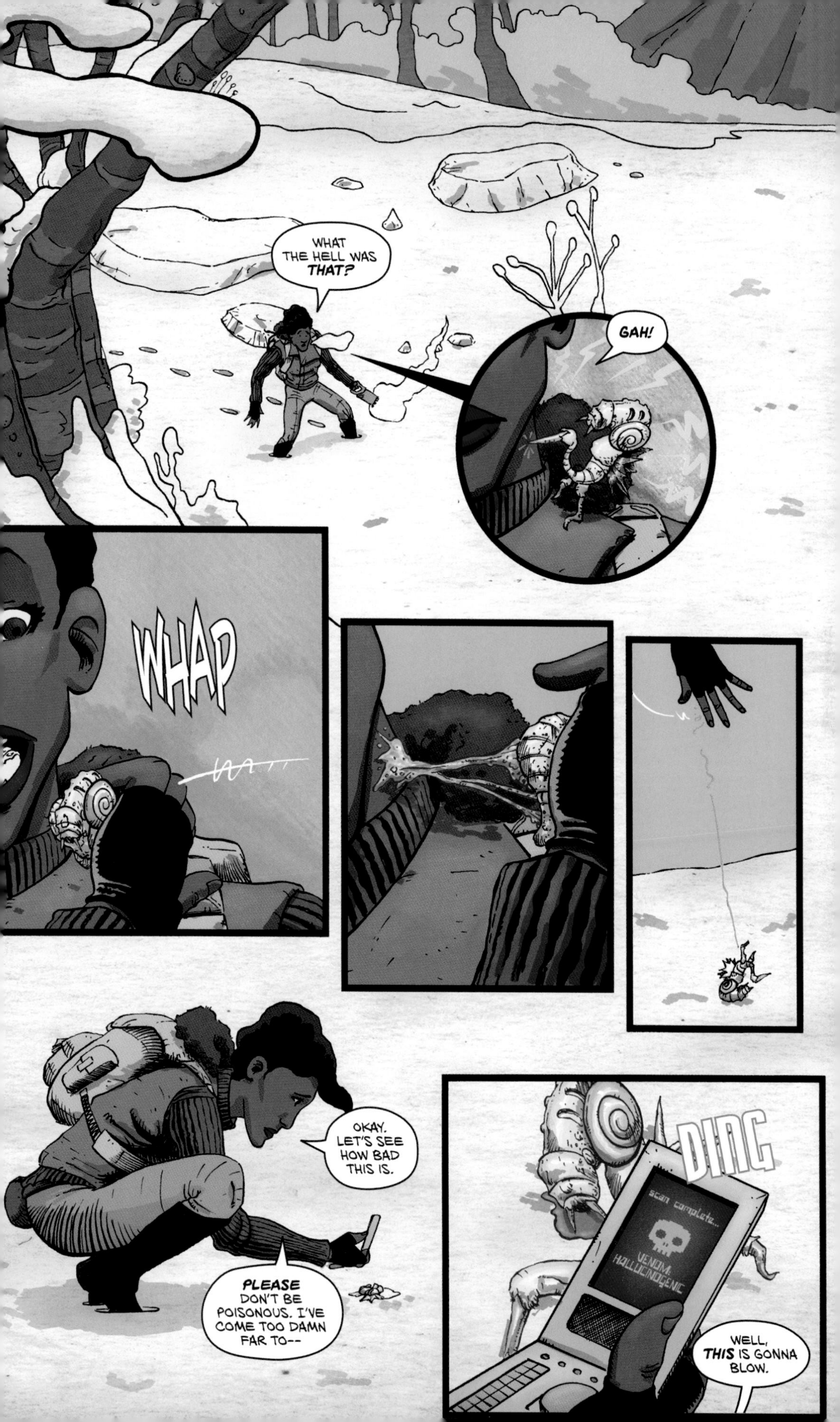
WHAT THE HELL WAS *THAT?*
GAH!
WHAP
OKAY. LET'S SEE HOW BAD THIS IS.
PLEASE DON'T BE POISONOUS. I'VE COME TOO DAMN FAR TO--
DING
scan complete...
VENOM: HALLUCINOGENIC
WELL, *THIS* IS GONNA BLOW.

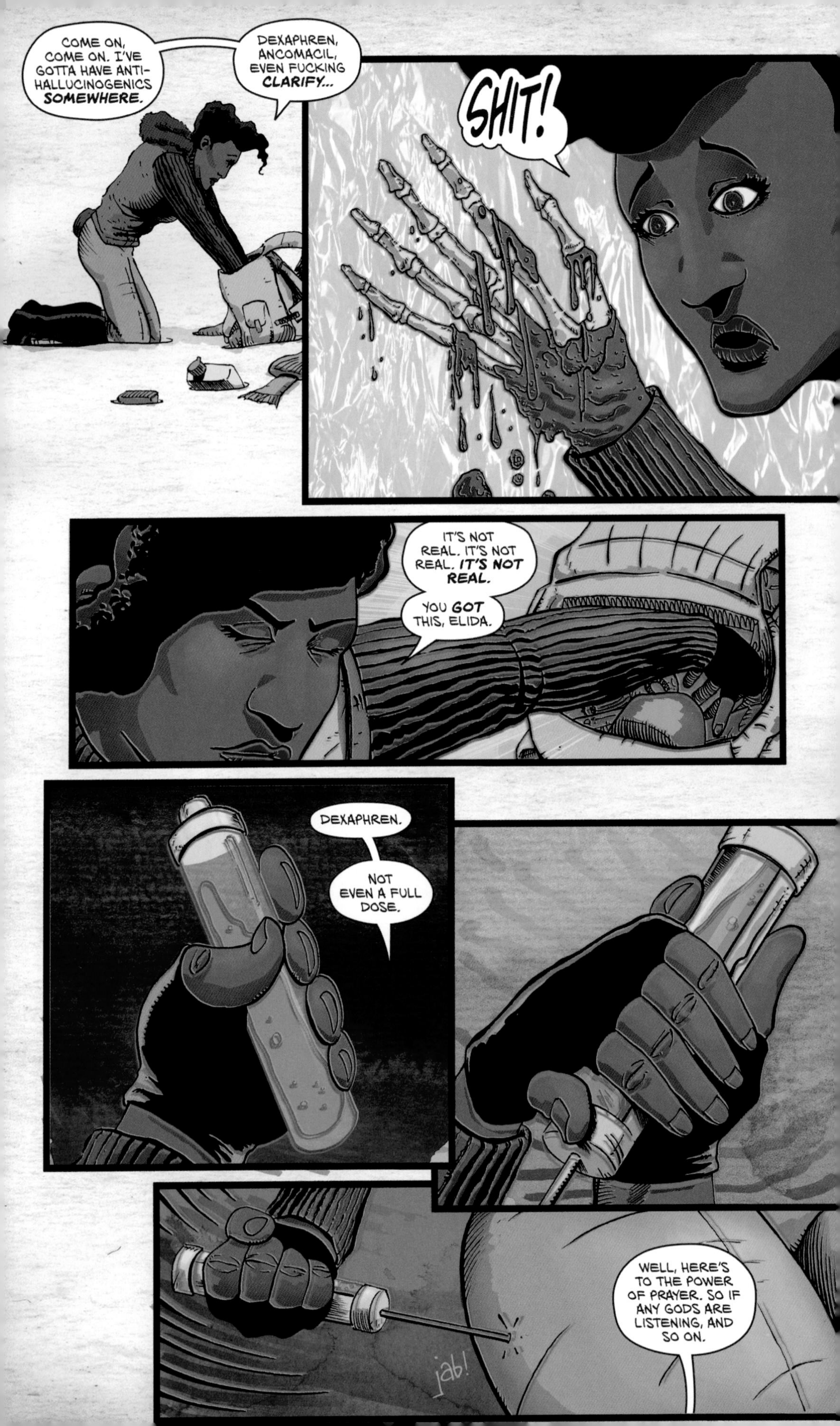
COME ON, COME ON. I'VE GOTTA HAVE ANTI-HALLUCINOGENICS SOMEWHERE.
DEXAPHREN, ANCOMACIL, EVEN FUCKING CLARIFY...
SHIT!
IT'S NOT REAL. IT'S NOT REAL. IT'S NOT REAL.
YOU GOT THIS, ELIDA.
DEXAPHREN.
NOT EVEN A FULL DOSE.
jab!
WELL, HERE'S TO THE POWER OF PRAYER. SO IF ANY GODS ARE LISTENING, AND SO ON.

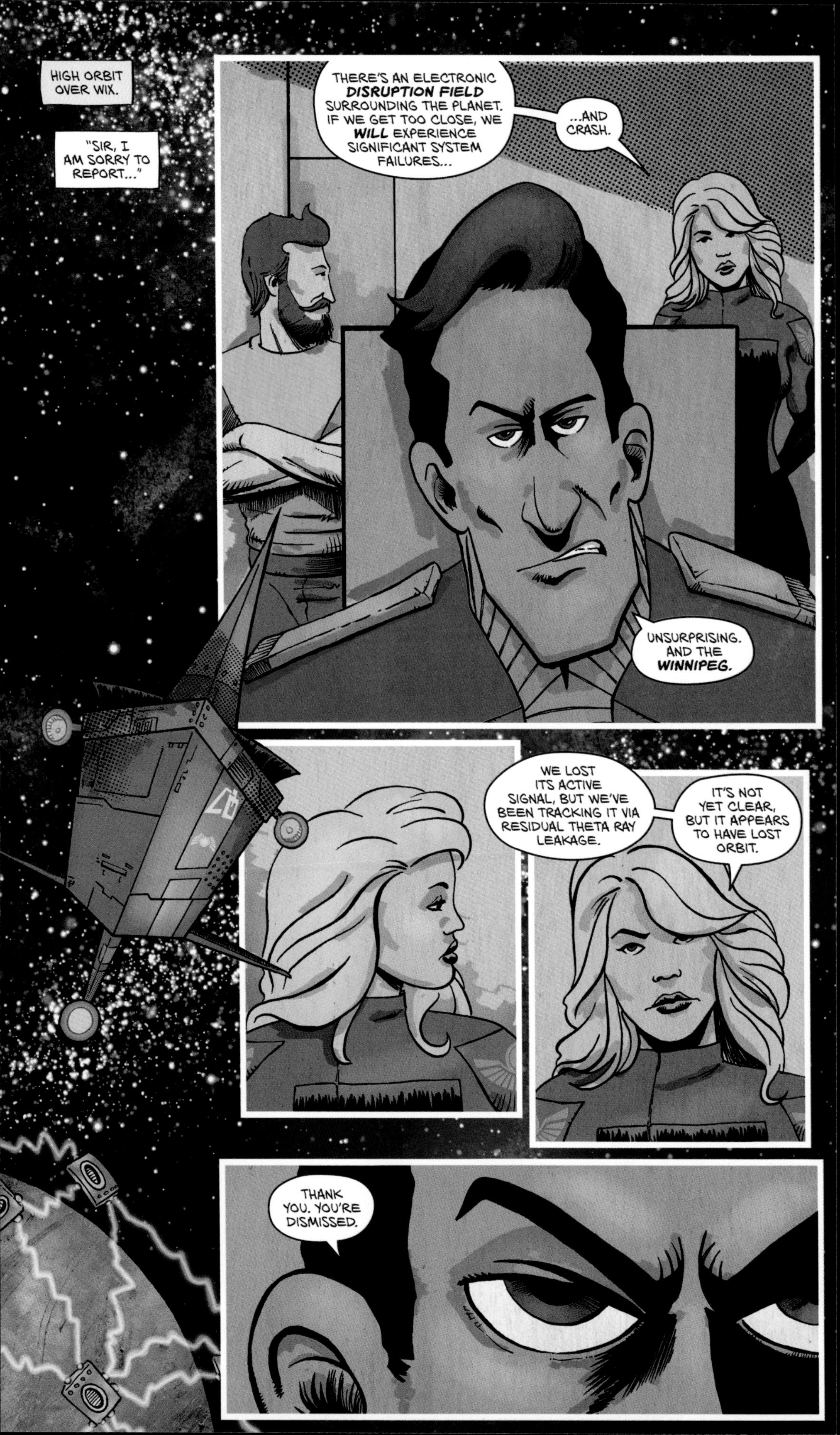

HIGH ORBIT OVER WIX.
"SIR, I AM SORRY TO REPORT..."
THERE'S AN ELECTRONIC **DISRUPTION FIELD** SURROUNDING THE PLANET. IF WE GET TOO CLOSE, WE **WILL** EXPERIENCE SIGNIFICANT SYSTEM FAILURES...
...AND CRASH.
UNSURPRISING. AND THE ***WINNIPEG.***
WE LOST ITS ACTIVE SIGNAL, BUT WE'VE BEEN TRACKING IT VIA RESIDUAL THETA RAY LEAKAGE.
IT'S NOT YET CLEAR, BUT IT APPEARS TO HAVE LOST ORBIT.
THANK YOU. YOU'RE DISMISSED.

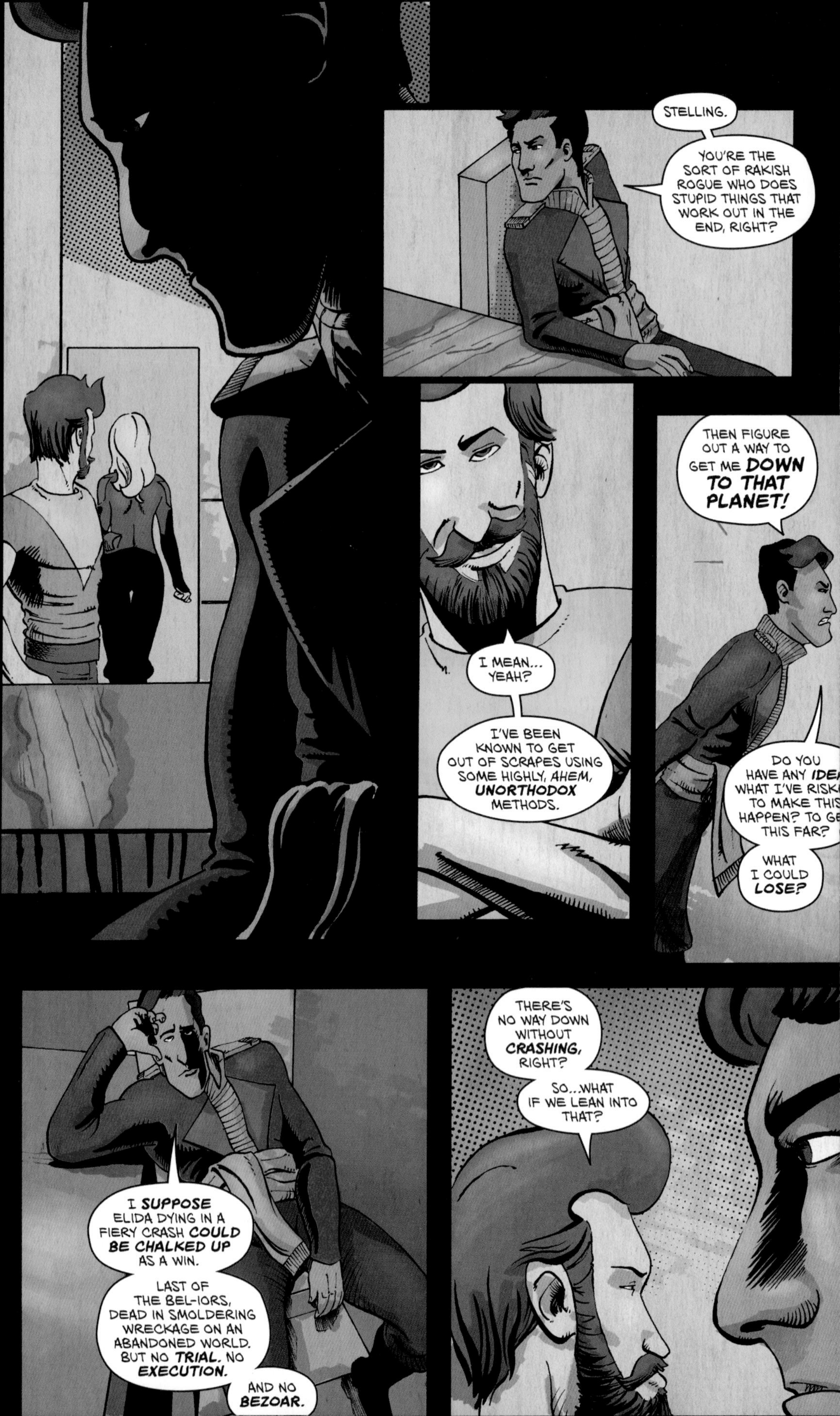
STELLING.
YOU'RE THE SORT OF RAKISH ROGUE WHO DOES STUPID THINGS THAT WORK OUT IN THE END, RIGHT?
I MEAN... YEAH?
I'VE BEEN KNOWN TO GET OUT OF SCRAPES USING SOME HIGHLY, *AHEM,* **UNORTHODOX** METHODS.
THEN FIGURE OUT A WAY TO GET ME **DOWN TO THAT PLANET!**
DO YOU HAVE ANY IDEA WHAT I'VE RISKED TO MAKE THIS HAPPEN? TO GET THIS FAR?
WHAT I COULD **LOSE?**
I **SUPPOSE** ELIDA DYING IN A FIERY CRASH **COULD BE CHALKED UP** AS A WIN.
LAST OF THE BEL-IORS, DEAD IN SMOLDERING WRECKAGE ON AN ABANDONED WORLD. BUT NO **TRIAL.** NO **EXECUTION.**
AND NO **BEZOAR.**
THERE'S NO WAY DOWN WITHOUT **CRASHING,** RIGHT?
SO...WHAT IF WE LEAN INTO THAT?

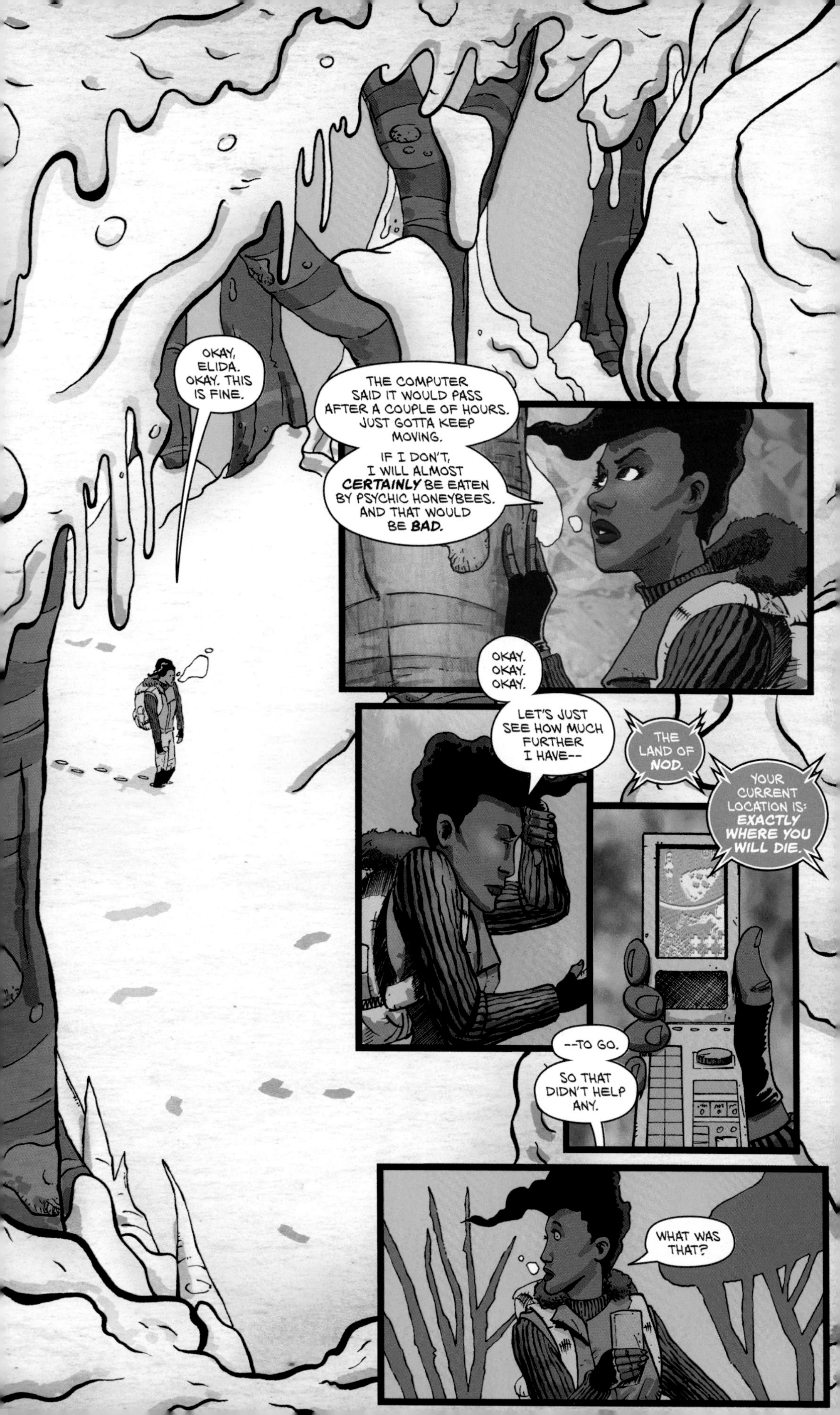
OKAY, ELIDA. OKAY. THIS IS FINE.
THE COMPUTER SAID IT WOULD PASS AFTER A COUPLE OF HOURS. JUST GOTTA KEEP MOVING.
IF I DON'T, I WILL ALMOST CERTAINLY BE EATEN BY PSYCHIC HONEYBEES. AND THAT WOULD BE BAD.
OKAY. OKAY. OKAY.
LET'S JUST SEE HOW MUCH FURTHER I HAVE--
THE LAND OF NOD.
YOUR CURRENT LOCATION IS: EXACTLY WHERE YOU WILL DIE.
--TO GO.
SO THAT DIDN'T HELP ANY.
WHAT WAS THAT?

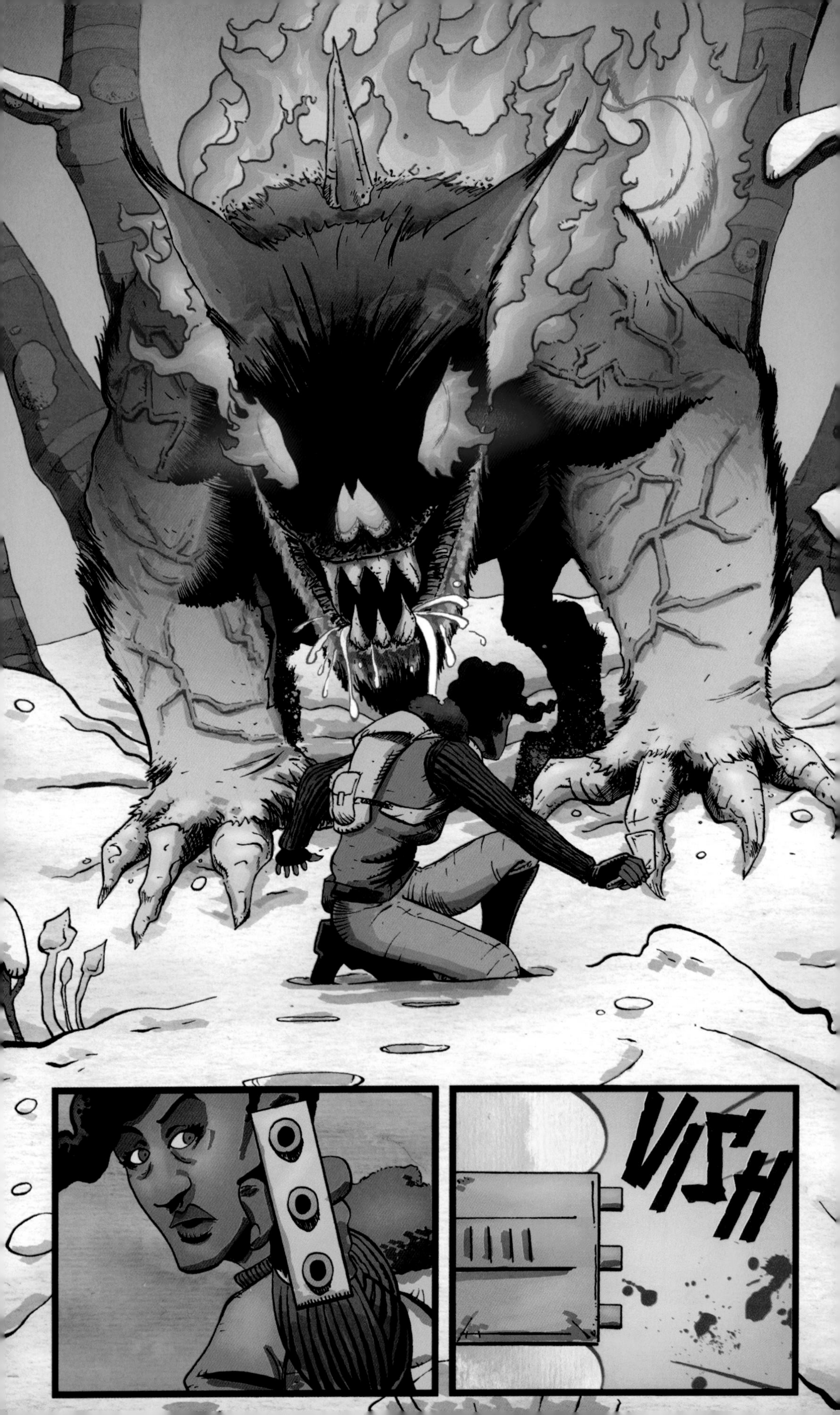
VISH

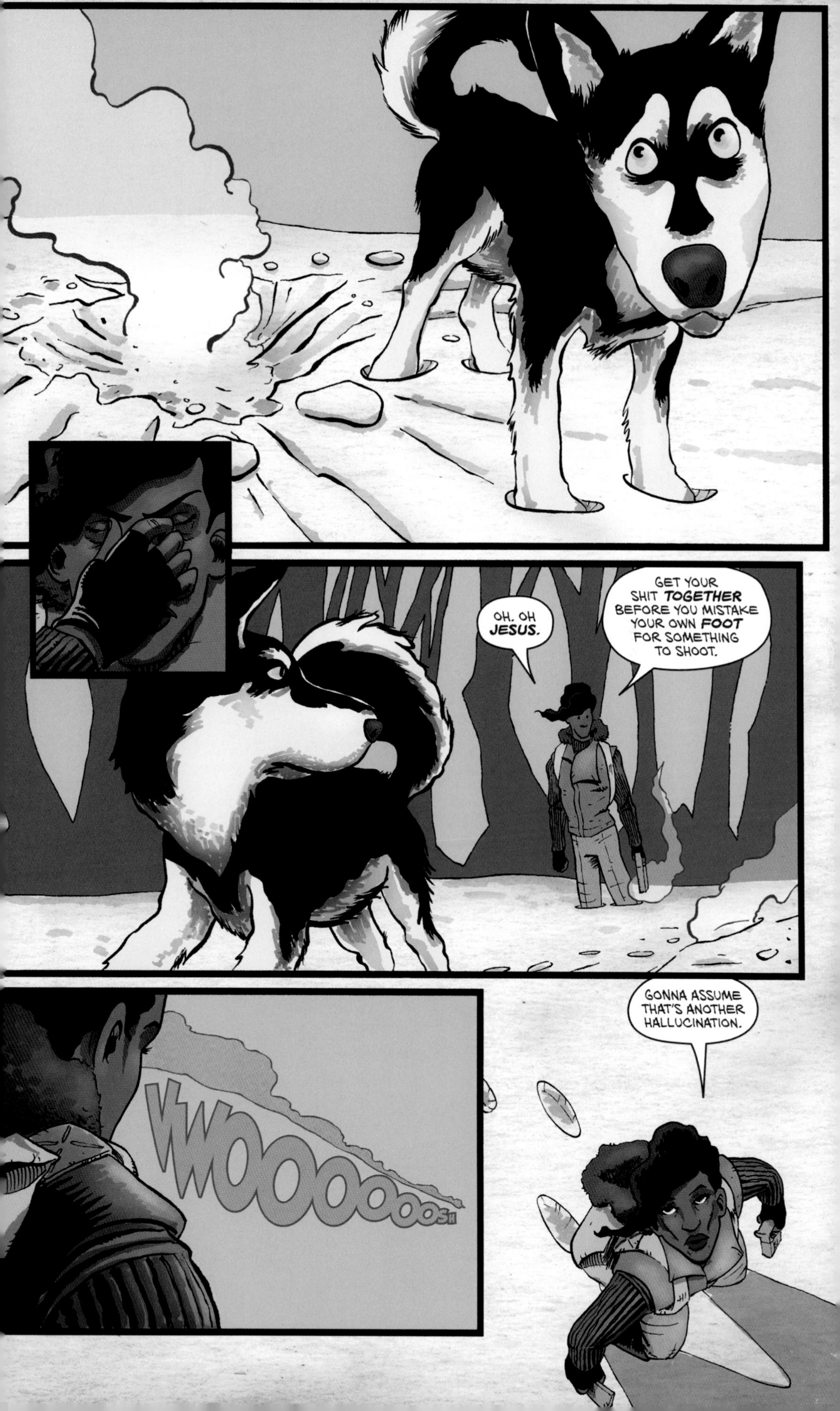
OH. OH JESUS.
GET YOUR SHIT TOGETHER BEFORE YOU MISTAKE YOUR OWN FOOT FOR SOMETHING TO SHOOT.
VWOOOOoosh
GONNA ASSUME THAT'S ANOTHER HALLUCINATION.

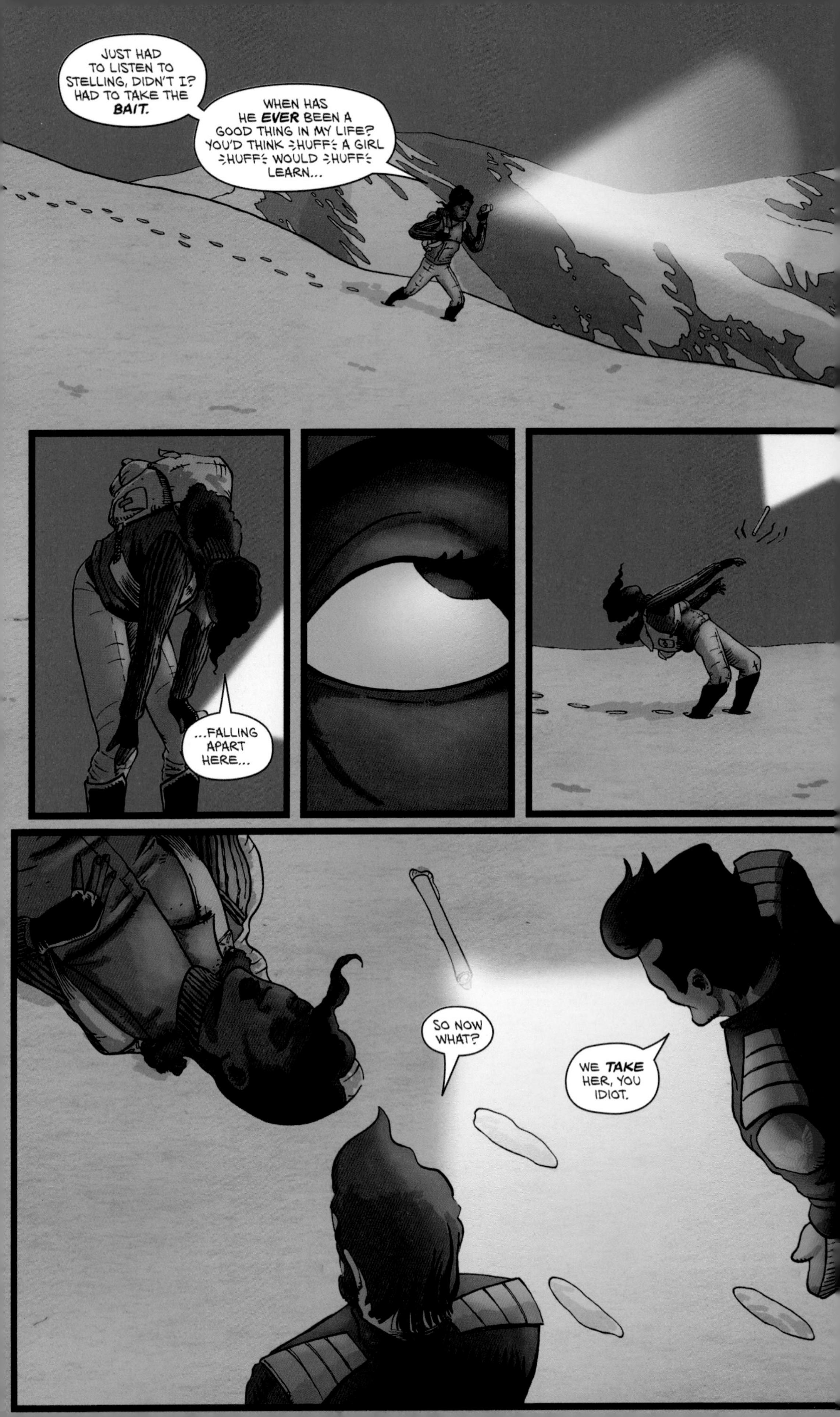
JUST HAD TO LISTEN TO STELLING, DIDN'T I? HAD TO TAKE THE **BAIT.**
WHEN HAS HE **EVER** BEEN A GOOD THING IN MY LIFE? YOU'D THINK ⪡HUFF⪢ A GIRL ⪡HUFF⪢ WOULD ⪡HUFF⪢ LEARN...
...FALLING APART HERE...
SO NOW WHAT?
WE **TAKE** HER, YOU IDIOT.

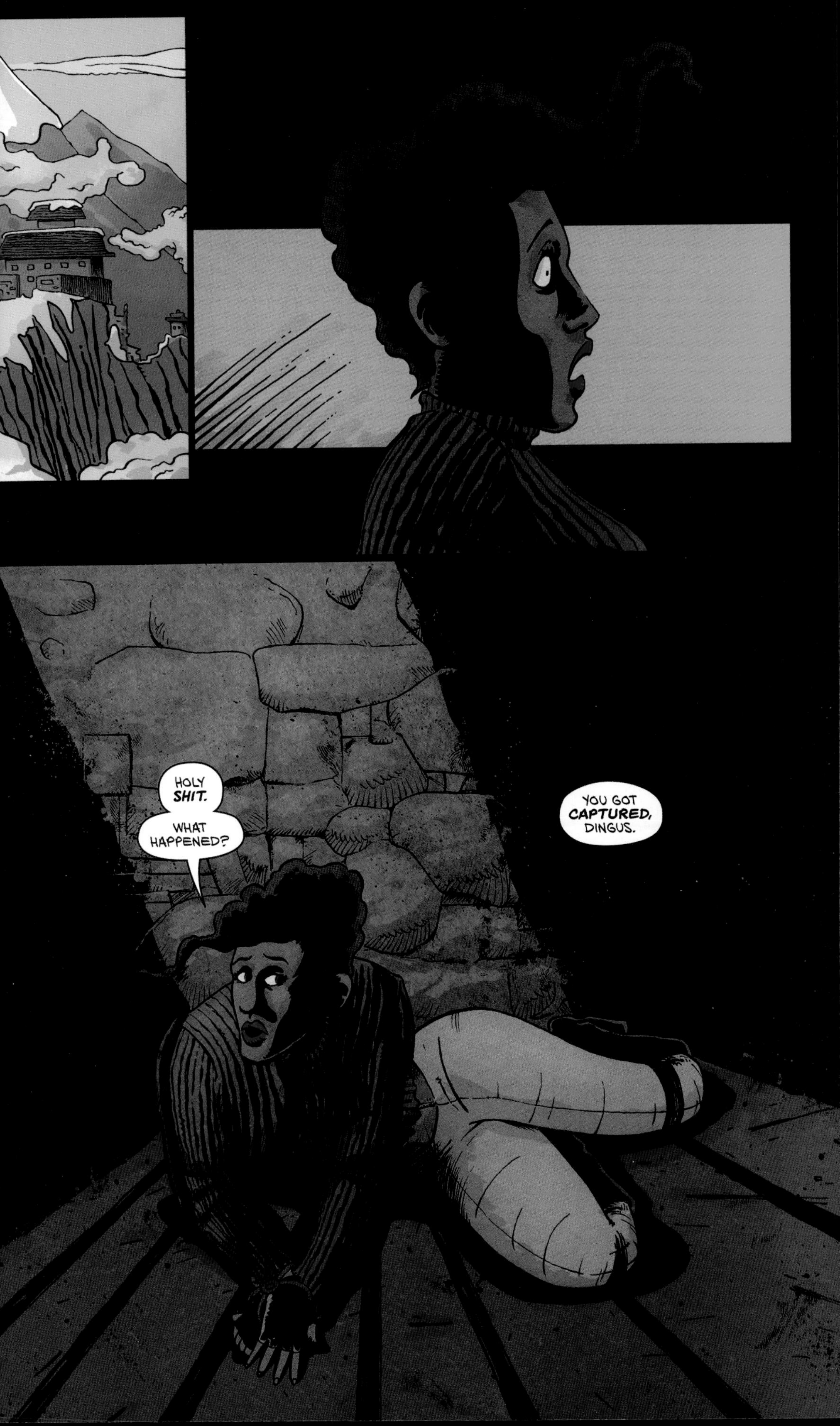
HOLY **SHIT.**
WHAT HAPPENED?
YOU GOT **CAPTURED,** DINGUS.

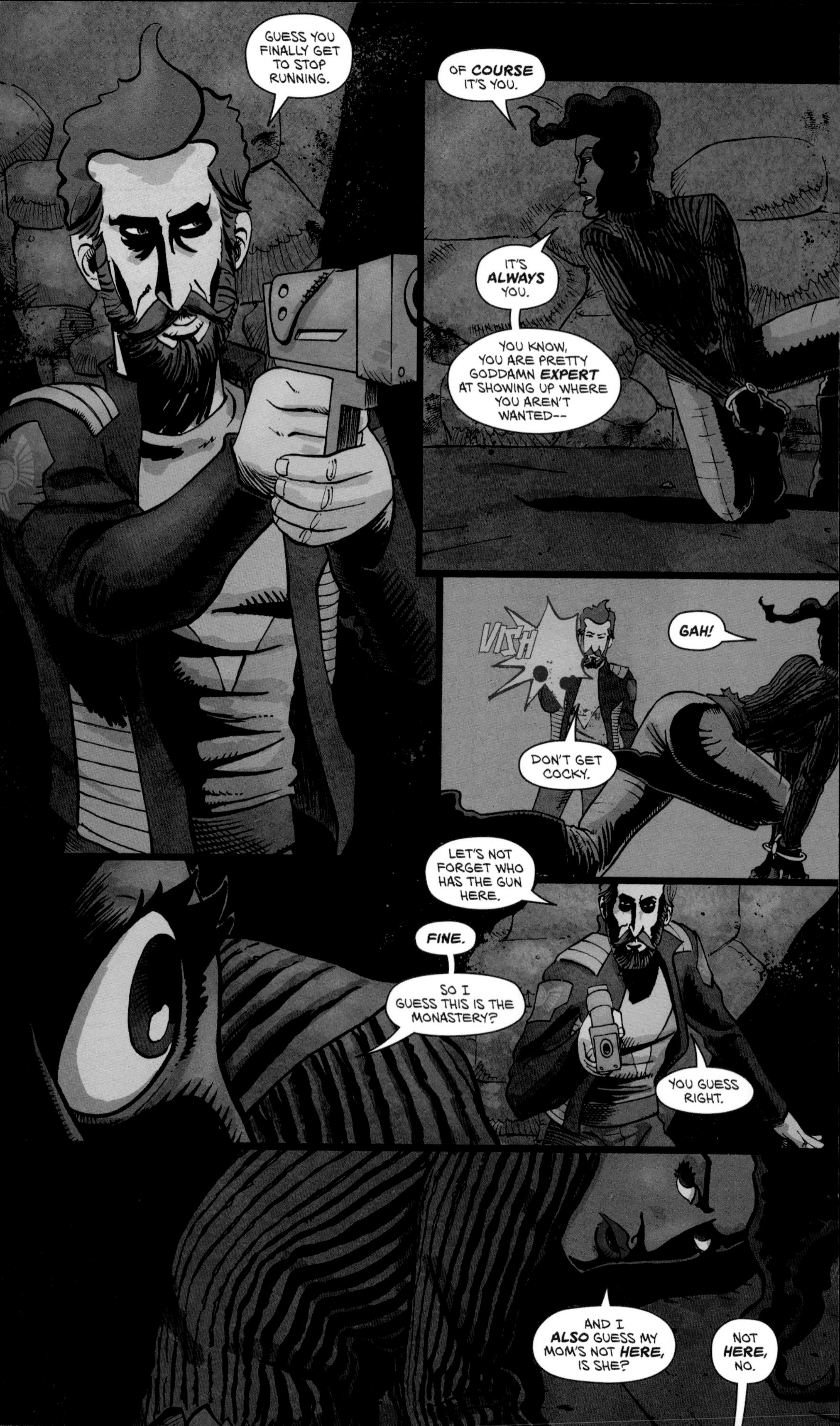
GUESS YOU FINALLY GET TO STOP RUNNING.
OF **COURSE** IT'S YOU.
IT'S **ALWAYS** YOU.
YOU KNOW, YOU ARE PRETTY GODDAMN **EXPERT** AT SHOWING UP WHERE YOU AREN'T WANTED--
VISH
GAH!
DON'T GET COCKY.
LET'S NOT FORGET WHO HAS THE GUN HERE.
FINE.
SO I GUESS THIS IS THE MONASTERY?
YOU GUESS RIGHT.
AND I **ALSO** GUESS MY MOM'S NOT **HERE,** IS SHE?
NOT **HERE,** NO.

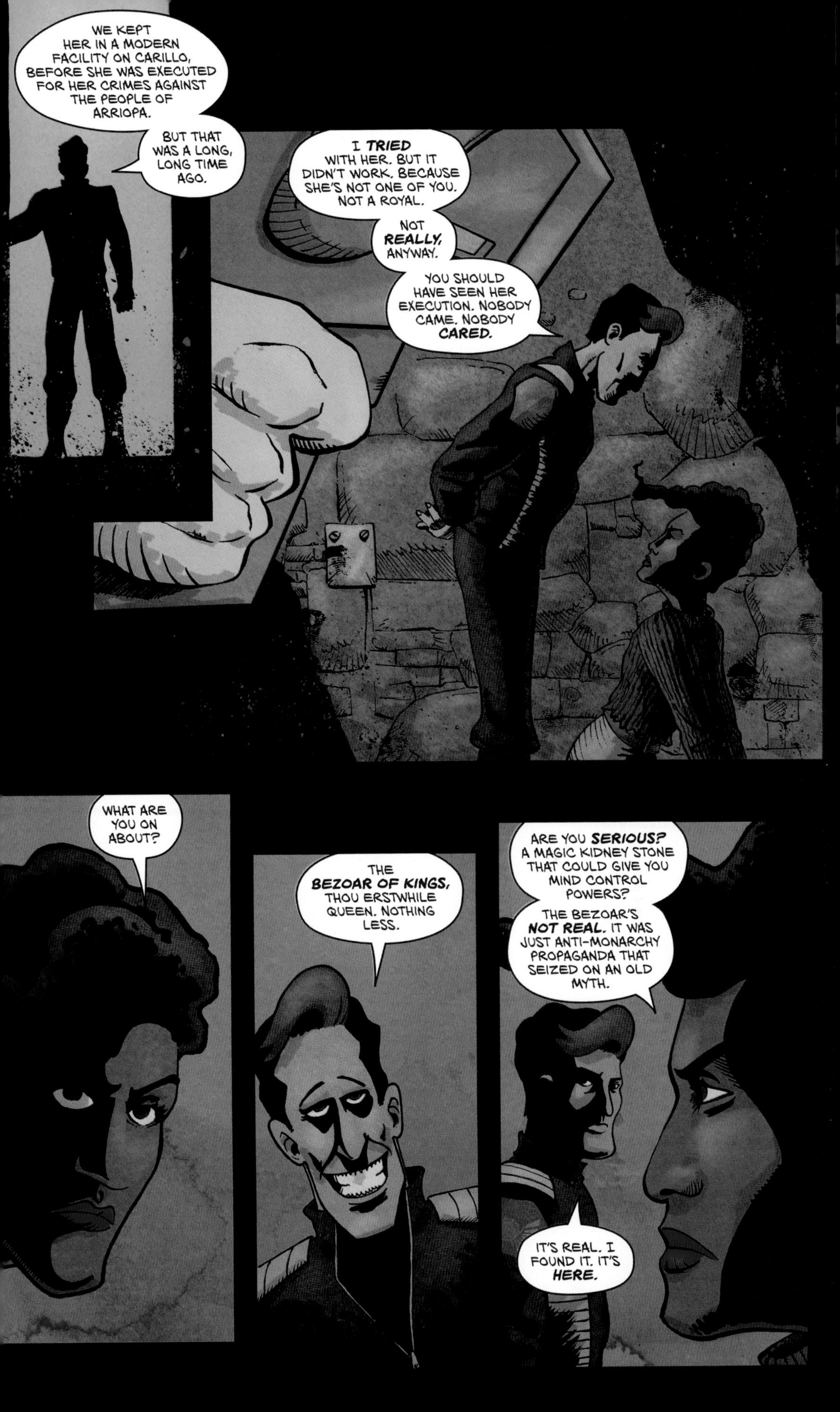
WE KEPT HER IN A MODERN FACILITY ON CARILLO, BEFORE SHE WAS EXECUTED FOR HER CRIMES AGAINST THE PEOPLE OF ARRIOPA.
BUT THAT WAS A LONG, LONG TIME AGO.
I TRIED WITH HER. BUT IT DIDN'T WORK. BECAUSE SHE'S NOT ONE OF YOU. NOT A ROYAL.
NOT REALLY, ANYWAY.
YOU SHOULD HAVE SEEN HER EXECUTION. NOBODY CAME. NOBODY CARED.
WHAT ARE YOU ON ABOUT?
THE BEZOAR OF KINGS, THOU ERSTWHILE QUEEN. NOTHING LESS.
ARE YOU SERIOUS? A MAGIC KIDNEY STONE THAT COULD GIVE YOU MIND CONTROL POWERS?
THE BEZOAR'S NOT REAL. IT WAS JUST ANTI-MONARCHY PROPAGANDA THAT SEIZED ON AN OLD MYTH.
IT'S REAL. I FOUND IT. IT'S HERE.

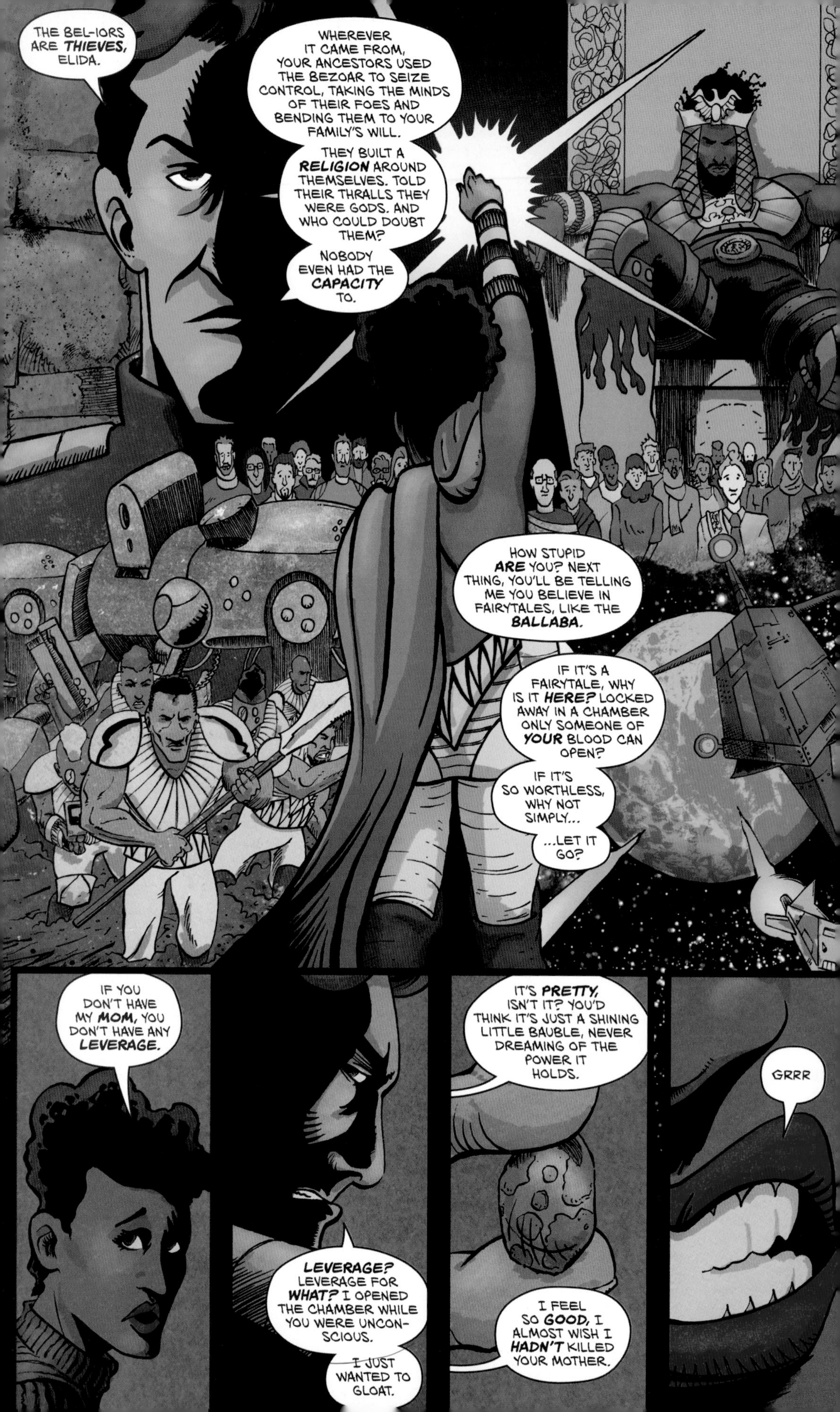
THE BEL-IORS ARE THIEVES, ELIDA.
WHEREVER IT CAME FROM, YOUR ANCESTORS USED THE BEZOAR TO SEIZE CONTROL, TAKING THE MINDS OF THEIR FOES AND BENDING THEM TO YOUR FAMILY'S WILL.
THEY BUILT A RELIGION AROUND THEMSELVES. TOLD THEIR THRALLS THEY WERE GODS. AND WHO COULD DOUBT THEM?
NOBODY EVEN HAD THE CAPACITY TO.
HOW STUPID ARE YOU? NEXT THING, YOU'LL BE TELLING ME YOU BELIEVE IN FAIRYTALES, LIKE THE BALLABA.
IF IT'S A FAIRYTALE, WHY IS IT HERE? LOCKED AWAY IN A CHAMBER ONLY SOMEONE OF YOUR BLOOD CAN OPEN?
IF IT'S SO WORTHLESS, WHY NOT SIMPLY...
...LET IT GO?
IF YOU DON'T HAVE MY MOM, YOU DON'T HAVE ANY LEVERAGE.
LEVERAGE? LEVERAGE FOR WHAT? I OPENED THE CHAMBER WHILE YOU WERE UNCON-SCIOUS.
I JUST WANTED TO GLOAT.
IT'S PRETTY, ISN'T IT? YOU'D THINK IT'S JUST A SHINING LITTLE BAUBLE, NEVER DREAMING OF THE POWER IT HOLDS.
I FEEL SO GOOD, I ALMOST WISH I HADN'T KILLED YOUR MOTHER.
GRRR

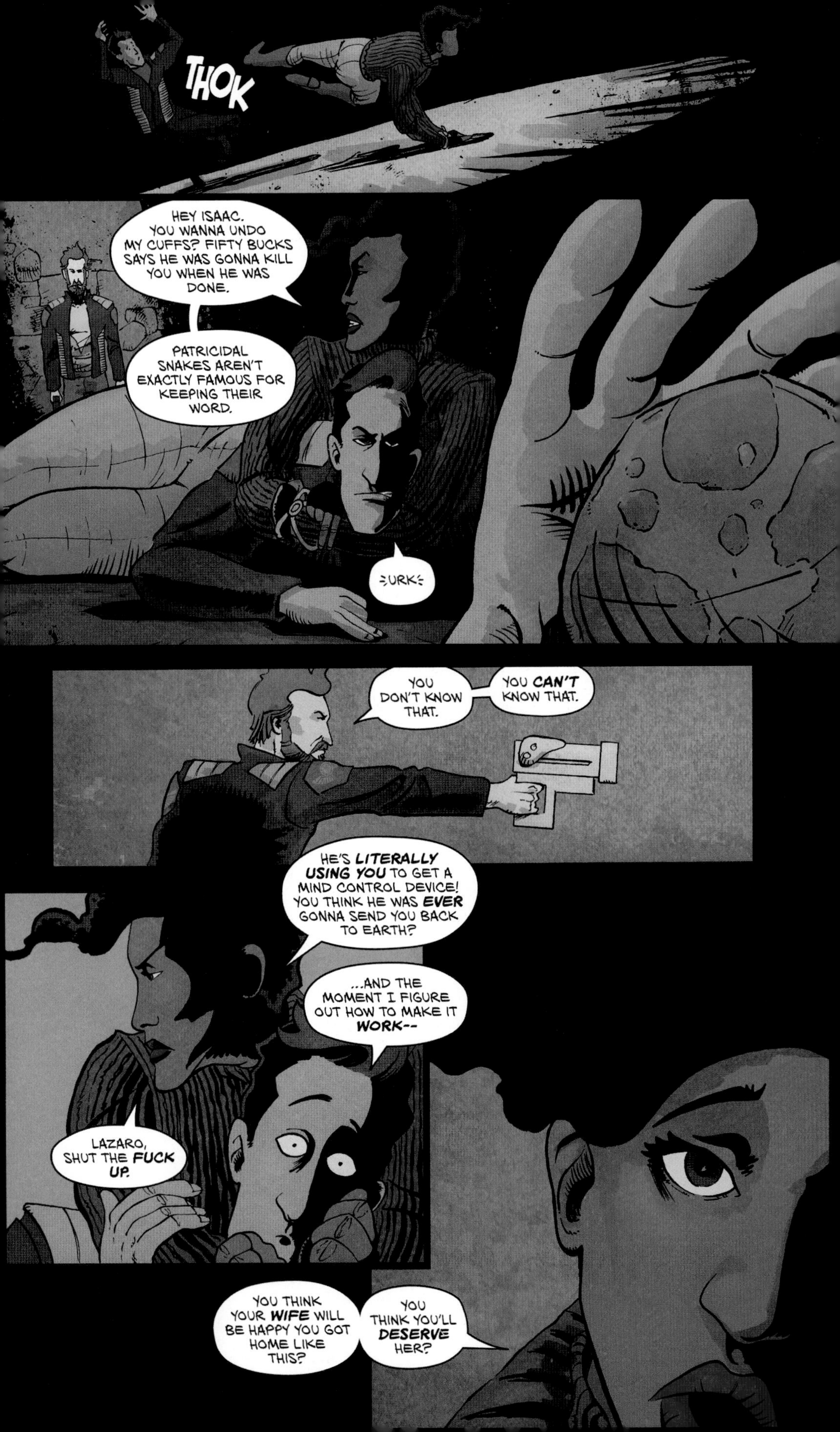
THOK
HEY ISAAC. YOU WANNA UNDO MY CUFFS? FIFTY BUCKS SAYS HE WAS GONNA KILL YOU WHEN HE WAS DONE.
PATRICIDAL SNAKES AREN'T EXACTLY FAMOUS FOR KEEPING THEIR WORD.
URK
YOU DON'T KNOW THAT.
YOU CAN'T KNOW THAT.
HE'S LITERALLY USING YOU TO GET A MIND CONTROL DEVICE! YOU THINK HE WAS EVER GONNA SEND YOU BACK TO EARTH?
...AND THE MOMENT I FIGURE OUT HOW TO MAKE IT WORK--
LAZARO, SHUT THE FUCK UP.
YOU THINK YOUR WIFE WILL BE HAPPY YOU GOT HOME LIKE THIS?
YOU THINK YOU'LL DESERVE HER?

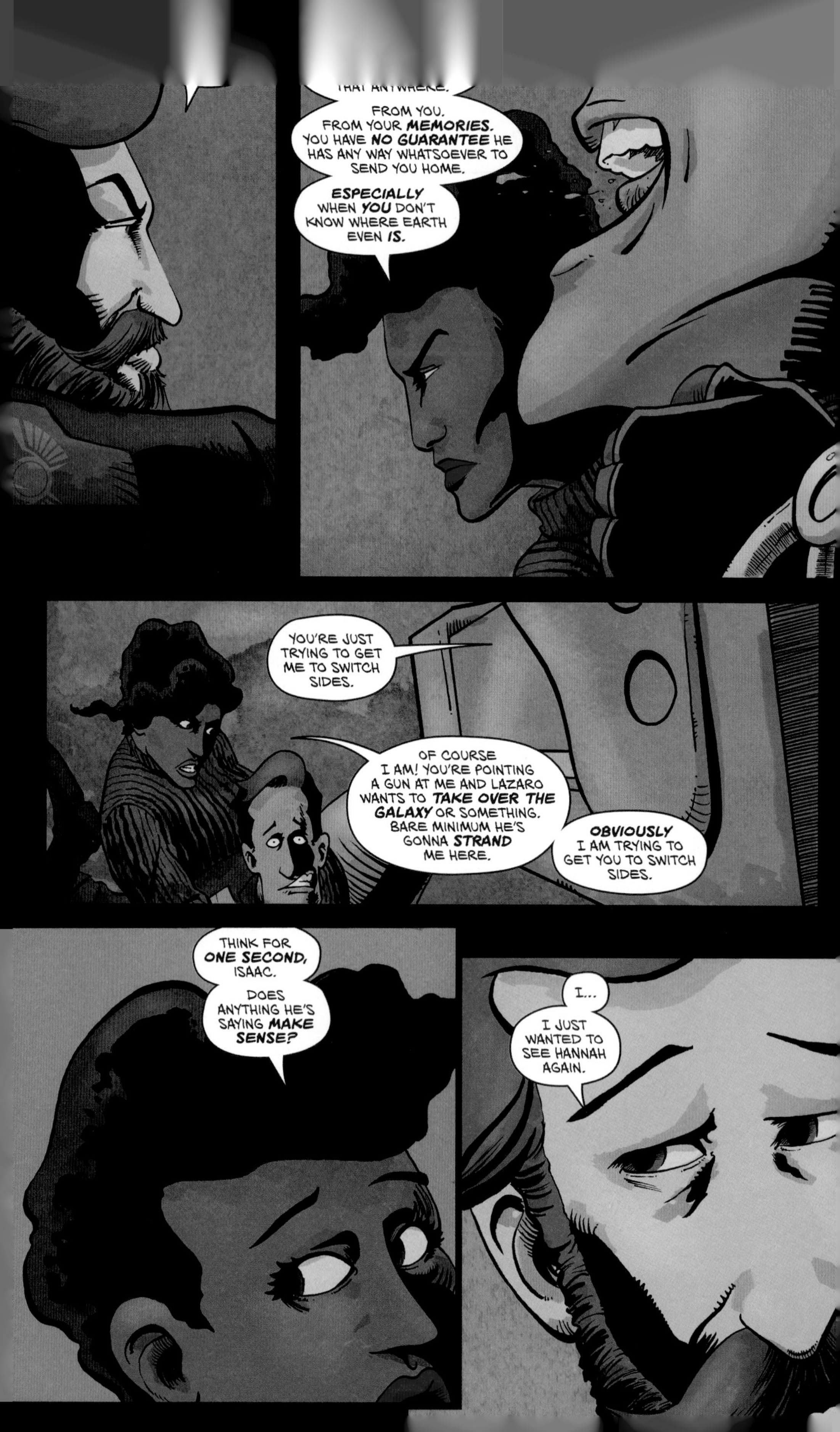

THAT ANYWHERE.
FROM YOU. FROM YOUR MEMORIES. YOU HAVE NO GUARANTEE HE HAS ANY WAY WHATSOEVER TO SEND YOU HOME.
ESPECIALLY WHEN YOU DON'T KNOW WHERE EARTH EVEN IS.
YOU'RE JUST TRYING TO GET ME TO SWITCH SIDES.
OF COURSE I AM! YOU'RE POINTING A GUN AT ME AND LAZARO WANTS TO TAKE OVER THE GALAXY OR SOMETHING. BARE MINIMUM HE'S GONNA STRAND ME HERE.
OBVIOUSLY I AM TRYING TO GET YOU TO SWITCH SIDES.
THINK FOR ONE SECOND, ISAAC.
DOES ANYTHING HE'S SAYING MAKE SENSE?
I...
I JUST WANTED TO SEE HANNAH AGAIN.

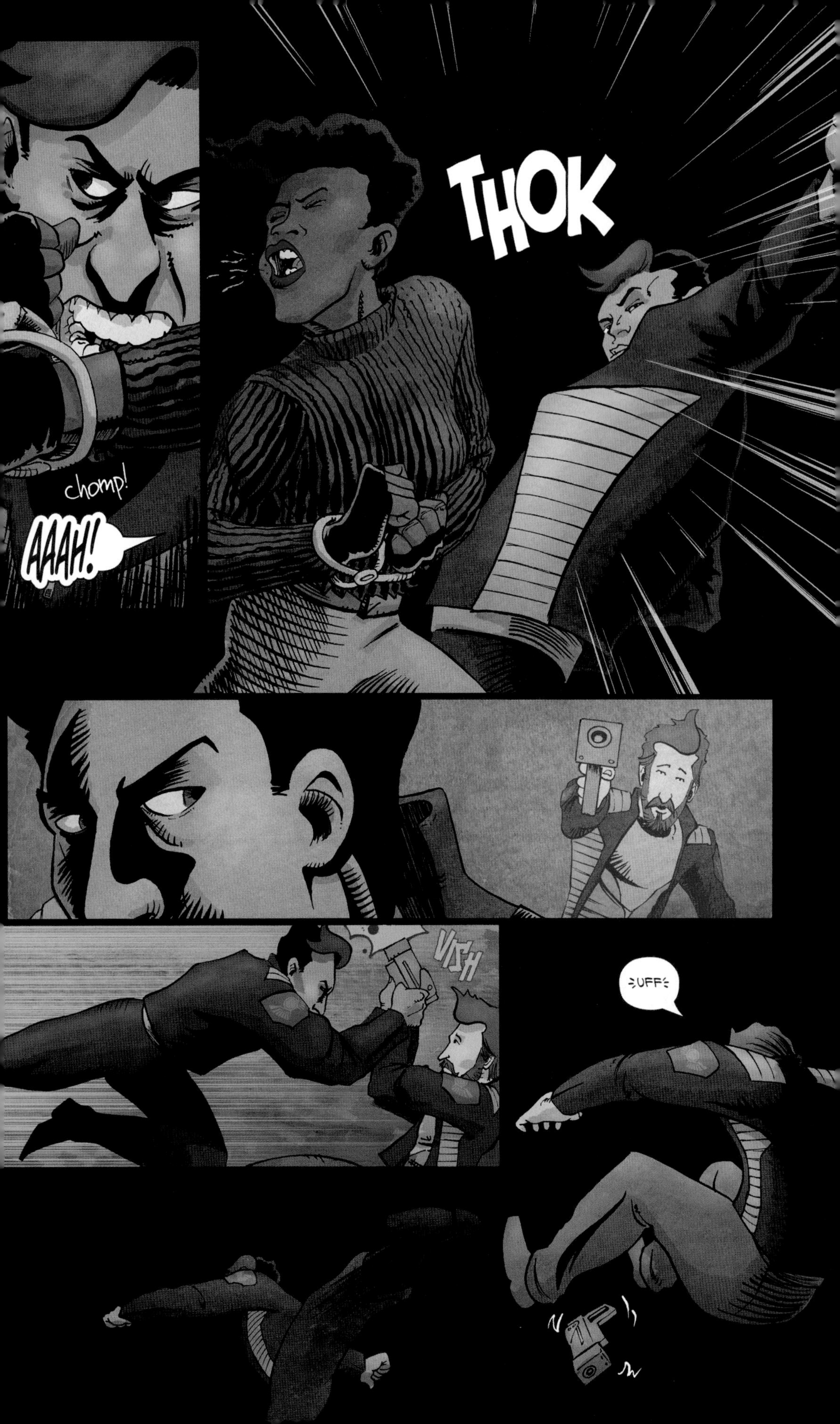
chomp!
AAAH!
THOK
VISH
UFF

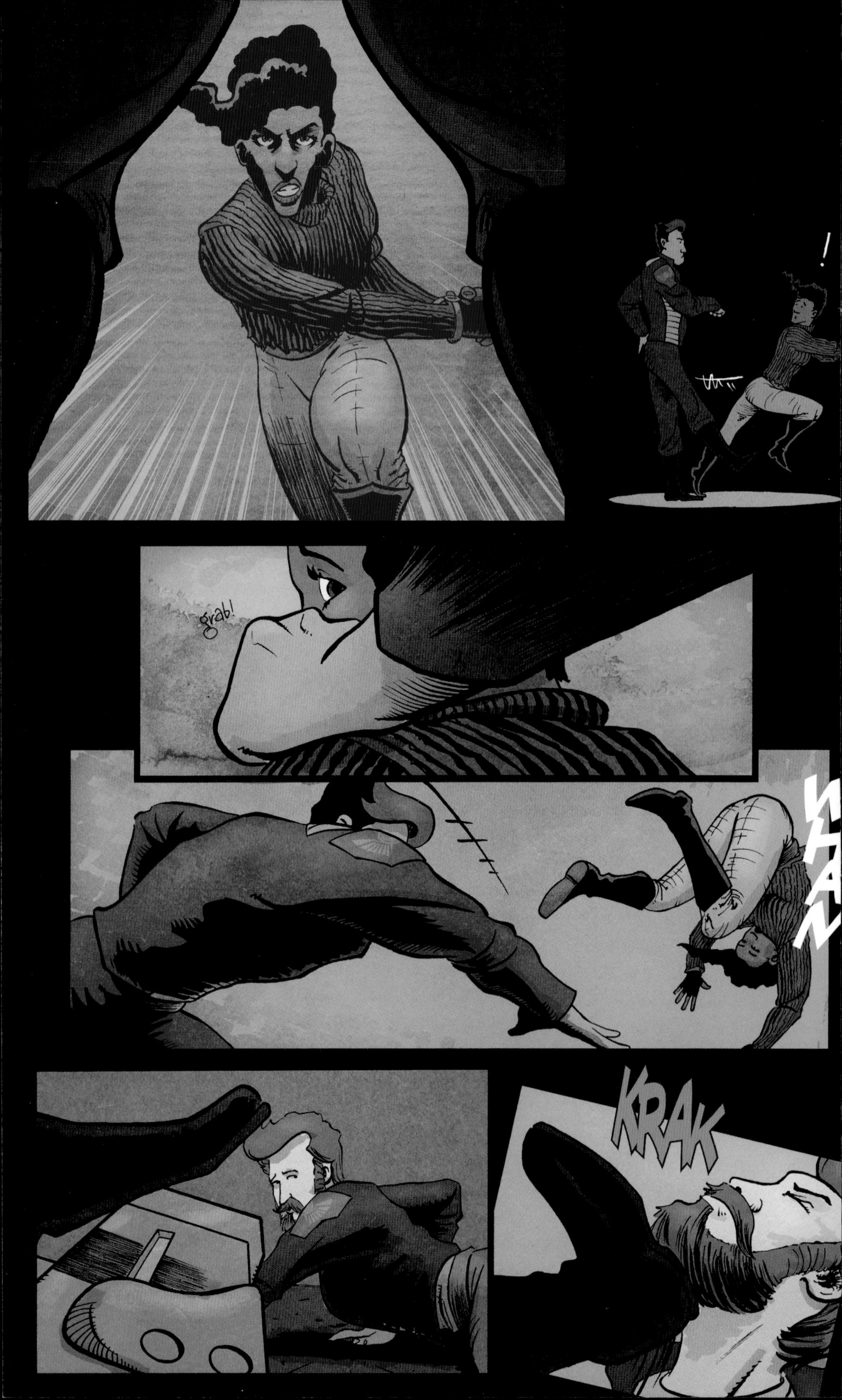
!
grab!
WHAM
KRAK

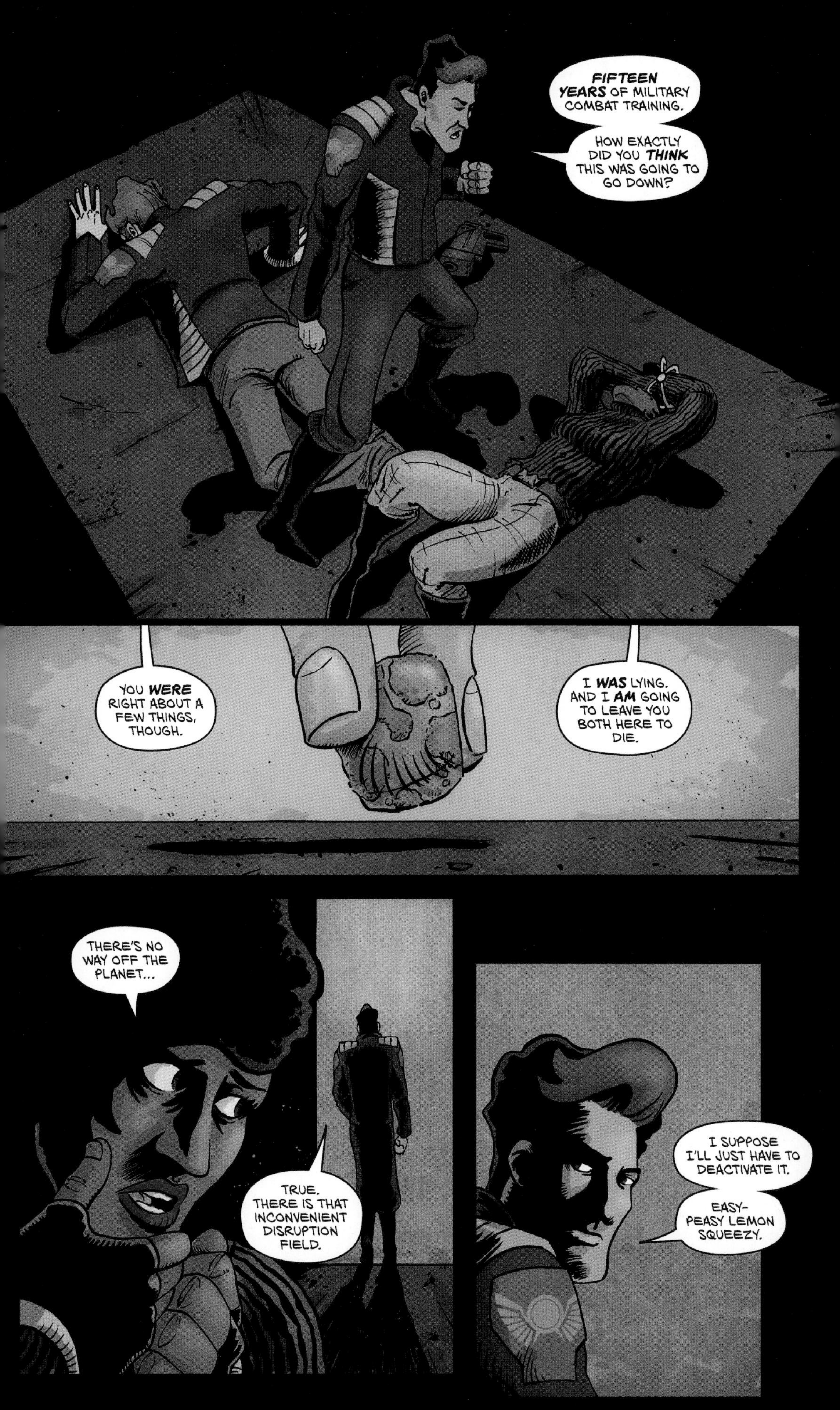
FIFTEEN YEARS OF MILITARY COMBAT TRAINING.
HOW EXACTLY DID YOU THINK THIS WAS GOING TO GO DOWN?
YOU WERE RIGHT ABOUT A FEW THINGS, THOUGH.
I WAS LYING. AND I AM GOING TO LEAVE YOU BOTH HERE TO DIE.
THERE'S NO WAY OFF THE PLANET...
TRUE. THERE IS THAT INCONVENIENT DISRUPTION FIELD.
I SUPPOSE I'LL JUST HAVE TO DEACTIVATE IT.
EASY-PEASY LEMON SQUEEZY.

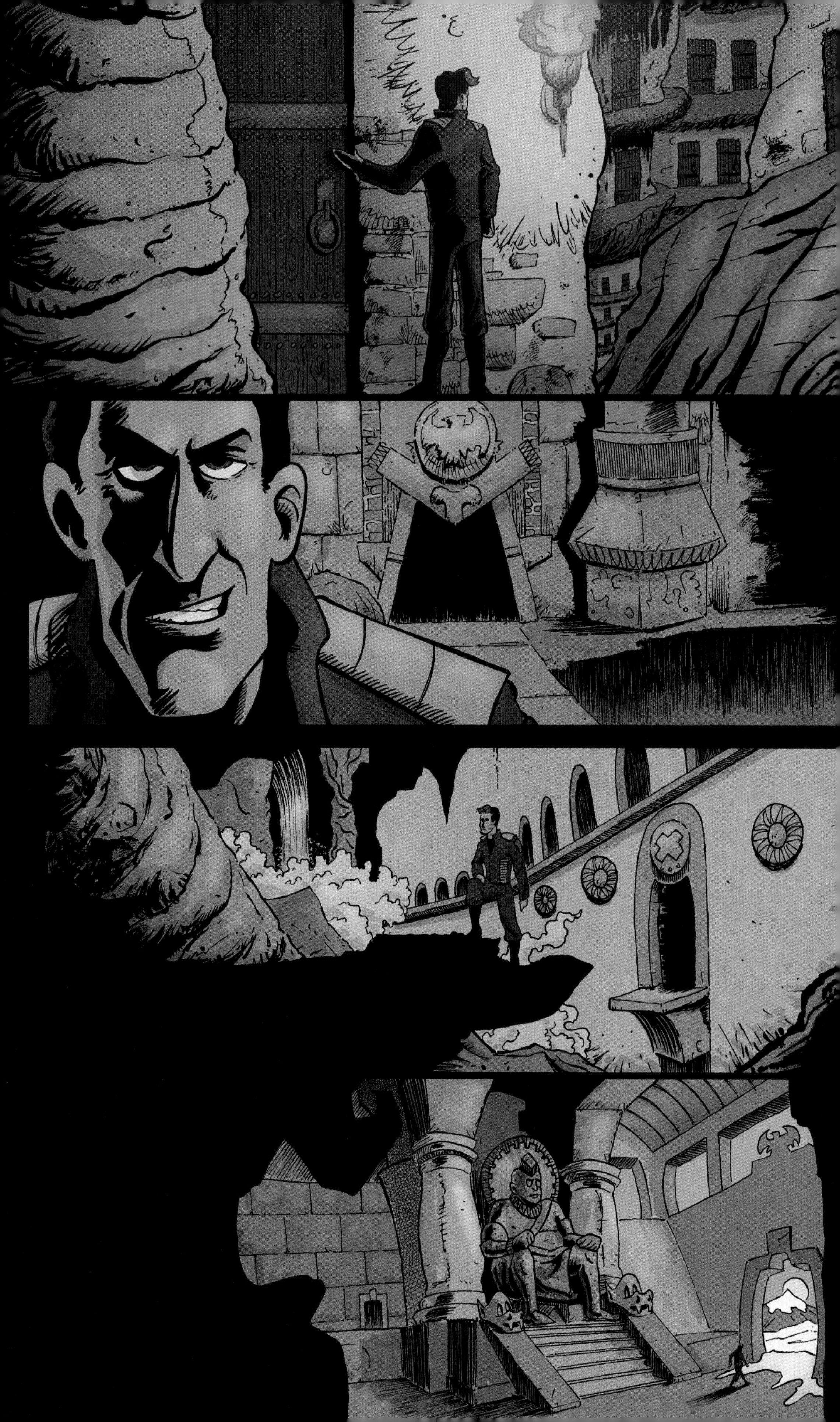

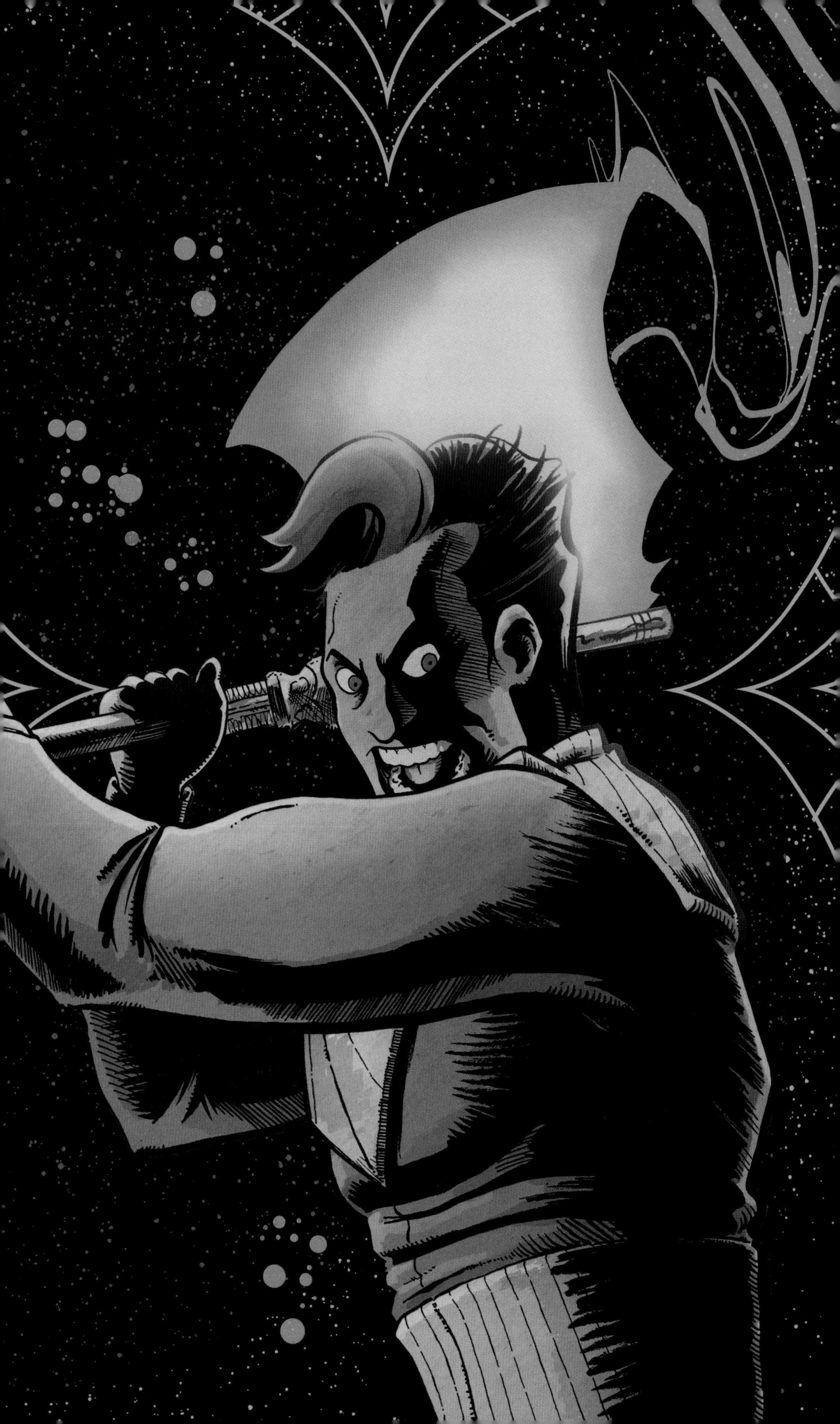

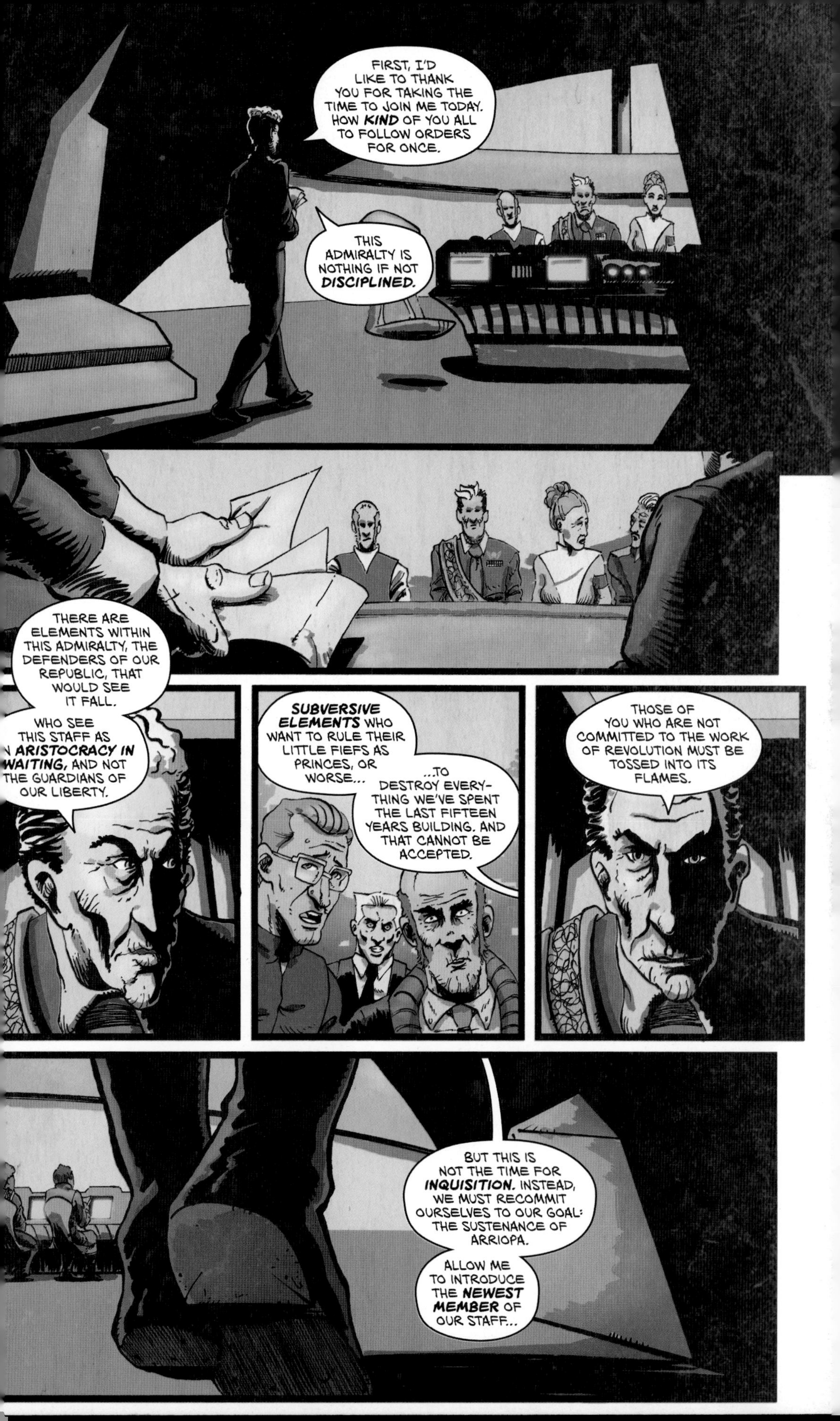

FIRST, I'D LIKE TO THANK YOU FOR TAKING THE TIME TO JOIN ME TODAY. HOW KIND OF YOU ALL TO FOLLOW ORDERS FOR ONCE.
THIS ADMIRALTY IS NOTHING IF NOT DISCIPLINED.
THERE ARE ELEMENTS WITHIN THIS ADMIRALTY, THE DEFENDERS OF OUR REPUBLIC, THAT WOULD SEE IT FALL.
WHO SEE THIS STAFF AS ARISTOCRACY IN WAITING, AND NOT THE GUARDIANS OF OUR LIBERTY.
SUBVERSIVE ELEMENTS WHO WANT TO RULE THEIR LITTLE FIEFS AS PRINCES, OR WORSE...
...TO DESTROY EVERYTHING WE'VE SPENT THE LAST FIFTEEN YEARS BUILDING. AND THAT CANNOT BE ACCEPTED.
THOSE OF YOU WHO ARE NOT COMMITTED TO THE WORK OF REVOLUTION MUST BE TOSSED INTO ITS FLAMES.
BUT THIS IS NOT THE TIME FOR INQUISITION. INSTEAD, WE MUST RECOMMIT OURSELVES TO OUR GOAL: THE SUSTENANCE OF ARRIOPA.
ALLOW ME TO INTRODUCE THE NEWEST MEMBER OF OUR STAFF...

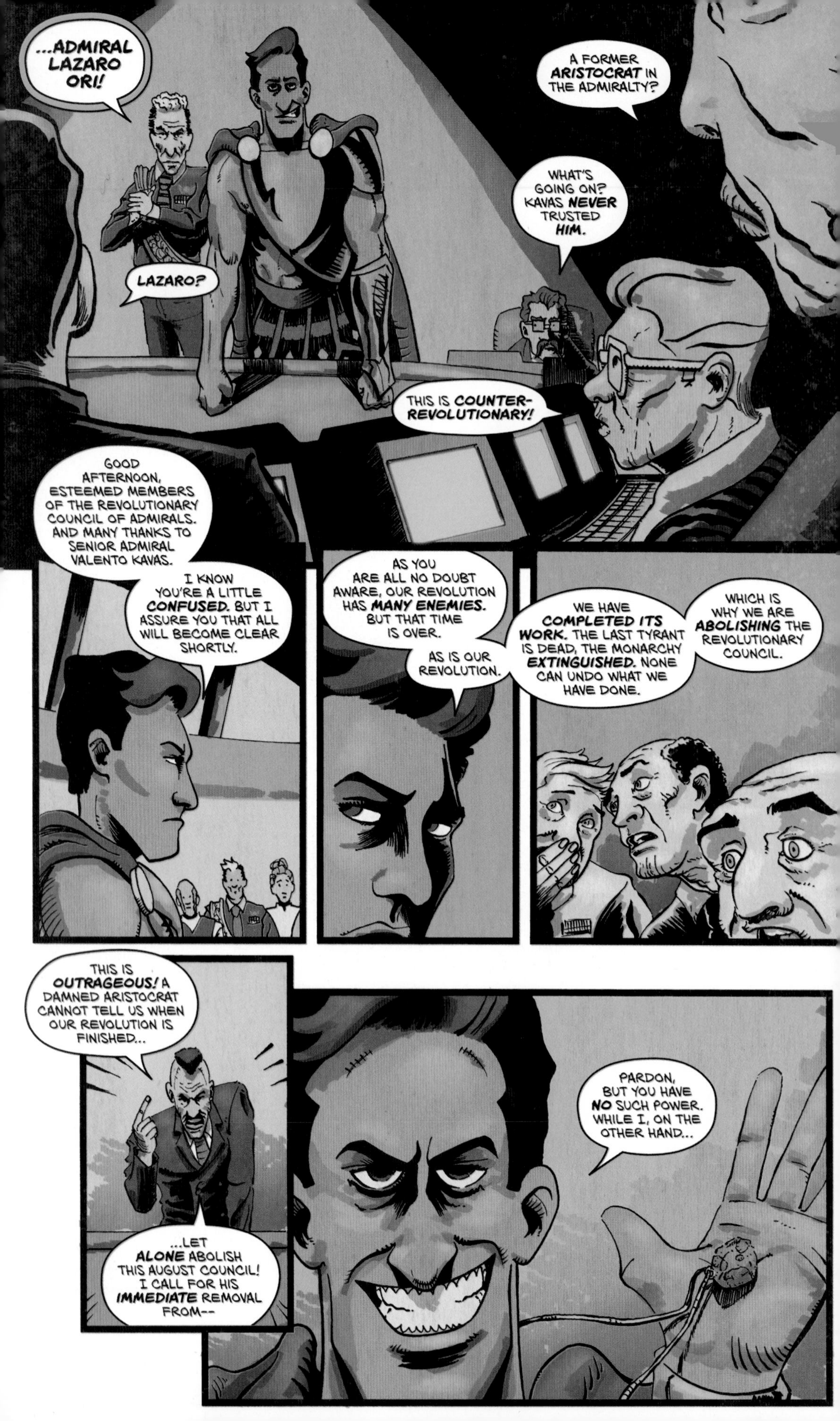

...ADMIRAL LAZARO ORI!
A FORMER ARISTOCRAT IN THE ADMIRALTY?
WHAT'S GOING ON? KAVAS NEVER TRUSTED HIM.
LAZARO?
THIS IS COUNTER-REVOLUTIONARY!
GOOD AFTERNOON, ESTEEMED MEMBERS OF THE REVOLUTIONARY COUNCIL OF ADMIRALS. AND MANY THANKS TO SENIOR ADMIRAL VALENTO KAVAS.
I KNOW YOU'RE A LITTLE CONFUSED. BUT I ASSURE YOU THAT ALL WILL BECOME CLEAR SHORTLY.
AS YOU ARE ALL NO DOUBT AWARE, OUR REVOLUTION HAS MANY ENEMIES. BUT THAT TIME IS OVER.
AS IS OUR REVOLUTION.
WE HAVE COMPLETED ITS WORK. THE LAST TYRANT IS DEAD, THE MONARCHY EXTINGUISHED. NONE CAN UNDO WHAT WE HAVE DONE.
WHICH IS WHY WE ARE ABOLISHING THE REVOLUTIONARY COUNCIL.
THIS IS OUTRAGEOUS! A DAMNED ARISTOCRAT CANNOT TELL US WHEN OUR REVOLUTION IS FINISHED...
...LET ALONE ABOLISH THIS AUGUST COUNCIL! I CALL FOR HIS IMMEDIATE REMOVAL FROM--
PARDON, BUT YOU HAVE NO SUCH POWER. WHILE I, ON THE OTHER HAND...

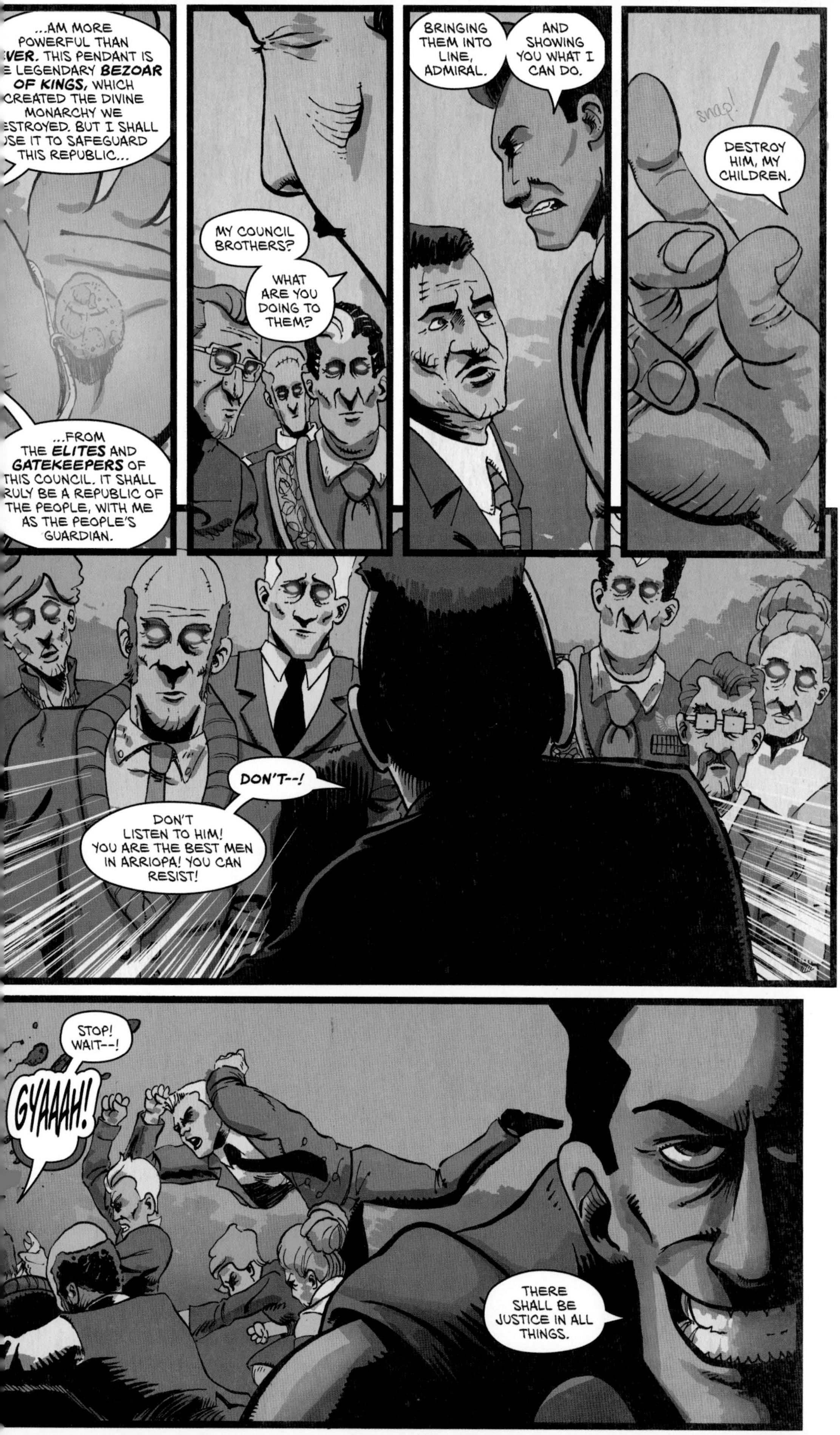
...AM MORE POWERFUL THAN
EVER. THIS PENDANT IS
E LEGENDARY BEZOAR OF KINGS, WHICH CREATED THE DIVINE MONARCHY WE ESTROYED. BUT I SHALL USE IT TO SAFEGUARD THIS REPUBLIC...
...FROM THE ELITES AND GATEKEEPERS OF THIS COUNCIL. IT SHALL RULY BE A REPUBLIC OF THE PEOPLE, WITH ME AS THE PEOPLE'S GUARDIAN.
MY COUNCIL BROTHERS?
WHAT ARE YOU DOING TO THEM?
BRINGING THEM INTO LINE, ADMIRAL.
AND SHOWING YOU WHAT I CAN DO.
snap!
DESTROY HIM, MY CHILDREN.
DON'T--!
DON'T LISTEN TO HIM! YOU ARE THE BEST MEN IN ARRIOPA! YOU CAN RESIST!
STOP! WAIT--!
GYAAAH!
THERE SHALL BE JUSTICE IN ALL THINGS.

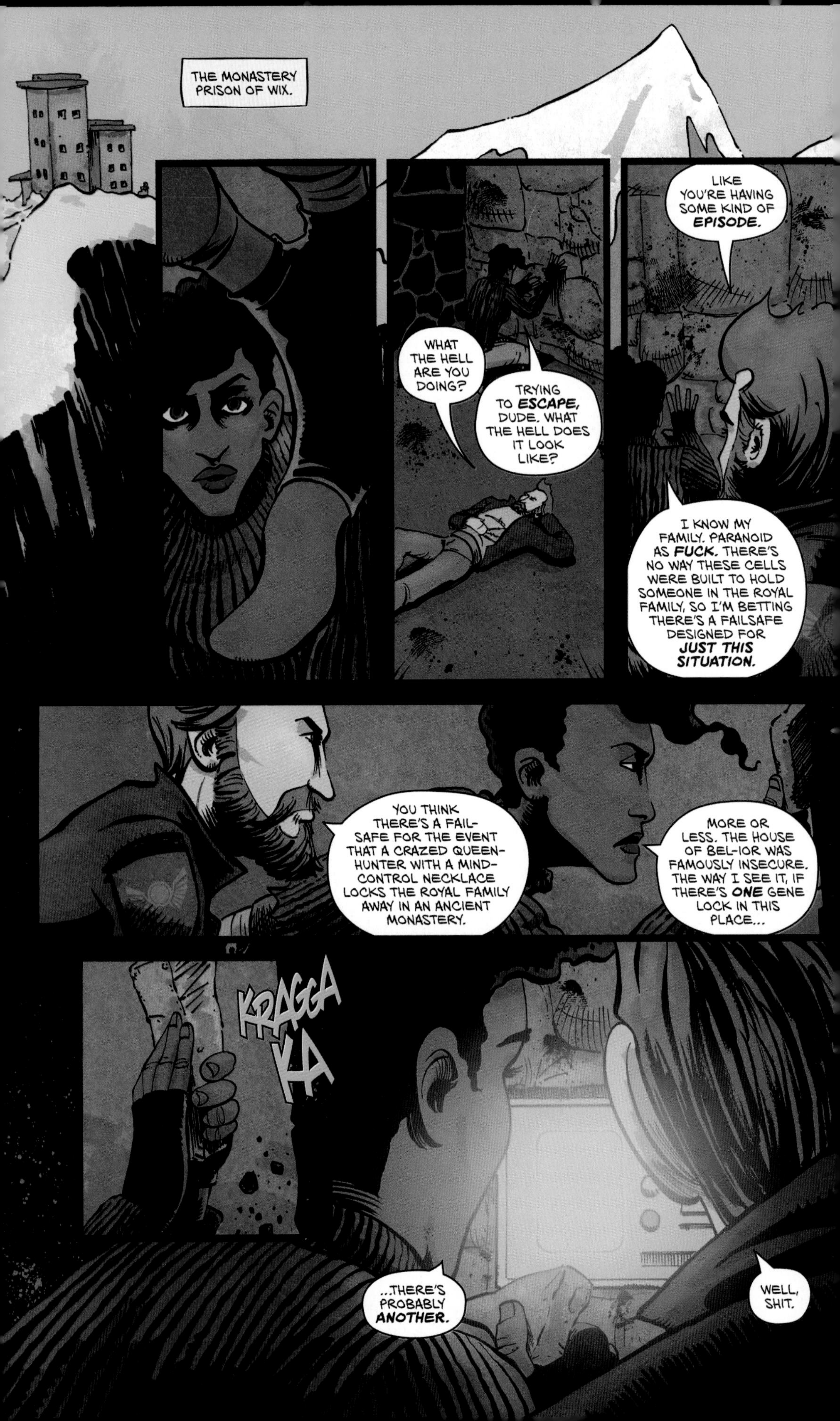
THE MONASTERY PRISON OF WIX.
WHAT THE HELL ARE YOU DOING?
TRYING TO **ESCAPE,** DUDE. WHAT THE HELL DOES IT LOOK LIKE?
LIKE YOU'RE HAVING SOME KIND OF **EPISODE.**
I KNOW MY FAMILY. PARANOID AS **FUCK.** THERE'S NO WAY THESE CELLS WERE BUILT TO HOLD SOMEONE IN THE ROYAL FAMILY, SO I'M BETTING THERE'S A FAILSAFE DESIGNED FOR **JUST THIS SITUATION.**
YOU THINK THERE'S A FAIL-SAFE FOR THE EVENT THAT A CRAZED QUEEN-HUNTER WITH A MIND-CONTROL NECKLACE LOCKS THE ROYAL FAMILY AWAY IN AN ANCIENT MONASTERY.
MORE OR LESS. THE HOUSE OF BEL-IOR WAS FAMOUSLY INSECURE. THE WAY I SEE IT, IF THERE'S **ONE** GENE LOCK IN THIS PLACE...
KRAGGA KA
...THERE'S PROBABLY **ANOTHER.**
WELL, SHIT.

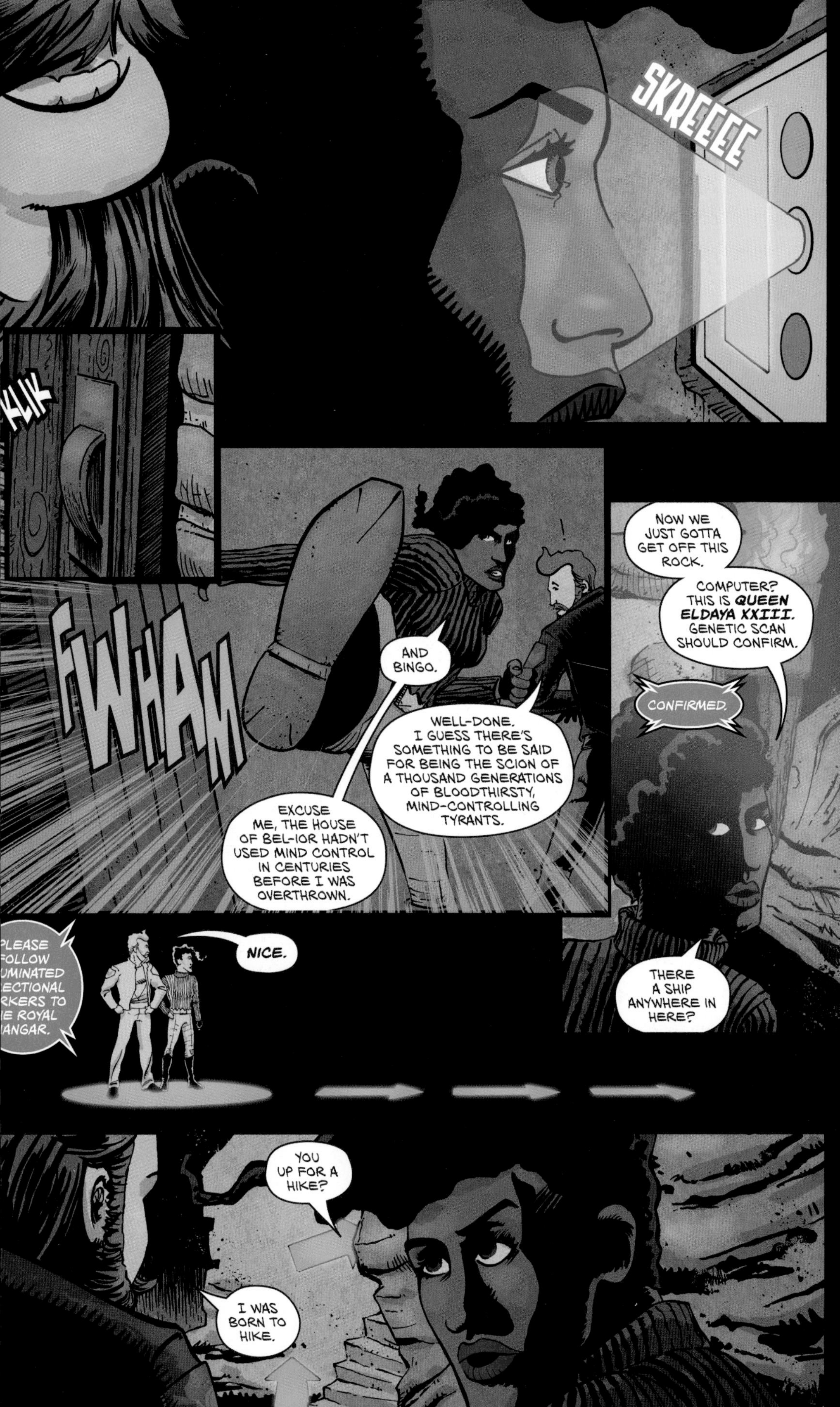
SKREEEEE
KLIK
FWHAM
AND BINGO.
WELL-DONE. I GUESS THERE'S SOMETHING TO BE SAID FOR BEING THE SCION OF A THOUSAND GENERATIONS OF BLOODTHIRSTY, MIND-CONTROLLING TYRANTS.
EXCUSE ME, THE HOUSE OF BEL-IOR HADN'T USED MIND CONTROL IN CENTURIES BEFORE I WAS OVERTHROWN.
NOW WE JUST GOTTA GET OFF THIS ROCK.
COMPUTER? THIS IS QUEEN ELDAYA XXIII. GENETIC SCAN SHOULD CONFIRM.
CONFIRMED.
THERE A SHIP ANYWHERE IN HERE?
NICE.
YOU UP FOR A HIKE?
I WAS BORN TO HIKE.

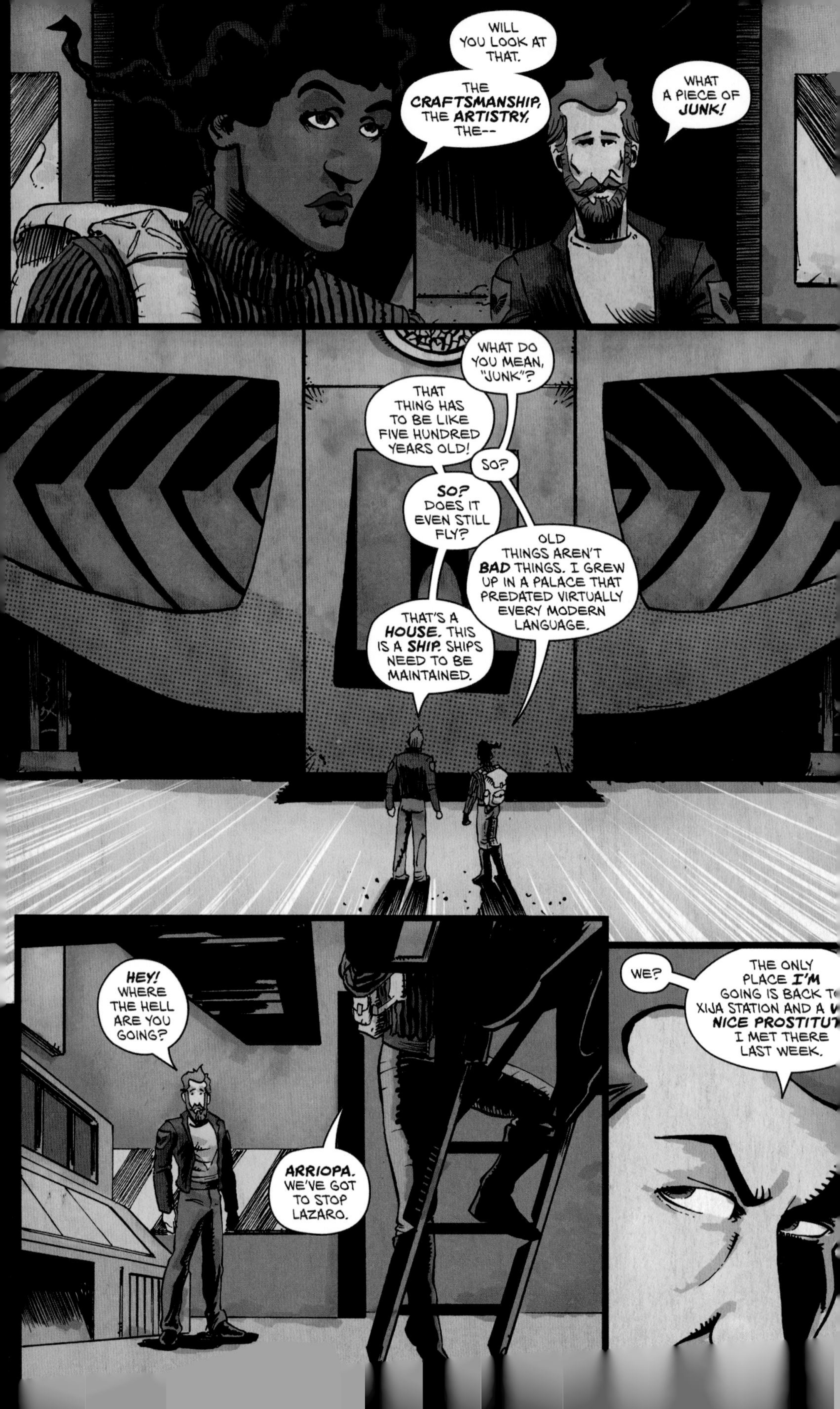

WILL YOU LOOK AT THAT.
THE **CRAFTSMANSHIP,** THE **ARTISTRY,** THE--
WHAT A PIECE OF **JUNK!**
WHAT DO YOU MEAN, "JUNK"?
THAT THING HAS TO BE LIKE FIVE HUNDRED YEARS OLD!
SO?
SO? DOES IT EVEN STILL FLY?
OLD THINGS AREN'T **BAD** THINGS. I GREW UP IN A PALACE THAT PREDATED VIRTUALLY EVERY MODERN LANGUAGE.
THAT'S A **HOUSE.** THIS IS A **SHIP.** SHIPS NEED TO BE MAINTAINED.
HEY! WHERE THE HELL ARE YOU GOING?
ARRIOPA. WE'VE GOT TO STOP LAZARO.
WE?

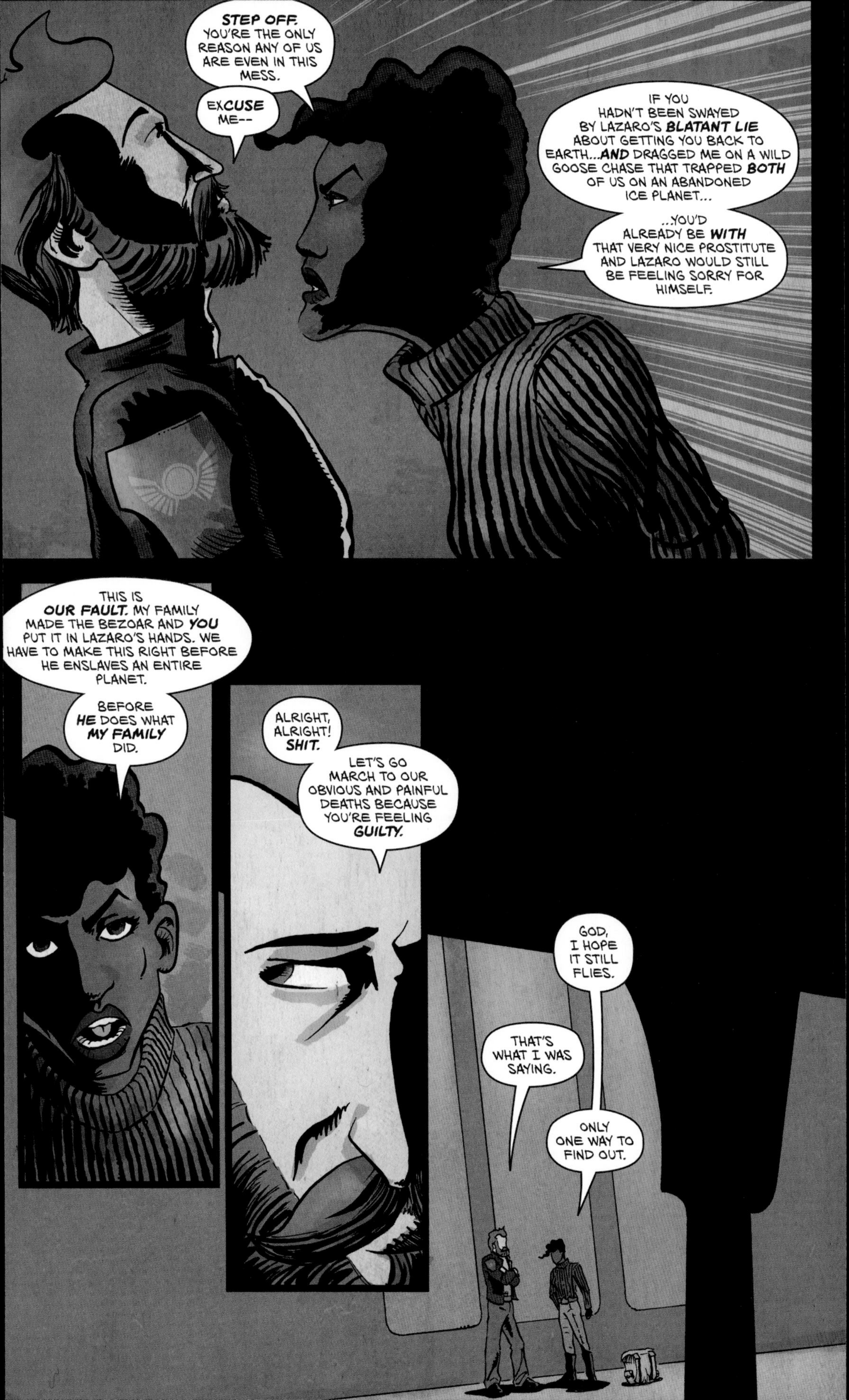
STEP OFF. YOU'RE THE ONLY REASON ANY OF US ARE EVEN IN THIS MESS.
EXCUSE ME--
IF YOU HADN'T BEEN SWAYED BY LAZARO'S BLATANT LIE ABOUT GETTING YOU BACK TO EARTH...AND DRAGGED ME ON A WILD GOOSE CHASE THAT TRAPPED BOTH OF US ON AN ABANDONED ICE PLANET...
...YOU'D ALREADY BE WITH THAT VERY NICE PROSTITUTE AND LAZARO WOULD STILL BE FEELING SORRY FOR HIMSELF.
THIS IS OUR FAULT. MY FAMILY MADE THE BEZOAR AND YOU PUT IT IN LAZARO'S HANDS. WE HAVE TO MAKE THIS RIGHT BEFORE HE ENSLAVES AN ENTIRE PLANET.
BEFORE HE DOES WHAT MY FAMILY DID.
ALRIGHT, ALRIGHT! SHIT.
LET'S GO MARCH TO OUR OBVIOUS AND PAINFUL DEATHS BECAUSE YOU'RE FEELING GUILTY.
GOD, I HOPE IT STILL FLIES.
THAT'S WHAT I WAS SAYING.
ONLY ONE WAY TO FIND OUT.

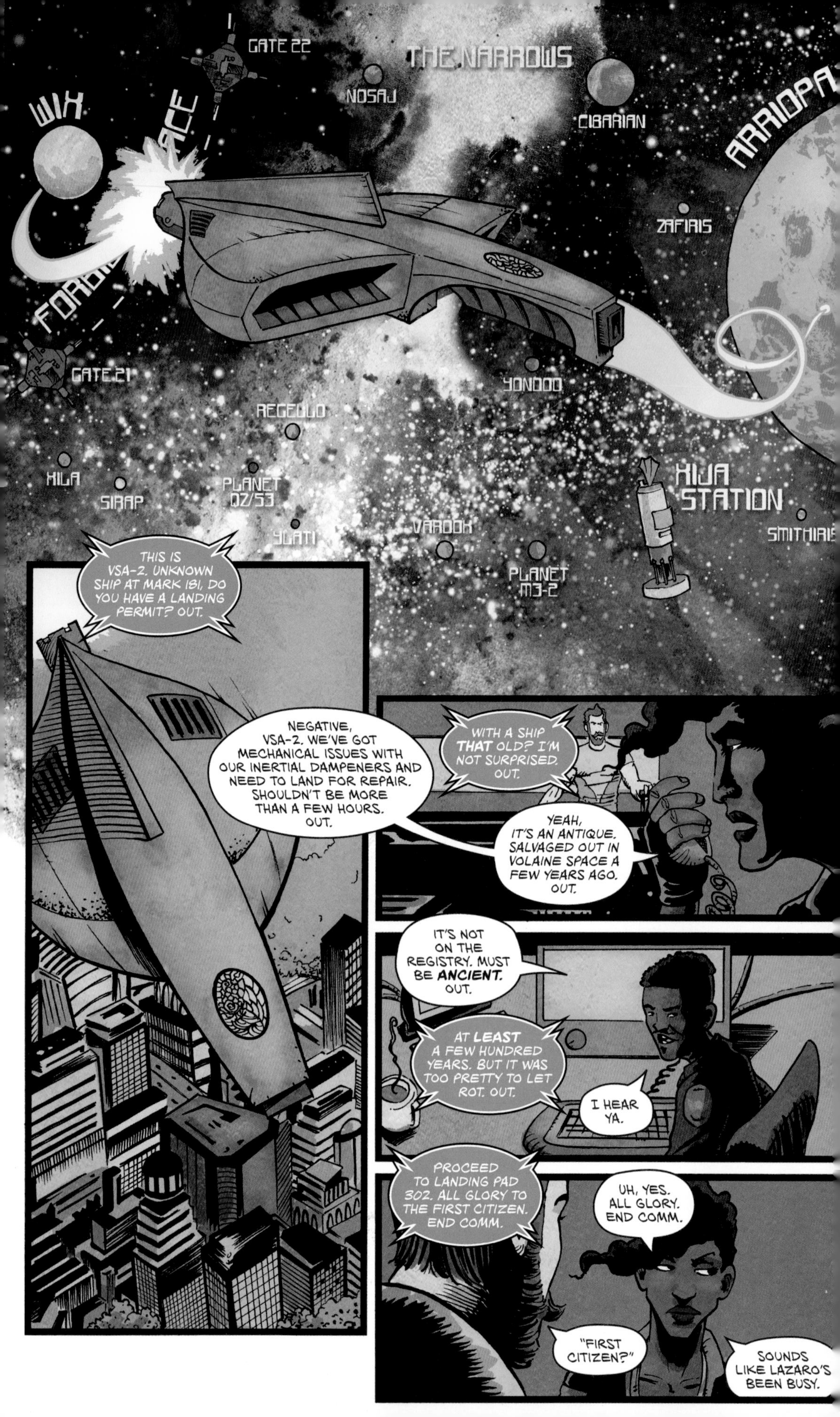
THE NARROWS
GATE 22
WIX
NOSAJ
CIBARIAN
ARRIOPA
ZAFIRIS
GATE 21
YONDOO
REGEULO
XILA
SIRAP
PLANET Q2/53
YLATI
VARDOX
XIJA STATION
SMITHIRIS
PLANET M3-2
THIS IS VSA-2. UNKNOWN SHIP AT MARK 181, DO YOU HAVE A LANDING PERMIT? OUT.
NEGATIVE, VSA-2. WE'VE GOT MECHANICAL ISSUES WITH OUR INERTIAL DAMPENERS AND NEED TO LAND FOR REPAIR. SHOULDN'T BE MORE THAN A FEW HOURS. OUT.
WITH A SHIP THAT OLD? I'M NOT SURPRISED. OUT.
YEAH, IT'S AN ANTIQUE. SALVAGED OUT IN VOLAINE SPACE A FEW YEARS AGO. OUT.
IT'S NOT ON THE REGISTRY. MUST BE ANCIENT. OUT.
AT LEAST A FEW HUNDRED YEARS. BUT IT WAS TOO PRETTY TO LET ROT. OUT.
I HEAR YA.
PROCEED TO LANDING PAD 302. ALL GLORY TO THE FIRST CITIZEN. END COMM.
UH, YES. ALL GLORY. END COMM.
"FIRST CITIZEN?"
SOUNDS LIKE LAZARO'S BEEN BUSY.

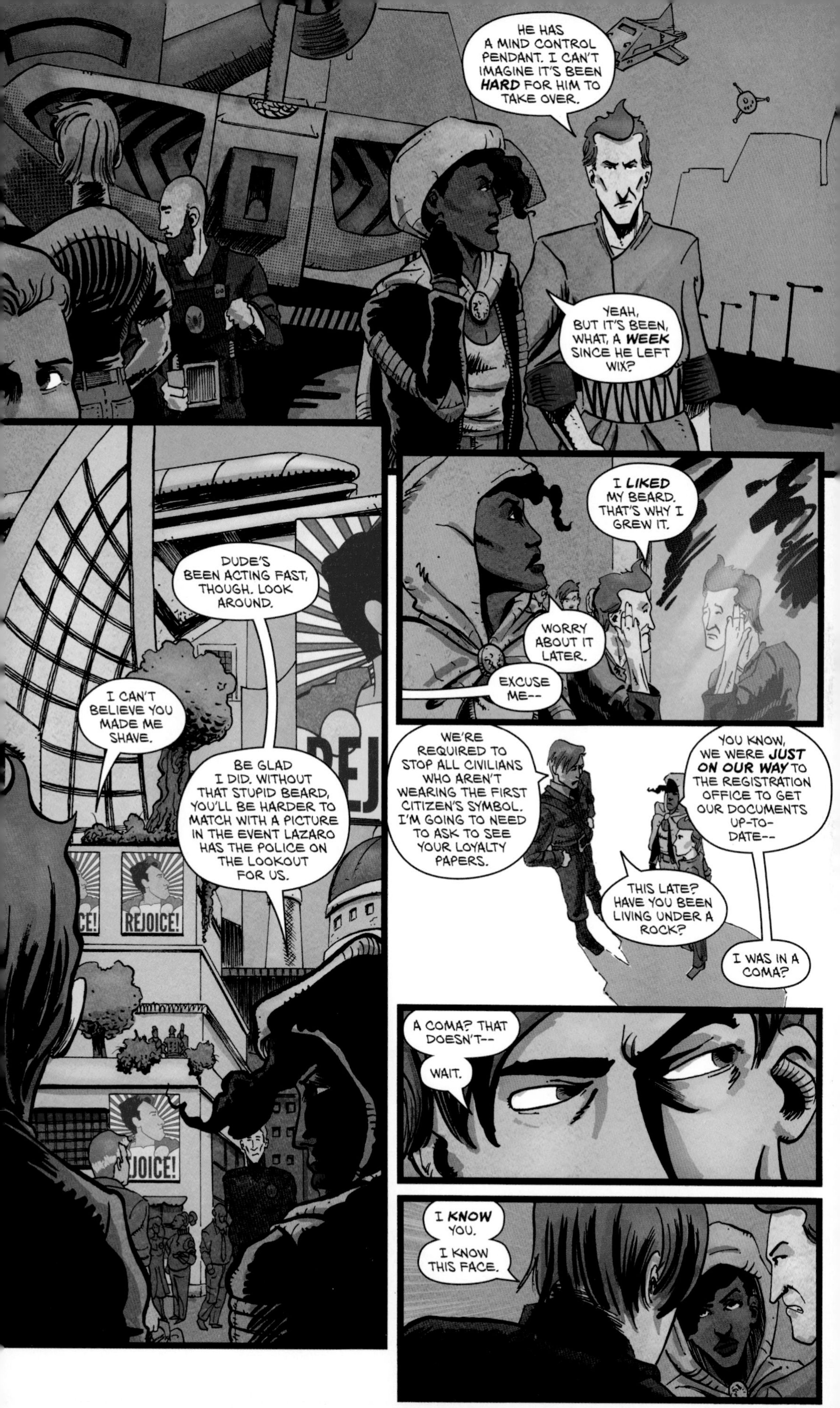
HE HAS A MIND CONTROL PENDANT. I CAN'T IMAGINE IT'S BEEN **HARD** FOR HIM TO TAKE OVER.
YEAH, BUT IT'S BEEN, WHAT, A **WEEK** SINCE HE LEFT WIX?
DUDE'S BEEN ACTING FAST, THOUGH. LOOK AROUND.
I CAN'T BELIEVE YOU MADE ME SHAVE.
BE GLAD I DID. WITHOUT THAT STUPID BEARD, YOU'LL BE HARDER TO MATCH WITH A PICTURE IN THE EVENT LAZARO HAS THE POLICE ON THE LOOKOUT FOR US.
REJOICE!
REJOICE!
I **LIKED** MY BEARD. THAT'S WHY I GREW IT.
WORRY ABOUT IT LATER.
EXCUSE ME--
WE'RE REQUIRED TO STOP ALL CIVILIANS WHO AREN'T WEARING THE FIRST CITIZEN'S SYMBOL. I'M GOING TO NEED TO ASK TO SEE YOUR LOYALTY PAPERS.
YOU KNOW, WE WERE **JUST ON OUR WAY** TO THE REGISTRATION OFFICE TO GET OUR DOCUMENTS UP-TO-DATE--
THIS LATE? HAVE YOU BEEN LIVING UNDER A ROCK?
I WAS IN A COMA?
A COMA? THAT DOESN'T--
WAIT.
I **KNOW** YOU.
I KNOW THIS FACE.

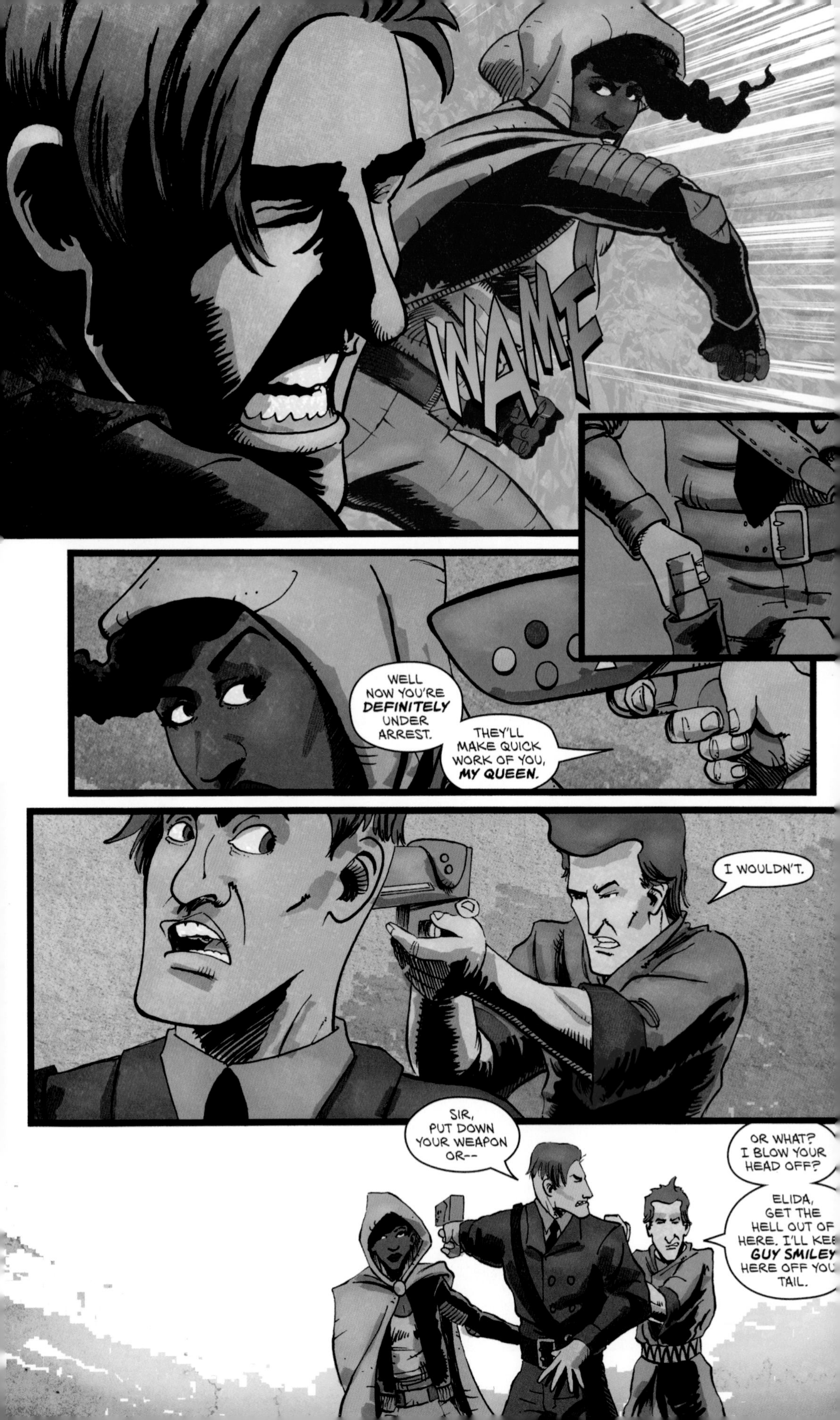
WAMF
WELL NOW YOU'RE DEFINITELY UNDER ARREST.
THEY'LL MAKE QUICK WORK OF YOU, MY QUEEN.
I WOULDN'T.
SIR, PUT DOWN YOUR WEAPON OR--
OR WHAT? I BLOW YOUR HEAD OFF?
ELIDA, GET THE HELL OUT OF HERE. I'LL KEE GUY SMILEY HERE OFF YOU TAIL.

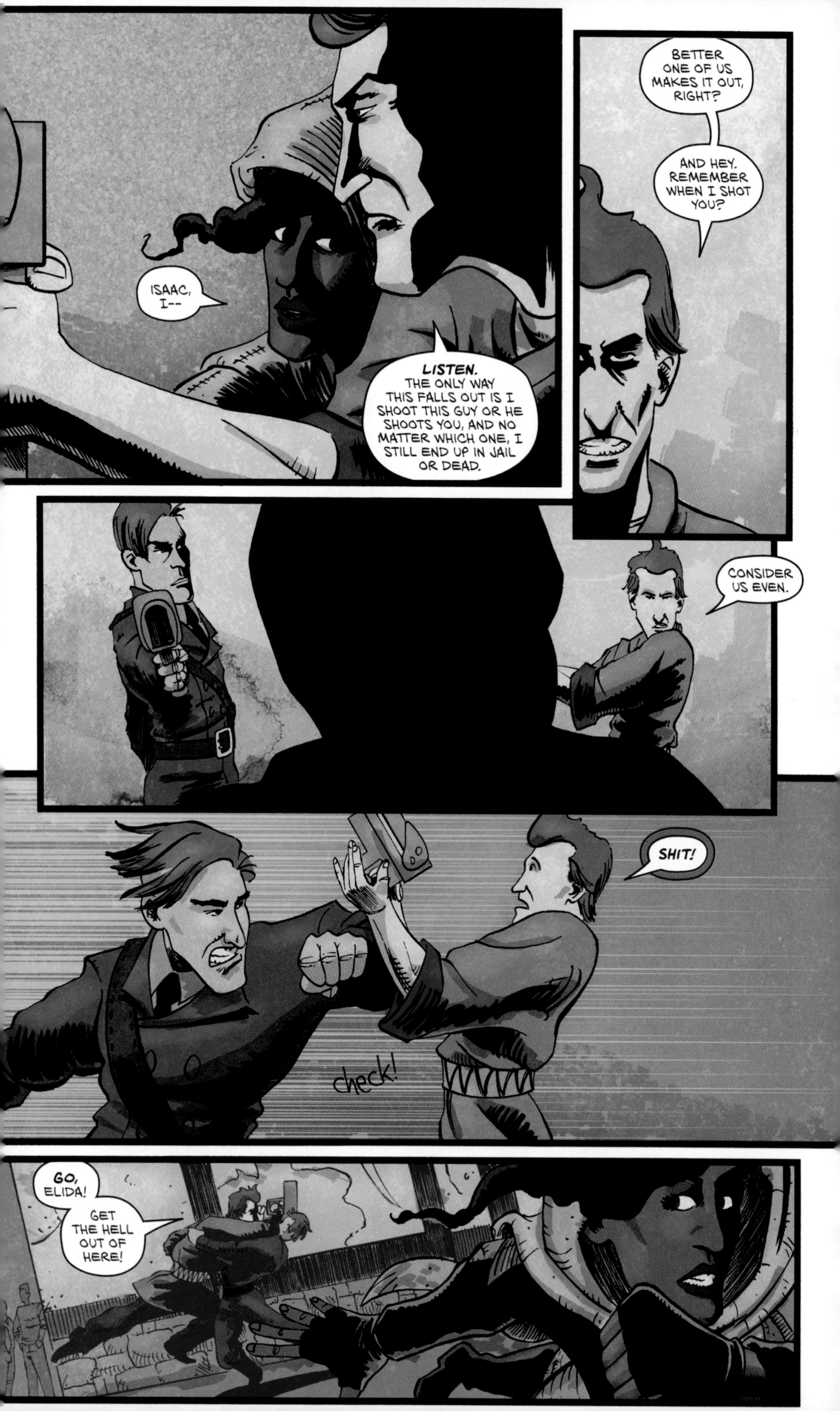
ISAAC, I--
LISTEN. THE ONLY WAY THIS FALLS OUT IS I SHOOT THIS GUY OR HE SHOOTS YOU, AND NO MATTER WHICH ONE, I STILL END UP IN JAIL OR DEAD.
BETTER ONE OF US MAKES IT OUT, RIGHT?
AND HEY. REMEMBER WHEN I SHOT YOU?
CONSIDER US EVEN.
SHIT!
check!
GO, ELIDA!
GET THE HELL OUT OF HERE!

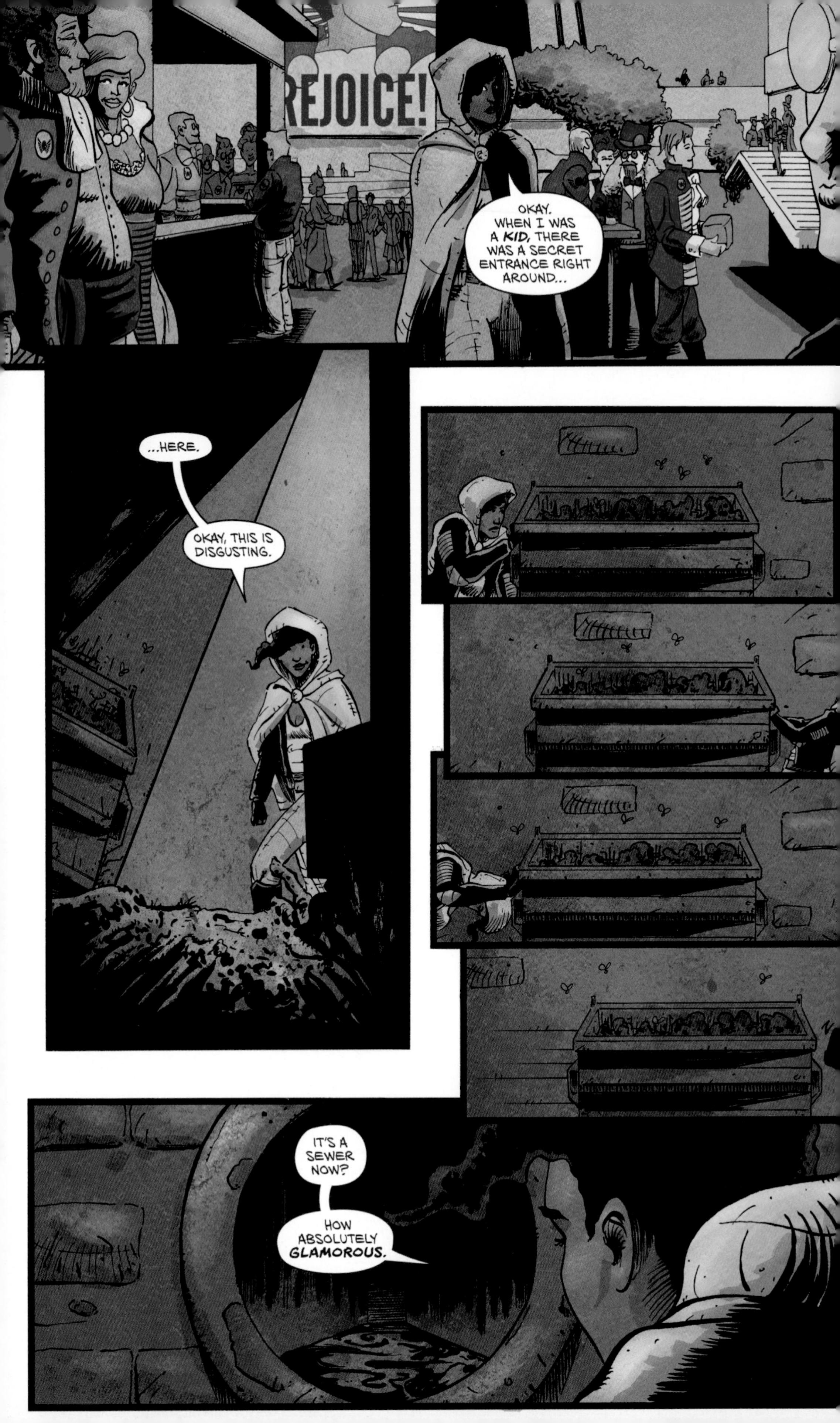
REJOICE!
OKAY. WHEN I WAS A KID, THERE WAS A SECRET ENTRANCE RIGHT AROUND...
...HERE.
OKAY, THIS IS DISGUSTING.
IT'S A SEWER NOW?
HOW ABSOLUTELY GLAMOROUS.

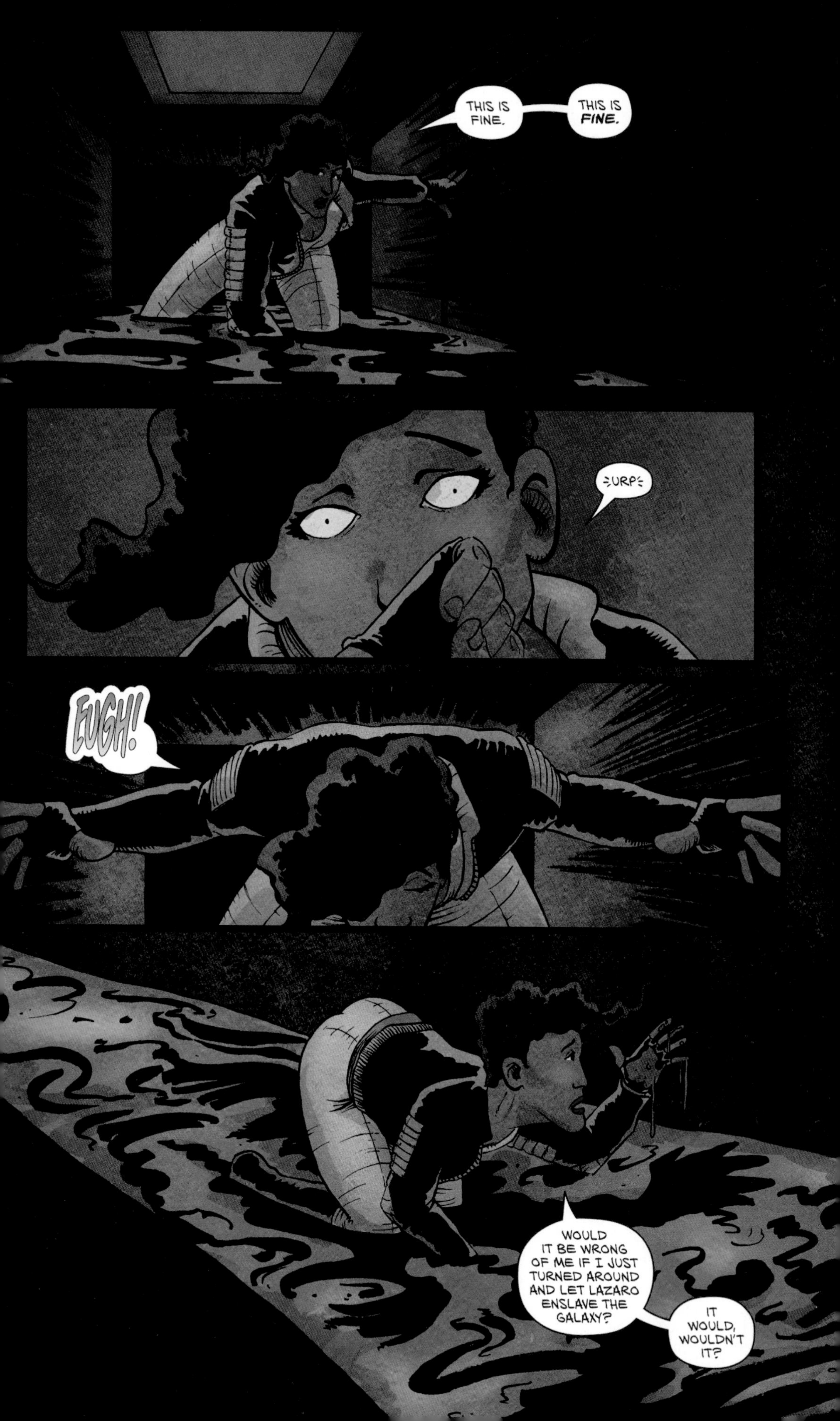
THIS IS FINE.
THIS IS FINE.
URP
EUGH!
WOULD IT BE WRONG OF ME IF I JUST TURNED AROUND AND LET LAZARO ENSLAVE THE GALAXY?
IT WOULD, WOULDN'T IT?

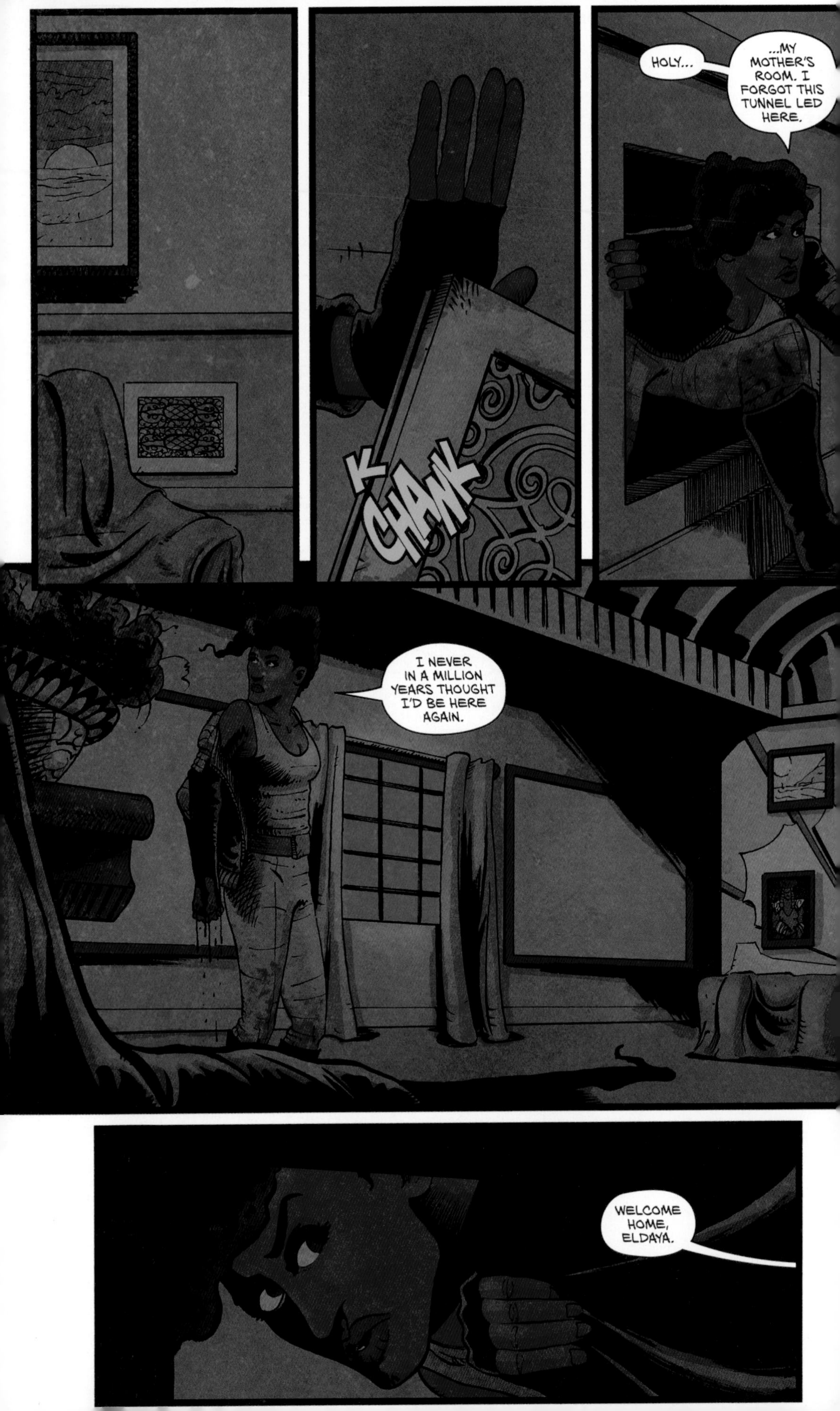
K
CHANK
HOLY...
...MY MOTHER'S ROOM. I FORGOT THIS TUNNEL LED HERE.
I NEVER IN A MILLION YEARS THOUGHT I'D BE HERE AGAIN.
WELCOME HOME, ELDAYA.

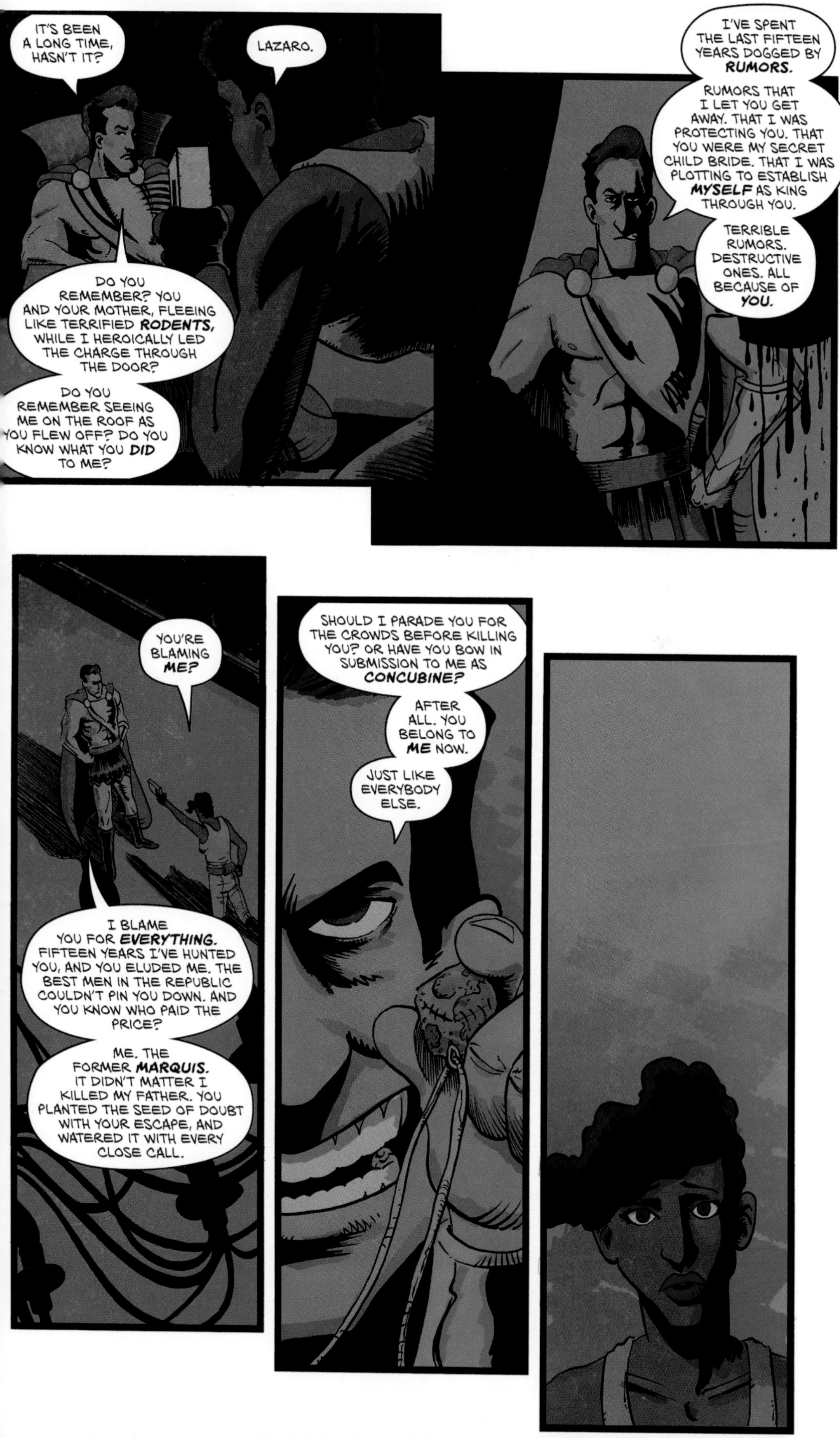
IT'S BEEN A LONG TIME, HASN'T IT?
LAZARO.
DO YOU REMEMBER? YOU AND YOUR MOTHER, FLEEING LIKE TERRIFIED **RODENTS,** WHILE I HEROICALLY LED THE CHARGE THROUGH THE DOOR?
DO YOU REMEMBER SEEING ME ON THE ROOF AS YOU FLEW OFF? DO YOU KNOW WHAT YOU **DID** TO ME?
I'VE SPENT THE LAST FIFTEEN YEARS DOGGED BY **RUMORS.**
RUMORS THAT I LET YOU GET AWAY. THAT I WAS PROTECTING YOU. THAT YOU WERE MY SECRET CHILD BRIDE. THAT I WAS PLOTTING TO ESTABLISH **MYSELF** AS KING THROUGH YOU.
TERRIBLE RUMORS. DESTRUCTIVE ONES. ALL BECAUSE OF **YOU.**
YOU'RE BLAMING **ME?**
I BLAME YOU FOR **EVERYTHING.** FIFTEEN YEARS I'VE HUNTED YOU, AND YOU ELUDED ME. THE BEST MEN IN THE REPUBLIC COULDN'T PIN YOU DOWN. AND YOU KNOW WHO PAID THE PRICE?
ME. THE FORMER **MARQUIS.** IT DIDN'T MATTER I KILLED MY FATHER. YOU PLANTED THE SEED OF DOUBT WITH YOUR ESCAPE, AND WATERED IT WITH EVERY CLOSE CALL.
SHOULD I PARADE YOU FOR THE CROWDS BEFORE KILLING YOU? OR HAVE YOU BOW IN SUBMISSION TO ME AS **CONCUBINE?**
AFTER ALL. YOU BELONG TO **ME** NOW.
JUST LIKE EVERYBODY ELSE.

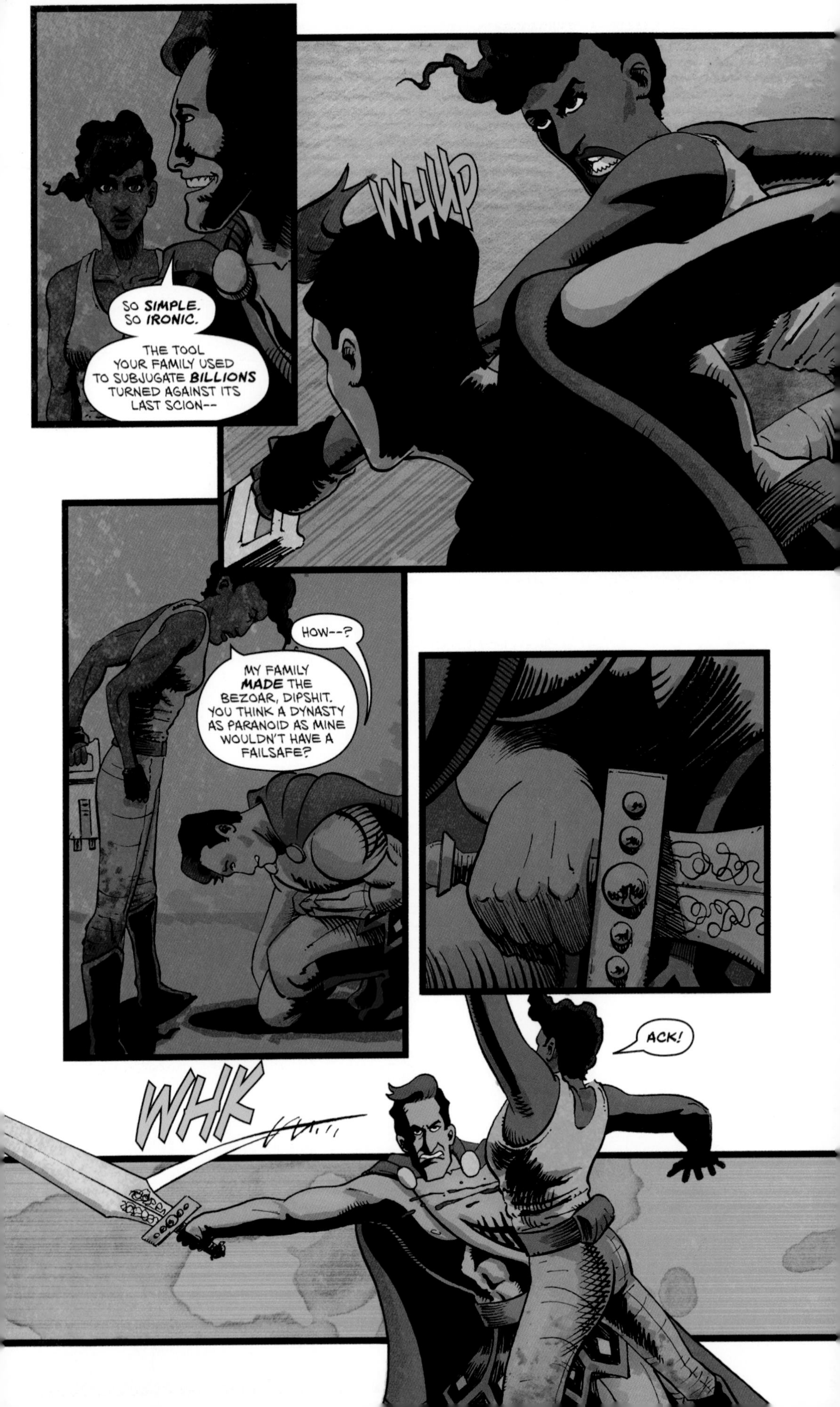
SO SIMPLE. SO IRONIC.
THE TOOL YOUR FAMILY USED TO SUBJUGATE BILLIONS TURNED AGAINST ITS LAST SCION--
WHUP
HOW--?
MY FAMILY MADE THE BEZOAR, DIPSHIT. YOU THINK A DYNASTY AS PARANOID AS MINE WOULDN'T HAVE A FAILSAFE?
ACK!
WHK

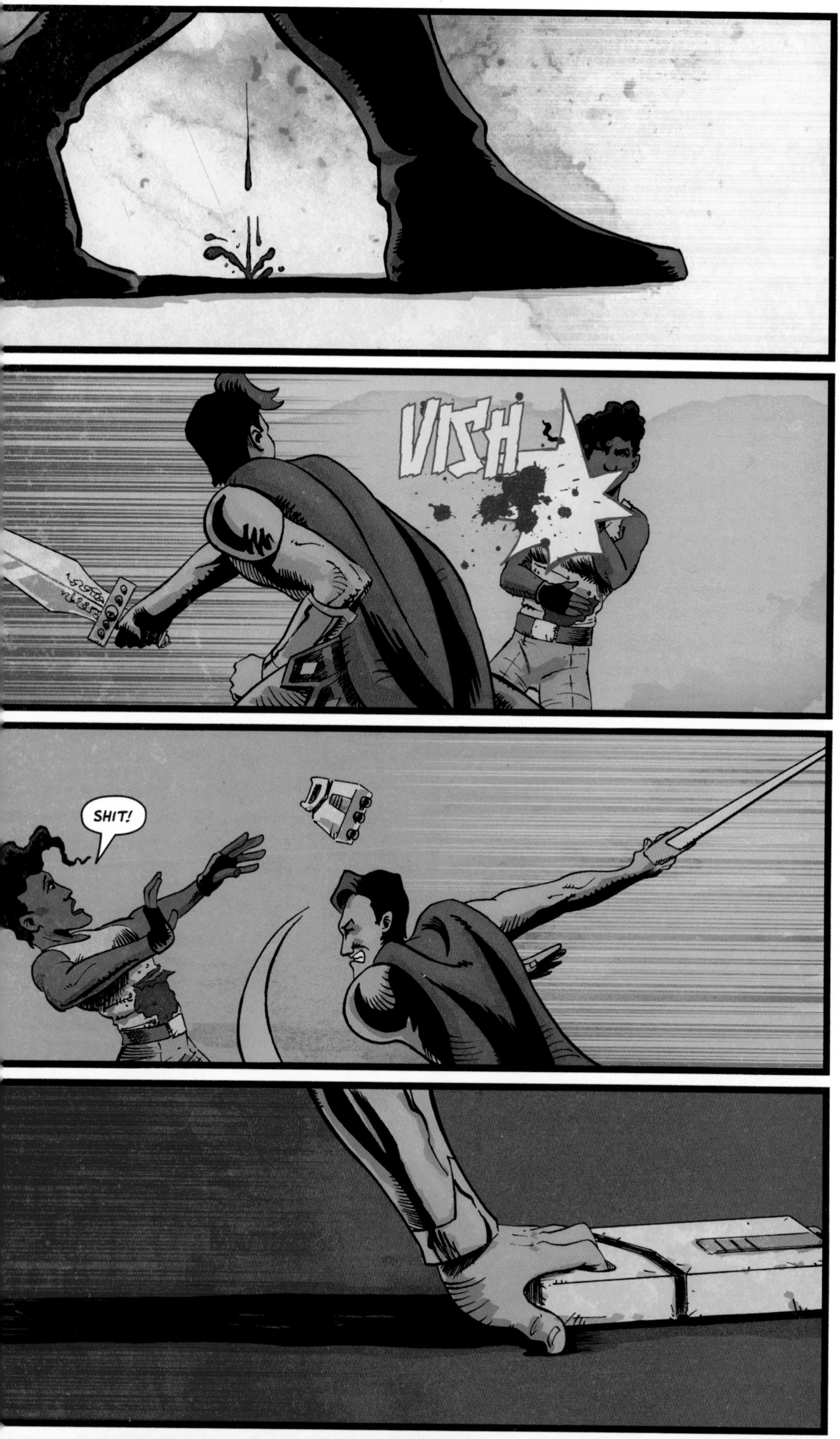
VISH
SHIT!

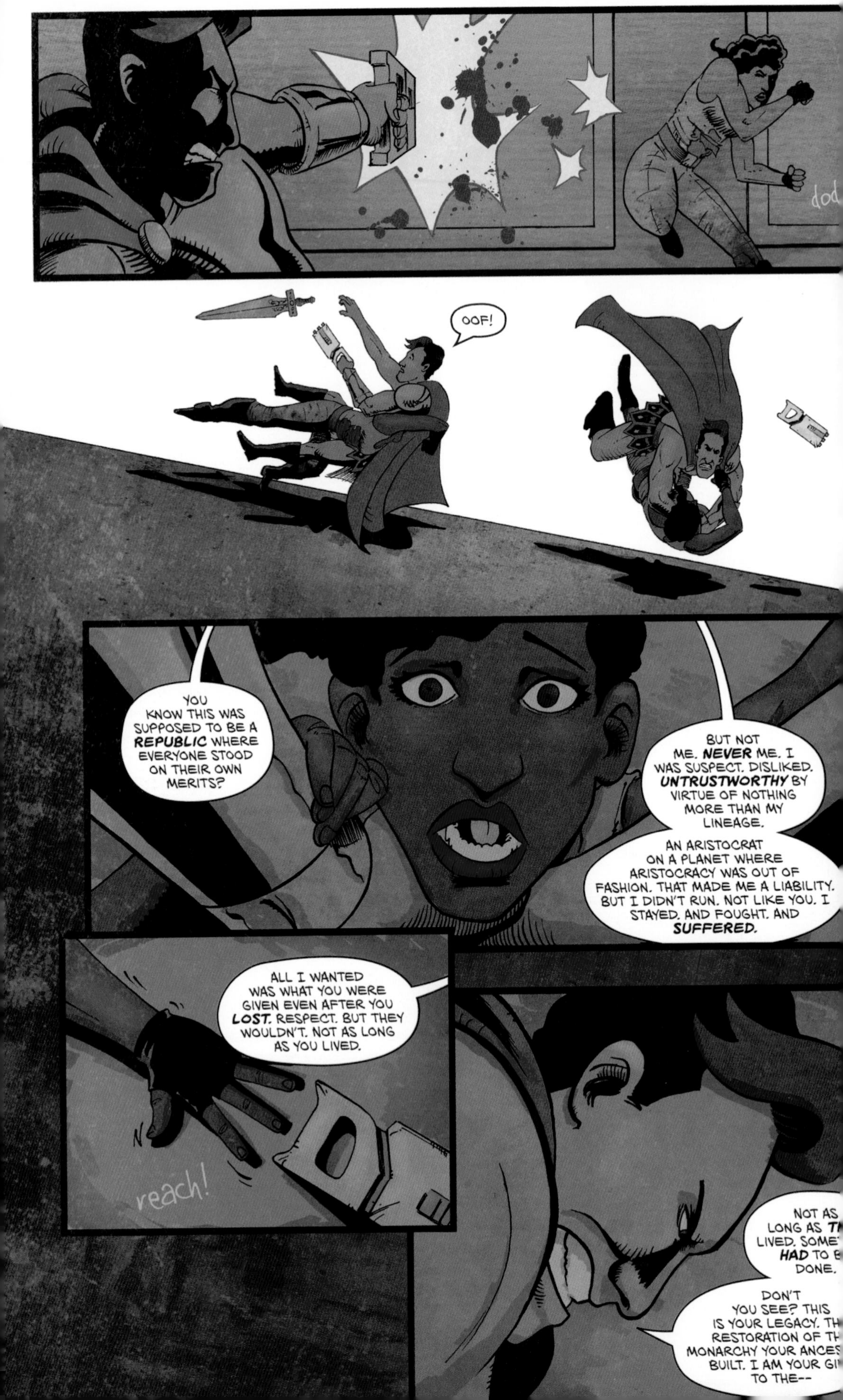
dod
OOF!
YOU KNOW THIS WAS SUPPOSED TO BE A REPUBLIC WHERE EVERYONE STOOD ON THEIR OWN MERITS?
BUT NOT ME. NEVER ME. I WAS SUSPECT. DISLIKED. UNTRUSTWORTHY BY VIRTUE OF NOTHING MORE THAN MY LINEAGE.
AN ARISTOCRAT ON A PLANET WHERE ARISTOCRACY WAS OUT OF FASHION. THAT MADE ME A LIABILITY. BUT I DIDN'T RUN. NOT LIKE YOU. I STAYED. AND FOUGHT. AND SUFFERED.
ALL I WANTED WAS WHAT YOU WERE GIVEN EVEN AFTER YOU LOST. RESPECT. BUT THEY WOULDN'T. NOT AS LONG AS YOU LIVED.
reach!
NOT AS LONG AS TH LIVED. SOMET HAD TO B DONE.
DON'T YOU SEE? THIS IS YOUR LEGACY. TH RESTORATION OF TH MONARCHY YOUR ANCES BUILT. I AM YOUR GI TO THE--

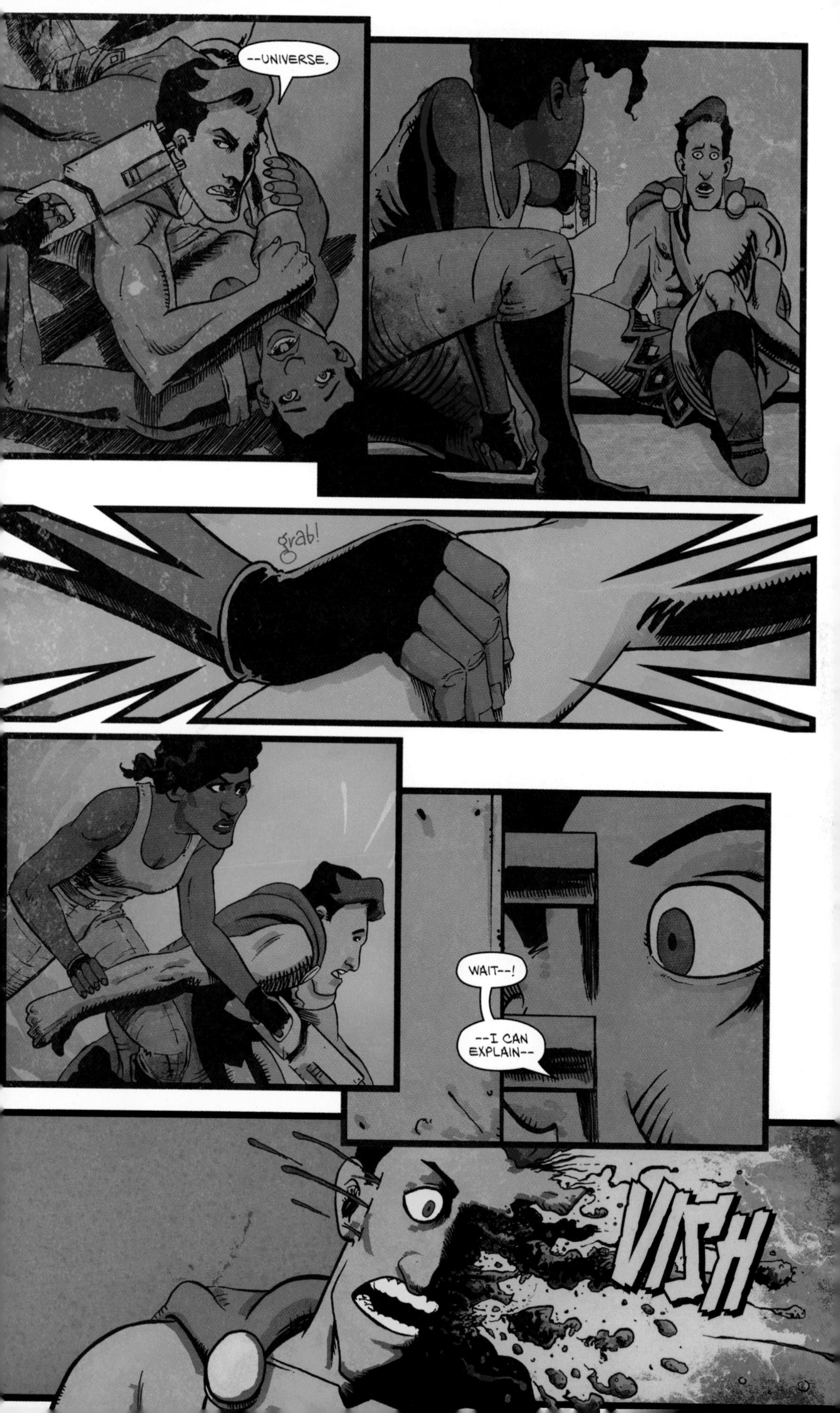
--UNIVERSE.
grab!
WAIT--!
--I CAN EXPLAIN--
VISH

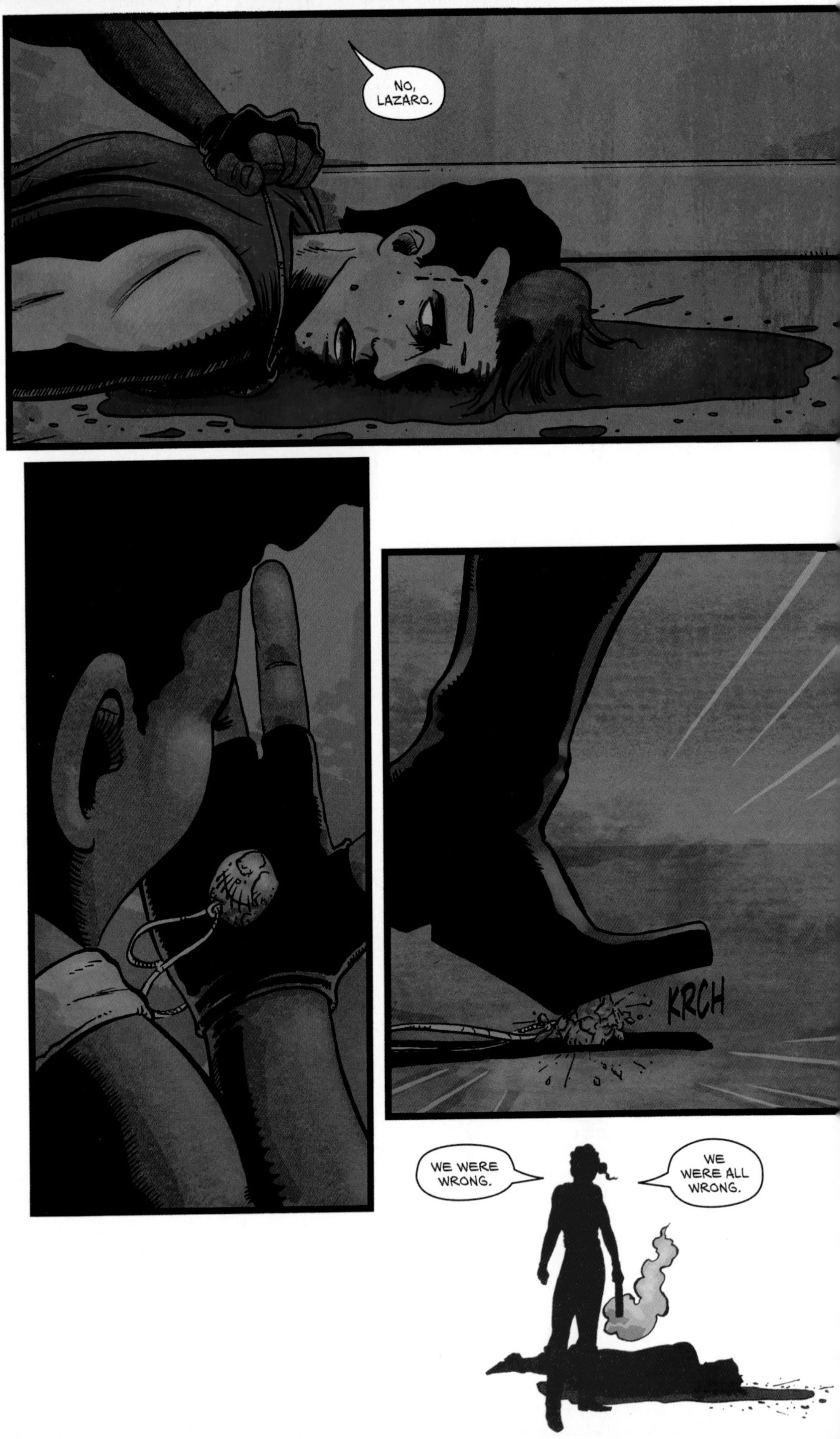
NO, LAZARO.
KRCH
WE WERE WRONG.
WE WERE ALL WRONG.

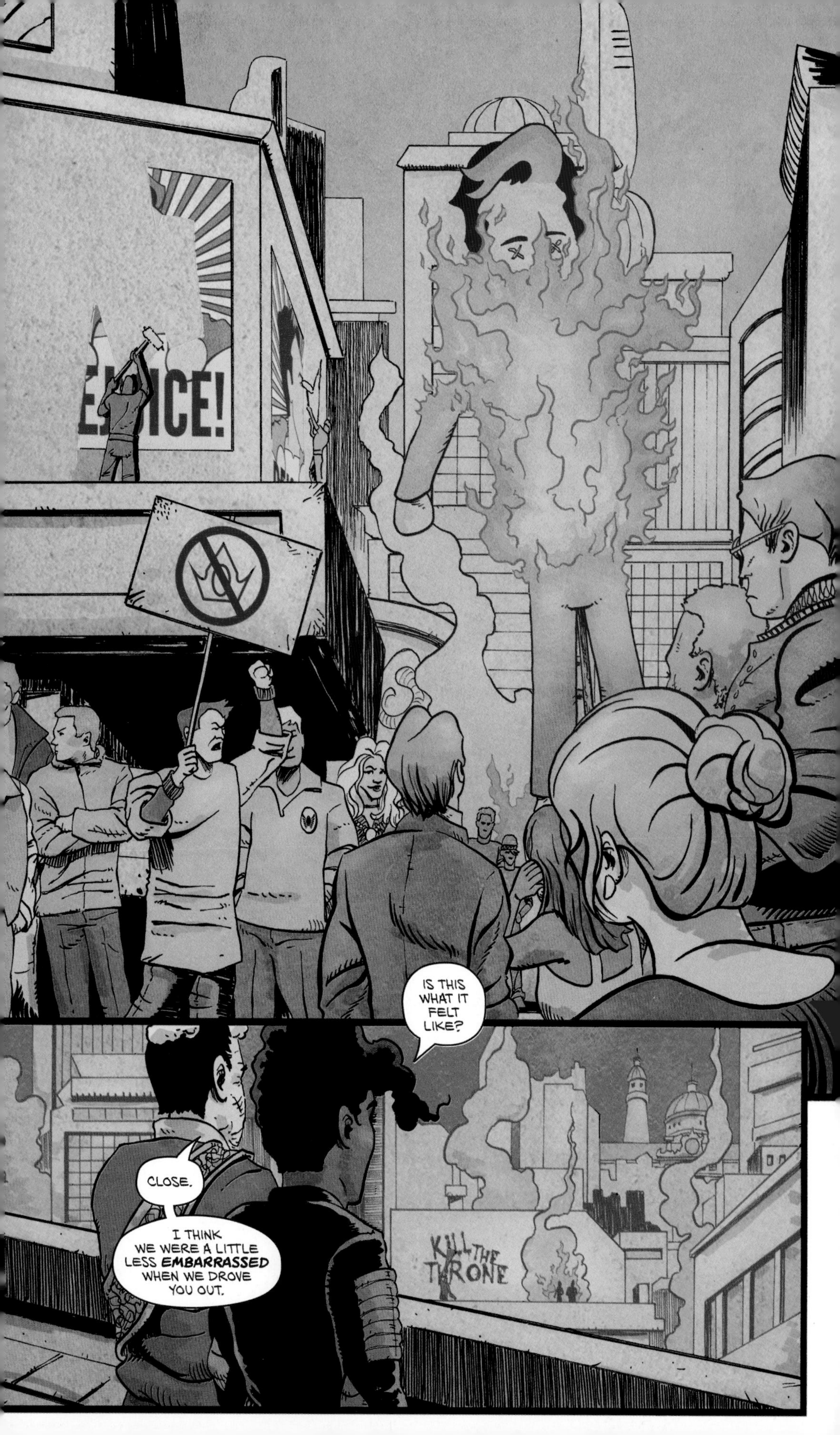
E...ICE!
IS THIS WHAT IT FELT LIKE?
CLOSE.
I THINK WE WERE A LITTLE LESS EMBARRASSED WHEN WE DROVE YOU OUT.
KILL THE THRONE

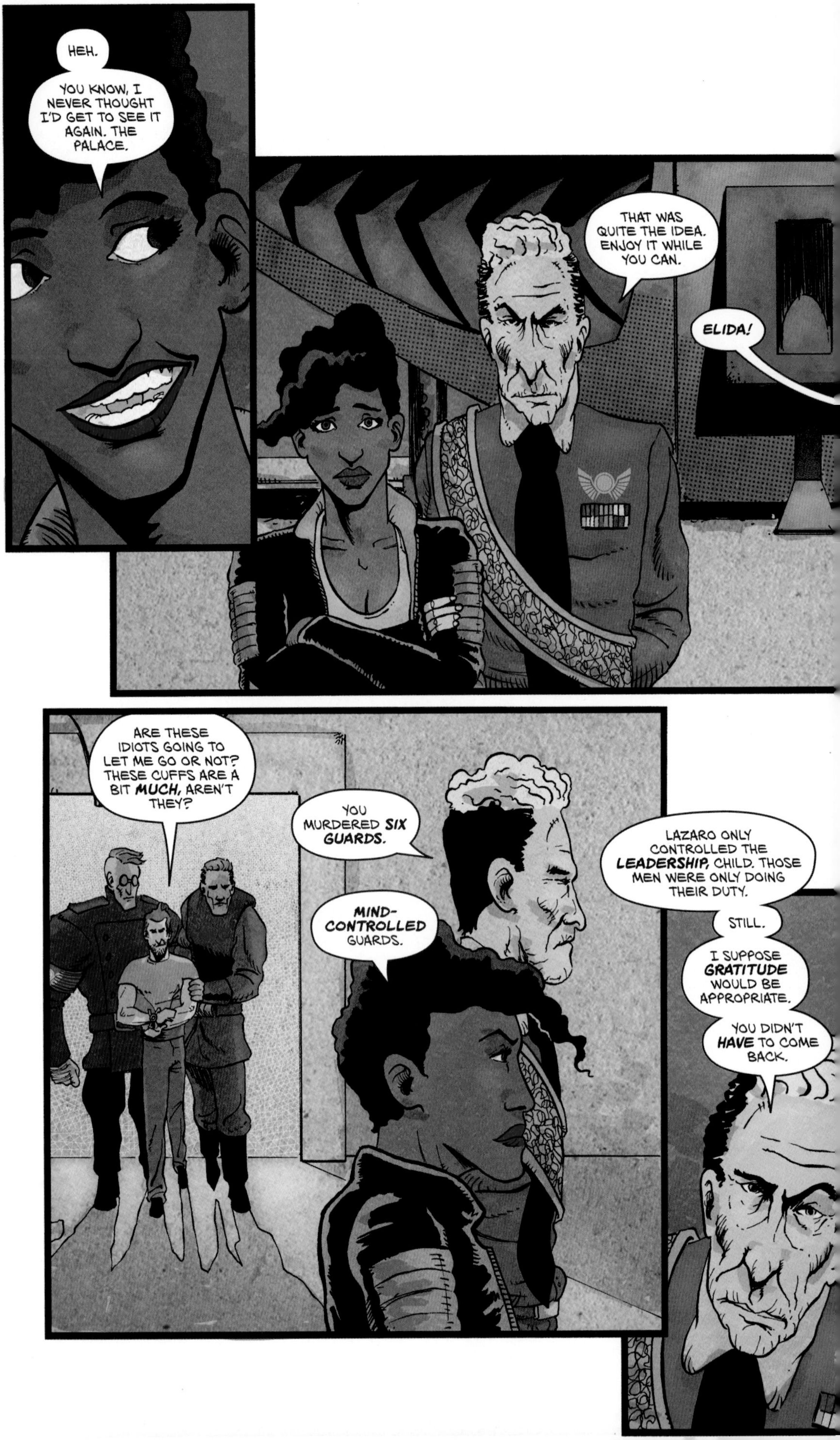
HEH.
YOU KNOW, I NEVER THOUGHT I'D GET TO SEE IT AGAIN. THE PALACE.
THAT WAS QUITE THE IDEA. ENJOY IT WHILE YOU CAN.
ELIDA!
ARE THESE IDIOTS GOING TO LET ME GO OR NOT? THESE CUFFS ARE A BIT MUCH, AREN'T THEY?
YOU MURDERED SIX GUARDS.
MIND-CONTROLLED GUARDS.
LAZARO ONLY CONTROLLED THE LEADERSHIP, CHILD. THOSE MEN WERE ONLY DOING THEIR DUTY.
STILL.
I SUPPOSE GRATITUDE WOULD BE APPROPRIATE.
YOU DIDN'T HAVE TO COME BACK.

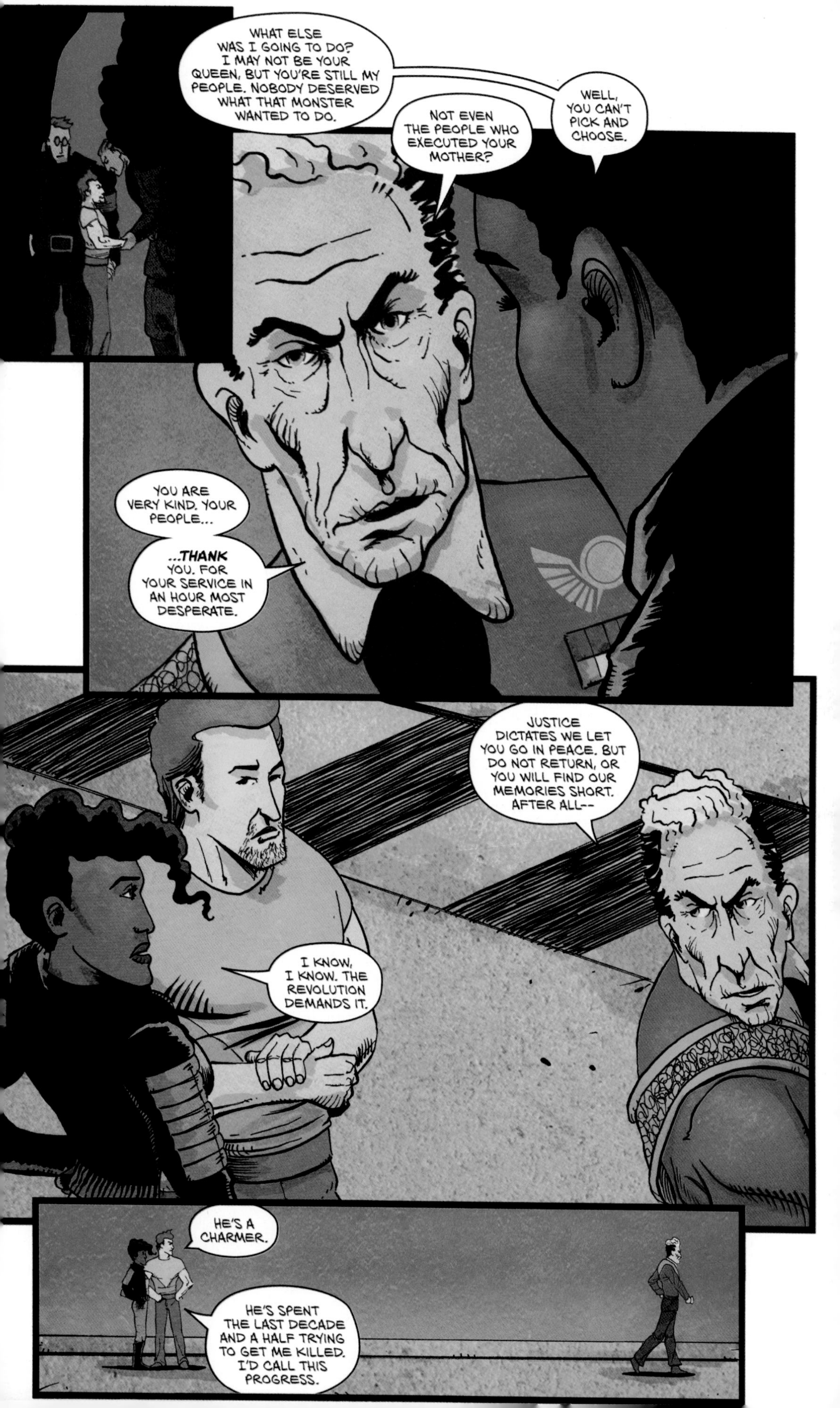
WHAT ELSE WAS I GOING TO DO? I MAY NOT BE YOUR QUEEN, BUT YOU'RE STILL MY PEOPLE. NOBODY DESERVED WHAT THAT MONSTER WANTED TO DO.
NOT EVEN THE PEOPLE WHO EXECUTED YOUR MOTHER?
WELL, YOU CAN'T PICK AND CHOOSE.
YOU ARE VERY KIND. YOUR PEOPLE...
...THANK YOU. FOR YOUR SERVICE IN AN HOUR MOST DESPERATE.
JUSTICE DICTATES WE LET YOU GO IN PEACE. BUT DO NOT RETURN, OR YOU WILL FIND OUR MEMORIES SHORT. AFTER ALL--
I KNOW, I KNOW. THE REVOLUTION DEMANDS IT.
HE'S A CHARMER.
HE'S SPENT THE LAST DECADE AND A HALF TRYING TO GET ME KILLED. I'D CALL THIS PROGRESS.

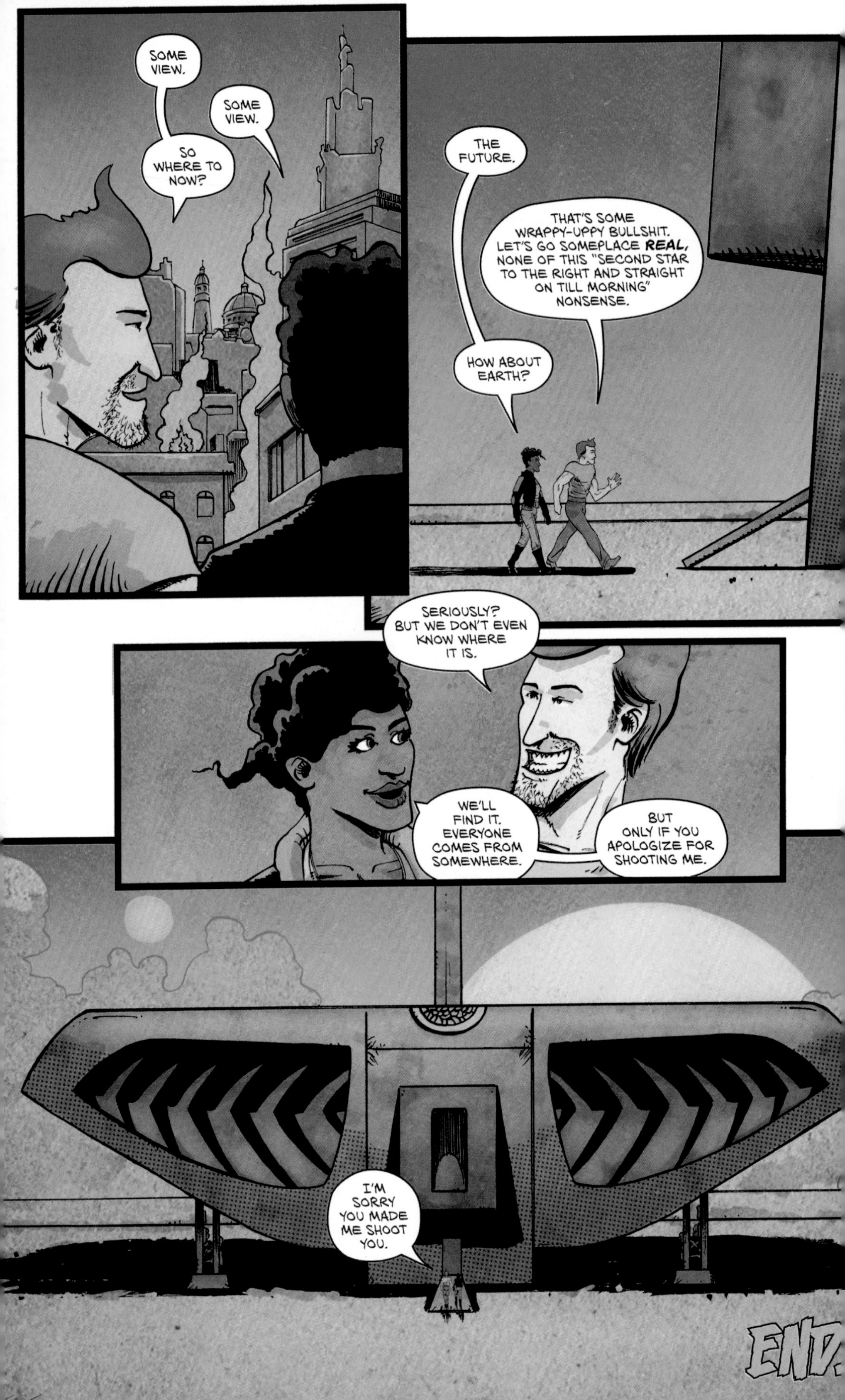
SOME VIEW.
SOME VIEW.
SO WHERE TO NOW?
THE FUTURE.
THAT'S SOME WRAPPY-UPPY BULLSHIT. LET'S GO SOMEPLACE **REAL,** NONE OF THIS "SECOND STAR TO THE RIGHT AND STRAIGHT ON TILL MORNING" NONSENSE.
HOW ABOUT EARTH?
SERIOUSLY? BUT WE DON'T EVEN KNOW WHERE IT IS.
WE'LL FIND IT. EVERYONE COMES FROM SOMEWHERE.
BUT ONLY IF YOU APOLOGIZE FOR SHOOTING ME.
I'M SORRY YOU MADE ME SHOOT YOU.
END.

COVER GALLERY

FEATURING THE ART OF:
NATASHA ALTERICI
JASON SMITH & HARRY SAXON

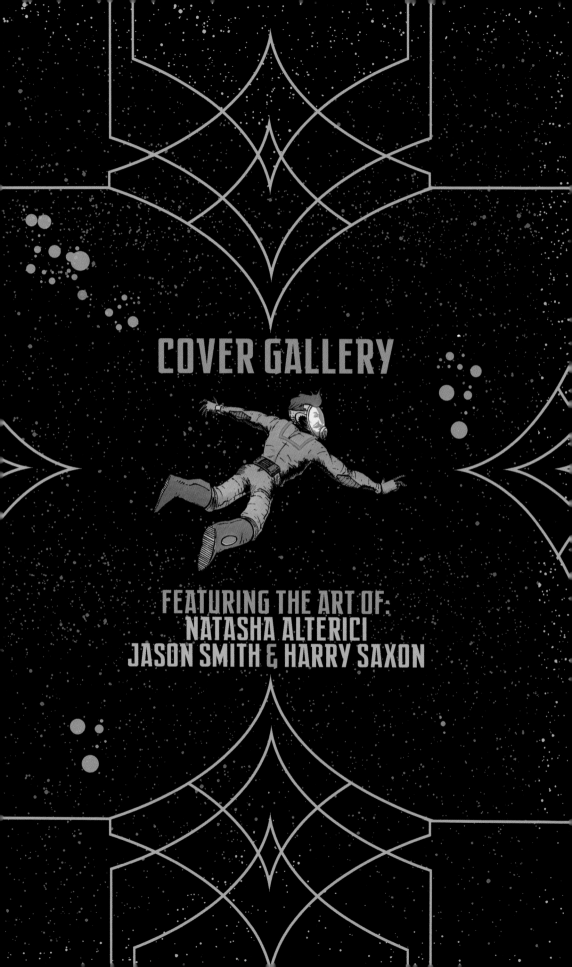

ISSUE 1 COVER

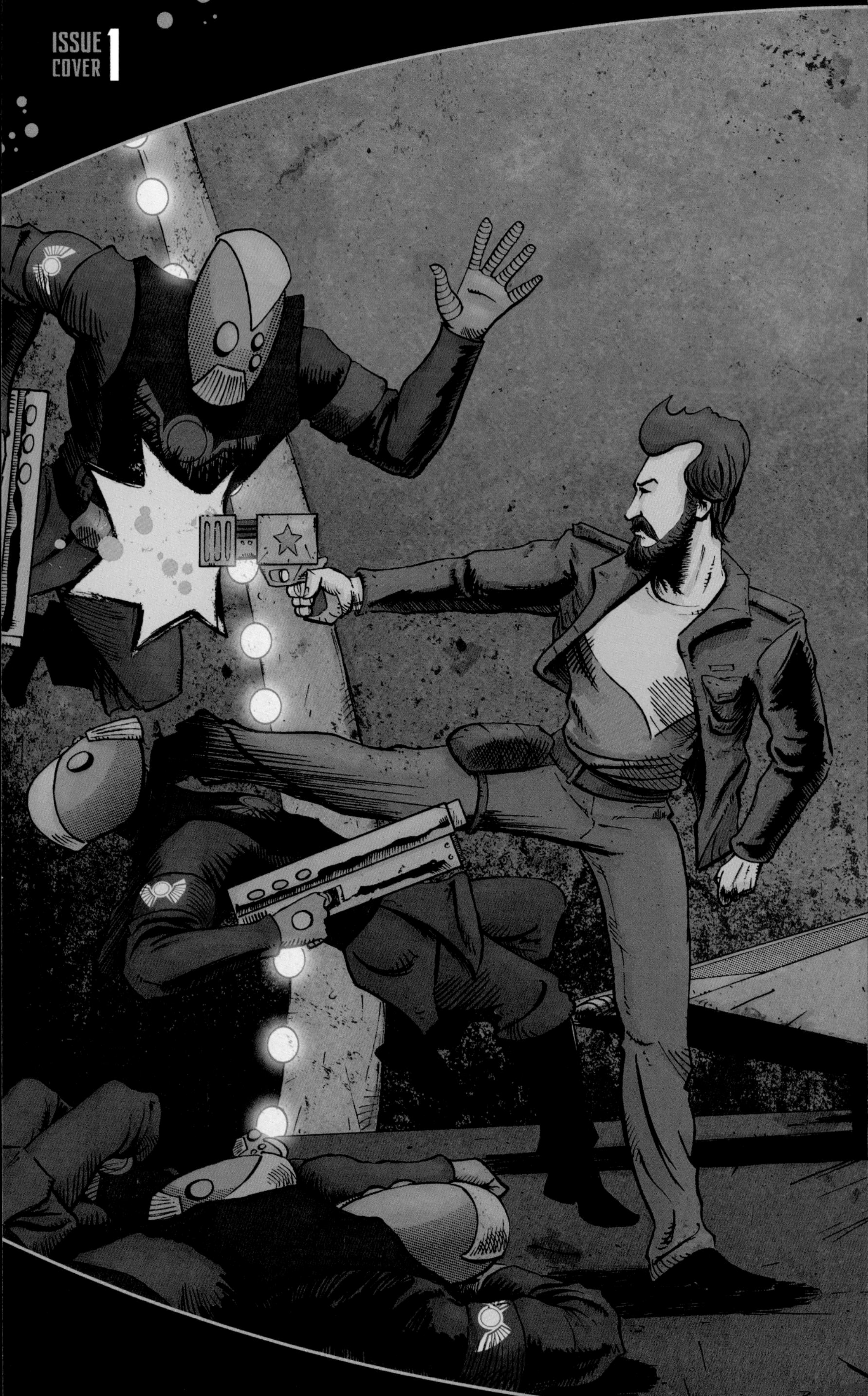

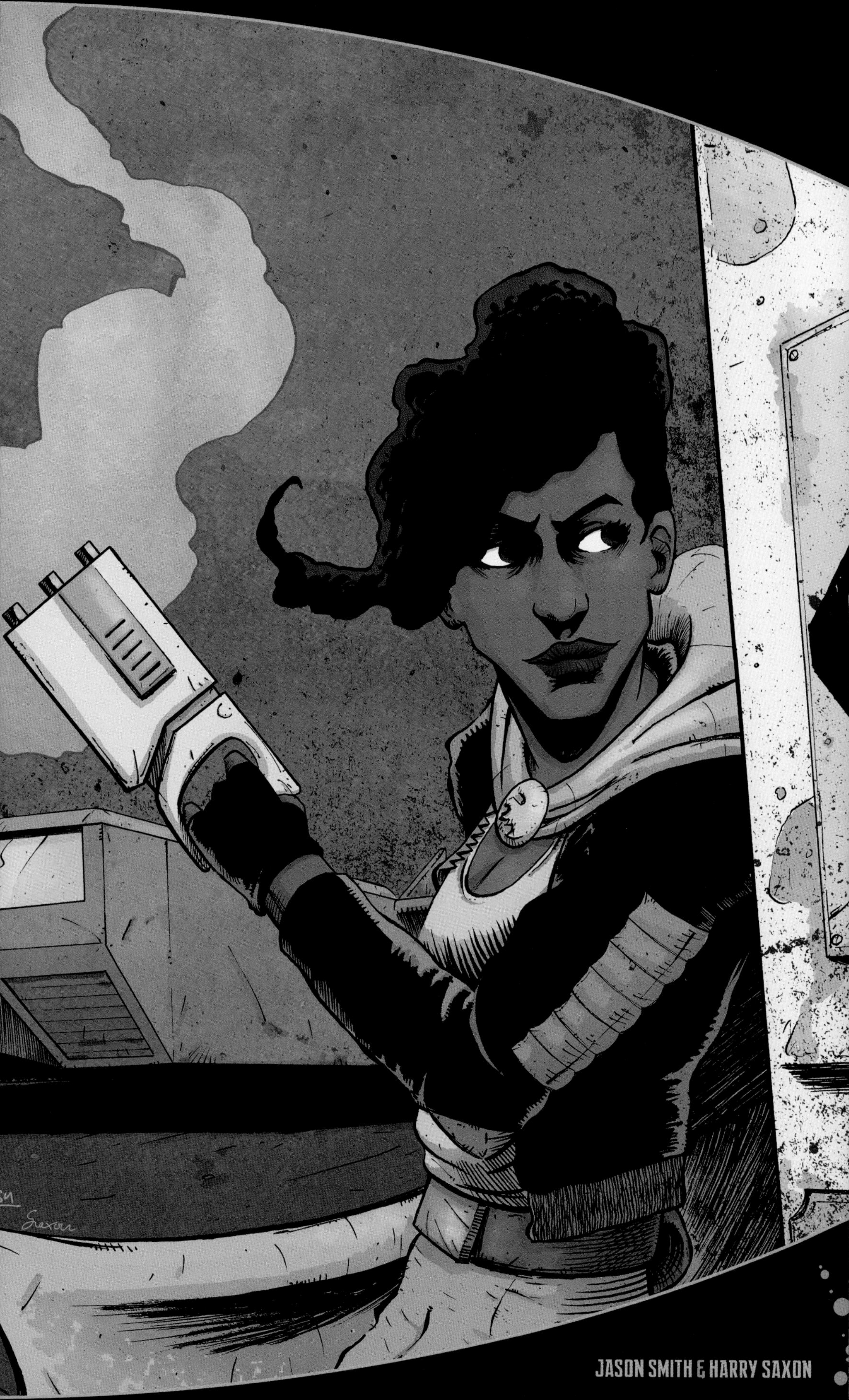

JASON SMITH & HARRY SAXON

ISSUE COVER 2

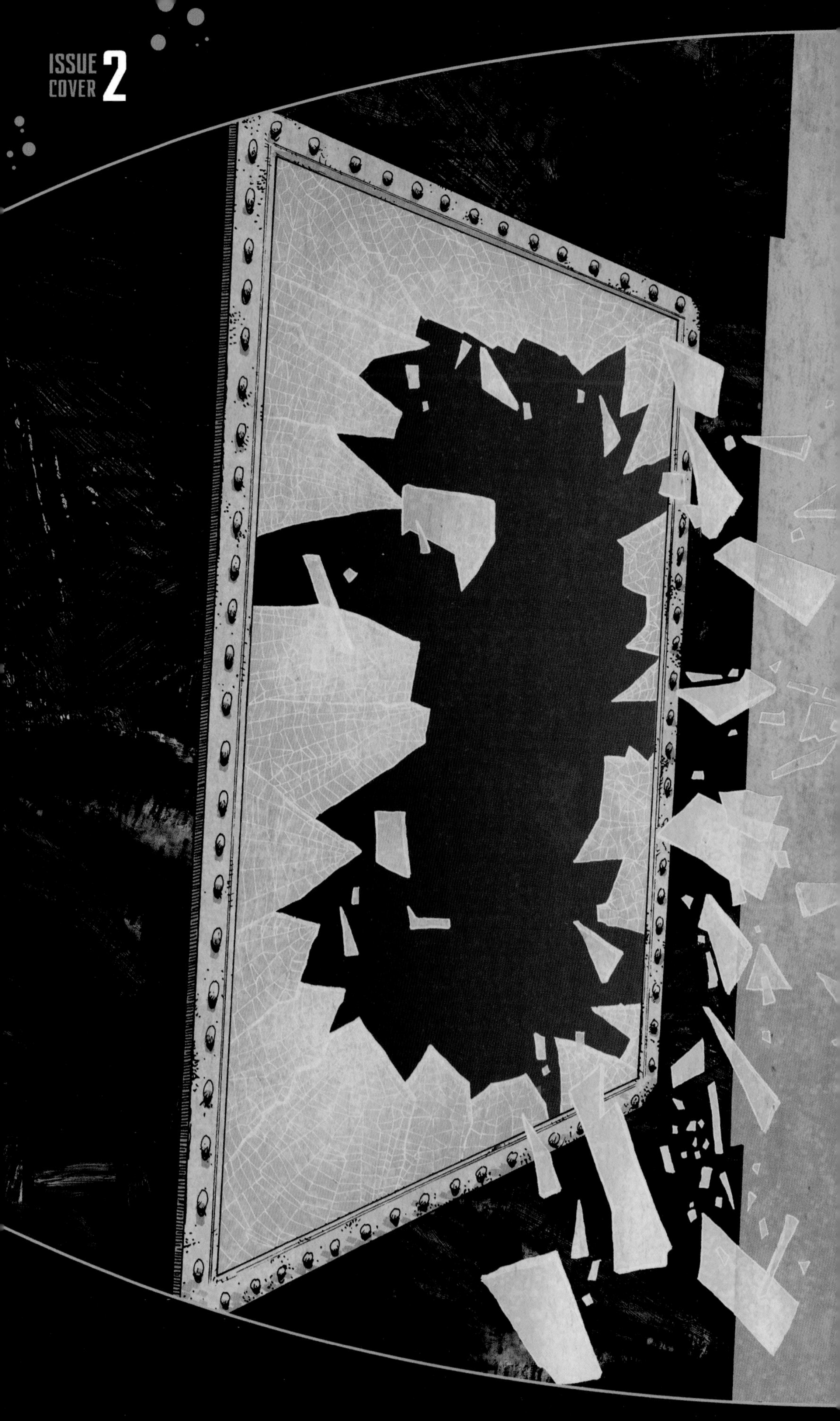

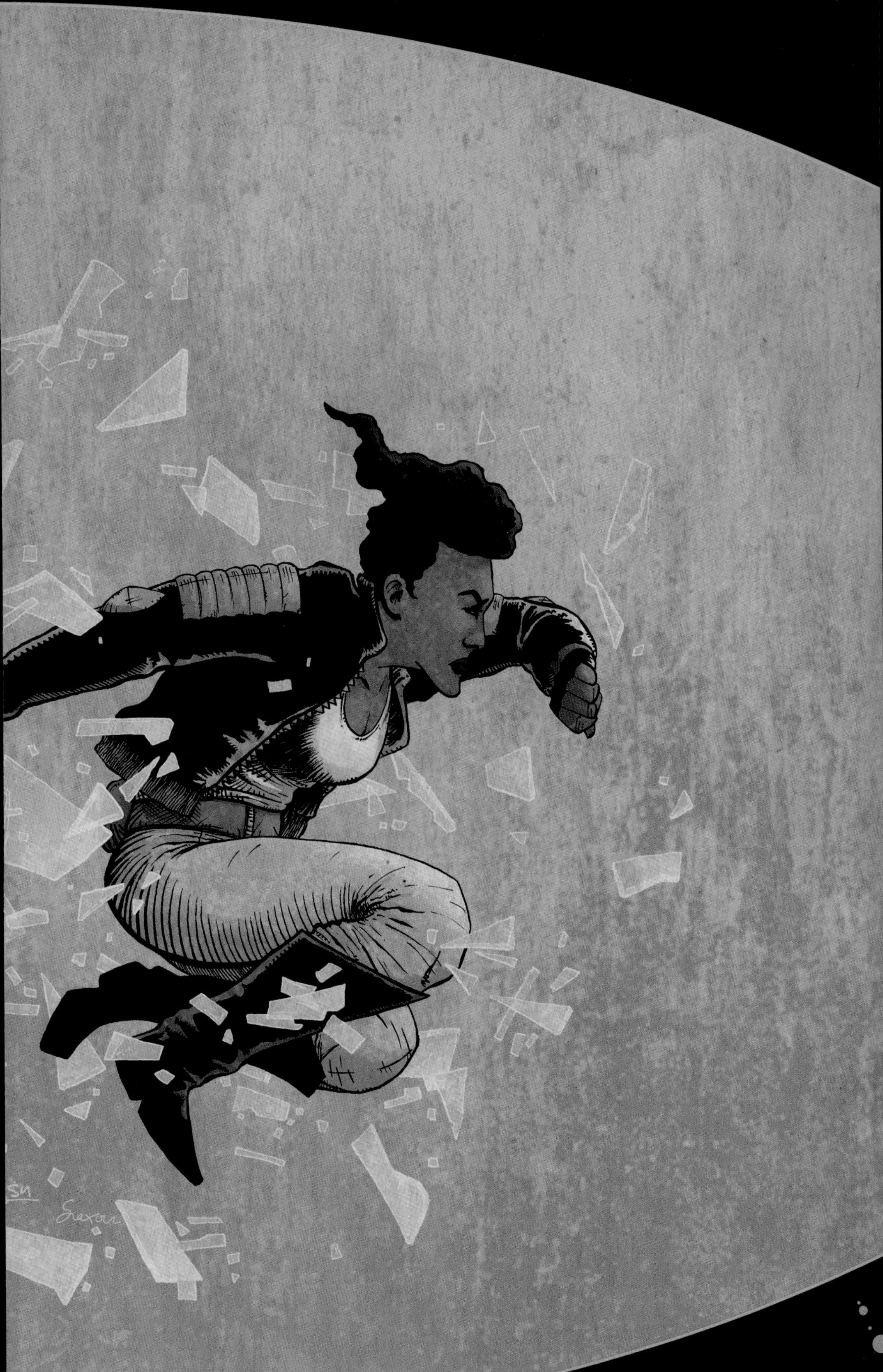

JASON SMITH & HARRY SAXON

ISSUE COVER 3

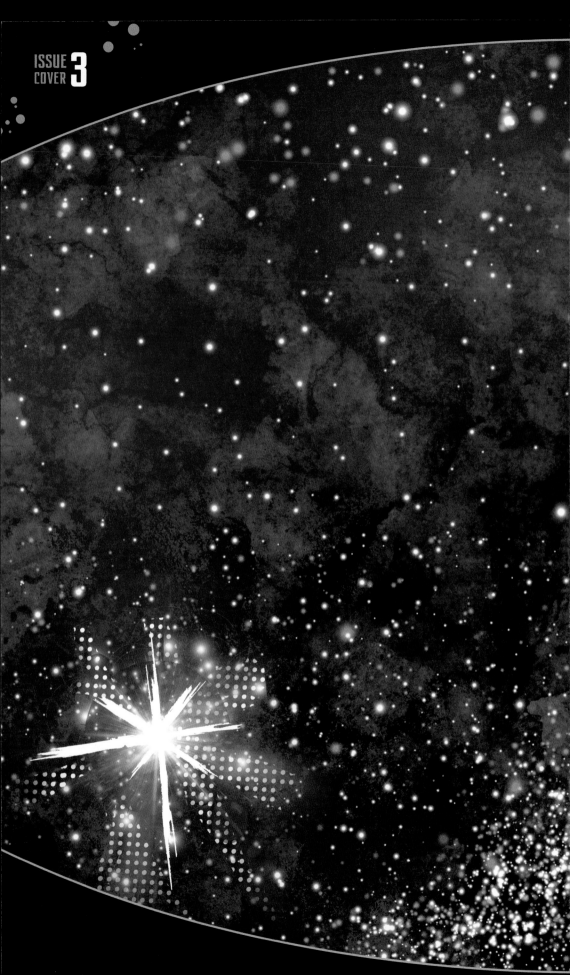

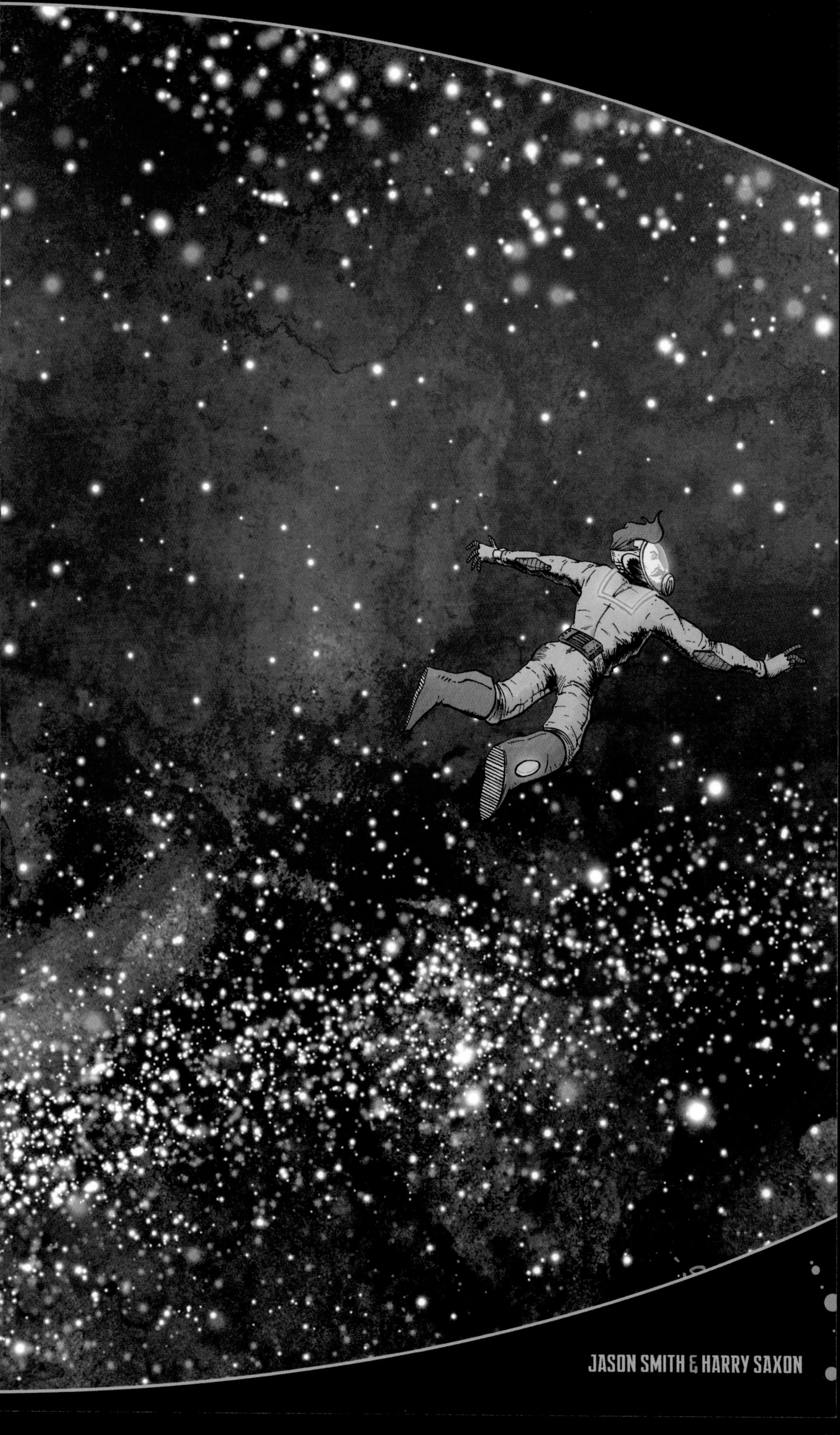
JASON SMITH & HARRY SAXON

ISSUE COVER 4

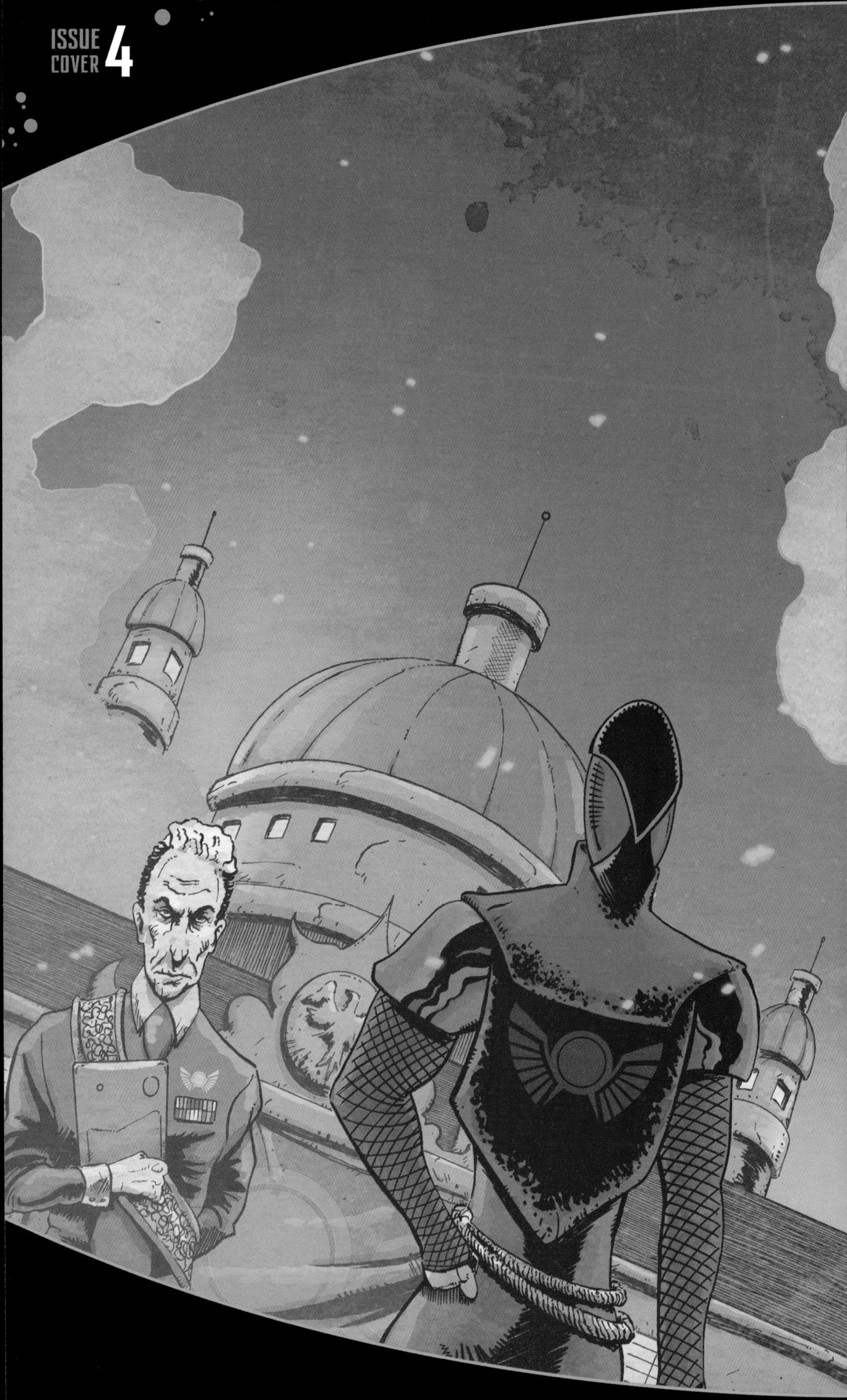

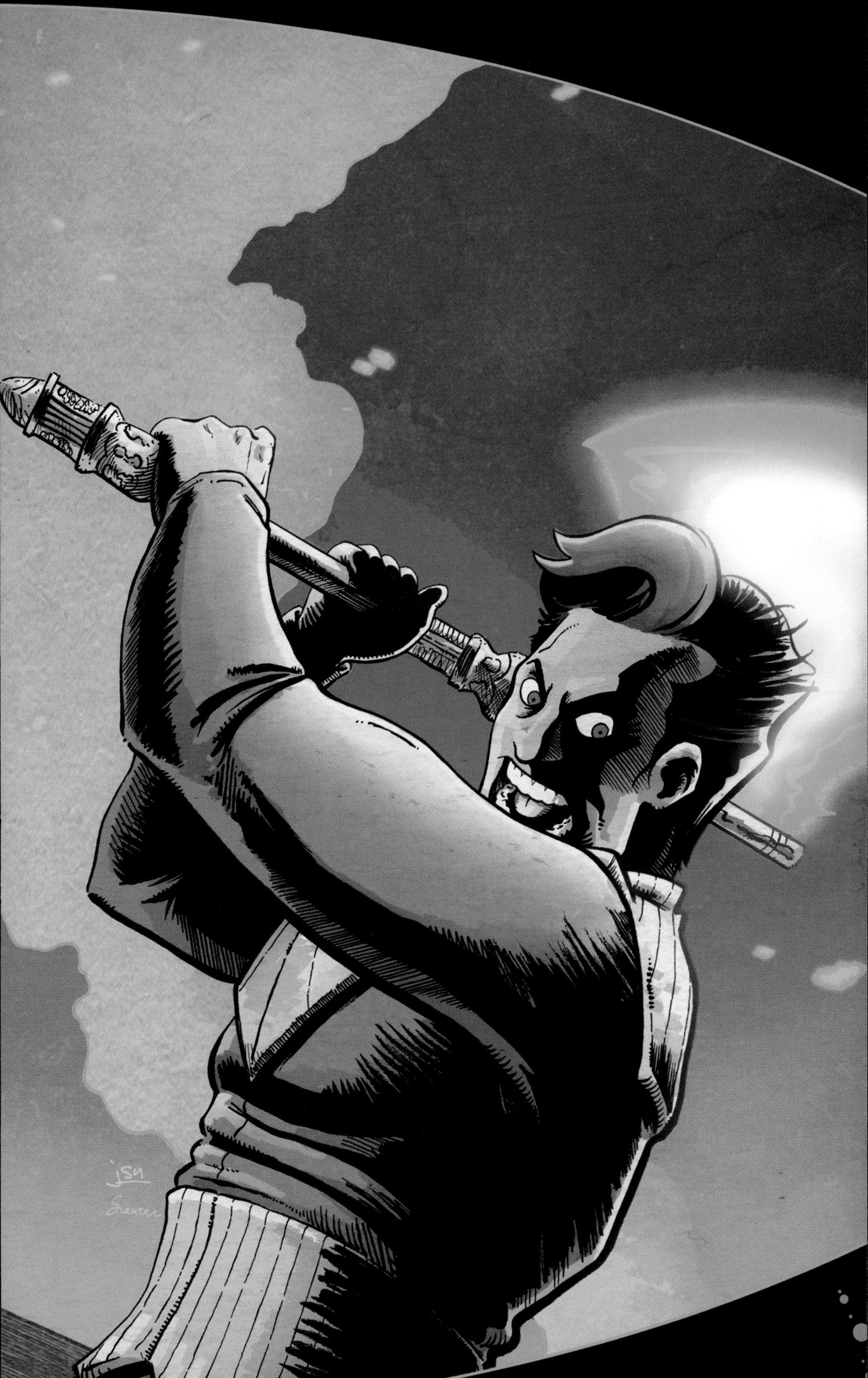

JASON SMITH & HARRY SAXON

ISSUE 5
COVER

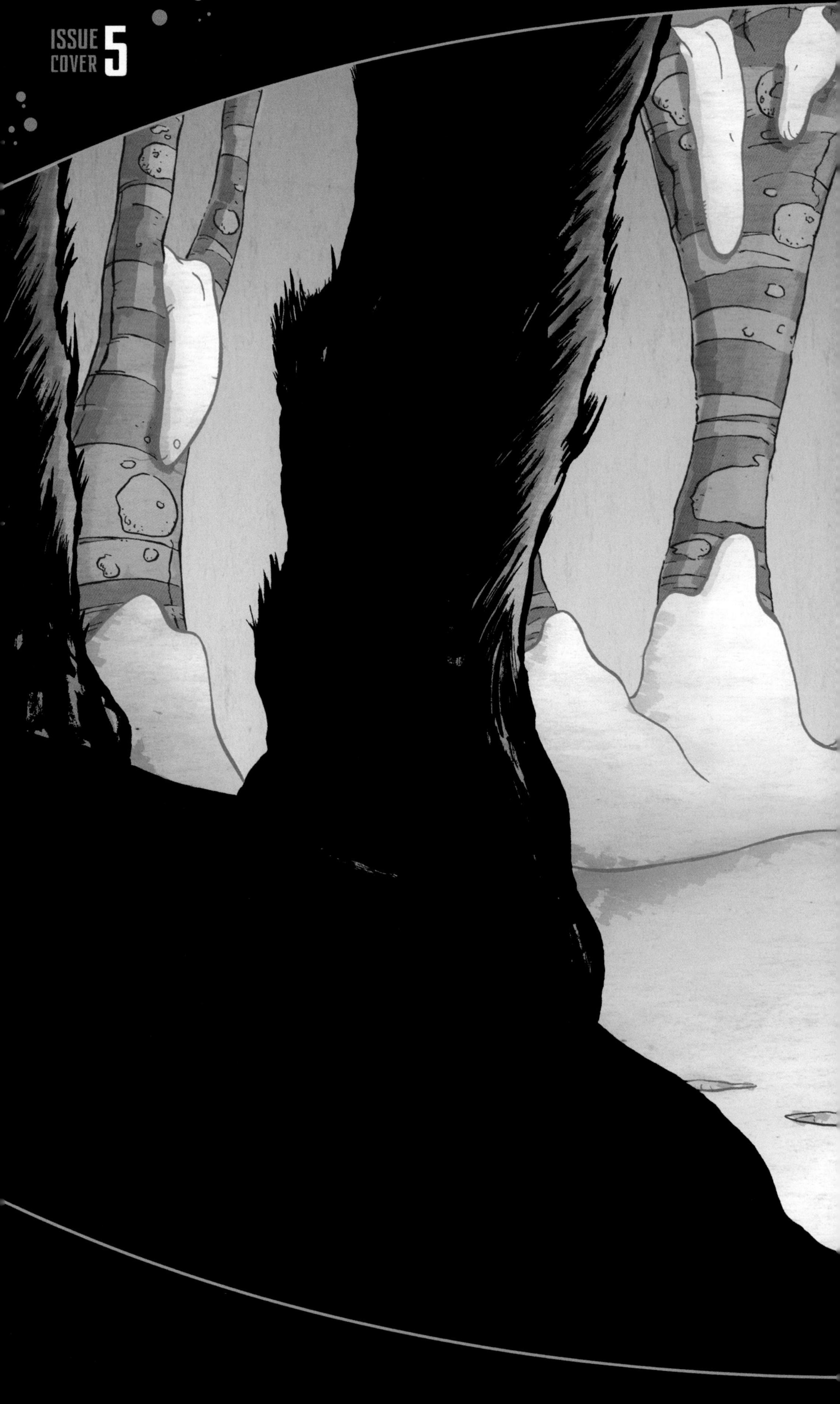

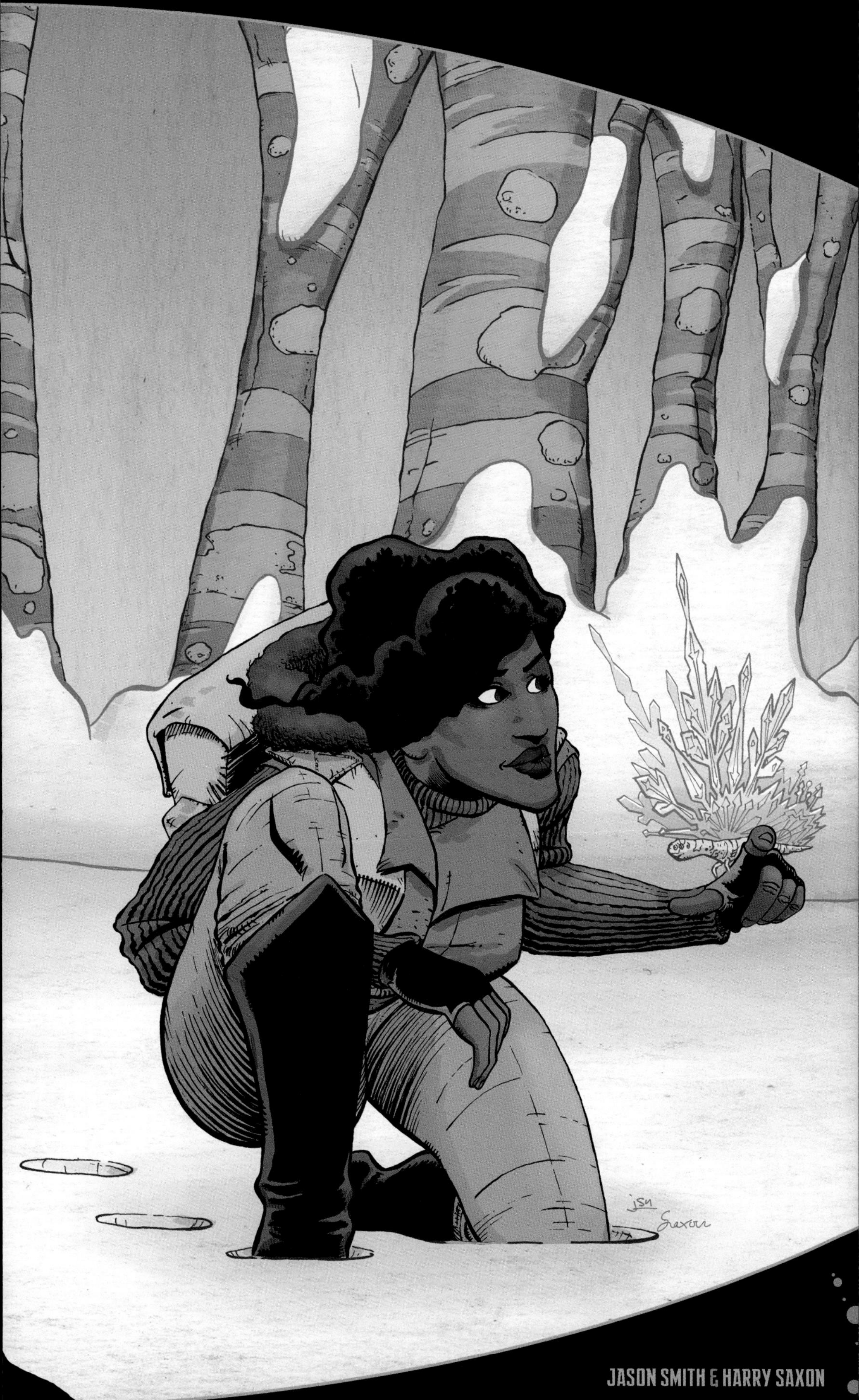
jsn
Saxon

JASON SMITH & HARRY SAXON

ISSUE 6 COVER

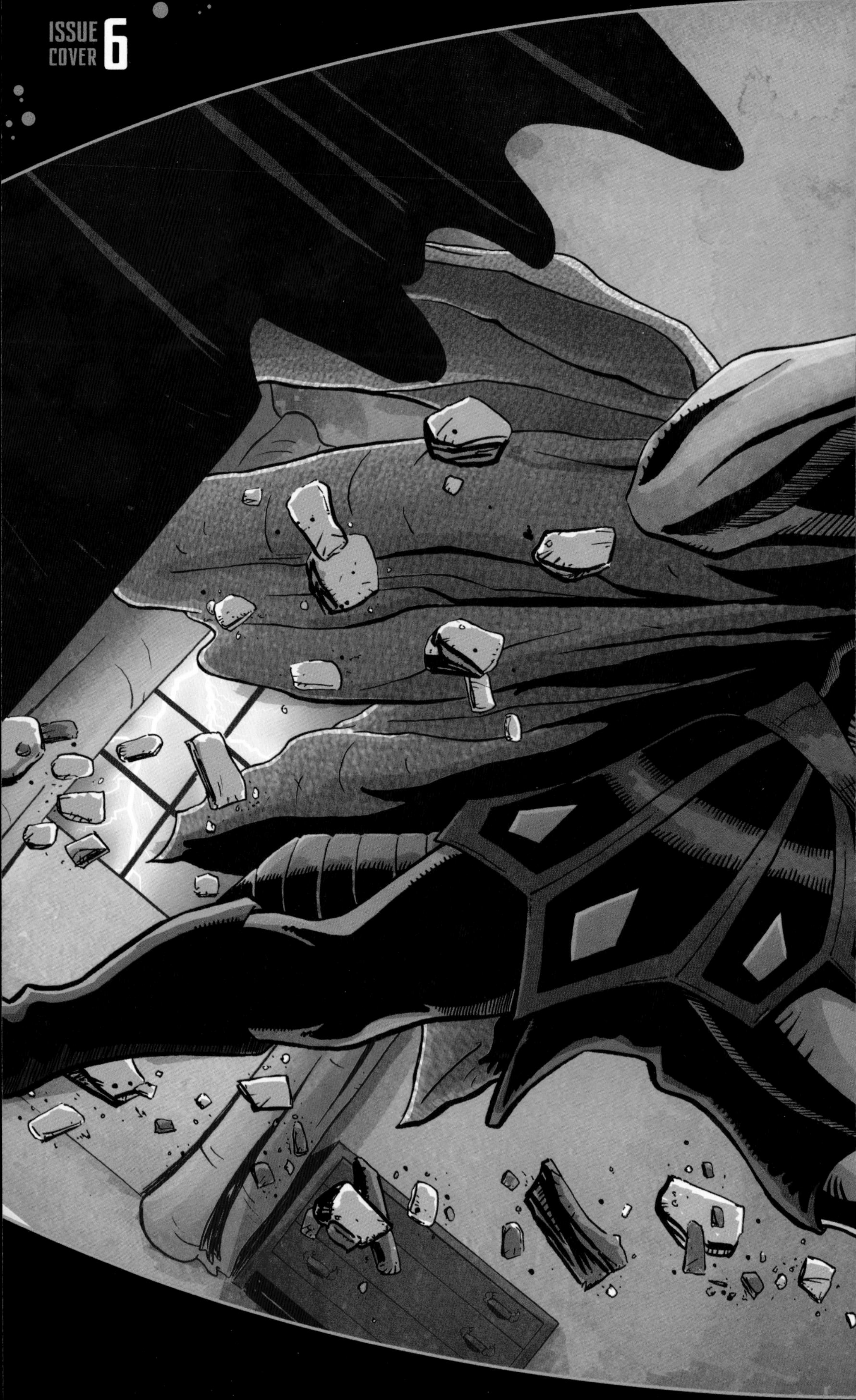

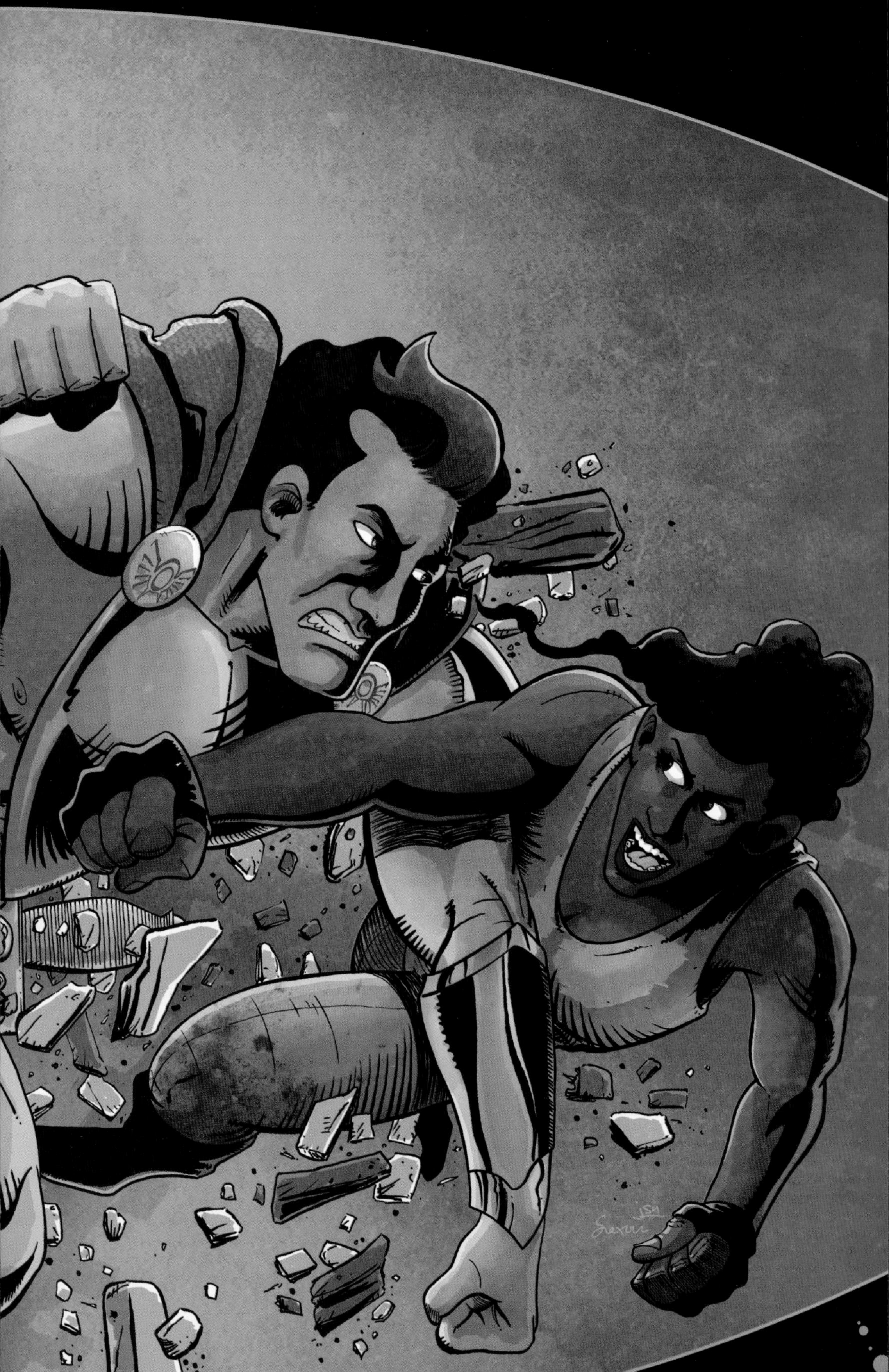

JASON SMITH & HARRY SAXON

ISSUE 1 COVER

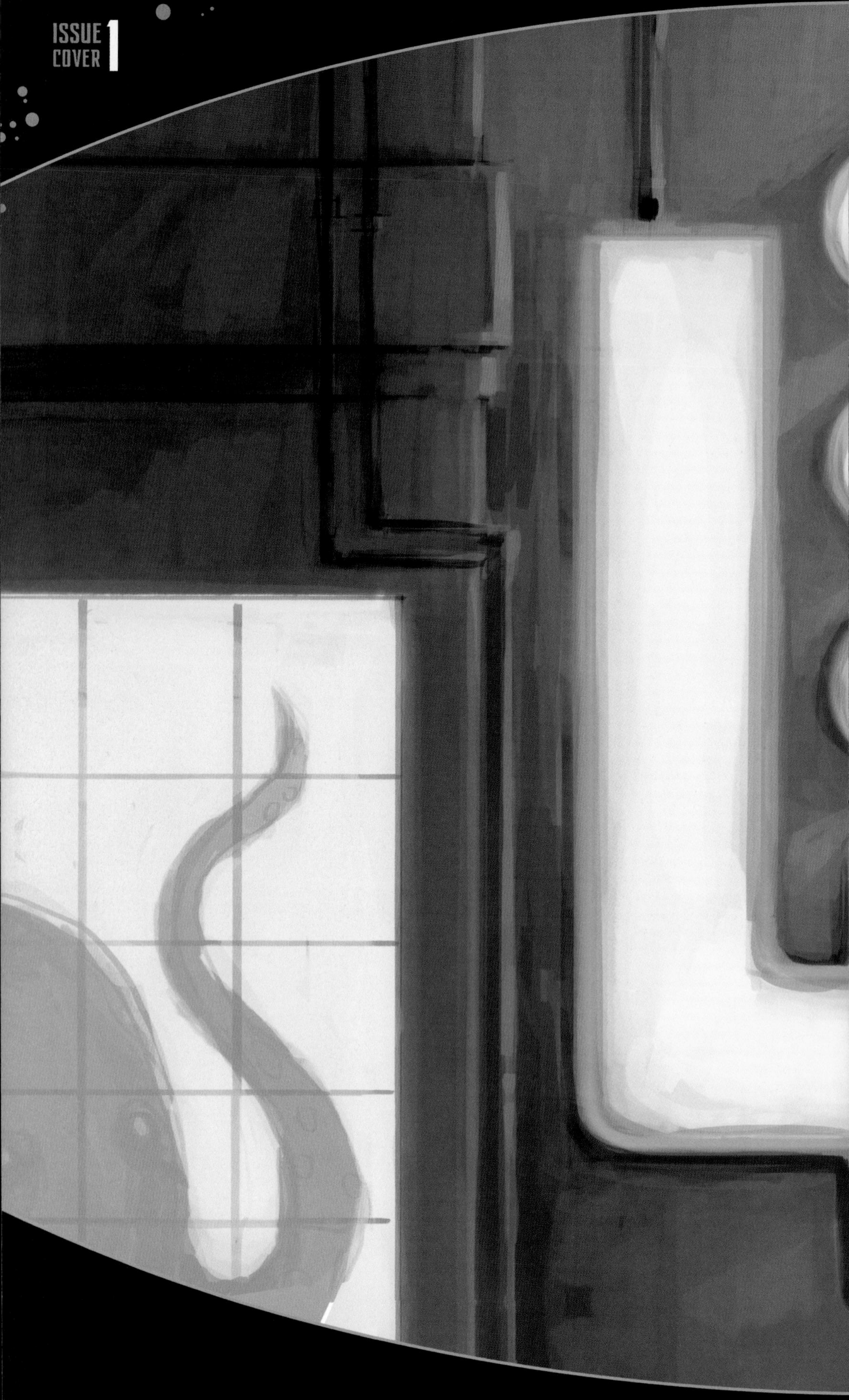

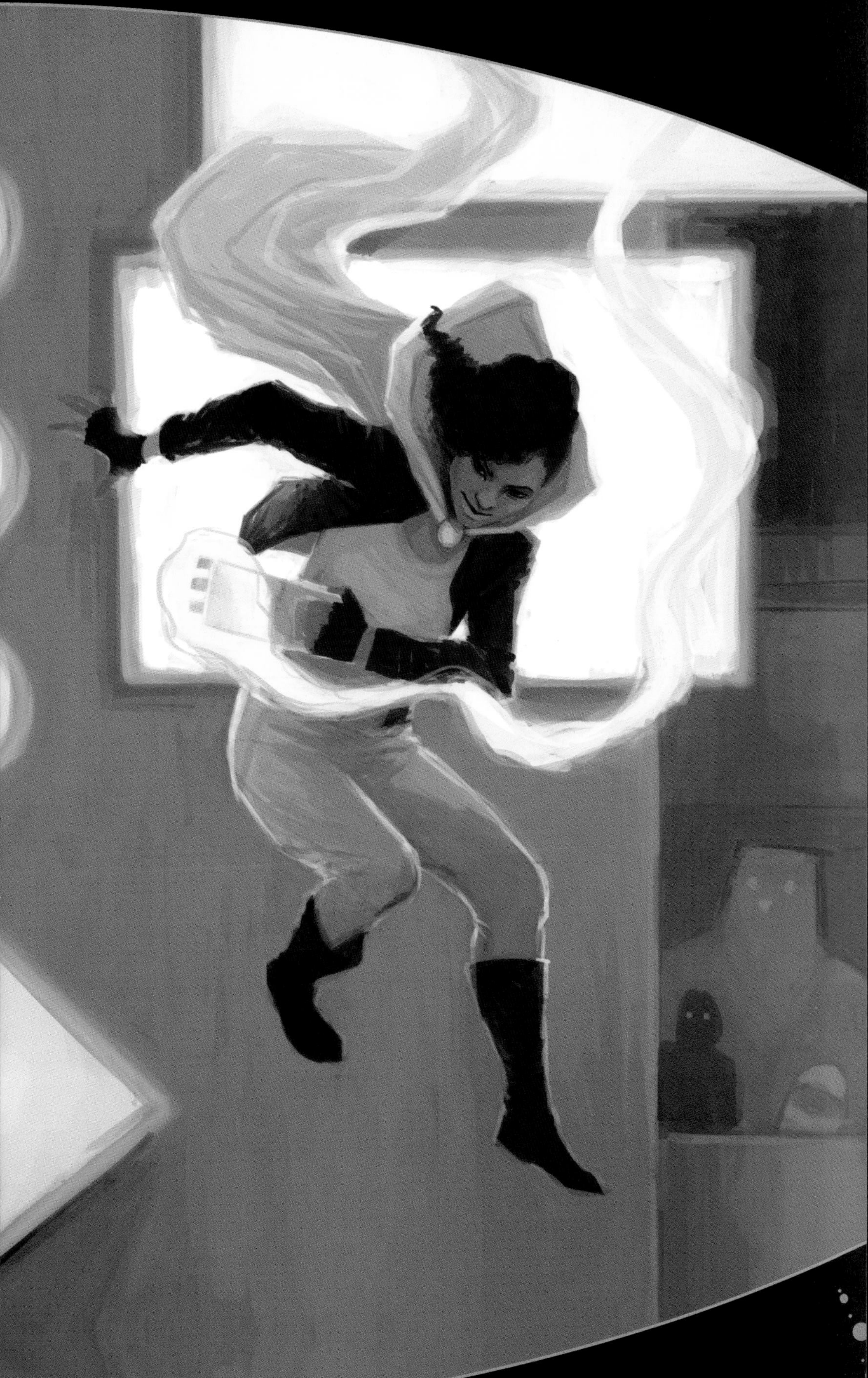

NATASHA ALTERICI

ISSUE COVER 2

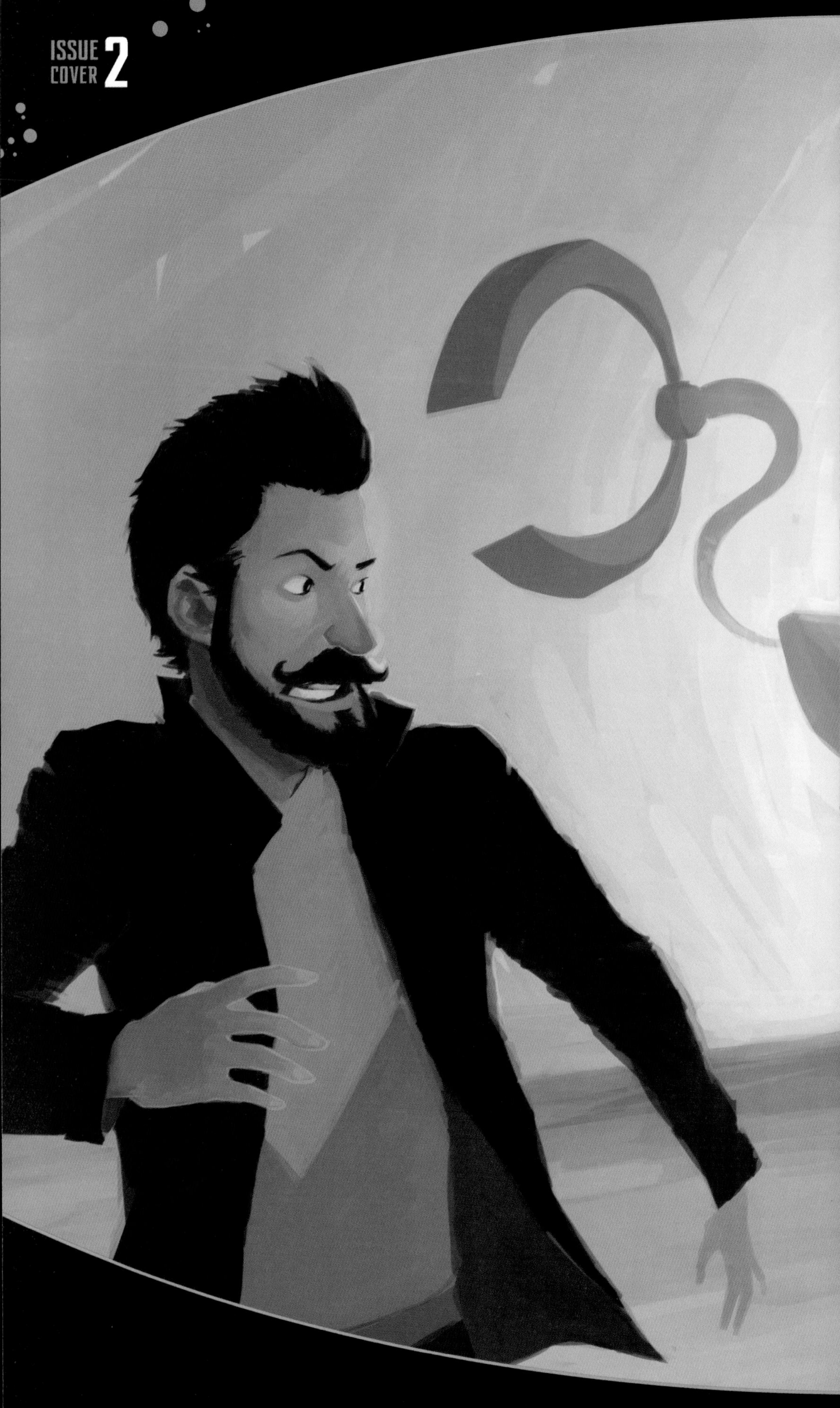

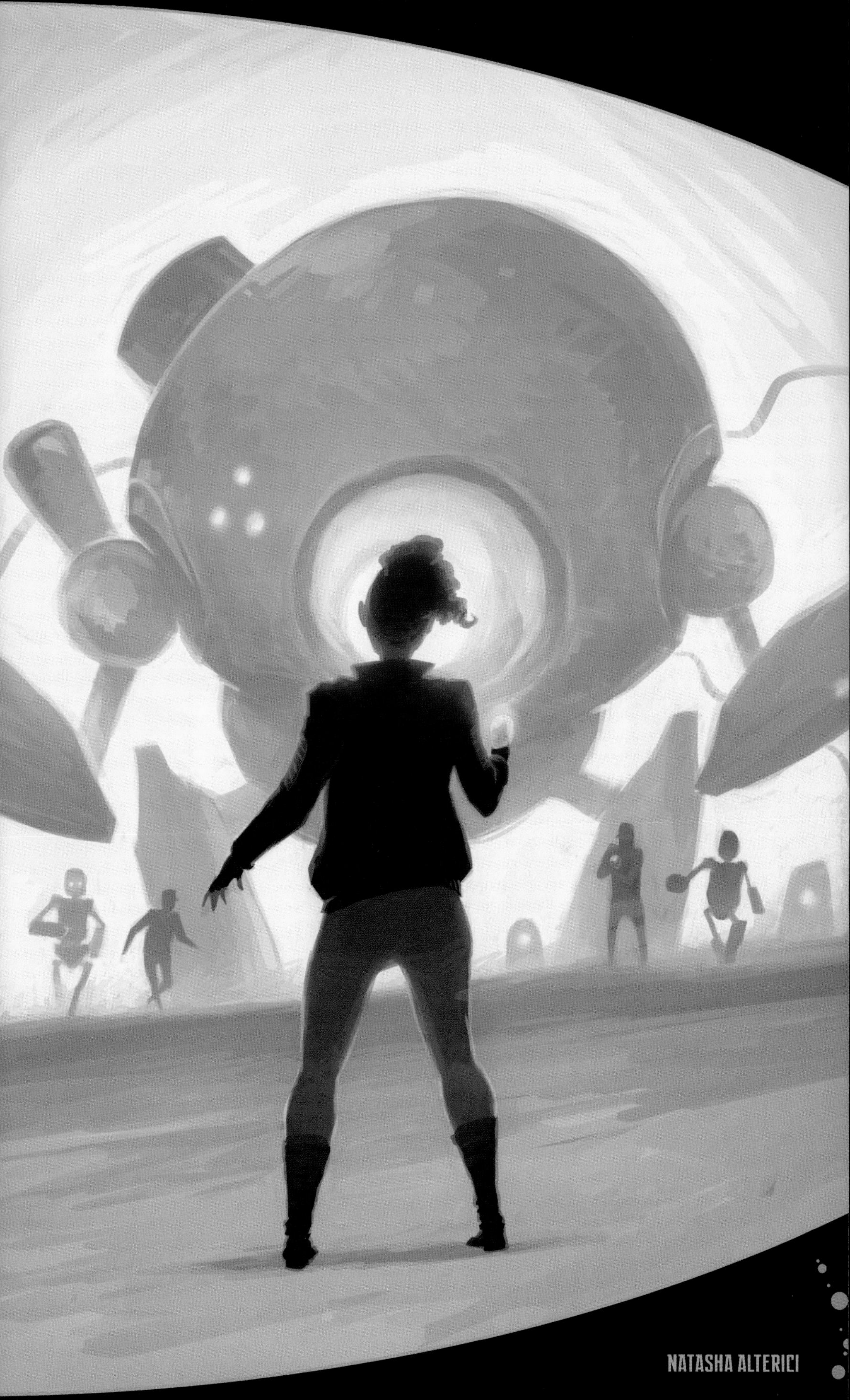

NATASHA ALTERICI

ISSUE COVER 3

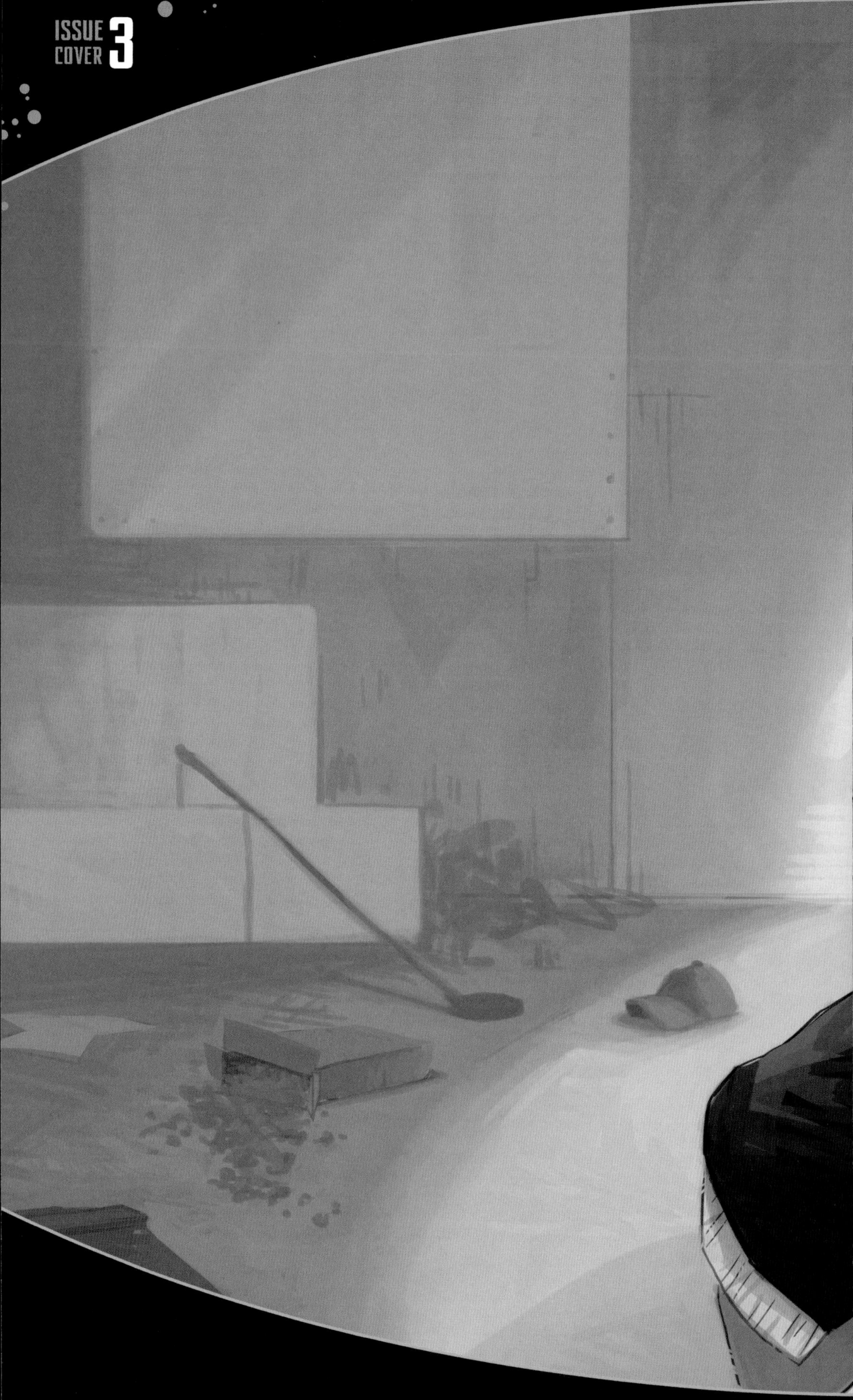

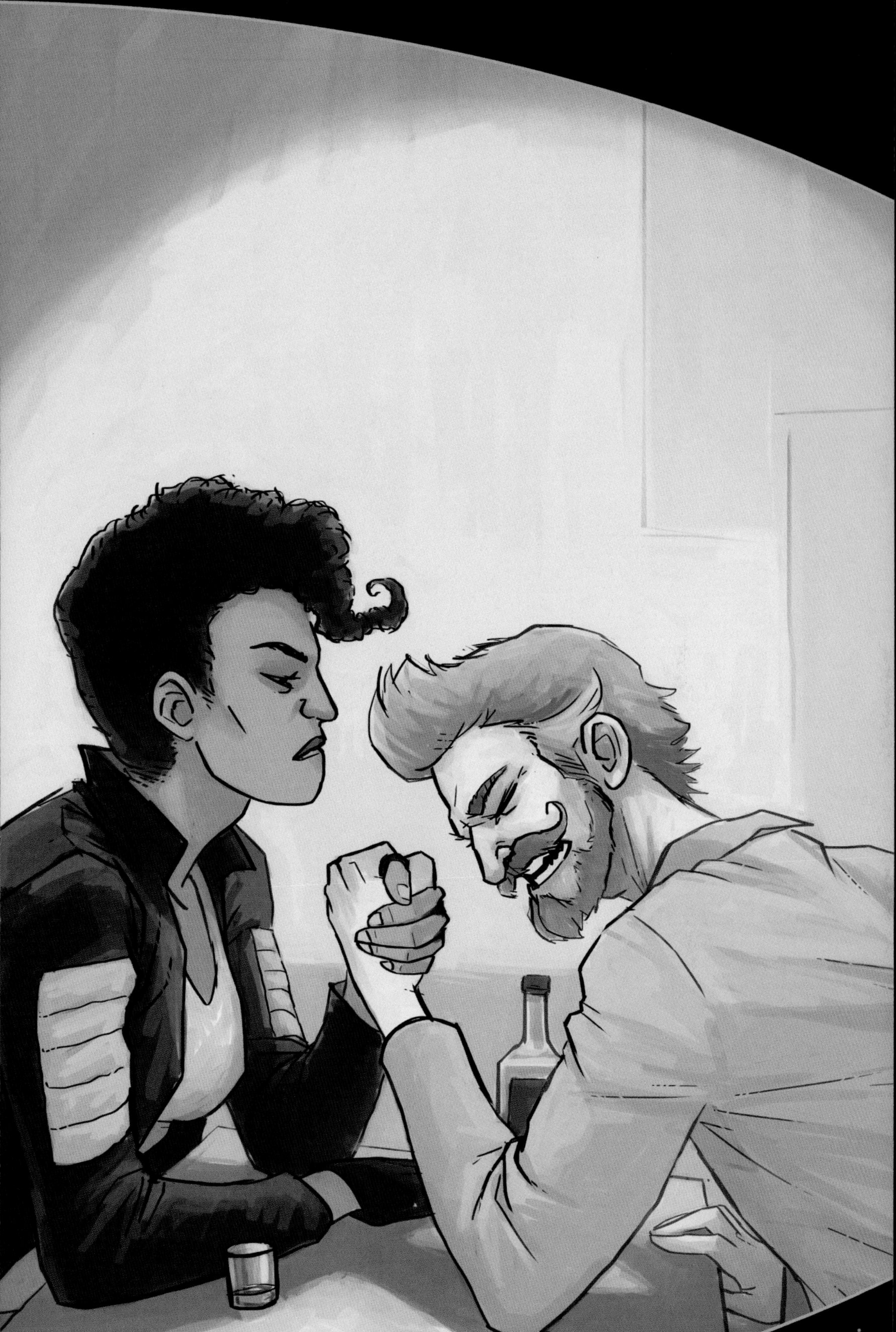

NATASHA ALTERICI

ISSUE 4 COVER

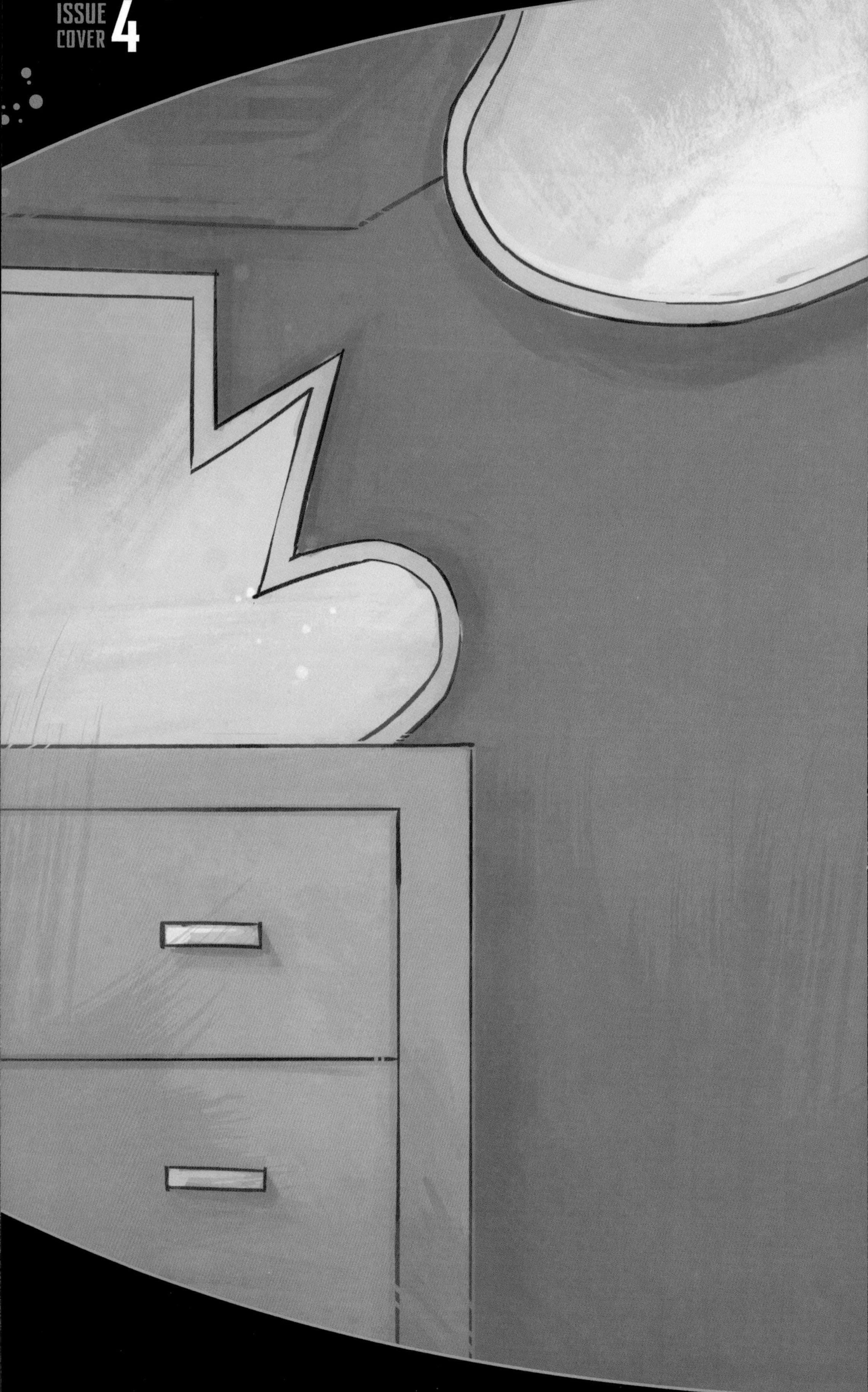

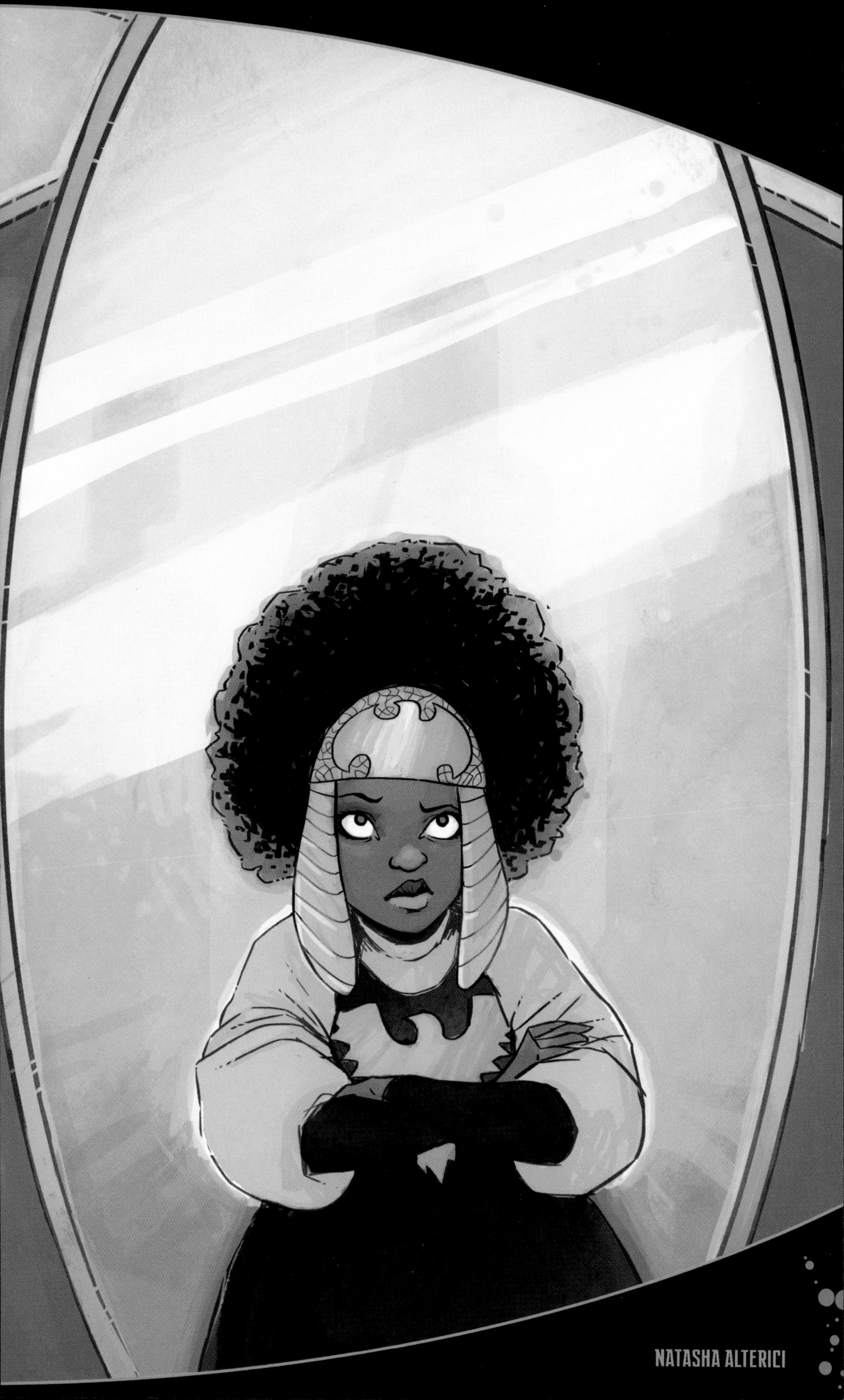

NATASHA ALTERICI

ISSUE COVER 5

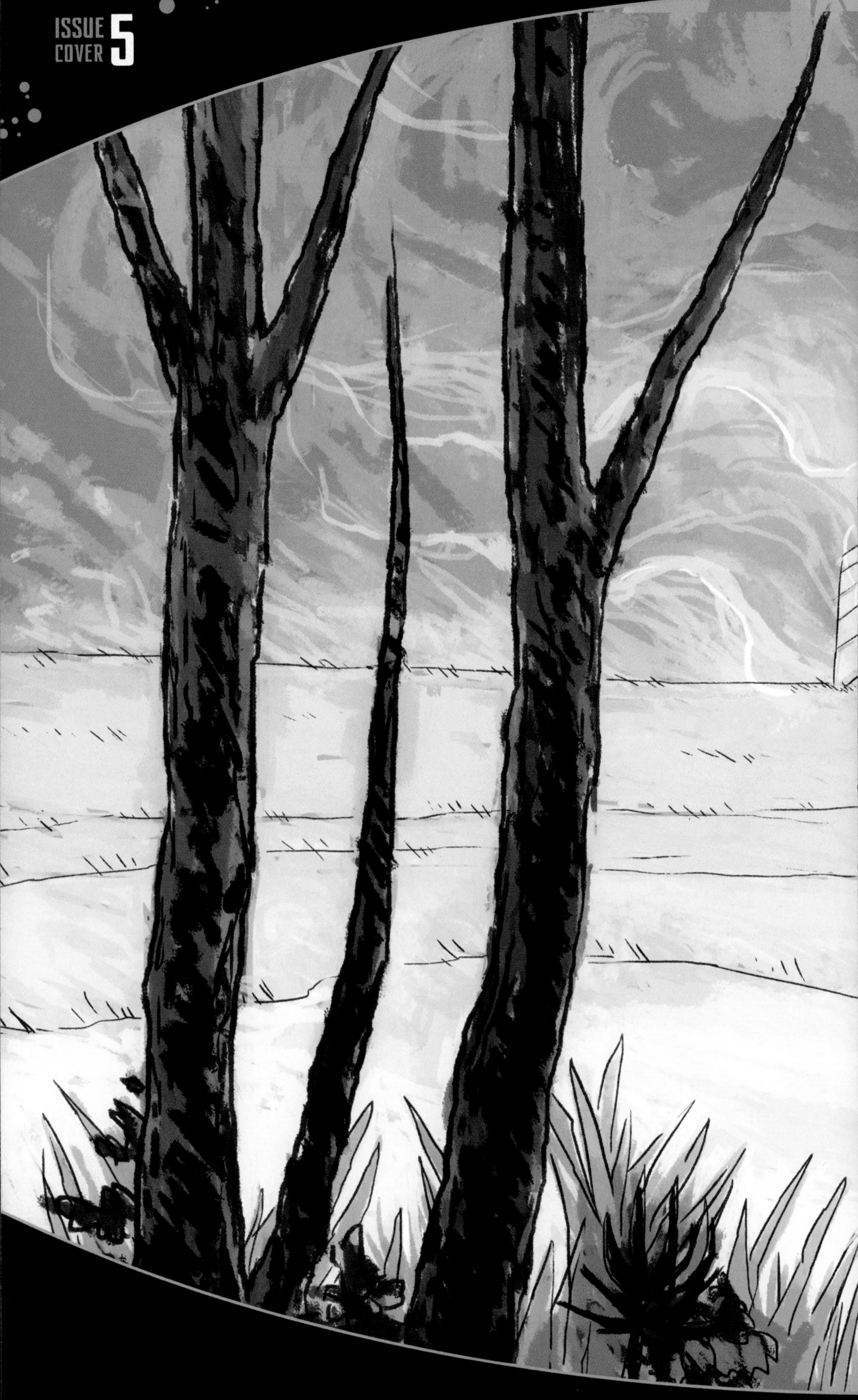

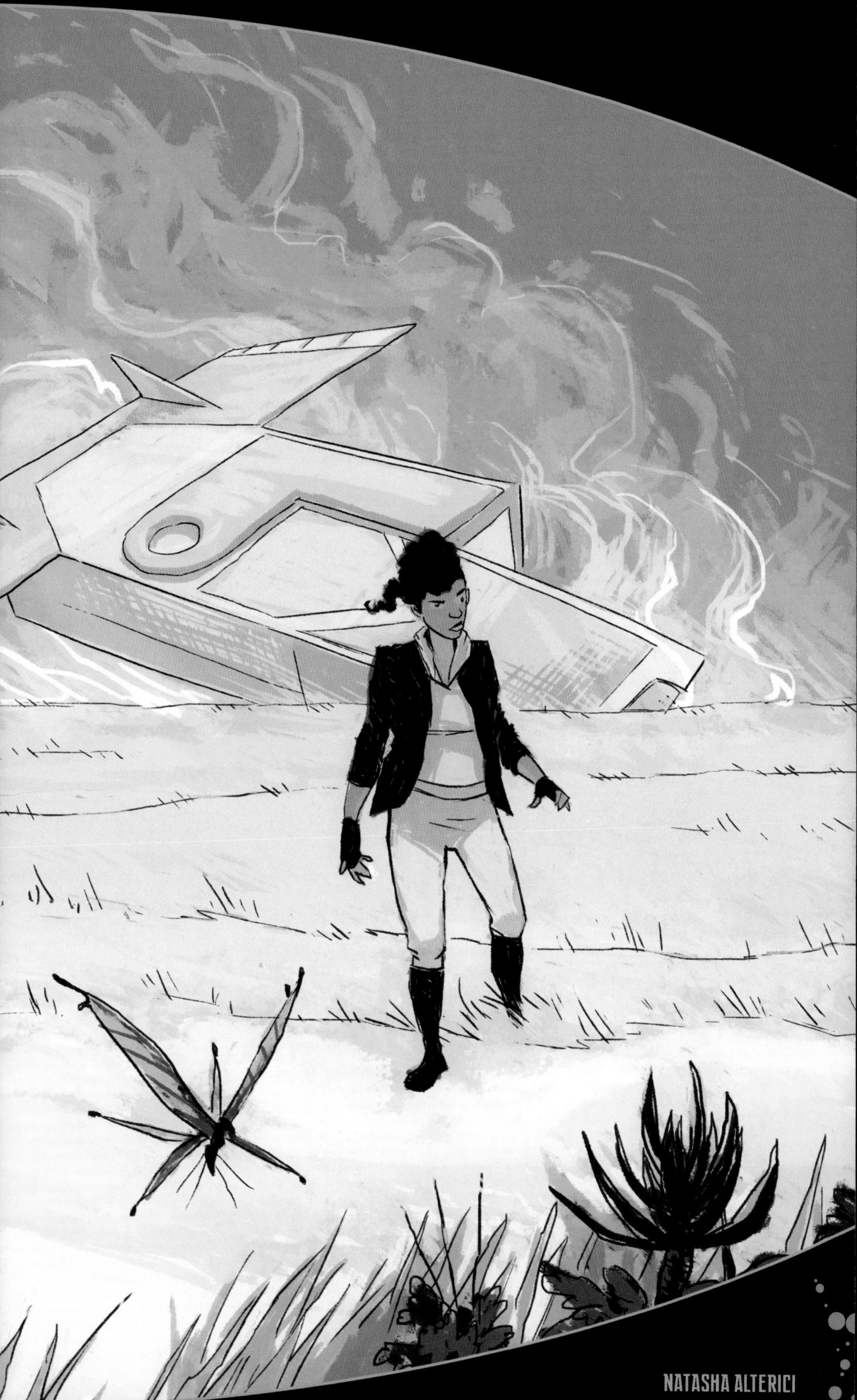

NATASHA ALTERICI

MAKING OF A QUEEN

FEATURING THE ART OF JASON SMITH

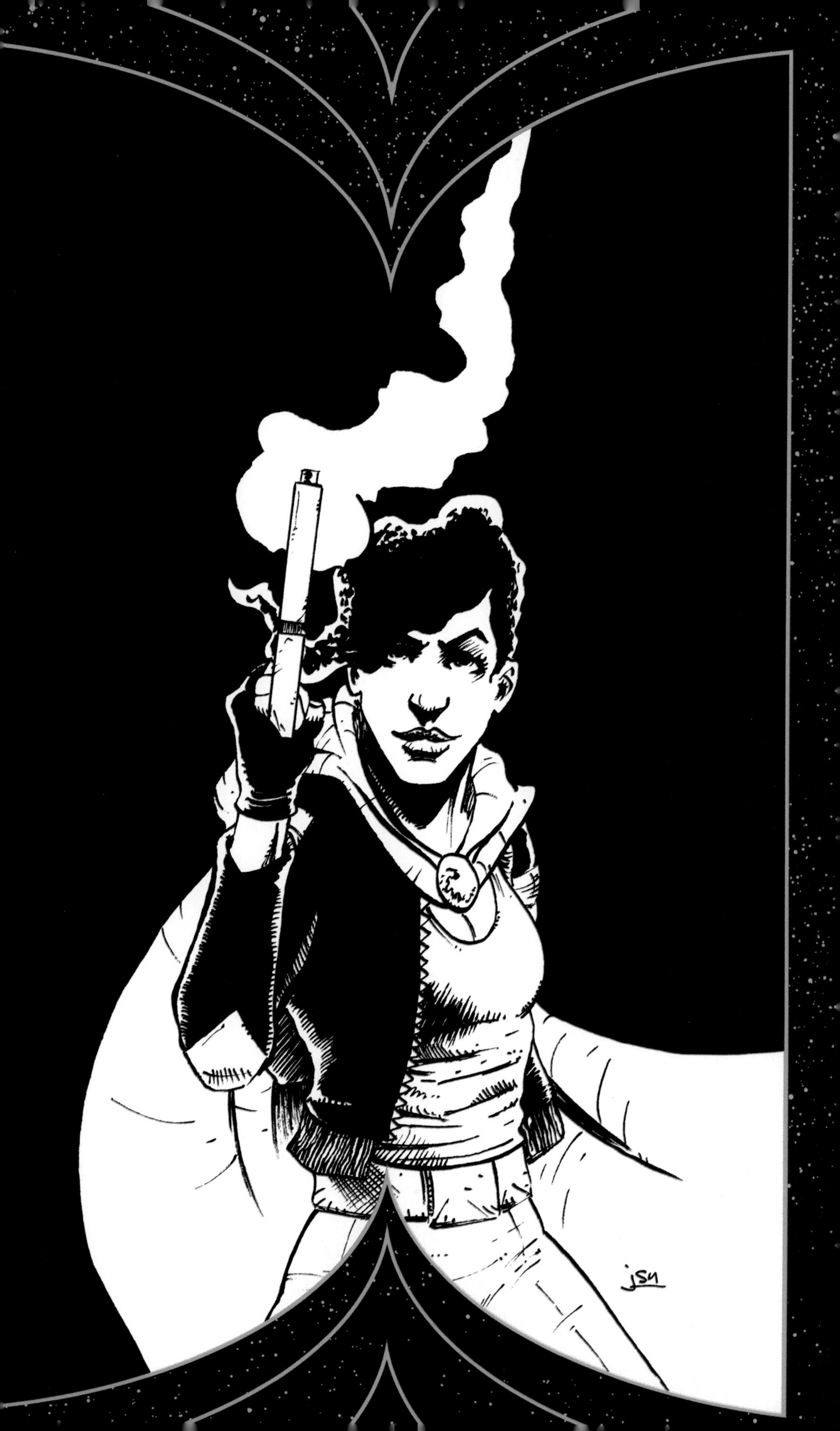

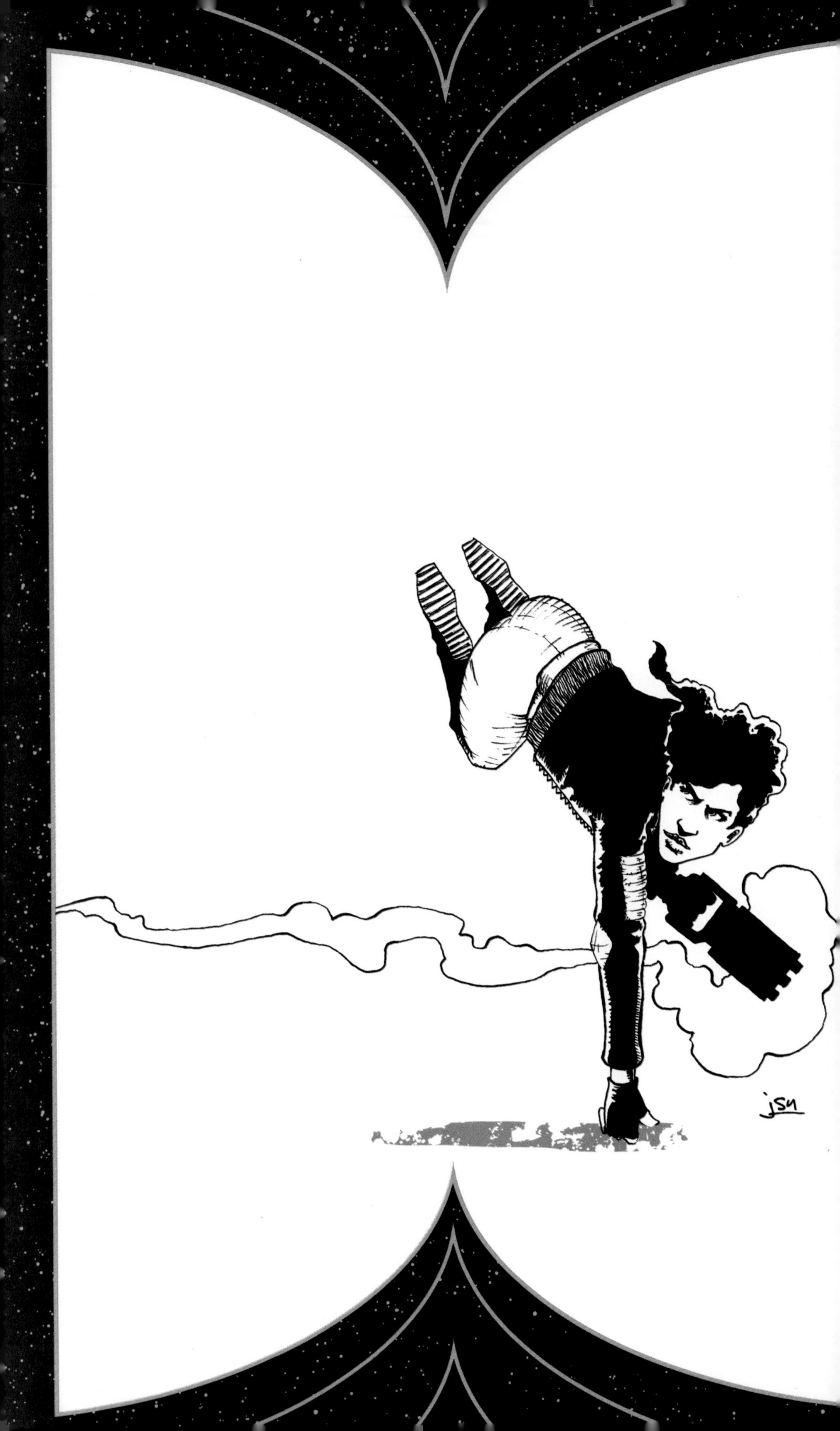
jsn

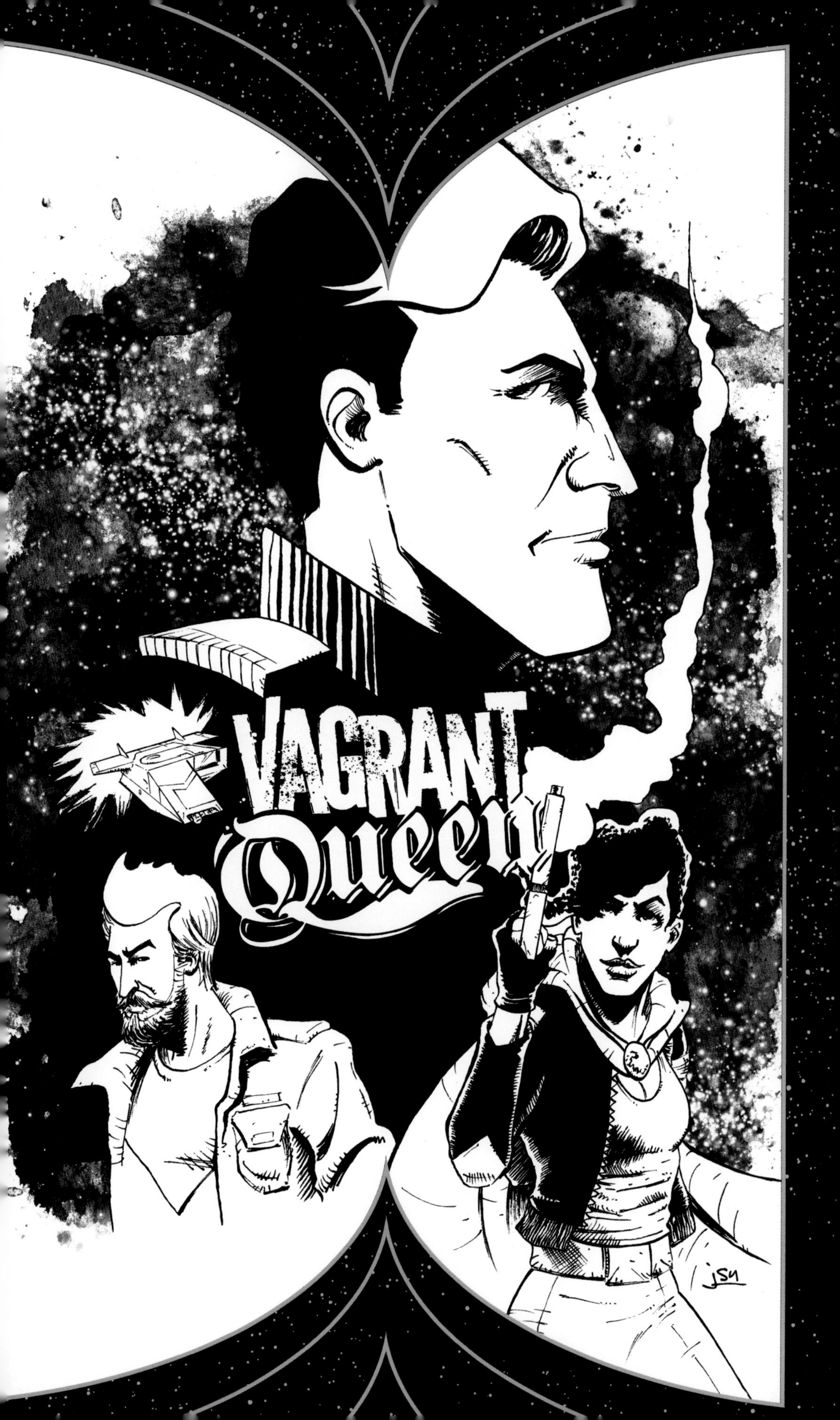
VAGRANT
Queen

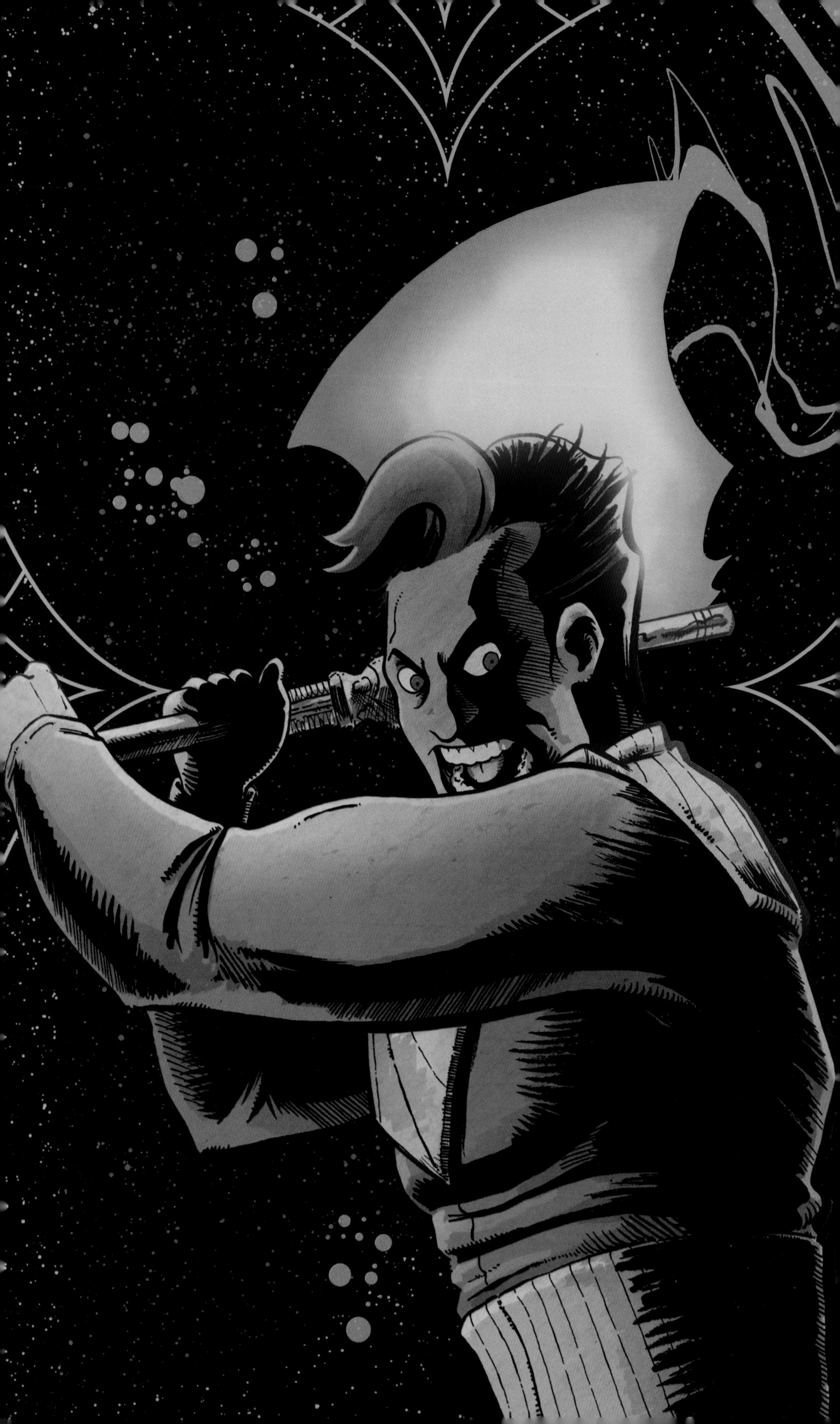